目錄 # Table of Contents

U0154319

P. 18

題目範例 中文翻譯　TRACK 08

女： 亞當先生，請發言。我想你可以開始董事會議了。

男： 謝謝妳，強森女士。首先，我很榮幸能獲選為主席。我作為主席的第一項動議就是成立委員會，其職責為在九月以前改善銷售量。為了要執行那項動議，我需要在座大多數的各位舉手支持。

女： 在座各位都舉手了。此項動議一致通過，並於明日起開始實施。

男： 謝謝各位。在任何情況下，我都不會使我們的營利下滑。

P. 22

考題範例│題組 1 中文翻譯　TRACK 09

男： 這間房子根本不能住。瓦斯漏氣、地板破洞、牆壁有裂縫——妳家的屋況可能是我看過最糟糕的。妳請我來檢查是對的。

女： 露臺和門框之間的縫隙呢？至少有五公分吧！

男： 對，有這麼大的縫隙，可以想見小動物——蠕蟲、甲蟲、蜘蛛、蝸牛——都會跑進來。妳住在這間房子多久了？它是什麼時候蓋的？

女： 我們住這裡還不到一年！它是我們搬進來的幾個月前蓋好的。

P. 23

考題範例│題組 2 中文翻譯　TRACK 10

女： 我剛訂了我們去摩洛哥馬拉喀什的機票。

男： 摩洛哥？妳為什麼選摩洛哥作為我們度假的地點？

女： 嗯，首先，摩洛哥以眾多美食及購物聞名。而且真的很便宜！你看！從倫敦到馬拉喀什的來回機票一人只要一百元美金！而且，這些飯店看起來都很棒，價格也是最低價。

男： 是啊。我記得有看過拉巴特非洲藝術節的介紹。好吧，聽起來妳做了個不錯的選擇！

P. 24

考題範例│題組 3 中文翻譯　TRACK 11

女：哈囉，賽門。有什麼需要我幫忙的嗎？

男：嗯，我弟弟下個月要在佛羅里達結婚，我希望能請假去參加。我已經填好申請表了。

女：你想請什麼時候？

男：我想請十七號的那一整個禮拜。那樣的話，我還可以帶我的孩子們去迪士尼樂園。

女：可以啊。只要確保你在幾天前先發出不在辦公室的通告，並向凱倫說明你目前在進行的案子。你不在時，她可以替你負責你的客戶。

男：沒問題。有大家的幫忙，<u>我知道一切會很順利的</u>。就好像我從來沒離開過！

PART 4 Short Talks 簡短獨白

P. 25

題目範例｜中文翻譯 TRACK 12

這裡是電視城的史密斯城市分部，電視城是您電視、電腦與其他電子產品的首選。我們現在似乎無法接聽您的電話。我們目前沒有營業，正在重新整修以提供您更優質的服務。我們將在下個月的十七號舉辦盛大的重新開幕派對，詳情請參考我們的網站。我們的正常上班時間為星期一至星期六，早上十點至晚上九點。如果您有急事，可以按下 * 字鍵與數字 1，留言告知您的名字、想聯絡的對象，以及您想說的內容。您也可以寄電子郵件至 help@tvtvcity.com。

P. 28

考題範例｜題組 1 中文翻譯 TRACK 13

大衛·華格納先生，我是瓊斯水電公司的莎拉。我們很遺憾無法與您取得聯繫。此通留言是要提醒您，您尚未繳納帳單。您的帳戶顯示您積欠 154.26 美元。此事非常重要，請記得立即繳納您的帳單。這是我們最後一次通知您。若您未於兩天內支付應繳款項，您的水電將被停用，並被索取 25 美元的延滯金。若您已支付您的帳單並認為這過程中出了差錯，請前往本公司填寫帳單不符表格。直至您填寫完表格並經本公司審核確認錯誤前，您仍必須按時繳納您的帳單與相關費用。感謝您的寶貴時間，華格納先生。

P. 29

考題範例｜題組 2 中文翻譯 TRACK 14

費斯克先生，謝謝您撥空來到這裡參觀我們的運作。<u>我希望我們能澄清產品瑕疵的問題。</u>首先，在左邊的是我們的收貨倉庫，貨品會被送到這裡。右邊是我們的製模區。再過去是組裝區。產品組裝後會送到這間房間密封與上漆。這是您說想檢查生產問題的房間。接著，工人會將成品放在乾燥架上。之後，會在那間小房間裡做產品測試。最後但同樣重要的是，如果產品通過品質檢查，會從後面的出貨室出貨。有任何問題嗎？

考題範例│題組 3 中文翻譯　TRACK 15

嘿，謝謝你跟我會面。我記得去年你推薦我買一些美金，因為當時匯率是最好的。你的建議讓我賺了不少錢。嗯，根據去年匯率的變化，看起來現在是我用美金買回一些歐元的好時機。你覺得如何？去年此時它漲到最高點，隔月又暴跌。我想我最好快點行動，以免後悔錯失良機。

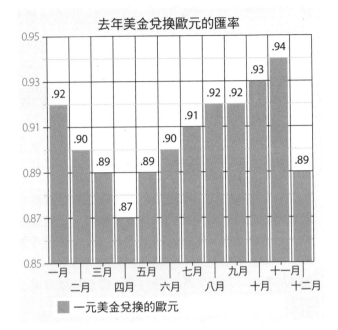

去年美金兌換歐元的匯率

一月 .92　二月 .90　三月 .89　四月 .87　五月 .89　六月 .90　七月 .91　八月 .92　九月 .92　十月 .93　十一月 .94　十二月 .89

■ 一元美金兌換的歐元

PART 6 Text Completion 段落填空

題目範例 中文翻譯

致我們珍視的顧客：

「親愛的動物」在經營二十二年後，準備要結束營業了。我們想要謝謝您的惠顧，包括您和您的寵物，其中許多已經變得像我們的家人一樣。從十月一日起，各位將在店內看到許多折扣，因為我們開始要處理掉我們的存貨。從十二月一日起，全部的存貨將要拿出來出清。<u>別錯過這麼棒的買賣，恰巧能趕上耶誕節喔！</u>我們歡迎舊雨新知在十二月二十日，星期六上午十點到下午五點和我們一起慶祝最後一個營業日。我們會有來店禮抽獎、茶點，以及在下午三點鐘舉行所有剩餘商品的熱鬧拍賣會，包括層架和展示桌。

謹致，
大衛‧哈金斯

PART 7 Reading Comprehension 閱讀測驗

P. 56

考題範例｜題組 1 中文翻譯

收件人：arthurbryk@houseofpanes.com
寄件人：edover@clifftonconsultants.org
主　旨：工作狀態

親愛的亞瑟：

我寫這封信時心裡無比沉重。我們合作多年，但我恐怕最終要中止我們之間的關係了。

老實說，你之前幫我們辦公室進行的那次裝修是完全讓人無法接受的。非但玻璃的品質有很大的改進空間，讓我們很驚訝的是，才過了幾天，窗玻璃片就開始出現裂縫了。

由於這只不過是長期一連串類似事件中最近期的一件，我別無選擇，只能下這個決定。我們之間的關係將立即結束。

謹致，
愛琳

P. 57

考題範例｜題組 2 中文翻譯

麥可 S. [下午 1:14 分]
嘿，大夥兒。我要提醒你們。影印機旁邊的碎紙機暫時不能使用。在它修好前，要用伺服器機房旁邊的那一台。

席琳娜 W. [下午 1:15 分]
喔，讓我來猜猜。又有人放太多紙進去了嗎？那已經發生好幾次了。遵守規定很難嗎？我不敢相信我跟能力這麼差的人一起工作。

崔弗 B. [下午 1:15 分]
哇，哇，哇。席琳娜，冷靜下來。我相信那只是意外。沒有人故意弄壞它。

席琳娜 W. [下午 1:16 分]
我知道。很明顯不是那樣。但即使是意外，還是很糟糕。大家需要注意自己的行為。

普席娜 C. [下午 1:17 分]
我有個主意。或許我們應該在機器上面貼張標示。那樣的話，可以提醒大家每次使用時要按照正確的操作方法。

麥可 S. [下午 1:17 分]
我喜歡那個主意。普席娜，我欣賞妳有建設性的態度。妳可以製作標示嗎？

普席娜 C. [下午 1:18 分]
當然可以。我馬上處理。標示會在機器修好前弄好。

麥可 S. [下午 1:18 分]
太好了。我預計機器會在幾天內修好。妳可以有充裕的時間製作。

考題範例｜題組 3 中文翻譯

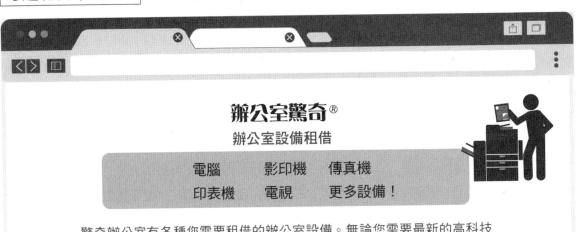

辦公室驚奇®

辦公室設備租借

電腦	影印機	傳真機
印表機	電視	更多設備！

驚奇辦公室有各種您需要租借的辦公室設備。無論您需要最新的高科技設備，或只是尋求暫時的解決方案，我們都能提供支援。無須擔心！

我們的設備租借以月、週或日為單位。顧客亦可選擇購買所租借的設備。設備的售價將可扣除已支付的租金。此外，我們提供一個限時的超級優惠！如果您租借四種或以上不同的設備，您的帳單可再折抵一百元。

使用我們的線上試算系統來獲取租金的報價

辦公室驚奇® 線上報價試算系統

印表機		數量	傳真機		數量
	每月 ($300)			每月 ($250)	
	每週 ($85)			每週 ($75)	
	每日 ($15)	10		每日 ($12)	10
電腦	每月 ($700)		影印機	每月 ($900)	
	每週 ($200)			每週 ($300)	
	每日 ($35)	30		每日 ($50)	30
會議電話	每月 ($100)		電視	每月 ($200)	
	每週 ($30)			每週 ($60)	
	每日 ($8)	10		每日 ($10)	10

有問題嗎？請寄電子郵件至
inquiries@officesurprise.net.

總計 ~~$1,800~~
$1,700

寄件人：jeff.thomas@crealtech.com
收件人：manager@officesurprise.net
主　旨：每小時的價格？
日　期：五月十二日

致辦公室驚奇的經理：

我是創造現實科技公司的傑夫・湯瑪士。我的公司下個月要辦一個活動，我們將需要許多設備（我已附上你們網站提供的估價）。你們的網站表示可以按日租借設備。那麼可以按小時嗎？我們需要大量的設備，但只需要在早上使用。你們公司可以接受比日租費用價格更低的租借嗎？我認為以租借不到半天而言，將我的總費用打六折是合理的。

P. 73~82

Part 1: Photographs

TRACK 17

1 (A) The badge has been left on a desk.
(B) The employees are swiping their badges.
(C) The employee is showing his badge.
(D) The document is hanging around his neck.

(A) 識別證被放在桌上。
(B) 員工們正在刷他們的識別證。
(C) 那位員工正在展示他的識別證。
(D) 這份文件正掛在他的脖子上。

正解 **(C)**
圖中的男子手上正拿著識別證朝向前方，因此符合圖片的敘述為 (C)「那位員工正在展示他的識別證。」

(B) swipe *(v.)* 刷（卡）。

2 (A) Ink cartridges are being replaced.
(B) The printer is out of paper.
(C) A document is being printed.
(D) The documents have been stapled.

(A) 墨水匣正在更換中。
(B) 印表機沒紙了。
(C) 一份文件正被列印出來。
(D) 那些文件已用釘書機釘好了。

正解 **(C)**
圖中可見印表機正在印出一份資料，故正確答案為 (C)。print *(v.)* 列印。

(B) be/run out of sth. *(phr.)* 用光某物。

Part 2: Question and Response

❸ The company's administration has an office on the second floor, doesn't it?

(A) I saw the secretary at her desk.

(B) They can administer the drug.

(C) Yes, next to the conference room.

公司行政部門在二樓有間辦公室,對吧?

(A) 我看到秘書在她的座位上。

(B) 他們可以給藥。

(C) 是的,就在會議室旁邊。

正解 **(C)**

本句為「附加問句」題型,意思是「公司行政部門在二樓有間辦公室,對吧?」合適的回應為 (C)「是的,就在會議室旁邊。」

(A) 選項與題意無關。

(B) 以與題目中 administration「行政」同字根的 administer「給予」一字試圖影響作答,實為與題意無關的答案。administer the drug/medicine 指「(醫護人員等)給藥」。

---

❹ Can you put me through to marketing?

(A) Sure, I will connect you now.

(B) We can't put it off any longer.

(C) I can put it in the mail for you.

你可以幫我轉接到行銷部嗎?

(A) 沒問題,我現在就幫您轉接。

(B) 我們不能再拖延了。

(C) 我可以幫你放在郵件裡。

正解 **(A)**

本題為以 Can 開頭的一般是非問句,詢問對方是否可以幫忙轉接電話。(A) 雖未直接以 Yes/No 回答,但表示沒問題馬上幫忙轉接,符合邏輯故為正解。

(B) put it off 是「拖延」之意,與題目無關。

(C) 此處的 put 是「放置」,答非所問。

---

❺ The stationery is kept in the supply room.

(A) There's a stationery store downtown.

(B) OK, I'll get some printing paper.

(C) The cars were stationary at the crossing.

文具放在儲藏室。

(A) 市中心有家文具店。

(B) 好的,我會去拿些影印紙。

(C) 車陣在十字路口動彈不得。

正解 **(B)**

本題為直述句,說明「文具放在儲藏室」。選項中唯一符合邏輯之回應為 (B)「好的。我會去拿些影印紙。」

(A) 題目與文具店無關。

(C) 企圖以發音相同字 stationary 混淆作答,但該字是形容詞表「靜止不動的」,與題意無關。

---

❻ Why do I need this swipe card?

(A) He's in the committee.

(B) Please wear your badge.

(C) To clock in and out.

我為何需要這張刷卡卡片?

(A) 他是委員會的一員。

(B) 請佩戴你的識別證。

(C) 為了要打卡上下班。

正解 **(C)**

本題以 Why 詢問需要這張刷卡卡片的原因,回答應說明理由。(C) 回答「為了要打卡上下班」,為符合邏輯之可能理由,故為正解。

(A) 與題意無關。

(B) 並未回答需要卡片的原因。

Part 3: Short Conversations

Questions 7-9 refer to the following conversation.

W: Hey Joe, this is Chloe in Accounts. I received your e-mail just now, but I couldn't open the attachments.

M: That's strange. No one else seems to have had a problem opening them.

W: I know. My colleague, Janice, opened them just fine. I guess I'll have to get the IT guy on it. **In the meantime**, could you print the documents for me? I will need them for the meeting with the CEO tomorrow.

M: Yeah, sure. I'll print them this afternoon and put them in the internal mail. You should have them first thing in the morning.

W: That would be great, thanks.

• in the meantime *(phr.)* 同時

女：嘿，喬，我是會計部的克蘿伊。我剛收到你的電子郵件，但我打不開附件。

男：怪了。別人似乎都可以打開。

女：我知道。我的同事珍妮絲就順利打開了。我想我得請資訊人員來看看了。與此同時，你可以幫我把文件印出來嗎？我明天跟執行長開會會需要它們。

男：好，當然。我下午會印出來放在內部郵件裡。妳應該明天一早就會拿到了。

女：那太棒了，謝啦。

---

7 What is the purpose of the woman's call to the man?
(A) To ask him to check his e-mails
(B) To invite him to a meeting with the CEO
(C) To ask him to fix her computer
(D) To inform him of a problem

女子打電話給男子的目的為何？
(A) 為了要他查看他的電子郵件
(B) 為了邀請他一起和執行長開會
(C) 為了要他修理她的電腦
(D) 為了通知他一個問題

正解 **(D)**

本題詢問女子打給男子的目的。由女子所說 I received your e-mail just now, but I couldn't open the attachments. 「我剛收到你的電子郵件，但我打不開附件。」可知她有郵件方面的問題要告訴他，答案選 (D)。

---

8 What does the man plan to do?
(A) Send the e-mail again
(B) Print the attachments
(C) Speak to the IT guy
(D) Photocopy some documents

男子計畫做什麼？
(A) 再寄一次電子郵件
(B) 把附件列印出來
(C) 跟資訊人員談談
(D) 影印一些文件

正解 **(B)**

本題詢問男子計畫做什麼。由男子所說 I'll print them this afternoon and put them in the internal mail. 「我下午會印出來放在內部郵件裡。」可知他會把附件印出來，故選 (B)。

⑨ When will the woman get the documents?

(A) Tomorrow morning
(B) This afternoon
(C) Tonight
(D) Just now

女子何時會拿到文件？

(A) 明天早上
(B) 今天下午
(C) 今晚
(D) 就是現在

正解 **(A)**

題目問女子何時會拿到文件。由男子所說 You should have them first thing in the morning. 可知她明天早上就會拿到了，故正確答案為 (A)。

Questions 10-12 refer to the following conversation and inventory list.

M: Gina, before the start of the new school year, I would like you to check the stockroom to see if we need to order anything.

W: Sure thing. I can print out an inventory list for you so that you will be able to **see at a glance** what we need.

M: That would be great, thanks. We especially need to make sure we have at least a hundred books in stock for our kindergartners, as they take longer to be delivered from the publisher.

W: OK, got it. I will go check right now and send you an e-mail with an attachment of the inventory list. Then I will go ahead and order more stock, if that's OK with you.

M: Yes, please. That would be very helpful.

• see (sth.) at a glance *(phr.)* 一眼就能看出……

男：吉娜，在新學年開始之前，我想要妳查看一下儲藏室，看看我們是否需要訂購什麼東西。

女：沒問題。我可以幫您把庫存清單印出來，好讓您一眼就能看出我們需要什麼。

男：那太好了，謝謝。我們特別需要確保幼兒園學生使用的書至少要有一百本庫存，因為它們從出版商那裡運送過來要花比較長的時間。

女：好的，知道了。我現在就去看看，並寄給您一封附上庫存清單的電子郵件。然後我會著手訂購更多的存貨，如果您覺得這樣進行沒問題的話。

男：好的，就請這麼做。妳幫了大忙。

INVENTORY LIST—STATIONERY & EDUCATIONAL SUPPLIES

ITEM #	DESCRIPTION	LOCATION	UNITS (PER PACK)	QUANTITY
SP7076	Early Readers (Books)	Aisle 1, shelf 1	x5	10 units
TR8765	Pencils (HB)	Aisle 2, shelf 1	x10	50 units
SY4545	Colored Pencils	Aisle 2, shelf 1	x10	20 units
XZ3124	Markers	Aisle 2, shelf 1	x6	10 units
AH9787	Colored Paper	Aisle 3, shelf 2	X100	3 units

庫存清單——文具和教育用品

品項編號	敘述	位置	單位（每包）	數量
SP7076	初階讀者（書）	一號走道、一號書架	五本	十包
TR8765	鉛筆（HB）	二號走道、一號書架	十枝	五十包
SY4545	彩色鉛筆	二號走道、一號書架	十枝	二十包
XZ3124	馬克筆	二號走道、一號書架	六枝	十包
AH9787	彩色紙	三號走道、二號書架	一百張	三包

⑩ What is the woman's occupation?
(A) Principal   **(B) Secretary**
(C) Deliveryman   (D) Publisher

女子的職業是什麼？
(A) 校長   **(B) 秘書**
(C) 送貨員   (D) 出版商

正解 **(B)**

題目問女子的職業是什麼。對話中男子吩咐女子工作事項，可推知女子應是男子的秘書，答案選 (B)。

---

⑪ What does the man say about the books for kindergartners?
(A) They are not kept in the stockroom.
(B) They are too hard for kindergartners.
(C) They are no longer in stock.
(D) They take longer to arrive.

關於為幼兒園學生準備的書，男子說了什麼？
(A) 它們沒有放在儲藏室裡。
(B) 它們對幼兒園學生來說太難了。
(C) 已經沒有庫存了。
(D) 它們要花較長的時間送達。

正解 **(D)**

本題詢問關於幼兒園學生使用的書，男子說了什麼。由男子所說 . . . as they take longer to be delivered from the publisher. 可知這些書要花較長的運送時間，故選 (D)。

12 Look at the graphic. How many new kindergarten books does the woman need to buy?

(A) 5   (B) 10

(C) 50   (D) 90

看圖表。女子需要購買多少本幼兒園新書？

(A) 五本   (B) 十本

(C) 五十本   (D) 九十本

正解 (C)

本題詢問秘書需要買多少本幼兒園新書。由男子所說 . . . make sure we have at least a hundred books in stock for our kindergartners . . .「……確保幼兒園學生使用的書至少要有一百本庫存……」，又根據圖表，目前書的庫存有五十本（一包有五本，共有十包，所以為五十本），因此推知秘書還要再買五十本，才能湊齊男子所說的一百本書，答案選 (C)。

Part 4: Short Talks

TRACK 20

Questions 13-15 refer to the following telephone message.

Good afternoon, Mr. Johnson. This is Elaine, one of the receptionists downstairs in the lobby. A couple of minutes ago, <u>I signed for a delivery</u> of bulk mail from QuickPrint Printing Company. It seems to be a large number of advertizing brochures, but the box doesn't state who the recipient should be. Maybe I should just go ahead and send the box up to the marketing department on the 5th floor, but I don't want to do that if it's not for them. I was hoping you might know who the order belongs to. If you do, could you give me a call on extension 001 or leave me a voicemail message? Thanks.

強森先生午安。我是伊蓮，樓下大廳的其中一位接待員。幾分鐘前，<u>我簽收了</u>快印印刷公司送來的大宗郵件。看起來好像是大量的宣傳小冊子，但箱子上沒寫收件人是誰。也許我應該就把箱子送到五樓的行銷部就好，但如果不是給他們的話我就不想那樣做。我在想你也許會知道這筆訂貨是屬於誰的。如果你知道的話，可以打分機 001 給我或是留言到我的語音信箱嗎？謝謝。

13 What problem does the speaker have?

(A) She doesn't know where the marketing department is.

(B) She doesn't know what is inside the box.

(C) She doesn't know who a delivery belongs to.

(D) She doesn't know how to place an order.

說話者有什麼問題？

(A) 她不知道行銷部在哪裡。

(B) 她不知道箱子裡有什麼東西。

(C) 她不知道送達的貨物是屬於誰的。

(D) 她不知道如何下訂單。

正解 (C)

本題詢問說話者有什麼問題。由關鍵句 I was hoping you might know who the order belongs to.「我在想你也許會知道這筆訂貨是屬於誰的。」可知答案應選 (C)。

⑭ What does the speaker mean when she says, "I signed for a delivery"?
- (A) She put a sign up in the lobby.
- (B) She sent out a delivery.
- (C) She signed up for an activity.
- **(D) She provided a signature.**

說話者提到 "I signed for a delivery" 的意思為何？
- (A) 她在大廳設置了一塊招牌。
- (B) 她把一件貨物寄送出去。
- (C) 她報名參加一場活動。
- **(D) 她提供了她的簽名。**

正解 (D)

sign 作動詞時指「簽（名）」，sign for sth. 則是指「簽收」，delivery 是指「遞送之物」。因此符合本對話情境的答案為 (D)。

(C) sign up for (phr.) 報名……（活動、組織等）。

---

⑮ What will the speaker do next?
- (A) Send the box up to marketing
- (B) Return the box to QuickPrint
- **(C) Wait for a call from Mr. Johnson**
- (D) Give out the brochures to visitors

說話者接下來會做什麼事？
- (A) 把箱子送到行銷部
- (B) 把箱子退回快印印刷公司
- **(C) 等強森先生的電話**
- (D) 把冊子分發給訪客

正解 (C)

本題詢問說話者接下來會做什麼事。由倒數第二句 If you do, could you give me a call on extension 001 or leave me a voice mail message?「如果你知道的話，你可以打分機 001 給我或是留言到我的語音信箱嗎？」可知她接下來會等強森先生回電，答案選 (C)。

Questions 16-18 refer to the following announcement and table.

Hello, everyone. Thanks for attending this briefing. First, I just want to remind everyone about the board meeting which will be taking place this Friday. As well as myself, all five of our board of directors have confirmed that they will be attending the meeting, and Celine will be taking minutes. We need to make sure that a suitable conference room is ready for the meeting. We'll be needing a projector so that we can all view my presentation, but I have already photocopied the necessary documents. Of course, we'll need coffee throughout the morning. Can you all make sure everything's ready? It would be great if you could tidy up your workstations and dress suitably on Friday, as I will be starting with a tour of the office. Then the board meeting will follow, at around 10:00 a.m. Is everything clear?

大家好。感謝各位參加這場簡報會。首先，我只是想要提醒各位這禮拜五有董事會議要開。除了我之外，所有五個董事會成員也確認會出席會議，而席琳會做會議記錄。我們得確保為這場會議準備好一間適合的會議室。我們會需要一台投影機，這樣所有人才能看到我的簡報，但我已經影印好必要的文件了。當然，我們整個上午都會需要咖啡。你們可以一起確保一切都準備就緒嗎？如果各位能整理一下你們的工作區域並在禮拜五穿著合宜那就太棒了，因為我會先帶他們參觀辦公室。然後十點左右董事會議就會接著開始。大家都清楚了嗎？

Room	Seating Capacity	Facilities
Reception area, 1st floor	4	Water cooler
Room A, 1st floor	5	Projector
Room B, 2nd floor	10	Projector, Coffee maker
Room C, 5th floor	12	Whiteboard, Photocopier, Coffee maker

房間	可容納座位	設備
接待區，一樓	四	飲水機
A 室，一樓	五	投影機
B 室，二樓	十	投影機、咖啡機
C 室，五樓	十二	白板、影印機、咖啡機

⑯ Who most likely is the speaker?
(A) A cleaner
(B) A secretary
(C) A receptionist
(D) A company director

說話者最有可能是誰？
(A) 清潔工
(B) 秘書
(C) 接待員
(D) 公司主管

正解 (D)

本題詢問說話者的身分。由關鍵句 As well as myself, all five of our board of directors have confirmed that they will be attending the meeting . . .「除了我之外，所有五個董事會成員也確認會出席會議……」以及他吩咐大家一起為董事會議做好準備，可推知他應是公司主管，答案選 (D)。

⑰ What is implied about the upcoming meeting?
(A) It will be casual.
(B) It will be important.
(C) It will be brief.
(D) It will include lunch.

關於即將到來的會議，說話者有什麼暗示？
(A) 它會是非正式的。
(B) 它將會很重要。
(C) 它將很短暫。
(D) 它會提供午餐。

正解 (B)

本題詢問關於即將到來的會議，說話者有何暗示。由關鍵句 First, I just want to remind everyone about the board meeting which will be taking place this Friday. 可知禮拜五要開董事會議，又倒數第三句 It would be great if you could tidy up your workstations and dress suitably on Friday . . . 可知說話者要求大家在禮拜五那天要穿著合宜，暗示那場董事會議很重要，答案選 (B)。

⑱ Look at the graphic. On which floor will the meeting be held?
(A) In the reception area
(B) On the 1st floor
(C) On the 2nd floor
(D) On the 5th floor

看圖表，會議會在哪一樓舉行？
(A) 在接待區　　　　(B) 一樓
(C) 二樓　　　　　(D) 五樓

正解 **(C)**

本題詢問會議會在哪一樓舉行。由關鍵句 We'll be needing a projector . . .「我們會需要一台投影機……」以及 Of course, we'll need coffee throughout the morning.「當然，我們整個上午都會需要咖啡。」，再對照圖表，可得知只有二樓同時有投影機和咖啡機，且可容納座位超過六人（說話者加上五位董事會成員），故 (C) 為正解。

Part 5: Incomplete Sentences

⑲ In order to track working hours, employees are given a special card so that they can punch _____ every day.
(A) back
(B) on
(C) in
(D) at

為了追蹤工時，員工會拿到一張特殊卡片，這樣他們就能每天打卡。
(A) 無 punch back 之搭配用法。
(B) 無 punch on 之搭配用法。
(C) punch in 指「上班打卡」。
(D) 無 punch at 之搭配用法。

正解 **(C)**

本題考動詞片語。punch in 表示「打卡上班」，合乎句意，故 (C) 為正確答案。

⑳ If we _____ out of stock of ink cartridges, we would need to order some more from our supplier.
(A) are
(B) is
(C) was
(D) were

如果我們的墨水匣用完了，我們就需要向供應商再訂一些。
(A) 是（現在式第二人稱單數或各人稱複數 be 動詞）
(B) 是（現在式第三人稱單數 be 動詞）
(C) 是（過去式單數 be 動詞）
(D) 是（過去式複數 be 動詞）

正解 **(D)**

本題考文法。句子開頭有 If，可知這是測驗假設語氣，又由後面主要子句的 would need 可推知這是與現在事實相反的假設，if 子句動詞要用過去式，而當動詞是 be 動詞，不論主詞為第幾人稱均使用 were，答案選 (D)。

21 Mr. Lee _____ for an important business trip to Shanghai last Monday.

(A) **left**

(B) was leaving

(C) leave

(D) leaves

李先生上週一為了重要事務去上海出差。

(A) 離開（過去式）

(B) 離開（過去進行式）

(C) 離開（原形動詞）

(D) 離開（現在式第三人稱單數動詞）

本題考時態。句子最後面有時間副詞 last Monday，可知這是過去發生的事，又根據句意，此處不是表達過去某時正在進行的動作，而是過去某時已完成的動作，因此動詞應用過去式，正確答案為 (A)。

• leave for *(phr.)* 出發去（某地）

---

22 There has been a lot of _____ between the company and the tax office.

(A) correspondent

(B) corresponding

(C) **correspondence**

(D) corresponded

那間公司和國稅局一直以來有很多書信往返。

(A) 通訊記者（名詞）

(B) 對等的（形容詞或現在分詞）

(C) **書信往返（名詞）**

(D) 符合；對應（動詞 correspond 的過去式）

本題考詞性。空格前方為介系詞 of，可推知空格內應為名詞；又根據句意，那間公司和國稅局一直以來有很多「往返書信」，故答案應選 (C)。

---

23 The executive committee passed the _____ with a vote of five to one in favor.

(A) recipient

(B) **resolution**

(C) receptionist

(D) requirement

執行委員會以五票對一票通過了那項決議。

(A) 接受者

(B) **決議**

(C) 接待員

(D) 需求

本題考字義。依照句意可知空格處填入 (B) resolution 指「決議」，表示執行委員會通過了那項決議。

Part 6: Text Completion

Questions 24-27 refer to the following notice.

NOTICE TO ALL STAFF

Our administration department has noticed a great increase in the amount of ---24--- being produced in this office recently, which has led to rising costs for ink and paper. This notice is to let everybody know that we will no longer automatically replace ---25--- in individual printers. The decision has ---26--- by the directors that, once the ink has run out on your personal desktop printers, the ink will not be replaced. ---27--- Desktop printers that are no longer in use will be donated to the local junior high school. Thank you for your understanding and remember to think before you print!

公告全體員工

我們的行政部門已經注意到最近這間辦公室所產生的印刷品數量大為增加,這造成墨水和紙的花費上升。這份公告是要讓大家知道我們將不再自動更換個人印表機的墨水匣。主管們已做出這項決定,一旦你個人桌上型印表機的墨水用完,其墨水匣將不會替換。<u>反之,你的印刷需求將會由中央行政團隊處理。</u>不再使用的桌上型印表機將捐贈給當地的國中。感謝你的理解,並記得在列印之前先好好想想!

---

24 (A) swipe cards　　(B) voicemails
  (C) printed matter　(D) board meetings

(A) 刷卡卡片　　(B) 語音信箱
(C) 印刷品　　(D) 董事會議

正解 (C)
本題考單字。原句提到行政部門已經注意到最近辦公室所產生的＿＿＿數量大為增加,這造成墨水和紙的花費上升,故依句意可知最適合的答案為 (C)。

---

25 **(A) ink cartridges**　(B) junk mail
  (C) shareholders　　(D) stock

(A) 墨水匣　　(B) 垃圾郵件
(C) 股東　　　(D) 存貨

正解 (A)
本題考單字。原句提到,這份公告是要讓大家知道我們將不再自動更換個人印表機的＿＿＿,可知符合句意的答案為 (A)。

---

26 (A) made　　　(B) make
  (C) been made　(D) be made

(A) 做（過去式）　(B) 做（原形動詞）
(C) 已被做　　(D) 被做

正解 (C)
本題考文法。該句主詞為 The decision,後面有 by the directors,可知該句動詞須使用被動語態,表示這項決定是「被」主管們做出的,又因為空格前方有助動詞 has,可知空格內應填 been made 形成現在完成式的被動語態,故答案應選 (C)。

27 (A) Instead, the ink will be replaced for you so you can carry on printing.

(B) Rather, your printing needs will be handled by the central administration team.

(C) However, you will be able to use your swipe card to enter the building.

(D) Nevertheless, you will still be able to forward your junk mail to our department.

(A) 相反地，會幫你更換墨水，好讓你能繼續列印。

(B) 反之，你的印刷需求將會由中央行政團隊處理。

(C) 然而，你將可以用你的刷卡卡片進入這棟建築。

(D) 然而，你將仍能轉寄你的垃圾郵件到我們部門。

正解 **(B)**

本空格的前一句說「一旦你個人桌上型印表機的墨水用完，其墨水將不會替換。」，可推測下一句應會說明在此情況下，員工要如何列印所需的資料，故 (B) 應為正選。

Part 7: Reading Comprehension

Questions 28-30 refer to the following letter.

Dear colleagues,

It is with some sadness that I am informing you all of my decision to leave the company after ten memorable years. This is a subject that I have been thinking about for a while, but yesterday I finally took the leap and informed the board of directors of my decision to resign. It wasn't an easy decision, but I decided that the time was right for me to spend more time with my young family.

As I will be away on my final business trip for the company next week, I may not have the chance to say goodbye to you all in person. However, I am happy to give you my personal e-mail, which is sally.taylor@tmail.com. Charles in HR has my address if you need to forward any mail that may arrive for me by post.

Finally, I would like to thank everyone for making my time here so pleasant and I hope to see you all soon.

All the best,

Sally

親愛的同事們：

我帶著一絲感傷，想在這裡通知大家，在經過十個難忘的寒暑之後，我決定要離開公司了。我考慮這件事已經有一段時間了，但昨天我終於付諸實行通知董事會我辭職的決定了。這不是個容易的決定，但我認為現在正是多花點時間陪伴我年幼家人的時機。

由於下個禮拜我要為公司出最後一次差，我也許沒機會親自跟大家道別了。然而，我很樂意給你們我的個人電子郵件：sally.taylor@tmail.com。如果你們需要轉交任何以郵件寄來給我的信件，人資部的查爾斯有我的地址。

最後，我想要感謝大家讓我在這裡過得如此愉快，我希望能早日跟大家見面。

祝一切順利，

莎莉

28 The phrase "took the leap" in paragraph 1, line 3, is closest in meaning to

(A) jumped over

(B) took control

(C) changed one's mind

(D) made a decision

第一段第三行的片語 took the leap 意思最接近

(A) 跳過   (B) 掌控

(C) 某人改變主意   **(D)** 做出決定

| 正解 **(D)** |

本題為同義字詞。詢問第一段的 took the leap 意思相近於何者。take the leap 指「放手嘗試做某事」，意思近於 (D)「做出決定」。

---

29 What is NOT mentioned in the letter?

(A) The date she will be leaving

(B) Her decision for leaving

(C) How long she has worked there

(D) Her personal e-mail address

信裡沒有提到哪一件事？

(A) 她將要離開的日期

(B) 她要離開的決定

(C) 她在那裡工作多久

(D) 她的個人電子郵件地址

| 正解 **(A)** |

本題為除外題，詢問信裡沒有提到哪一件事。(B) 由第一段第一句的 leave the company 與第二句的 my decision to resign 可知她要離職了；(C) 由第一段第一句 leave the company after ten memorable years 可知她在那裡工作十年；(D) 由第二段第二句可知她的電子郵件是 sally.taylor@tmail.com。唯 (A) 她將要離開的日期內文沒有提及，答案選 (A)。

---

30 What is implied about the letter writer?

(A) She has elderly relatives.

(B) She needs a break from traveling.

(C) She has children at home.

(D) She doesn't like her employer.

關於信件作者，文中有何暗示？

(A) 她有年長的親戚。

(B) 她需要去旅遊休息一下。

(C) 她家裡有小孩。

(D) 她不喜歡她的僱主。

| 正解 **(C)** |

本題為推論題，詢問該信作者的狀況。解題關鍵在第一段最後一句 . . . the time was right for me to spend more time with my young family.「對我來說現在正是多花點時間陪伴我年幼家人的時機」，可知她家裡有小孩要照顧，故選 (C)。

Questions 31-35 *refer to the following e-mail and instructions.*

To:	allstaff@elt.com
From:	toby@Qcopiers.com
Re:	Installation and use of new photocopier

Dear ELT Staff,

Q-Copiers are very pleased to be your new vendor and servicing company of your brand new ADX4009 photocopier. Yesterday, our team visited your office to set up the new machine and it is now ready to use.

We think you will be pleased with the many excellent features of the ADX4009, which include the ability to copy color as well as black and white, the capacity to produce bulk mail as well as individual documents, and various options to staple and finish your photocopies. The ADX4009 is also one of the most user-friendly machines and you will have no trouble getting the hang of it. To help you, I am attaching a brief summary of the instructions and access codes for you to punch in when you want to make copies.

We will be servicing the photocopier every six months and Rob Lane in your Administration Department is the person responsible for the day-to-day operation of the photocopier. So, if you have any problems, you can call him on extension 203.

Best Regards,

Toby Smart
Sales & Servicing Manager
Q-Copiers Inc.

收件者：allstaff@elt.com
寄件者：toby@Qcopiers.com
主　旨：新影印機的安裝和使用

親愛的 ELT 全體員工：

Q-Copiers 很高興能成為貴公司全新 ADX4009 影印機的新供應商及檢修公司。昨天我們團隊造訪您的辦公室安裝新機器，而它現在已可供使用了。

我們認為諸位將會對 ADX4009 許多絕佳的功能十分滿意，這包括了可以彩色及黑白影印、可以產生大量郵件以及個別文件，並具有多種選項來裝訂完成各位的影印文件。ADX4009 同時也是最方便用戶使用的機器之一，諸位將能輕鬆地熟悉它的操作方法。為了協助各位，我附上一份簡短的操作說明摘要，以及各位影印時需要輸入的通行碼。

我們每六個月會檢修一次影印機，而貴公司行政部門的羅伯·雷恩則會負責影印機的日常操作。所以諸位若有任何問題，可以打分機 203 找他。

謹致，

托比·史馬特
銷售服務經理
Q-Copiers 股份有限公司

Company: ELT Inc.
Installation Date: January 3rd
Model: ADX4009

BASIC INSTRUCTIONS FOR USE

1. Photocopier will usually be in standby mode, so you will not need to turn on the power.

2. Ensure paper trays are full. Stocks of paper can be found in the supply room where the stationery is kept.

3. Place your document(s) face-up in the paper feeder (for multiple pages) or lift the lid and place your document on the glass face-down (for single pages).

4. The menu screen will guide you through the steps for photocopying. Here you will select paper size, number of copies, color, and printing options, and position of staples.

5. Press the green "Copy" button.

ADDITIONAL INFORMATION

• If pages get stuck, contact extension 203.

• If the resolution of your copies is not adequate, please call a member of our servicing team on 1-800-555-992.

• Check your employee badge for code, or see table on the right.

Department	Code
Administration	0985
Marketing	0986
Sales	0987

公司：ELT 股份有限公司
安裝日期：一月三日
型號：ADX4009

基本使用說明

1. 影印機通常會處於待機模式，所以您不用打開電源。

2. 請確保紙盤是滿的。影印紙的存貨可在儲藏室找到，就在放文具的地方。

3. 請將您的文件朝上放在送紙盤上（影印多頁時），或是抬起蓋子並將您的文件朝下放在玻璃上（影印單頁時）。

4. 選單螢幕會引導您進行影印步驟。在這裡您要選擇紙張尺寸、影本份數、顏色和影印選項，以及裝訂位置。

5. 按下綠色的「影印」鍵。

補充說明

• 如果卡紙，請聯絡分機 203。

• 如果您影本的解析度不足，請打 1-800-555-992 聯絡我們檢修團隊的成員。

• 查看您的員工名牌以獲得密碼，或是看右側的表格。

部門	密碼
行政	0985
行銷	0986
業務	0987

31 What is the main purpose in writing the e-mail?

(A) To sell the company a new photocopier

(B) To send instructions for use of new photocopier

(C) To introduce a photocopier supplier

(D) To tell people about various photocopiers

撰寫這封電子郵件的主要目的為何？

(A) 為了賣新的影印機給該公司

(B) 為了寄新影印機的使用說明

(C) 為了介紹一間影印機供應商

(D) 為了告訴人們有關不同影印機的事

正解 **(B)**

本題為主旨題，詢問此封電子郵件的主要目的。由電郵一開頭的 Re: Installation and use of new photocopier 可知這是關於新影印機的安裝和使用，又第二段最後一句 To help you, I am attaching a brief summary of the instructions and access codes for you to punch in when you want to make copies. 「為了協助各位，我附上一份簡短的操作說明摘要，以及各位影印時需要輸入的通行碼。」可知此郵件的目的就是要寄新的影印機的使用說明，答案選 (B)。

(C) supplier (n.) 供應商。

---

32 What is NOT mentioned in the e-mail?

(A) The number of people that installed the machine

(B) The features of the new machine

(C) The model number of the machine

(D) The name of the vendor company

下列哪一項沒有在電子郵件中提及？

(A) 安裝機器的人數

(B) 新機器的特色

(C) 該機器的型號

(D) 供應商的名稱

正解 **(A)**

本題為除外題，詢問下列哪一項沒有在電子郵件中提及。(B) 可見第二段的 ... which include the ability to copy color as well as black and white, the capacity to produce bulk mail as well as individual documents, and various options to staple and finish your photocopies.；(C)、(D) 可見郵件的第一句 Q-Copiers are very pleased to be your new vendor and servicing company of your brand new ADX4009 photocopier.。唯獨 (A) 未提及，故 (A) 為正選。

㉝ What are the code numbers on the instructions?

(A) Telephone extensions

(B) Model numbers

(C) Maximum number of copies

(D) Access codes

在使用說明上的密碼是什麼？

(A) 電話分機

(B) 型號

(C) 影印的最大印量

(D) 通行碼

正解 **(D)**

本題為細節題，詢問使用說明上的密碼是什麼。由郵件上的關鍵句 I am attaching a brief summary of the instructions and access codes for you to punch in when you want to make copies. 可知這個密碼是員工影印時需要輸入的通行碼，答案選 (D)。

㉞ In what month will the photocopier next be serviced?

(A) January

(B) March

(C) June

(D) July

影印機下次檢修是在哪一個月？

(A) 一月

(B) 三月

(C) 六月

(D) 七月

正解 **(D)**

本題為整合題，詢問影印機下次檢修是在哪一個月。由郵件第三段第一句 We will be servicing the photocopier every six months ... 可知每六個月會檢修一次，又根據使用說明的 Installation Date: January 3rd 可知安裝日期是在一月，因此六個月後就是七月，答案選 (D)。

㉟ What is the access code for Rob Lane?

(A) 0986

(B) ADX4009

(C) 0985

(D) 0987

羅伯‧雷恩的通行碼是多少？

(A) 0986

(B) ADX4009

(C) 0985

(D) 0987

正解 **(C)**

本題是整合題，詢問羅伯‧雷恩的通行碼是多少。由郵件最後一段第一句 ... and Rob Lane in your Administration Department is the person responsible for ... 可知羅伯‧雷恩屬於行政部門，又對照基本使用說明中的表格，行政部門的密碼為 0985，因此答案為 (C)。

P. 96~104

Part 1: Photographs

TRACK 22

1 (A) A man is demonstrating a product to his coworkers.
(B) The coworkers are meeting in the boardroom.
(C) A projector is hanging on the wall.
(D) A woman is giving a presentation in the office.

(A) 一名男子正在對他的同事展示產品。
(B) 員工們正在會議室開會。
(C) 一台投影機懸掛在牆上。
(D) 一名女子正在辦公室發表簡報。

正解 **(B)**

圖中的員工們坐在會議室裡談話，因此符合圖片的敘述為 (B)「員工們正在會議室開會。」

(D) presentation *(n.)* 簡報；報告。

2 (A) The businessman is submitting a report.
(B) Some documents have been filed in the cabinet.
(C) The businessmen are comparing graphs.
(D) A contract is being signed by the businessmen.

(A) 那名商人正在提交一份報告。
(B) 一些文件已被歸檔在櫃子裡。
(C) 商人們正在比較圖表。
(D) 一份合約正被商人們簽署。

正解 **(D)**

圖中可見雙方正在簽署一份合約，故正確答案為 (D)。sign *(v.)* 簽署。
(B) file *(v.)* 把……歸檔；cabinet *(n.)* 檔案櫃。
(C) compare *(v.)* 比較。

Part 2: Question and Response

❸ Why has our company faced such stiff competition this year?
  (A) Five people competed for first place.
  (B) Consumers really like our products best.
  (C) Two rival companies released similar products.

為什麼我們公司今年面臨如此激烈的競爭？
(A) 五個人為爭取第一而相互競爭。
(B) 消費者真的最愛我們的產品。
(C) 有兩家競爭對手推出了相似的產品。

正解 (C)

本題以 Why 詢問今年競爭如此激烈的原因，回答應說明理由。(C) 回答「有兩家競爭對手推出了相似的產品」，為符合邏輯之可能理由，故為正選。

(A) 句意與公司的競爭無關。
(B) 消費者若最愛公司的產品，公司便不須擔憂競爭激烈，故非正確答案。

---

❹ Have you reached an agreement on the marketing strategy?
  (A) Yes, but we couldn't agree on anything.
  (B) Yes, we're going to use social media.
  (C) No, we need to hire more people.

你們對於行銷策略取得一致的意見了嗎？
(A) 是的，但我們對任何事都無法取得一致的意見。
(B) 是的，我們將會使用社群媒體。
(C) 不，我們需要雇用更多人。

正解 (B)

題目問「你們對於行銷策略取得一致的意見了嗎？」亦即詢問他們是否意見一致，(B) 回答「是的，我們將會使用社群媒體。」合乎題意。

(A) 開頭說 Yes 表示已取得共識，但是後面又說意見不一致，前後矛盾。
(C) 題目並未詢問是否要雇用更多人。

---

❺ Will the advertisement appear on billboards or in the newspaper?
  (A) Some newspapers are more widely read than others.
  (B) We think advertising on signs is a better strategy.
  (C) The movie star will not appear in our advertisement.

那則廣告會在大型廣告看板上出現還是在報紙出現？
(A) 有些報紙比其他報紙享有更高的閱讀率。
(B) 我們覺得在招牌上打廣告是個比較好的策略。
(C) 那位電影明星不會出現在我們的廣告裡。

正解 (B)

本題為選擇疑問句，詢問廣告會在大型廣告看板或報紙上出現。可能的回答是「兩者皆是」、「兩者擇一」或「兩者皆非」。(B) 擇一回應，表示會刊登在招牌，也就是廣告看板上，故答案選 (B)。

(A) 句意與廣告無關。
(C) 題目並未詢問電影明星是否會出現在廣告裡。

❻ I think the company will be downsizing next year.
(A) So we will probably get a lot of new coworkers.
(B) That's good because their sizes don't fit me.
(C) That's too bad, but I guess they need to cut costs.

我想明年公司將會縮編。
(A) 那麼我們也許會有很多新同事。
(B) 那很好，因為它們的尺寸不適合我。
(C) 那太糟了，但我想他們需要削減成本。

正解 **(C)**

本題為直述句，題目說明年公司將會縮編。最可能的回應為 (C)「那太糟了，但我想他們需要削減成本。」表示公司為了省錢才會縮小規模，合乎邏輯。
(A) 縮小規模和招募新同事相互矛盾。
(B) 題目和尺寸適合與否無關。

Part 3: Short Conversations

TRACK 24

Questions 7-9 refer to the following conversation.

W: So, if we are successful in this location, we can open franchises elsewhere. We are projecting that <u>we will be able to expand</u> in at least five major cities.

M: I am sure this enterprise will be a success, so I am certain others will be interested in being a part of it.

W: Yes, owning a franchise is a great way to start a business, and there is less risk involved than starting a business from scratch.

M: I agree. It's good for the franchise owners and for us too, as we will get a percentage of their profits.

女：那麼，如果我們在這個地點成功的話，<u>我們在其他地方也可以開加盟店</u>。我們預計將至少能在五座大城市擴展生意。

男：我確定這項事業會成功，所以我敢肯定其他人會有興趣成為其中的一份子。

女：是啊，擁有一間加盟店是創業的一個絕佳方法，比白手起家創業的風險低。

男：我同意。這對加盟店跟我們來說都很好，因為我們會從他們的獲利中抽成。

❼ What are the speakers mainly discussing?
   (A) The company's advertising campaign
   (B) The financial state of the business
   (C) The success of the company's first store
   (D) The advantages of franchise businesses

   說話者主要在談論何事？
   (A) 公司的廣告宣傳活動
   (B) 企業的財務狀況
   (C) 公司第一家店的成功
   (D) 加盟事業的優勢

正解 (D)

本題詢問說話者主要在談論何事。由女子所說 Yes, owning a franchise is a great way to . . . 及男子回答 I agree. It's good for the franchise owners and for us too . . . 表示他們在討論加盟事業的優點，答案選 (D)。

❽ What does the woman mean when she says, "we will be able to expand"?
   (A) The company will be able to open more stores.
   (B) The coworkers will be able to start their own business.
   (C) The company will be able to negotiate a new deal.
   (D) The company will rent a bigger office.

   女子提到 "we will be able to expand" 的意思為何？
   (A) 公司將可以開更多店。
   (B) 同事們將可以開創自己的事業。
   (C) 公司將可以商談一筆新的交易。
   (D) 公司將會租用更大間的辦公室。

正解 (A)

從關鍵句 . . . we can open franchises elsewhere. We are projecting that we will be able to expand in at least five major cities. 可知他們預計將至少能在五座大城市擴展生意，也就是開更多家加盟店，故答案選 (A)。

❾ Why does the man think opening franchises is a good idea?
   (A) He will get a promotion.
   (B) His company will earn money from them.
   (C) He likes traveling around the city.
   (D) He will be able to retire early.

   為何男子認為開加盟店是個好主意？
   (A) 他會得到晉升。
   (B) 他的公司會從中賺錢。
   (C) 他喜歡遊覽全城。
   (D) 他將可以提早退休。

正解 (B)

本題詢問為何男子認為開加盟店是個好主意。由最後一句 It's good for the franchise owners and for us too, as we will get a percentage of their profits. 得知他們會從加盟店的獲利中抽成，因此答案選 (B)。

Questions 10-12 *refer to the following conversation and chart.*

M: I wanted to discuss with you how well our merchandise is selling in the various markets and how well it is likely to sell over the next two years.

W: Sure. I have some retail sales figures for you as well as this graph showing last year's global sales.

M: That's great. Thanks for preparing the figures for me.

W: No problem. It looks like Asia will continue to be our strongest retail market.

M: Yes. It's not really surprising since Asian consumers are buying so many electronics right now. So, over the next two years, I would like to shift our focus to another market that is showing great potential. Let's aim to increase the sales in that market by 1 million so that it can reach the 5 million mark.

W: I agree. I have already set up a brainstorming meeting with the Marketing Department.

男：我想和妳討論一下我們的商品在不同市場的銷售狀況，以及在未來兩年可能會有的表現。

女：好的。我這裡也有一些零售銷售數字要給你看，以及這張顯示了去年全球銷量的圖表。

男：那太棒了。謝謝妳為我準備這些數字。

女：這沒什麼。看來亞洲持續會是我們最強勁的零售市場。

男：是的。這不太令人意外，因為現在亞洲消費者正購買超多的電器用品。所以在未來兩年，我想要把我們的焦點轉移到另一個嶄露極大潛力的市場。讓我們努力把該市場的銷售提高一百萬，那麼它就能達到五百萬的目標了。

女：我同意。我已和行銷部門安排了一場腦力激盪會議。

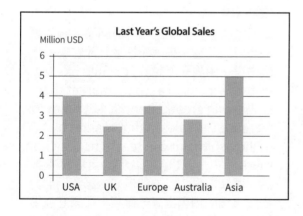

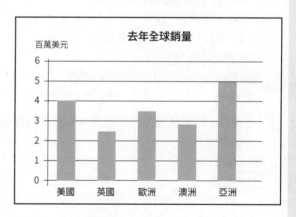

⑩ What line of work are the speakers in?
(A) Advertising　　(B) **Sales**
(C) Publishing　　(D) Education

說話者的工作領域為何？
(A) 廣告　　(B) 銷售
(C) 出版　　(D) 教育

正解 (B)

本題詢問說話者的工作領域為何。從關鍵字詞 retail sales figures「零售銷售數字」、last year's global sales「去年的全球銷量」、Let's aim to increase the sales「讓我們把目標定在增加銷售量」可知他們在討論銷量及銷售目標，因此最可能的工作領域為 (B)。

⑪ What does the man say about the Asian market?
(A) It has been unexpectedly strong.
(B) It should be the main focus in future.
(C) **It's strong because people are buying more electronics.**
(D) It's not worth the company investing in.

男子對於亞洲市場發表了何種看法？
(A) 它超乎預期地表現強勁。
(B) 它應在未來成為主要焦點。
(C) **它表現強勁，因為人們購買更多電器用品。**
(D) 它不值得公司進行投資。

正解 (C)

本題詢問男子對於亞洲市場發表了何種看法。女子先表達亞洲將持續會是他們最強勁的零售市場，男子接著回應 Yes. It's not really surprising since Asian consumers are buying so many electronics right now.，可得知男子同意其說法，因為許多人都在買電器用品，答案選 (C)。

⑫ Look at the graphic. Which market does the man want the company to focus on over the next two years?
(A) Europe　　(B) **USA**
(C) UK　　(D) Australia

看圖表。男子想要公司在未來兩年把重點放在哪一個市場？
(A) 歐洲　　(B) **美國**
(C) 英國　　(D) 澳洲

正解 (B)

本題須結合對話與圖表內容回答。詢問男子想要公司在未來兩年把重點放在哪一個市場。由男子所說 . . . I would like to shift our focus to another market that is showing great potential. Let's aim to increase the sales in that market by 1 million so that it can reach the 5 million mark.「……我想要把我們的焦點轉移到另一個嶄露極大潛力的市場。讓我們努力把該市場的銷售提高一百萬，那麼它就能達到五百萬的目標了。」，可推知他所說的那個市場銷售額現在應是四百萬，對照圖表可知是美國，答案選 (B)。

Part 4: Short Talks

Questions 13-15 refer to the following talk.

Welcome! Thank you all for attending this month's meeting. I know you are all really busy and I don't expect today's meeting to be too lengthy. I just wanted to keep you all informed about our new direct marketing campaign. Thanks to the efforts of our excellent Marketing team, the campaign is really paying off. Since the launch, we have been able to reach out to thousands of customers by phone, e-mail, and letter. The response has been amazing and many new customers have taken up our offer of a free trial. Our telephone marketers really have excellent persuasion skills! Of course this means that in the coming months we will be extra busy, as we need to ensure that these new customers remain committed. Thanks for an excellent month and keep up the good work!

歡迎！感謝大家參加這個月的會議。我知道各位都很忙，我想今天的會議不會開很久。我只是想要讓大家知道我們新的直效行銷活動。多虧了我們優秀行銷團隊的努力，宣傳活動很成功。活動起跑後，我們便得以透過手機、電子郵件和書信將觸角延伸至數千名客戶。客戶的回應很棒，且很多新客戶開始接受我們提供的免費試用。我們電話行銷人員的說服技巧真的很棒！當然這意味著在接下來的幾個月我們將會更加忙碌，因為我們需要確保這些新客戶維持忠誠度。感謝這個月優秀的表現，繼續保持下去吧！

SECTION B 試題練習

UNIT 2 General Business 一般商務

---

13 What is the main purpose of the talk?

(A) To launch a new product

(B) To report on a successful marketing campaign

(C) To discuss ways to keep new customers

(D) To discuss how customers will be contacted

這段談話的主要目的是？

(A) 推出新產品

(B) 報告一個成功的行銷活動

(C) 討論留住新客戶的方法

(D) 討論如何聯繫到客戶

正解 (B)

題目是問「這段談話的主要目的」。關鍵句是 I just wanted to keep you all informed about our new direct marketing campaign . . . the campaign is really paying off.「我只是想要讓大家都知道我們新的直效行銷活動……宣傳活動很成功。」故知答案應為 (B)。

---

14 Who is being addressed?

(A) The employees

(B) The competitors

(C) The retailers

(D) The customers

這段談話的對象是誰？

(A) 員工

(B) 競爭對手

(C) 零售商

(D) 客戶

正解 (A)

本題詢問這段談話的對象。由開頭說 Thank you all for attending this month's meeting. I know you are all really busy and I don't expect today's meeting to be too lengthy.「感謝大家參加這個月的會議。我知道各位都很忙，我想今天的會議不會開很久。」以及後面提到行銷團隊及電話行銷人員的表現，得知是在對內部員工談話，故答案為 (A)。

⑮ Why does the speaker say that the following months will be extra busy?
- (A) Because they will be launching a new direct marketing campaign
- (B) Because they will have to contact a lot of people by telephone
- **(C) Because they need to make sure they keep the new customers**
- (D) Because they will be busy celebrating their successes

為何說話者會說接下來的幾個月會更加忙碌？
- (A) 因為他們將會推出新的直效行銷活動
- (B) 因為他們將必須用電話聯繫很多人
- **(C) 因為他們需要確保能留住他們的新顧客**
- (D) 因為他們將會忙著慶祝他們的成功

正解 (C)

題目問「為何說話者會說接下來的幾個月會更加忙碌？」從倒數第二句說到 Of course this means that in the coming months we will be extra busy, as we need to ensure that these new customers remain committed.「當然這意味著在接下來的幾個月我們將會更加忙碌，因為我們需要去確保這些新客戶維持忠誠度。」因此答案選 (C)。

Questions 16-18 *refer to the following talk and chart.*

Hi everyone. Thanks for attending this brainstorming session. As you know, the purpose of this session will be to come up with ideas on how we can become the leading sportswear company in Asia. To begin with, let's take a look at some facts and figures to see how we compare with our competitors. As you can see, we are in a strong position, mainly because our merchandise is appealing to people who are active in many different sports. We are now the second most popular sportswear brand. However, our goal is to be number one, which is why I have asked you to come to this meeting. So, let's get started, shall we?

嗨，各位。感謝你們參加這個腦力激盪會議。如同大家所知道的，這個會議的目的是要激發出一些想法，看我們能如何成為主導亞洲運動服裝的公司。一開始，讓我們看看一些實例和數據，以便了解與競爭對手相比之下，我們的表現如何。你們可以看到，我們的地位很穩固，主要是因為我們的商品吸引從事多種不同運動的人。我們現在是第二受歡迎的運動服裝品牌。然而，我們的目標是要成為第一，這就是為何我要大家來開這個會。所以，我們就開始吧，好嗎？

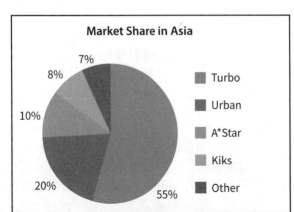

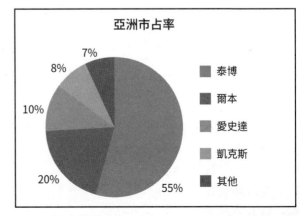

16 Who does the company's merchandise appeal to most?

(A) People who go running

(B) People who do different sports

(C) People who practice yoga

(D) People who like swimming

該公司的商品最吸引誰？

(A) 跑步的人

(B) 從事不同種運動的人

(C) 練習瑜珈的人

(D) 喜歡游泳的人

正解 **(B)**

本題詢問最受該公司商品吸引的對象。由關鍵句 . . . because our merchandise is appealing to people who are active in many different sports.「……因為我們的商品吸引從事多種不同運動的人」，所以得知答案是 (B)。

---

17 Look at the graphic. Which company does the speaker work for?

(A) A*Star

(B) Turbo

(C) Kiks

(D) Urban

看圖表。說話者是在哪間公司上班？

(A) 愛史達

(B) 泰博

(C) 凱克斯

(D) 爾本

正解 **(D)**

本題是圖表題。詢問說話者在哪間公司上班。由關鍵句 We are now the second most popular sportswear brand.「我們現在是第二受歡迎的運動服裝品牌。」，對照圖表可知市占率第二高的為爾本公司，故答案為 (D)。

---

18 What will happen next?

(A) They will go for lunch.

(B) They will look at graphs.

(C) They will discuss ideas.

(D) They will end the meeting.

接下來會發生什麼？

(A) 他們會去吃午餐。

(B) 他們會看圖表。

(C) 他們會討論想法。

(D) 他們會結束會議。

正解 **(C)**

本題問接下來會做的事。談話一開始便提到這是一個腦力激盪會議（brainstorming session），目的是討論如何成為主導亞洲運動服裝的公司。而最後說話者說 So, let's get started, shall we? 可知他們即將開始在會議上集思廣益討論想法，故答案為 (C)。

Part 5: Incomplete Sentences

⑲ We will hold a follow-up _____ after the initial brainstorming meeting to present our ideas to the Board of Directors.

(A) compromise   (B) strategy

(C) session   (D) consumer

一開始的腦力激盪會議結束後，我們會開一個後續會議來把我們的想法呈現給董事會。

(A) 妥協   (B) 策略

(C) 會議   (D) 消費者

正解 **(C)**

本題為字義題。依照句意可知空格處應填入 (C) session「會議」，表示接下來會有一個後續會議。

---

⑳ The coworkers held a highly _____ meeting in the boardroom in which they finalized their sales strategy.

(A) productive   (B) commercial

(C) rival   (D) brief

同事們在會議室開了一個高效能的會議，定下了他們的銷售策略。

(A) 有成效的   (B) 商業的

(C) 競爭的；對手   (D) 簡短的

正解 **(A)**

本題考字義。由於後半句提到同事們在會議中所達成的進展，故空格處應填入 (A) productive「有成效的」，以便順暢地帶出後面的語意。

㉑ The _____ brochure will tell you all about the services we offer, our prices, and what special discounts are available.

(A) enclose

(B) encloses

(C) enclosed

(D) enclosing

附上的小冊子會告訴你我們所提供的所有服務、我們的價格，以及有哪些特別折扣。

(A) 附上（原形動詞）

(B) 附上（現在式第三人稱單數動詞）

(C) 附上的（過去式或過去分詞）

(D) 附上（現在分詞或動名詞）

正解 **(C)**

本題考詞性。空格後方為名詞 brochure，可知空格處應填入形容詞以便修飾 brochure。(C) enclosed 為過去分詞時，可作形容詞表示「已附上的」，因此 (C) 為正確答案。

㉒ The contract was given to a large construction _____ based in Taichung, as they had the most experience with this type of building.

(A) boardroom   (B) competition

(C) distribution   **(D) firm**

那間公司合約簽給了一間在台中的大型建設公司，因為他們對於這類的建築最有經驗。

(A) 會議室   (B) 競爭

(C) 分發   **(D) 公司**

正解 **(D)**

本題考字義。依照句意可知空格處應填入 (D) firm 指「公司」。construction firm 即「建設公司」。

㉓ The advertising agency came up with a TV commercial _____ would appeal to young professionals.

(A) who

(B) that

(C) when

(D) where

該廣告公司構思出一個應能吸引年輕行家的電視廣告。

(A) （表人的關係代名詞）他（們）；她（們）

(B) （表人或物的關係代名詞）那個；那些

(C) （表時間的關係副詞）當……時

(D) （表地點的關係副詞）在那裡

正解 **(B)**

觀察選項可知本題考關係詞。空格前方為名詞 TV commercial，空格後接「助動詞＋原形動詞」，可知空格處應填入表物的主格關係代名詞，引導形容詞子句修飾前方名詞（即先行詞）commercial，故答案為 (B)。

Part 6: Text Completion

Questions 24-27 refer to the following e-mail.

To:	stern.greg@telltech.com
From:	tinaquick@tca.tw
Re:	Invitation to Digital Marketing Workshop

Dear Greg Stern,

It is our pleasure to invite you to our Digital Marketing Workshop, ---**24**--- we are looking forward to hosting during the Technology Trade Fair in San Jose. Make time in your busy trade fair schedule to attend our informative workshop in which you will hear ---**25**--- and take part in discussions on how to market your products, drive traffic to your website through SEO (Search Engine Optimization), and increase sales by utilizing social media. This year, we are delighted to welcome the highly-successful ---**26**--- Bill Grange, who will be giving a talk on How to Market in the Digital Age. If you would like to attend, please click on the link below to request tickets.

---**27**--- We look forward to welcoming you!

Attend Digital Marketing Workshop

Kind Regards,

Tina Quick
Technology Companies Association

收件者：stern.greg@telltech.com
寄件者：tinaquick@tca.tw
主　旨：邀請您參加數位行銷專題討論會

格雷・史登先生您好：

很榮幸邀請您來參加我們滿心期盼於聖荷西的科技貿易展期間舉辦的數位行銷專題討論會。在您繁忙的看展行程中請騰出時間來參加我們充滿豐富資訊的專題討論會，您在會中將能聽取簡報並參與討論，了解如何行銷您的產品、如何透過SEO（優化搜尋引擎）來提升您網站的流量，以及藉由使用社群媒體來增加銷售。今年，我們很開心邀請到非常成功的企業家比爾・格蘭杰，他將會發表一段關於「在數位時代如何行銷」的演說。若您有意參加，請點擊以下連結索取票券。

門票將在貿易展的前一週發放。我們期待迎接您的到來！

參加數位行銷專題討論會

謹致問候，

蒂娜・奎克
科技公司協會

㉔ (A) which　　　　(B) when
(C) whose　　　　(D) who

(A)（表物的主格或受格關係代名詞）它；它們
(B)（表時間關係副詞）當……時
(C)（表人或物的所有格關係代名詞）它的；它們的
(D)（表人的主格關係代名詞）他（們）；她（們）

正解 (A)

本題考關係詞。空格前方為名詞 our Digital Marketing Workshop（先行詞），後方為缺少受詞的不完整子句，可判斷空格處須填入表物的受格關係代名詞，以引導形容詞子句來修飾先行詞，故答案為 (A)。

㉕ (A) presentations
(B) advertisements
(C) agreements
(D) enterprises

(A) 簡報
(B) 廣告
(C) 協議
(D) 企業

正解 (A)

本題考字義。依照句意可知空格處應填入 (A) presentation「簡報」，表示受邀者將在會中聽取簡報。

㉖ (A) contract
(B) entrepreneur
(C) franchise
(D) headquarters

(A) 契約
(B) 企業家
(C) 連鎖企業
(D) 總部

正解 (B)

本題為字義題。由空格後的人名可知空格處應填入 (B) entrepreneur「企業家」。

㉗ (A) There are no more tickets available for this event.
(B) Tickets will be issued in the week before the Trade Fair.
(C) You'll receive credits each time you click on an ad.
(D) The brainstorming session is open to everyone.

(A) 這個活動已經沒有多的票券。
(B) 門票將在貿易展的前一週發放。
(C) 您每次點擊廣告都將獲得點數。
(D) 這個腦力激盪會議開放給每個人參加。

正解 (B)

空格的前一句說「若您有意參加，請點擊以下連結索取票券。」而後一句為「我們期待迎接您的到來！」，選項 (B) 提及貿易展門票的相關資訊，與前後文語意連貫，故為正解。

Part 7: Reading Comprehension

Questions 28-30 *refer to the following direct marketing letter.*

The Great Chariot Hotel
New York City, New York, USA

Dear Sir/Madam,

I am writing on behalf of Real Event Solutions Ltd. We are an established events company that has worked on projects ranging from **high street** retail store annual banquets to movie wrap-up parties. When it comes to production, there is no requirement that Real cannot meet, and we pride ourselves on our high levels of efficiency and professionalism.

Should you be interested in hiring us for your event, I would be delighted to come in and give you a short presentation, free of charge. You can also reach me at mick@realeventsolutions.com or on 0981 410 0150.

Please also visit our website, where you can learn more about our past projects, as well as read **testimonials** from previous clients we've collaborated with.

Thank you and I hope to hear from you at your earliest convenience.

Yours sincerely,

Mick Vance
Senior Marketing Executive
Real Event Solutions Ltd.

戰車大酒店
美國紐約州紐約市

敬啟者您好：

我謹代表瑞爾活動策劃公司撰寫此信。我們是一間著名的活動籌辦公司，辦過的專案從商店街零售商的年度餐會到電影的殺青派對都有。在活動籌辦上，沒有瑞爾達不到的要求，且我們以高效率和專業水準自豪。

若您有興趣雇請我們來籌辦活動，我會很樂意走一趟，給您一段免費的簡短報告。您也可以透過 mick@realeventsolutions.com 或是打電話到 0981 410 0150 來聯繫我。

也請您參訪我們的網站，您可以在網站上得知更多有關我們過去的專案，也可以讀到之前和我們合作過的客戶的推薦信。

謝謝您並希望能盡早收到您的聯繫。

謹致，

米克・凡斯
資深行銷經理
瑞爾活動策劃公司

• high street *(n.)* （位於重要商業區的）大街；商業街
• testimonial *(n.)* 證明書；推薦信

28 What is the purpose of this letter?

(A) To request product information

(B) To follow up on a payment

(C) To promote a company

(D) To apologize for an error

這封信的目的是什麼？

(A) 索取產品資訊

(B) 後續追蹤帳款

(C) 推銷一間公司

(D) 為錯誤致歉

正解 **(C)**

本題為主旨題，詢問此信的主要目的。信件作者在第一句便表明來自一間活動策劃公司，並接著介紹過去的經驗，且在第二段開頭表示：Should you be interested in hiring us for your event, I would be delighted to … 「若您有興趣雇請我們來籌辦活動，我會很樂意⋯⋯」，由此可知此信目的是在推銷自家公司，所以答案選 (C)。

---

29 What does the writer offer to give the recipient?

(A) A free presentation

(B) A discount on equipment

(C) A free banquet

(D) An invitation to his store

寫這封信的人提供什麼給收件者？

(A) 免費的簡報

(B) 設備的折扣

(C) 免費的宴會

(D) 他商店的邀請卡

正解 **(A)**

本題為細節題，詢問寫這封信的人提供給收件者什麼東西。解題關鍵在第二段說 I would be delighted to come in and give you a short presentation, free of charge. 「我很會很樂意走一趟，給您一段免費的簡短報告。」可知會提供免費的簡報，故答案為 (A)。

---

30 The word "retail" in paragraph 1, line 2, is closest in meaning to

(A) franchise

(B) selling

(C) location

(D) session

第一段第二行的 "retail" 意義最接近

(A) 連鎖企業

(B) 銷售

(C) 地點

(D) 會議

正解 **(B)**

本題考同義字，詢問文中第二句 retail 意思最近似何者。retail 此處為「零售；零賣」，意近於 (B) selling。

Questions 31-33 *refer to the following news report.*

BLAZE DEMONSTRATES RECOVERY

This week, Blaze Electronics reported better than expected quarterly profits, surprising the analysts who predicted the collapse of the company. These profits are the ultimate proof that, after a difficult few years, the company is on the road to recovery. ---[1]--- Blaze, once one of the most profitable electronics manufacturers, has seen steady losses during the past few years due to increased competition from new markets. Their newly appointed CEO, John Mitchell, was hired with the hope that he could reverse the downward trend. ---[2]--- Certainly figures for this quarter seem to back up his optimism. Unfortunately, while Mitchell is working towards shifting the company in a profitable direction, many remain doubtful that it is possible in the long term. ---[3]--- Competitors in Asia, with low labor and manufacturing costs, are pushing more established firms out. Mitchell attributes recent profitability to the company's strategy of building on its long-standing reputation for quality. ---[4]--- He points out that, in the long term, consumers are more likely to choose quality over price.

布雷茲展現復甦跡象

本週,布雷茲電子公布季度盈利收優於預期,讓曾預測該公司將倒閉的分析師十分意外。這些營收最終證明該公司在歷經幾年的困難之後,正在復甦當中。布雷茲曾是獲利最高的電子製造商之一,過去幾年因為新興市場的競爭愈加激烈而持續虧損。其新任執行長,約翰‧米歇爾,被延請來希望可以翻轉衰退的趨勢。讓米歇爾上任看來得到很好的結果,且他堅定相信公司會成功。本季的數字確實證實了他的樂觀。不幸的是,當米歇爾致力讓公司走向獲利的同時,很多人仍然質疑長期下來這是否可能。亞洲的競爭者有低廉的勞工和生產成本,這正迫使更多現有的公司被淘汰。米歇爾把最近的獲利歸功於公司策略是建立品質優良的長期名聲。他指出,長期下來消費者較可能選擇品質,而非價格。

31 What is the purpose of the article?
(A) To report on why Asian businesses are thriving
(B) To report on the appointment of a new CEO
(C) To report on a company's recent success
(D) To report a company's quarterly losses

本篇文章的目的為何？
(A) 報導為何亞洲商業會蓬勃
(B) 報導一位新執行長的任命
(C) 報導一間公司近來的成功
(D) 報導一間公司的季度虧損

正解 (C)

本題為主旨題。詢問此篇文章的目的。由標題 Blaze Demonstrates Recovery 與文中開頭說 This week, Blaze Electronics reported better than expected quarterly profits . . . 「本週，布雷茲電子公布季度盈利收優於預期……」，以及後續文章說明新任執行長帶領公司走向獲利，得知本篇文章目的為 (C)。

32 Why does John Mitchell believe the company will continue to be successful?
(A) Because the company will build more factories in Asia
(B) Because people will ultimately choose quality products over cheap ones
(C) Because he will reduce the company's labor and manufacturing costs
(D) Because the company's quarterly profits are demonstrating a recovery

為何約翰・米歇爾相信公司會持續成功？
(A) 因為公司會在亞洲成立更多工廠
(B) 因為人們最終會選擇優質產品而非便宜的產品
(C) 因為他會減少公司的勞工和生產成本
(D) 因為公司的季度獲利展現了復甦跡象

正解 (B)

本題解題關鍵句為最後一句 He points out that, in the long term, consumers are more likely to choose quality over price. 「他指出，長期下來消費者較可能選擇品質，而非價格。」所以答案為 (B)。

33 In which of the positions marked [1], [2], [3], and [4] does the following sentence best belong?
"Bringing Mitchell on board seems to be paying off and he firmly believes that the company can succeed."
(A) [1]　　　　　**(B) [2]**
(C) [3]　　　　　(D) [4]

下面的句子最適合放在標示 [1]、[2]、[3]、[4] 的哪個位置？
「讓米歇爾上任看起來得到很好的結果，且他堅定相信公司會成功。」
(A) [1]　　　　　**(B) [2]**
(C) [3]　　　　　(D) [4]

正解 (B)

本題為篇章結構題，題目句談論該新任執行長對該公司帶來正面的轉變，而根據上下文 [2] 的前方提到新任執行長被延請來希望可以翻轉衰退的趨勢，後方則說到本季的數字證實了他的樂觀，語意前後呼應，故答案選 (B)。

P. 116~124

Part 1: Photographs

TRACK 27

① (A) The glasses have been placed in the drawer.
(B) Some plants are being watered.
(C) The résumés are on the table.
(D) Someone has been promoted.

(A) 眼鏡被放在抽屜裡。
(B) 一些植物正在被澆水。
(C) 那些履歷表在桌上。
(D) 有一個人獲得了升遷。

正解 **(C)**
圖中可見桌上放著幾張履歷表，因此符合圖片的敘述為 (C)「那些履歷表在桌上。」

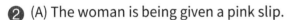

② (A) The woman is being given a pink slip.
(B) A woman is attending an interview.
(C) The woman is on maternity leave.
(D) A man is working overtime.

(A) 那名女子正收到一張解雇通知單。
(B) 一名女子正參加面試。
(C) 那名女子正在休產假。
(D) 一名男子正在加班。

正解 **(D)**
圖中可見女子面帶微笑在會議室和另一名男子握手，且圖中人物均著正式商務服裝，故最有可能的答案為 (B)。

Part 2: Question and Response

❸ When will you take your annual leave?
(A) Most likely in July.
(B) I need to leave early.
(C) I'll take you up on that.

你何時會休年假？
(A) 最有可能在七月。
(B) 我需要早退。
(C) 我會接受你的提議。

正解 **(A)**
本題以 When 詢問對方何時會休年假，回答應說明時間。(A) 回答「最有可能在七月」，故為正確答案。
(B) 題目與早退無關。
(C) take sb. up on sth. 指「接受（某人主動提出的幫助或提議）」之意，與題目無關。

---

❹ Did you apply for that job at Coffee & Cake?
(A) I have a degree in Applied Physics.
(B) Yes, a coffee would be great.
(C) No, the pay is not great.

你有應徵「咖啡與蛋糕」的那份工作嗎？
(A) 我有應用物理學的學位。
(B) 是的，來杯咖啡會很好。
(C) 沒有，薪水不太好。

正解 **(C)**
本題為以 Did 開頭的一般是非問句，詢問對方是否有應徵某家店的工作。(C) 回答「沒有，薪水不太好。」，直接以 No 回應並提出理由，故為正解。
(A) 題目並未詢問對方的學位。
(B) 題目並未詢問對方要不要喝咖啡。

---

❺ Would you prefer to work full-time or part-time?
(A) I would like to work less hours.
(B) I want to study full-time.
(C) Actually, I'm still full from breakfast.

你偏好做全職工作還是兼職工作？
(A) 我想要工作時數少一點。
(B) 我想要當全職學生。
(C) 其實，我吃完早餐現在還很飽。

正解 **(A)**
本題為選擇疑問句，詢問對方偏好做全職工作還是兼職工作，選項中唯一可能之回應為 (A)「我想要工作時數少一點。」，間接表示偏好的是兼職工作。
(B) 題目在問工作，而非求學（study）。
(C) 與題意不符。

---

❻ I would love a career in medicine.
(A) I would like to be a mechanic, too.
(B) You would need to study a lot.
(C) Being in love is wonderful.

我很想從事醫學的工作。
(A) 我也想要當技師。
(B) 你會需要念很多書。
(C) 墜入愛河是件很棒的事。

正解 **(B)**
本題為直述句，描述想要從事醫學相關的工作。選項中唯一符合邏輯之回應為 (B)「你會需要念很多書。」
(A) 題目說想從事醫學方面的工作，卻回答也想當技師，答非所問。
(C) 與題意無關。

Part 3: Short Conversations

Questions 7-9 *refer to the following conversation with three speakers.*

W: Hey, I saw a social media post last night that said that Core Tech has some job openings.

M1: Really? That's great. You've been waiting for a vacancy to come up there for a while.

M2: So, you're going to apply, right?

W: I want to, but I'm not sure if I have the right qualifications.

M2: I guess you could call the human resources department and ask them.

M1: Well, if you really want to work there, I think you should send them your résumé anyway. Even if you're not right for one of these job openings, you never know what might come up in the future.

女：嘿，我昨晚看到一則社群媒體貼文說核心科技公司有一些職缺。

男一：真的嗎？那太棒了。妳等職缺出現已經有一陣子了。

男二：那麼，妳會去應徵，對吧？

女：我想要應徵，但我不確定我的資格是否符合。

男二：我想妳可以打去人力資源部門詢問他們。

男一：嗯，如果妳真的想在那裡工作，我覺得妳應該就把履歷表寄給他們。就算這些職缺之中沒有一個適合妳，妳永遠不知道以後會出現哪些職缺。

⑦ What is this conversation mainly about?
(A) Where Core Tech have advertised their job openings
(B) How to contact human resources at Core Tech
(C) Whether the woman should apply for a job at Core Tech
(D) Whether the woman has the right qualifications for a vacancy

這段對話的主要關於什麼？
(A) 核心科技在哪裡刊登職缺
(B) 如何聯繫核心科技公司的人力資源部門
(C) 該女子是否應該應徵核心科技公司的工作
(D) 該女子是否符合職缺的條件

正解 (C)

本題詢問對話的主題。從女子說到的關鍵字詞 job openings「工作職缺」、right qualifications「符合的條件」，還有男二問道 you're going to apply, right?「妳會去應徵，對吧？」以及男一說的 send them your résumé anyway「就把履歷表寄給他們」等，可知三人在討論女子是否該應徵一份職缺，答案選 (C)。

8 How does the woman feel about applying for a job at Core Tech?

(A) She's confident that she'll get the job.

(B) She doesn't want to apply.

(C) She'd like to check other positions first.

(D) She's unsure if she has the right background.

女子對於應徵核心科技公司的工作有何想法？

(A) 她有信心會獲得這份工作。

(B) 她不想要應徵。

(C) 她想先看看其他職務。

(D) 她不確定自己是否具備合適的經歷。

正解 **(D)**

題目問女子對於應徵核心科技公司的工作有何想法。關鍵句為女子說 I want to, but I'm not sure if I have the right qualifications.「我想要應徵，但我不確定我的資格是否符合。」，所以答案選 (D)。

9 What is implied about Core Tech?

(A) The two men used to work there but quit.

(B) The woman has long wanted to work there.

(C) They don't have many employees.

(D) They only advertise on social media.

關於核心科技公司，對話中有何暗示？

(A) 那兩名男子曾在那裡工作，但辭職了。

(B) 女子很久以前就想要在那裡工作。

(C) 他們沒有很多員工。

(D) 他們只有在社群媒體上宣傳。

正解 **(B)**

本題詢問關於核心公司，對話有何暗示。由男一對女子說 You've been waiting for a vacancy to come up there for a while. 可知女子等這個職缺已有好一陣子了，所以答案為 (B)。

Questions 10-12 *refer to the following conversation and table.*

W: So we have now seen all the candidates for the job. I have a list here and some of the **comments** I wrote during the interview process.

M: That's great. We had some good interviewees this time; it's going to be hard to pick one.

W: That's true, although they all had quite different backgrounds and experience.

M: Well, I don't mind that too much. What I don't want, though, is someone who is **arrogant**, so I think there is one name we can **cross off** the list right away!

- comment *(n.)* 意見
- arrogant *(adj.)* 傲慢的
- cross (sb./sth.) off . . . *(phr.)* 從⋯⋯中劃掉（某人／某物）

女：好的，現在我們都已經看過這份工作的應徵者了。我這裡有份名單以及我在面試過程中寫下的一些評論。

男：那太棒了。我們這次有一些不錯的面試者；要挑選出一位會是件難事。

男：沒錯，雖然他們都具備相當不同的背景和經驗。

女：這個嘛，我不會太擔心那一點。不過我不想要一個傲慢的人，所以我想我們可以馬上劃掉名單上的一個名字！

NAME #	NOTES
Paul Lee	Experienced but nervous
Jock Green	Doesn't have degree required
Evan Isaacs	Qualified but over-confident
Sarah McAdams	Recent graduate so no experience

姓名	筆記
保羅·李	有經驗但緊張
喬克·格林	沒有所需的學位
伊凡·艾塞克	有資格但過度自信
莎拉·麥亞當斯	剛畢業所以缺乏經驗

10 What is the woman's likely occupation?

(A) Trainee

(B) Secretary

(C) Interviewee

(D) HR Manager

該名女子可能的職業為何？

(A) 練習生

(B) 秘書

(C) 面試者；應徵者

(D) 人資經理

正解 **(D)**

本題詢問人物身分，問「那名女子可能的職業為何？」。從女子所說 So we have now seen all the candidates for the job. I have a list here and some of the comments I wrote during the interview process.「好的，現在我們都已經看過這份工作的應徵者了。我這裡有份名單以及我在面試過程中我寫下的一些評論。」可推測她在負責面試新進人員，因此答案選 (D)「人資經理」。

11 What are the speakers doing?

(A) Checking résumés

(B) Deciding who to hire

(C) Interviewing candidates

(D) Appraising staff

說話者正在做什麼事？

(A) 核查履歷表

(B) 決定要雇用誰

(C) 面試應徵者

(D) 評估員工

正解 **(B)**

題目詢問說話者正在做的事。答題關鍵是男子所說 We had some good interviewees this time; it's going to be hard to pick one.「我們這次有一些不錯的面試者；要挑選出一位會是件難事。」可知他們正在決定要雇用哪一位面試者，答案選 (B)「決定要雇用誰」。

12 Look at the graphic. Which candidate will not be considered?

(A) Paul Lee

(B) Jock Green

(C) Evan Isaacs

(D) Sarah McAdams

看圖表。哪一位應徵者不會被考慮？

(A) 保羅・李

(B) 喬克・格林

(C) 伊凡・艾塞克

(D) 莎拉・麥亞當斯

正解 **(C)**

本題要結合對話和圖表來回答。題目問到哪一位應徵者不會被考慮。由對話得知男子不想要一個傲慢的人。而在圖表上伊凡・艾塞克被評為 Qualified but over-confident「有資格但過度自信」，over-confident 意近 arrogant，故 (C) 為正解。

Part 4: Short Talks

Questions 13-15 refer to the following speech.

Hello, everybody. It's great to see everyone gathered here today to celebrate Bob's retirement. As most of you know, Bob joined our company over 20 years ago and has been an exemplary employee. In fact, he's always treated his position here as more of a **vocation** than a job, and he's loved being out on the road for us, getting us those new customers. It's really going to be tough for someone else to **fill his shoes**! Anyway, now it's time for him to relax, put his feet up, and draw his **well-deserved** pension. So, Bob, thanks for everything and we wish you all the best. Please join me in a round of **applause** for Bob!

大家好。今天看到大家聚在這裡慶祝鮑伯的退休真是太棒了。大部分的你們都知道,鮑伯在二十多年前加入我們公司,一直以來都是模範員工。事實上,他總是把這裡的職位視為是一種使命,而非只是一份工作,而且他喜歡為了我們四處奔走,為我們爭取那些新客戶。其他人要接替他的工作真的會很辛苦!無論如何,現在是時候讓他放鬆休息,並領取他應得的退休金了。那麼鮑伯,謝謝你所做的一切,祝你萬事如意。請和我一起給鮑伯來點熱烈的掌聲吧!

- vocation *(n.)* 使命;(值得投入所有時間和精力的)職業
- fill sb.'s shoes *(phr.)* 取代某人;接替某人的工作(= step into sb.'s shoes)
- put one's feet up *(phr.)* 放鬆;休息
- well-deserved *(adj.)* 當之無愧的;應得的
- applause *(n.)* 掌聲

⓭ What is the purpose of this talk?

(A) **To say farewell to someone who is leaving the company**

(B) To congratulate someone on a promotion

(C) To evaluate an employee's successes at the company

(D) To explain how an employee was able to get new customers

這段談話的目的為何?

(A) 為了和即將離開公司的某人道別

(B) 為了恭喜某人升職

(C) 為了評估某位員工在公司的成功

(D) 為了要解釋某位員工如何爭取到新客戶

正解 (A)

本題問獨白目的。由關鍵句 It's great to see everyone gathered here today to celebrate Bob's retirement.「今天看到大家聚在這裡慶祝鮑伯的退休真是太棒了。」可知談話目的是 (A)「為了和即將離開公司的某人道別」。

- farewell *(n.)* 再見

14 What is implied about Bob's position at the company?

(A) The job will no longer exist.

(B) It was a relatively new post.

(C) His track record wasn't good.

(D) It involved a lot of traveling.

對於鮑伯在公司的職位有何暗示？

(A) 該工作將不復存在。

(B) 它相對來說是個新的職位。

(C) 他以往的紀錄並不好。

(D) 它需要經常外出。

正解 (D)

本題是推論題，問「對於鮑伯在公司的職位有何暗示？」。答題關鍵在 . . . and he's loved being out on the road for us, getting us those new customers. 「……而且他喜歡為了我們四處奔走，為我們爭取那些新客戶。」，可推測此職位需要常常出差去開發新客戶，因此答案選 (D)「它需要經常外出。」

• involve (v.) 涉及；包括

(B) relatively (adv.) 相對地。

(C) track record (n.) 以往的紀錄。

---

15 What does the man mean when he says, "It's really going to be tough for someone else to fill his shoes"?

(A) Bob's coworkers won't be familiar with his replacement.

(B) It will be impossible to find a replacement for Bob.

(C) It will be difficult for a new person to do such a good job.

(D) The company will need to provide new shoes for Bob.

當男子說 "It's really going to be tough for someone else to fill his shoes" 時，他的言下之意是？

(A) 鮑伯的同事不會熟悉代替他的人。

(B) 要找到代替鮑伯的人是不可能的事。

(C) 對新人來說要做得如此出色會很困難。

(D) 公司會需要提供鮑伯新鞋。

正解 (C)

本題考句意。在這句話之前，說話者在強調鮑伯傑出的工作表現，包括他一直以來是位模範員工（exemplary employee）、視自己的職位為使命（treated his position here as more of a vocation than a job）、四處奔波爭取客戶（being out on the road for us, getting us those new customers）等等，可推斷鮑伯退休後，接替他職位的人要做到如此出色並不容易，因此答案選 (C)。

(A) replacement (n.) 代替者。

Questions 16-18 refer to the following talk and paycheck.

Hi, Charles! Thanks for coming to see me. I wanted to see you in person to give you your paycheck and congratulate you once again on your recent promotion to **Licensing** Manager. Your recent evaluations have been excellent and you really **stood out** among all the other candidates for the department manager position, so this promotion is therefore well-deserved. So, as we discussed, your new position comes with more employee benefits, such as 15 days paid annual leave, transport **allowance**, and private medical insurance. These are in addition to your increase in salary of $300 per month. Here's your paycheck. Can you take a look at it to make sure everything is in order? If anything is wrong or missing, we can have the accounts department amend it right away.

嗨，查爾斯！謝謝你來見我。我想要當面把薪資支票交給你，並再次恭喜你最近榮升授權經理一職。你最近的評價都很棒，而且你真的在所有部門經理的候選人中脫穎而出，所以這次升職是實至名歸。那麼，正如我們討論過的，你的新職位會有更多的員工福利，像是十五天的帶薪年假、交通津貼以及私人醫療保險。這些是除了月薪加薪三百元之外的額外福利。這是你的薪資支票。你能看一下確保一切妥當嗎？如果有哪裡出錯或是少了什麼東西，我們可以請會計部門馬上修改。

- license *(v.)* 授權
- stand out *(phr.)* 變得很醒目、顯著；突出
- allowance *(n.)* （尤指為特定事項支付的）定期補貼；津貼
- deduction *(n.)* 扣除額

Name: Charles Marden	Title: Licensing Manager	
Description	**Earnings** (USD)	**Deductions** (USD)
Basic Salary	3,000.00	
Medical Allowance	300.00	
Company Pension Contribution	300.00	
Transport Allowance	200.00	
Meal Allowance	100.00	
Tax		100.00
TOTAL	**3,800.00**	

姓名：查爾斯·馬登	職稱：授權經理	
項目明細	**薪資**（美元）	**扣除額**（美元）
基本薪資	3,000.00	
醫療保險	300.00	
公司提撥退休金	300.00	
交通津貼	200.00	
伙食津貼	100.00	
稅		100.00
總計	**3,800.00**	

16 Who is being addressed?

(A) An employee who is being laid off

(B) An employee who has finished their probation

(C) An employee who has been promoted

(D) A contract employee

說話者的對象是誰？

(A) 要被解雇的員工

(B) 已結束試用期的員工

(C) 已被晉升的員工

(D) 約聘員工

正解 (C)

本題問「說話者的對象是誰？」。從說話者所說 I wanted to see you in person to give you your paycheck and congratulate you once again on your recent promotion to Licensing Manager. 「我想要當面把薪資支票交給你，並再次恭喜你最近榮升授權經理一職。」可推測其說話對象應是 (C)「已被晉升的員工」。

• address *(v.)* 對⋯⋯講話

---

17 What is implied about Charles Marden?

(A) He was the only candidate for the position.

(B) The company decided to give him another chance.

(C) He was much more suitable than the other candidates.

(D) He didn't need to have any evaluations.

關於查爾斯·馬登這個人，此談話有何暗示？

(A) 他是該職位的唯一候選人。

(B) 公司決定要給他另一次機會。

(C) 他遠比其他候選人更適合那份職務。

(D) 他不需要任何評價。

正解 (C)

本題是推論題，問「關於查爾斯·馬登這個人，此談話有何暗示？」。答題關鍵在於 . . . you really stood out among all the other candidates for the department manager position, so this promotion is therefore well-deserved. 可知他遠比其他候選人更適合擔任授權經理一職，故 (C) 為正選。

• suitable *(adj.)* 合適的

---

18 Look at the graphic. What was the employee's basic salary before the promotion?

(A) 3,500USD　　　(B) 3,000USD

(C) 2,900USD　　　**(D) 2,700USD**

看圖表。該員工在晉升之前的基本薪資是多少？

(A) 三千五百美元　　(B) 三千美元

(C) 兩千九百美元　　**(D) 兩千七百美元**

正解 (D)

這是圖表題，回答時須整合圖表與談話內容。題目問「該員工在晉升之前的基本薪資是多少？」，若單看圖表，他晉升後的基本薪資為美金三千元，而根據獨白 These are in addition to your increase in salary of $300 per month.「這些是除了月薪加薪三百元之外的額外福利。」，可知他這次加薪了三百元，因此晉升之前的基本薪資應該是兩千七百元，正確答案為 (D)。

Part 5: Incomplete Sentences

⑲ Personnel should fill out the necessary form once they return from _____ sick leave.

(A) **their**   (B) they

(C) them   (D) those

員工一旦休完病假重返工作岡位，就應填寫必要的表格。

(A) **他們的（所有格）**   (B) 他們（主格）

(C) 他們（受格）   (D) 那些

正解 (A)

本題考代名詞。本句主詞為 Personnel 「（總稱）員工」，而句子提到他們必須在結束病假回到工作崗位時填寫必要表格。根據語意，名詞 sick leave 是前面代名詞 they 的所有物，所以空格應填入 they 的所有格 their，答案選 (A)。

• fill out *(phr.)* 填寫（正式文件）

---

⑳ Only three people _____ for the chef position, probably due to the long hours they would have to work.

(A) apply

(B) applying

(C) **applied**

(D) applies

只有三個人應徵這份主廚的職位，可能是因為他們得要長時間工作的緣故。

(A) 應徵（原形動詞；現在式第一、二人稱動詞或第三人稱複數動詞）

(B) 應徵（動名詞或現在分詞）

(C) **應徵（過去式）**

(D) 應徵（現在式第三人稱單數動詞）

正解 (C)

本題考時態。根據句意，此處欲表達過去某時只有三人申請了這個職位，因此動詞應用過去式，正確答案為 (C)。

㉑ The job description says that it requires someone who is good at _____, doesn't it?

(A) personnel

(B) **multitasking**

(C) probation

(D) resignation

工作說明上寫著需要擅長同時處理多項任務的人，不是嗎？

(A) 員工

(B) **同時處理多項任務**

(C) 試用期

(D) 辭職

正解 (B)

本題考字義。依照句意可知空格處填入 (B) multitasking 指「同時處理多項任務」。其餘選項均非工作說明中可能會列出的條件。

22 For this job, you will need to be proficient in _____ Microsoft Office and Adobe Photoshop.
(A) neither
(B) both
(C) either
(D) not only

要從事這份工作，你會需要精通 Microsoft Office 和 Adobe Photoshop 這兩套軟體。
(A) 兩者皆不（常與 nor 連用）
(B) 兩者皆是（常與 and 連用）
(C) 兩者之一（常與 or 連用）
(D) 不但（常與 but also 連用）

正解 **(B)**
本題考連接詞。由後面的 and 得知空格當中應填入 (B) both。both A and B 表「A 和 B 都……」之意，須如本句用在肯定情境中（兩套軟體都要精通）。注意 (A) neither 須用在否定的情境，neither A nor B 表「A 與 B 皆不……」。

---

23 When you begin your internship, you will need to _____ Mr. Jenkins.
(A) retire from
(B) lay off
(C) compensate for
(D) report to

當你開始你的實習工作時，你將會是簡金斯先生的下屬。
(A) 從……退休
(B) 開除（某人）
(C) 補償……
(D) 向（某人）報告；為（某人的）下屬

正解 **(D)**
本題考片語動詞。依照句意可知空格處應填入 (D) report to，指「向（某人）報告」，也就是表示簡金斯先生將是其直屬主管。

Part 6: Text Completion

Questions 24-27 *refer to the following advertisement.*

JOB FAIR

August 10, 11, 12
The Convention Center

TAKE YOUR CAREER IN THE RIGHT DIRECTION

Would you like to have a new occupation? Are you looking for on-the-job training? Would you like to ---24--- a post with the best employers in your industry? ---25--- You will have the opportunity to connect with employers, recruiters, and ---26--- from at least 200 local and international companies. You will be able to communicate your career goals to potential employers and, in addition, you can sign up for **workshops** on career development, essential proficiencies for today's jobs market, and résumé-writing and interview skills.

Register online at mycityjobfair.com and don't forget ---27--- your professional profile summary, and copies of your résumé and cover letter.

就業博覽會

八月十日、八月十一日、八月十二日

會議中心

將您的生涯導向正確的方向

您想要擁有一份新職業嗎？您在尋找在職訓練嗎？您想要和您所處業界中最優秀的老闆一同工作嗎？那就別錯過今年的就業博覽會！您將有機會和來自至少兩百家當地與國際企業的老闆、招聘人員以及獵才專員互相交流。您將能和潛在雇主傳達您的生涯目標，另外，您還可以報名參加關於生涯發展、今日就業市場必備技能以及撰寫履歷與面試技巧的研討會。

在 mycityjobfair.com 線上註冊，而且別忘了攜帶您的專業個人簡介以及履歷表和求職信。

• workshop *(n.)* 研討會
• register *(v.)* 註冊

㉔ (A) take up
(B) take down
(C) take note
(D) take away

(A) 開始從事
(B) 拆除
(C) 作筆記
(D) 拿走

正解 **(A)**

本題考片語動詞。空格後方的受詞是 a post with the best employers in your industry，可推測是在問對方想不想「擔任」一份職務，故 (A)「開始從事」為最適合的答案。

25 (A) How would you like to get a postgraduate degree?

(B) Then don't miss this year's Job Fair!

(C) Where will your next adventure take you?

(D) Would you like to take early retirement?

(A) 您想要取得研究所的學位嗎？

(B) 那就別錯過今年的就業博覽會！

(C) 您下次要去哪裡冒險？

(D) 您想要提前退休嗎？

正解 (B)

本題須根據上下文脈絡填入適當句子。廣告開頭便連續提出數個與職涯發展有關的問題，而空格的下一句便開始列舉參加就業博覽會將能有哪些收穫，故應選 (B)「那就別錯過今年的就業博覽會！」，以便讓語意順暢連貫。

---

26 (A) headquarters

(B) headcounts

(C) headlines

(D) headhunters

(A) 總部

(B) 人數；人數清點

(C) 標題

(D) 獵才人員；獵人頭公司

正解 (D)

本題考單字。原句提到，你將有機會和來自至少兩百家當地與國際公司的老闆、招聘人員以及 ___ 互相交流。依句意可知最適合的答案為 (D)。

---

27 (A) brought

(B) to bring

(C) bringing

(D) have bring

(A) 帶來（過去式或過去分詞）

(B) 帶來（不定詞）

(C) 帶來（動名詞或現在分詞）

(D) 無 have bring 的用法。如要採現在完成式，have 後應接過去分詞 brought。

正解 (B)

本題考文法。按照句意，這裡是在提醒對方之後別忘了帶專業個人簡介、履歷表等資料。forget + to V. 表示「忘記要去做某事（動作尚未完成）」，forget + V-ing 是「忘記已做過某事（動作已完成）」，故依句意可知應選不定詞，答案為 (B)。

Part 7: Reading Comprehension

Questions 28-30 refer to the following e-mail.

To:	kelly@scholarsnote.com
From:	james@scholarsnote.com
Re:	Intern

Dear Kelly,

This is a quick message about our intern, Jeremy. Jeremy has been doing **fantastic** work down in our department and has been an **invaluable asset** since Caitlyn went on maternity leave. He is very friendly and efficient in his work and his communication skills are excellent. I really feel that he is able to take over any tasks that **come up** at the last minute and he never complains about the low wage or long working hours. I wanted to ask you about the possibility of offering Jeremy full-time employment at our company once his internship is up. I would hate to lose such a great team player to another company. What do you think? Do we have the **capacity** to offer him something?

Would love to know your thoughts, so please get back to me as soon as you can!

Thanks,

James

收件者：kelly@scholarsnote.com
寄件者：james@scholarsnote.com
回　覆：實習生

親愛的凱莉：

這是一則關於我們的實習生傑瑞米的簡短訊息。自從凱特琳休產假後，傑瑞米就一直在我們樓下的部門表現出色，也一直都是位寶貴的人才。他很友善，工作效率高，溝通能力也極好。我真的感覺他能接手任何臨時被交付的任務，而且他從不抱怨低薪或工時長。我想要問妳一旦傑瑞米的實習工作結束，公司提供他全職工作的可能性。我很不願意失去這樣的好隊友，而讓他到別間公司去。妳怎麼看？我們有能力給他一份工作嗎？

我很想知道妳的想法，所以請盡快回信給我！

謝謝，

詹姆士

- fantastic *(adj.)* 極好的
- invaluable *(adj.)* 寶貴的
- asset *(n.)* 人才；資產
- come up *(phr.)* （通常指意外地）發生
- capacity *(n.)* （指某人或某組織的）能力

28 What is the purpose of the e-mail?
(A) To ask for someone to be headhunted
(B) To offer someone leave without pay
(C) To discuss a potential job offer
(D) To communicate a salary decrease

這封電子郵件的目的為何？
(A) 為了要挖角某人
(B) 為了讓某人休無薪假
(C) 為了討論一份可能的工作機會
(D) 為了溝通減薪事宜

正解 **(C)**
本題是主旨題。解題關鍵為第一段第五句 I wanted to ask you about the possibility of offering Jeremy full-time employment at our company once his internship is up. 可以得知他想要跟凱莉討論有沒有機會給傑瑞米一份全職工作，故答案為 (C)。

29 What is NOT mentioned as being one of the intern's qualities?
(A) He is never sick.
(B) He never complains.
(C) He is good at communicating.
(D) He is efficient.

關於該位實習生的特質，何者未提及？
(A) 他從不生病。
(B) 他從不抱怨。
(C) 他擅長溝通。
(D) 他有效率。

正解 **(A)**
本題為除外題，詢問實習生的哪一個特質未被提及。(B) 由第一段第四句中 never complains 得知他從不抱怨；(C) 和 (D) 由第一段第三句中 communication skills are excellent 得知他擅長溝通，efficient in his work 得知他有效率。唯 (A)「他從不生病」沒有提及，答案選 (A)。

30 The word "up" in paragraph 1, line 7, is closest in meaning to
(A) awake
(B) started
(C) high
(D) completed

第一段第七行的 "up" 意義最接近
(A) 清醒的（形容詞）
(B) 開始的（過去分詞作形容詞）
(C) 高的（形容詞）
(D) 已完成的（過去分詞作形容詞）

正解 **(D)**
本題是考同義字。原文當中 once sth. is up 的 up 指「結束了的」，因此最接近該字意思的選項為 (D)「已完成的」。

Questions 31-34 *refer to the following online chat discussion.*

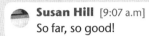

Tom Draper [9:05 a.m]
Hi guys. It's so great to have you two on board! I hope you are **settling in** well.

Susan Hill [9:07 a.m]
So far, so good!

Andy Hall [9:10 a.m]
It's great to be here. Everyone has been very helpful.

Tom Draper [9:11 a.m]
Good to know. Just a reminder that you will both have a 3-month probation period. After that, the sky's the limit! It's not hard to move up in this company if you work hard.

Susan Hill [9:15 a.m]
Good to know. Will you be doing an evaluation once our trial period is up?

Tom Draper [9:20 a.m]
That will be done by your supervisor in your department. We have employed a lot of new staff recently, so it makes sense to do it within each department.

Andy Hall [9:22 a.m]
Got it! Thanks.

Tom Draper [9:25 a.m]
OK, I'll let you **get on with** your work now. Unless you have any other questions for me?

Andy Hall [9:27 a.m]
Just one thing. My supervisor says there will be a lot of overtime hours this month due to the deadline. Will we be compensated for extra hours?

Tom Draper [9:30 a.m]
Of course! In addition to overtime payment, you can apply for an extra paid vacation day.

Susan Hill [9:35 a.m]
That's awesome!

湯姆・德雷珀 [9:05 a.m]
嗨，各位。你們兩位能夠加入真是太棒了！希望你們適應得很好。

蘇珊・希爾 [9:07 a.m]
到目前為止，一切都好！

安迪・霍爾 [9:10 a.m]
能來到這裡感覺很棒。大家都很願意幫忙。

湯姆・德雷珀 [9:11 a.m]
很高興聽到你這麼說。提醒你們一下，你們兩位都有三個月的試用期。之後的發展則有無限可能！如果你們努力工作，要在公司裡晉升並不困難。

蘇珊・希爾 [9:15 a.m]
很高興知道這件事。一旦我們的試用期結束，你會進行評估嗎？

湯姆・德雷珀 [9:20 a.m]
那會由你們的部門主管進行。我們最近雇用了很多新員工，所以在各部門內部進行評估很合理。

安迪・霍爾 [9:22 a.m]
知道了！謝謝。

湯姆・德雷珀 [9:25 a.m]
好的，我現在就讓你們回去繼續工作。除非你們有其他問題要問我？

安迪・霍爾 [9:27 a.m]
只有一件事。我主管說因為截止日的緣故，這個月會有很多加班時數。我們會因額外的工作時數得到補償嗎？

湯姆・德雷珀 [9:30 a.m]
當然會！除了加班費外，你們還可以申請額外的有薪年假。

蘇珊・希爾 [9:35 a.m]
那太棒了！

- settle in *(phr.)* 適應新環境
- get on with . . . *(phr.)* 開始或繼續（做某工作）

31 Why will there be a lot of extra work hours this month?

(A) Work has to be finished by a certain date.

(B) Because everyone wants to get paid more.

(C) Many people have gone on vacation.

(D) Someone has handed in their resignation.

為什麼這個月會有很多加班時數？

(A) 工作必須要在某特定日期前完成。

(B) 因為每個人都想要領更多錢。

(C) 許多人已去休假了。

(D) 某人已遞出辭呈。

正解 (A)

本題詢問這個月為何會有很多加班時數。由安迪‧霍爾在上午 9:27 寫道 . . . there will be a lot of overtime hours this month due to the deadline. 可知因為得在截止日前完成工作，所以這個月要時常加班，故答案為 (A)。

---

32 Who will be responsible for evaluations?

(A) Tom Draper

(B) A person from HR

(C) A manager of a department

(D) The CEO

誰會負責評估工作表現？

(A) 湯姆‧德雷珀　　(B) 人力資源部的人

(C) 部門主管　　(D) 執行長

正解 (C)

本題為細節題。解題關鍵是蘇珊‧希爾在上午 9:15 詢問湯姆‧德雷珀是否由他在其試用期後進行評估工作，而湯姆則在上午 9:20 回應 That will be done by your supervisor in your department. 「那會由你們的部門主管進行。」故知答案選 (C)。

---

33 What does Tom Draper imply about the company?

(A) Many people have retired recently.

(B) There are different options for compensation.

(C) The company had trouble hiring people.

(D) The company is doing poorly.

關於公司，湯姆‧德雷珀有何暗示？

(A) 最近有許多人退休了。　　**(B) 有不同補償方案。**

(C) 公司很難雇到人。　　(D) 公司現在的營運很差。

正解 (B)

本題為推論題，詢問關於公司，湯姆‧德雷珀有何暗示。解題關鍵在上午 9:27 安迪‧霍爾詢問加班是否有補償，而湯姆在上午 9:30 回覆 Of course! In addition to overtime payment, you can apply for an extra paid vacation day. 得知對於員工加班，公司提供加班費和有薪年假兩種補償方案，因此答案為 (B)。

---

34 At 9:11 a.m., what does Tom Draper mean when he writes "the sky's the limit"?

(A) Andy and Susan will have to fly a lot.

(B) The company's prospects are limited.

(C) It's hard to move up within the probation period.

(D) Anything is possible for the two newcomers.

在上午 9:11，湯姆‧德雷珀寫道 "the sky's the limit" 是何意？

(A) 安迪和蘇珊將要時常搭機出差。

(B) 公司前景有限。

(C) 試用期期間很難晉升。

(D) 對這兩位新人來說，任何事都有可能發生。

正解 (D)

本題考句意，題目問在上午 9:11，湯姆‧德雷珀寫道 "the sky's the limit" 有何用意。這個慣用語以「唯有天空才是盡頭」的字面意涵引伸指「未來無可限量；什麼事都可能發生」，因此答案為 (D)。

(B) prospect (n.) 前景。

P. 135~144

Part 1: Photographs

TRACK 32

1 (A) He's ordering some components.
(B) He's installing new software.
(C) He's working on an assembly line.
(D) He's packaging an item in the factory.

(A) 他正在訂購一些零件。
(B) 他正在安裝新的軟體。
(C) 他正在生產線上工作。
(D) 他正在工廠包裝物品。

正解 **(C)**
圖中的男子正在生產線上組裝汽車，因此符合圖片的敘述為 (C)「他正在生產線工作。」

2 (A) The bottles are stored in the warehouse.
(B) Some electronics are being inspected.
(C) Some gadgets are positioned around the building.
(D) The bottles are on the conveyor belt.

(A) 瓶子被儲存在倉庫裡。
(B) 有一些電子產品正在被檢查中。
(C) 有一些小機件被放置在大樓周圍。
(D) 瓶子在輸送帶上。

正解 **(D)**
圖中可見輸送帶上有很多瓶子，故正確答案為 (D)。

Part 2: Question and Response

❸ Will you call a mechanic for me?
   (A) Sure, I'll do it now.
   (B) No, I haven't seen him.
   (C) I don't know the model.

   你可以幫我打電話找技工嗎？
   (A) 當然，我現在就打。
   (B) 不，我沒有看到他。
   (C) 我不知道那個型號。

正解 (A)

本題為以 Will 開頭的一般是非問句，詢問對方是否可以幫忙打電話找技工。(A) 雖未直接以 Yes/No 回答，但表示沒問題會馬上幫忙，符合邏輯故為正解。

(B) 題目並非詢問有沒有看到某人。
(C) 此處的 model 指「型號」，答非所問。

---

❹ Has production been outsourced?
   (A) No, it's the best in the industry.
   (B) Yes, we have large numbers in stock.
   (C) Yes, a company in China is doing it.

   生產已經被外包了嗎？
   (A) 不，它是產業裡最好的。
   (B) 是，我們有很多庫存。
   (C) 是，中國的一間公司正在進行生產。

正解 (C)

本題為一般是非問句，詢問「是否已經外包生產」。可能的回答為「是，已外包」或「不，沒有外包」。(C) 回答「是，中國的一間公司正進行生產。」為符合邏輯之合理回應。

(A) 題目並非在討論優劣。
(B) 題目並未提到庫存狀況。

---

❺ The inventory has been checked, hasn't it?
   (A) Yes, it has been inspected.
   (B) Yes, it's in our product line.
   (C) No, they are automated.

   已經檢查過庫存了，不是嗎？
   (A) 是，它已經被仔細檢查了。
   (B) 是，它在我們的產品系列之內。
   (C) 不，它們是自動化的。

正解 (A)

本句為「附加問句」題型，詢問「已經檢查過庫存了，不是嗎？」合適的回應為 (A)「是，它已經被仔細檢查了。」

(B) 題目與產品系列的內容無關。
(C) 題目與自動化無關。

---

❻ The product was recalled due to a defect.
   (A) Actually, he hasn't called me back yet.
   (B) Customers should get their money back.
   (C) We've started increasing production.

   產品因為瑕疵而被召回。
   (A) 事實上，他還沒回電話給我。
   (B) 客戶應該要拿回他們的錢。
   (C) 我們已開始增加產量。

正解 (B)

本題為直述句，描述「產品因為瑕疵而被召回」。選項中唯一符合邏輯之回應為 (B)「客戶應該要拿回他們的錢。」

(A) 企圖以發音相似字 called 混淆作答，call sb. back 表「回電話給某人」，與題意無關。
(C) 題目已說產品有瑕疵，卻回答增加產量，與題目矛盾。

Part 3: Short Conversations

Questions 7-9 refer to the following conversation with three speakers.

M1: Unfortunately I think we will need to lay off some workers in the near future.

W: That will be very difficult. We are already short of staff on the assembly line.

M2: That's true. We are also struggling to package the goods at the end of the conveyor belts.

M1: I realize that, but the numbers just **don't add up**. We will need to let some people go and reduce our output.

W: That's a shame. Maybe we could **look into** automating the packaging so that we can maintain current output and still reduce costs.

M2: Yeah, I think we should look into that. But it won't **go down** well with the workers.

- not add up *(phr.)* 說不通；不合情理
- look into *(phr.)* 調查；探究
- go down *(phr.)* 引起某種反應

男一：很遺憾我想我們將要在近期裁減一些工人。

女：那會讓情況變得很艱困。我們的生產線已經人手短缺了。

男二：說得沒錯。我們輸送帶末端的產品包裝作業也很艱難地在進行。

男一：我了解，但是收支數字有些離譜。我們將需要裁掉一些人並且減少我們的產量。

女：那真的很遺憾。或許我們可以研究一下改採自動化包裝，這樣我們就能維持目前的產出但同樣能減低成本。

男二：沒錯，我想我們應該研究那個做法。但在工人間會出現反對聲浪。

❼ What are the speakers mainly discussing?
(A) Innovations in automation
(B) How to package goods
(C) Reducing their workforce
(D) Their factory's output

說話者主要是在討論什麼？
(A) 自動化的發明　　(B) 如何包裝貨品
(C) 減少他們的人力　(D) 他們工廠的產量

正解 **(C)**

本題為主旨題，詢問說話者討論的內容。由男一開頭時說 Unfortunately I think we will need to lay off some workers in the near future. 且接下來皆在討論裁員的原因和影響，得知答案要選 (C)。

❽ What does the woman suggest as a way to maintain output?
(A) Automating packaging
(B) Hiring more people
(C) Adding conveyor belts
(D) Laying people off

女子建議用什麼方法來維持產量？
(A) 自動化包裝　　(B) 雇用更多人
(C) 增加輸送帶　　(D) 裁員

正解 **(A)**

題目詢問維持產量的方法。由女子說 Maybe we could look into automating the packaging so that we can maintain current output and still reduce costs. 得知她建議採自動化包裝來維持產量同時減低成本，故答案為 (A)。

⑨ What is implied in the conversation?

   (A) The company is facing a lot of competition.

   (B) The workers in the factory are not happy.

   (C) The assembly line employees are too slow.

   (D) The company is struggling to make a profit.

此對話有何暗示？

   (A) 公司正面臨許多競爭。

   (B) 工廠裡的工人並不開心。

   (C) 生產線的員工動作太慢。

   (D) 公司努力要獲利。

正解 **(D)**

本題問此對話暗示了什麼。由男一說 I realize that, but the numbers just don't add up. We will need to let some people go and reduce our output. 得知公司收支失衡，所以考慮靠減少人事成本來增加獲利，答案應為 (D)。

Questions 10-12 refer to the following conversation and table.

W: We need to review how the products are coming off the production line, as some quality issues have been picked up by the team recently.

M: Sure. What are some of the issues?

W: Well, from looking at the table here, it seems like some products are coming off the line with paint **peeling** off or **scratches**. In addition, some items were damaged during the packaging process.

M: It sounds like we need to take a look at the machinery.

W: Definitely. But it looks as if we have an even bigger problem. And that is the question of why some of the products are not conforming to the standard size.

女：我們需要檢討產品下生產線時的狀況，因為團隊最近發現一些品質問題。

男：當然。有哪些問題呢？

女：嗯，從這裡的這個表格看來，有些產品似乎下生產線時就掉漆或刮到了。除此之外，一些品項在包裝過程中損壞了。

男：聽起來我們需要檢查一下機器。

女：沒錯。但看來我們好像有更嚴重的問題。那就是為何會某些產品的尺寸不符合標準規格。

• peel *(v.)* 剝落
• scratch *(n.)* 刮痕

REPORTED ISSUES	
Inspected by	**Issue found**
Tim Price	Paint peeling off
Greg Jones	Some scratches found
Alice Coulson	Size did not match standard
Peter Slane	Items damaged during packaging

通報問題	
檢查員	**發現的問題**
提姆・派斯	掉漆
葛雷・瓊斯	發現一些刮痕
愛麗絲・克勞森	尺寸不符標準規格
彼得・斯藍	品項在包裝時毀損

⑩ What does the woman inform the man about?

(A) **A list of quality control problems**

(B) A list of new machinery to buy

(C) A list of damaged goods

(D) A list of quality control inspectors

女子告知男子什麼事？

(A) 一連串的品管問題

(B) 需添購的新機器清單

(C) 一些受損的貨品

(D) 幾位品管稽核人員

正解 (A)

本題詢問女子告知男子什麼事。由女子開頭說 We need to review how the products are coming off the production line, as some quality issues have been picked up by the team recently. 得知最近發現一些品管方面的問題，故答案要選 (A)。

---

⑪ What does the man think they should do?

(A) Run a quality control test

(B) **Examine the machinery**

(C) Change the packaging

(D) Speak to the team

男子認為他們應該怎麼做？

(A) 進行品管測試

(B) 檢查機器

(C) 更換包裝

(D) 和團隊談談

正解 (B)

本題詢問男子認為該怎麼做。由男子說 It sounds like we need to take a look at the machinery. 可知他認為應該要檢查機器，故答案選 (B)。

---

⑫ Look at the graphic. Which inspector discovered the most serious problem?

(A) **Alice Coulson**

(B) Tim Price

(C) Greg Jones

(D) Peter Slane

看圖表。哪位檢查員發現了最嚴重的問題？

(A) 愛麗絲・克勞森

(B) 提姆・派斯

(C) 葛雷・瓊斯

(D) 彼得・斯藍

正解 (A)

本題為圖表題，詢問哪位檢查員發現了最嚴重的問題。由女子說 But it looks as if we have an even bigger problem . . . some of the products are not conforming to the standard size. 得知更大的問題是尺寸不符標準規格。對照圖表可知發現此問題的人是愛麗絲・克勞森，答案選 (A)。

Part 4: Short Talks

Questions 13-15 refer to the following announcement.

Good afternoon and thank you for joining me. Many of you will have heard **speculation** in recent weeks about a possible **merger** with Global Toys. I have asked you here today to confirm that the rumors are indeed correct. Following extensive negotiations between our Directors and the board of Global Toys, we have concluded that <u>this merger is in the best interest of our company</u>. As a small toy producer, we have struggled recently to produce the quality toys that we pride ourselves on. As part of Global Toys, currently the industry leader, we will be able to take advantage of their huge manufacturing plant in China. This will allow us to increase output and keep costs down. At the same time, the quality of our product lines will be maintained with extensive in-house quality control. I am confident that we will continue to produce products that parents can trust and kids will love.

- speculation *(n.)* 猜測；推測
- merger *(n.)* 合併

午安，謝謝大家的參與。在座的許多人在未來幾週會聽到我們可能和全球玩具公司合併的臆測。我今天召集各位到這裡，就是要向你們證實這個傳言的確是對的。經過本公司董事和全球玩具公司董事會的全面協商之後，我們的結論是<u>這場合併對公司而言是最有利的選擇</u>。身為一間小型玩具製造商，近來我們得奮力掙扎才得以製造出我們引以為傲的高品質玩具。成為目前產業龍頭全球玩具公司的一部分，我們將能利用他們在中國的大型製造工廠。這將使我們能夠增加產量且維持低成本。同時我們產品系列會透過全面的內部品管來維持品質。我有信心我們將會持續製造出父母信賴、孩子熱愛的產品。

---

⑬ What is the announcement about?
(A) An upcoming takeover
(B) The opening of a new plant
(C) A forthcoming merger
(D) The closure of the company

這個公告是關於什麼？
(A) 即將到來的收購
(B) 新工廠的開設
(C) 即將到來的合併
(D) 公司的倒閉

正解 (C)
本題是主旨題，詢問公告關於什麼。由關鍵字詞 possible merger「可能的合併」、the rumors are indeed correct「謠言的確是對的」可知是要向員工公告合併的消息，所以答案選 (C)。

⑭ What does the speaker mean when she says, "this merger is in the best interest of our company"?
(A) It will benefit the company.
(B) It will be good for Global Toys.
(C) It will be interesting.
(D) It is not necessary.

說話者說 "this merger is in the best interest of our company" 是什麼意思？
(A) 合併將對公司有好處。
(B) 合併將對全球玩具公司有好處。
(C) 合併將會很有趣。
(D) 合併是沒有必要的。

正解 **(A)**
本題問 "this merger is in the best interest of our company" 的句意。interest 在此是「利益」之意，原文中說話者說這句之後又接著闡述公司合併的好處，包括能夠增加產量且維持低成本等，因此答案為 (A)。

⑮ Who most likely is the speaker?
(A) An assembly line worker
(B) A company director
(C) A mechanic
(D) A subcontractor

誰最可能是說話者？
(A) 生產線工人　　　　**(B) 公司管理者**
(C) 技工　　　　　　　(D) 轉包商

正解 **(B)**
本題問說話者的身分。此公告乃在宣布公司合併消息並說明合併會帶來的好處，可以推測應為公司管理者對其員工說話，故答案為 (B)。

Questions 16-18 refer to the following talk and map.

Hello and welcome to our latest manufacturing facility. My name is Bob Wright and I'll be showing you around the magnificent new building and everything inside it. Following a tour of our offices, I will be taking you down to the factory floor where you will be able to see our state-of-the-art assembly lines, featuring all the newest technology available on the market. Unfortunately, I won't be able to show you where the goods end up right before delivery, as this part of the plant is not yet complete. However, we hope you will be impressed by our facility and that you will consider our plant for your future manufacturing needs. So, **without further ado**, let's get started. Please follow me.

哈囉，歡迎來參觀我們最新的製造設備。我的名字是鮑伯‧賴特，我會帶各位四處參觀這棟宏偉的新大樓以及內部的一切設施。在參觀我們的辦公室之後，我會帶各位到工廠樓層，您將能在那裡看到我們先進的生產線，它擁有所有市場上能取得的最新科技。可惜的是我將無法帶您參觀貨物在出貨之前的存放處，因為工廠的這個部分尚未完成。然而，我們希望各位會對我們的設備印象深刻，並考慮利用我們的工廠來滿足您未來的製造需求。那麼話不多說，我們馬上開始吧。請跟我來。

• without further ado *(phr.)* 不再浪費時間、精力；立即（ado 為名詞，表「忙亂；費力」）

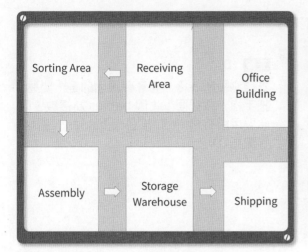

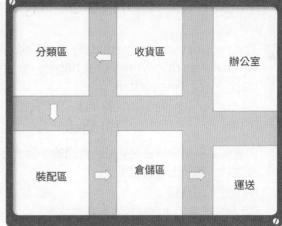

16 Who most likely are the listeners?
(A) Foreign tourists
(B) School students
(C) Potential clients
(D) Factory workers

誰最可能是聽這段談話的人？
(A) 外國觀光客　　　(B) 學校的學生
(C) 潛在的客戶　　(D) 工廠工人

正解 **(C)**
題目問這段談話的聽眾最有可能是誰。說話者帶領聽者參觀辦公室與新工廠，接著強調其設備擁有最新科技，然後在關鍵的一句說到 . . . we hope you will be impressed by our facility and that you will consider our plant for your future manufacturing needs.，可知說話者想讓聽者對新工廠留下好印象，並希望聽者未來考慮讓這間工廠承包製作，因此推測聽者應是潛在客戶，故答案為 (C)。

17 What would the speaker like the listeners to do?
(A) Think about using this facility
(B) Make an appointment in the office
(C) Tour the plant by themselves
(D) Only visit the assembly line

說話者希望聽者做什麼？
(A) 考慮使用這個設施　(B) 在辦公室預約
(C) 自己參觀工廠　　　　(D) 只參觀生產線

正解 **(A)**
本題詢問希望聽者做什麼。由 However, we hope you will be impressed by our facility and that you will consider our plant for your future manufacturing needs. 得知說話者希望對方可以考慮使用這間工廠的設備，所以答案為 (A)。

18 Look at the graphic. Where will the listeners be unable to go today?
(A) The office building
(B) The receiving area
(C) The storage warehouse
(D) The sorting area

看圖表。今天聽這段話的人不能去哪裡？
(A) 辦公室　　　　(B) 收貨區
(C) 倉儲區　　　(D) 分類區

正解 **(C)**
本題為圖表題，詢問今天聽這段話的人不能去哪裡。由關鍵句 Unfortunately, I won't be able to show you where the goods end up right before delivery 可知今天無法參觀貨品在出貨之前的存放區，原文中的 delivery 指「遞送；運送」，意同圖表中的 shipping，對照地圖在 shipping 之前的區域為倉儲區，所以答案是 (C)。

Part 5: Incomplete Sentences

19 The product was immediately recalled when it was discovered that babies could trap _____ fingers in it.

(A) them　　　　　　(B) his

(C) its　　　　　　　**(D) their**

當這個產品被發現會使嬰兒將他們的手指卡在裡面後，就馬上被回收了。

(A) 他們（受格）

(B) 他的（第三人稱陽性單數所有格）

(C) 它的（第三人稱中性單數所有格）

(D) 他們的（第三人稱複數所有格）

正解 (D)

本題測驗所有格。句意要表達的是「嬰兒把手指卡在裡面」，因 babies 為複數，因此要用所有格 their 來替代 babies'，所以答案為 (D)。

---

20 The new assembly line workers were shown how to _____ the products before they are packaged.

(A) put off　　　　　**(B) put together**

(C) put by　　　　　(D) put across

有人向這些新的生產線工人示範產品在包裝前該如何組裝。

(A) 延遲

(B) 組裝

(C) 存（錢）

(D) 表達清楚（想法或觀點）

正解 (B)

本題考片語動詞。空格後的受詞是 the products，故應選 (B) put together 表示「組裝」，才合乎句意。

---

21 The manufacturing costs will largely depend on the size of the _____.

(A) shortage　　　　**(B) batch**

(C) patent　　　　　(D) mechanic

生產成本絕大部分取決於產量的規模。

(A) 短缺　　　　　　**(B) 一批（生產量）**

(C) 專利　　　　　　(D) 技工

正解 (B)

本題考字義。依照句意可知空格處填入 (B) batch 指「一批（生產量）」，表示生產成本高或低取決於產量有多少。

---

22 A small factory was _____ to make some of the components for the production line.

(A) assembled　　　(B) customized

(C) subcontracted　(D) launched

一間小工廠被分包去製作一些生產線所需的零件。

(A) 組裝　　　　　　(B) 訂製

(C) 分包；轉包　　(D) 推出

正解 (C)

本題考字義。依照句意可知空格處填入 (C) subcontracted 指「分包」，亦即有其他公司將零件的製作分包給小工廠進行。

㉓ This Indian company sells fabrics _____ to retailers, fashion designers, and other manufacturers.

(A) **wholesale**　　(B) procedure
(C) maintenance　　(D) industry

這間印度公司將布料批發販售給零售商、時尚設計師和其他製造商。

(A) 批發　　　　(B) 程序
(C) 維修　　　　(D) 產業

正解 **(A)**

本題考字義。依照句意可知空格處填入 (A) wholesale 指「批發」，表示以批發的方式販售布料。

Part 6: Text Completion

Questions 24-27 refer to the following article.

In a recent interview, Chief Operating Officer of GDE Manufacturing, Andrew Norwood, discussed how manufacturing businesses can use production data to improve operations. ---24--- The concept means that businesses ---25--- their production output in order to identify the batch with the highest quality and strongest cost-to-revenue ratio. Analyzing production data will **reveal** the factors that resulted in the "ideal batch". These could include materials, temperature, ---26--- speeds, most **competent** assembly line workers, etc. These insights can then ---27--- **optimize** production, which will improve efficiency, reduce costs, raise quality, and support ongoing improvements.

在最近的訪問中，GDE 製造工廠的營運長安卓‧諾伍德談到製造業能如何利用生產數據來改善營運。諾伍德相信「理想批次」的概念可以被應用到大部分的產業。這個概念意味著公司審視其產出，找出具備最高品質與最大成本盈收比率的那批貨。分析生產數據將會揭露造就出「理想批次」的因素。這些因素包含原料、氣溫、機器的速度、最能幹的生產線工人等。這些見解可以被用在優化生產，而優化生產將能增進效率、減低成本、提高品質且維持不斷的進步。

- reveal *(v.)* 顯露；揭露
- competent *(adj.)* 能幹的；有能力的
- optimize *(v.)* 最佳化

24
(A) Norwood has installed new software to analyze the data from his manufacturing plant.

(B) Norwood believes that the concept of an "ideal batch" can be applied to most industries.

(C) Norwood has decided to share his expertise on raw materials with other manufacturers.

(D) Norwood believes that all assembly lines will be automated within the next ten years.

(A) 諾伍德已安裝新的軟體來分析他製造工廠的數據。

(B) 諾伍德相信「理想批次」的概念可以被應用到大部分的產業。

(C) 諾伍德已經決定與其他製造商分享他在原料上的專業知識。

(D) 諾伍德相信所有的生產線在未來十年內將會自動化。

正解 (B)

空格前方說到利用生產數據來改善營運，而空格後一句說「這個概念（concept）意味著……」。由於選項(B)提出一種稱為「理想批次」的概念，可知就是後一句談論的「這個概念」，語意連貫故為正確答案。

(C) expertise *(n.)* 專業知識。

25
(A) **examine**   (B) assemble

(C) install   (D) strike

(A) 審查
(B) 組裝
(C) 安裝
(D) 罷工

正解 (A)

本題考字義。原句提到「這個概念意味著公司 ＿＿＿ 其產量，找出具備最高品質與最大成本盈收比率的那批貨。」，可知符合句意的答案為 (A)。

26
(A) overproduction   (B) glitch

(C) inventory   **(D) machinery**

(A) 生產過剩
(B) 小故障
(C) 存貨
(D) 機器

正解 (D)

本題考單字。原句提到「這些包含了原料、氣溫、 ＿＿＿ 速度、最能幹的生產線工人等。」僅選項 (D) 符合本句句意。machinery speeds 即機器運轉的速度，關乎生產效能。

27
(A) get used to   **(B) be used to**

(C) used to   (D) use to

(A) 漸漸習慣於（＋N./V-ing）
(B) 被用來（＋V.）
(C) 過去經常（＋V.）
(D) 無 use to 的用法

正解 (B)

本題考文法及片語用法。因主詞為 These insights，可知本句要採被動語態，表示見解「被用來」優化生產，故答案應選 (B)。

Part 7: Reading Comprehension

Questions 28-29 refer to the following press release.

For Immediate Release

SUNCO OPENS MANUFACTURING PLANT INVIETNAM TO FULFILL DEMAND IN ASIA

Washington D.C., April 20th—SunCo Beverages International Holdings (SunCo) today celebrated the official opening of its new plant in Vietnam, in Hung Yen province. This plant is now the largest of the company's plants in Asia, with an area covering 103,000 square meters. It will mainly produce beverages in the **carbonated drinks** category.

Attending the opening ceremony were senior representatives of SunCo, local government leaders, and representatives of the Asian Beverage Industry Association (ABIA). Mr. Tony Lee, Executive Chairman of SunCo Beverages, said during his welcome speech, "SunCo has been focusing on the growing Asia market for the past decade. The Asia market has become a major growth area for the business and the opening of this new plant marks a significant milestone for our company."

Founded and based in Washington D.C., SunCo already has facilities in China and Singapore. SunCo is the owner of several successful brands of carbonated drinks and in the first quarter of this year they recorded a growth of 30% in the Asian market.

快訊

桑柯於越南設廠 以滿足亞洲需求

華盛頓特區，四月二十日電——桑柯飲料國際股份公司（桑柯）今天慶祝它在越南興安省的新廠正式啟用了。這座工廠現在是該公司在亞洲的最大廠，面積涵蓋十萬三千平方公尺。它將主要生產碳酸飲料。

參加開幕典禮有桑柯的資深代表、當地政府領導人和亞洲飲料產業協會的代表。桑柯飲料的執行董事湯尼 · 李先生在他的歡迎致詞中說：「桑柯致力壯大亞洲市場已有十年之久了。亞洲市場已成為這個產業的主要成長區域，這座新廠的啟用對我們公司來說是一個重大的里程碑。」

桑柯的創辦地與總部均位在華盛頓特區，它已進駐中國和新加坡。桑柯旗下擁有許多成功的碳酸飲料品牌，它們在今年第一季已於亞洲市場創下百分之三十的成長率。

• carbonated drink *(n.)* 碳酸飲料（carbonated 指「含二氧化碳的」）

28 What is the purpose of this press release?
(A) To inform people of the expansion of an existing manufacturing plant
(B) To inform people of a company's decision to enter the Asian market
(C) To inform people of the opening of a new manufacturing facility
(D) To inform people of a speech made by the chairman of SunCo Beverages

這篇新聞稿的目的是？
(A) 告知人們一間現有製造工廠的擴充
(B) 告知人們一間公司決定進入亞洲市場
(C) 告知人們一座新製造設施的啟用
(D) 告知人們桑柯飲料總裁的一段演說

正解 (C)

本題為主旨題，詢問新聞稿的目的。通常新聞稿一開頭就會說出主旨，因此解題關鍵在標題的 SunCo Opens Manufacturing Plant 與開頭第一句的 ... SunCo Beverages International Holdings (SunCo) today celebrated the official opening of its new plant in Vietnam, in Hung Yen province.，可知有一間新的工廠啟用，所以答案為 (C)。

29 Who was NOT mentioned as being present at this event?
(A) Local government leaders
(B) Local beverage suppliers
(C) Senior managers from SunCo
(D) ABIA representatives

誰未被提及出席這個活動？
(A) 當地政府領導人
(B) 當地飲料供應商
(C) 桑柯的資深經理
(D) 亞洲飲料產業協會的代表

正解 (B)

本題為除外題，詢問何者並為出席活動。(A)、(C)、(D) 均可見第二段第一句，唯獨 (B) 未提及，故為正選。

Questions 30-34 refer to the following e-mail and production cost outline.

To: Jack Greenfield

From: Justin Moore

Subject: Production cost outline

Dear Mr. Greenfield,

Following our meeting yesterday, I am hereby sending you the requested production cost outline. The proposed new line of in-ear headphones will be comprised of parts made in our own factories, unless stated **otherwise**. There is currently a big market for sports earphones and, as you know, our factories have the capacity to produce large batches that can ship worldwide. As well as large output capabilities, our factories also never compromise on quality and our quality control operations are some of the strictest in the manufacturing industry. Therefore, you can **rest assured** that what you are delivering to the consumer will adequately reflect your reputation for quality electronics.

Please note: Due to the fact that you are making a large order and in the hope we can do more business in future, I am pleased to inform you that I have lowered the cost per unit for each electronic component. Please see below for further details.

Please contact me once you have had a chance to review the cost outline and let me know if you have any questions.

Best Regards,

Justin Moore
Production Manager
LBJ Group Inc.

收件者：傑克‧格林菲爾
寄件者：賈斯汀‧摩爾
主　旨：生產成本概要

格林菲爾先生您好：

繼昨天的會議之後，我特此寄發您要求的生產成本概要。您提出的入耳式耳機的新產線，除非有另外聲明，否則將由敝公司的工廠所生產的零件組裝而成。目前運動耳機的市場很大，如您所知，敝公司的工廠有能力大量生產供給全世界。除了量產的能力之外，我們的工廠也從不在品質上妥協，而且我們的品管執行在製造業界中算是最嚴格的。因此，您可以放心您運送給消費者的產品將充分反映您優質電子產品的名聲。

請注意：由於您的訂單量很大而我們希望未來能有更多商業往來，我很開心地通知您我已經降低各電子零件的單件費用。請看以下的明細。

看完成本概要後請聯繫我，讓我知道您是否有任何疑問。

謹致，

賈斯汀‧摩爾
產品部經理
LBJ 集團股份有限公司

- otherwise *(adv.)* 在其他方面
- rest assured（用於安慰某人）請放心；別擔心

Planned Production Cost Outline for Elite Electronics	
Total Units: 10,000	
Cost Per Unit:	
Plastic casing	$2.00/unit
Rubber ear buds	$1.50/unit
Electronic components (supplied by X-Electronics)	$5.00/unit
Wire	$1.00/unit
Packaging (supplied by Excel Cardboard)	$0.20/unit
In-house labor (0.25 hours/unit)	$3.80/unit
Total Direct Cost/Unit	$13.50/unit
Direct Cost $13.50/unit x 10,000 units =	$135,000.00
Tax =	$13,500.00
Total Production Costs =	$148,500.00

艾立電子預計生產成本概要	
總數量：一萬件	
每件成本：	
塑膠套	2 元/件
橡膠耳塞	1.5 元/件
電子零件（由 X 電子公司供應）	5 元/件
電線	1 元/件
包裝（由優勝硬紙板公司供應）	0.2 元/件
內部勞工費用（0.25 小時／每件）	3.8 元/件
直接總成本／每件	13.50 元/件
直接成本 13.50 元/件 x 10,000 件 = 135,000 元	
稅金 = 13,500 元	
總生產成本 = 148,500 元	

30 What is the main purpose of Mr. Moore's e-mail?

(A) To state why the company should produce more earphones

(B) To provide a cost outline to a potential customer

(C) To invoice a customer for work that has been carried out

(D) To explain why some components cannot be made in-house

摩爾先生的電子郵件主要目的為何？

(A) 說明為何公司需要生產更多的耳機

(B) 提供成本概要給潛在客戶

(C) 為已完成的工作開立發票給客戶

(D) 解釋為何某些零件無法在內部生產

正解 (B)

本題為主旨題，詢問此電子郵件的主要目的。由電子郵件的主旨 Production cost outline 以及電子郵件的第二段第一句 Due to the fact that you are making a large order . . . I have lowered the cost per unit . . . 得知是為了給即將下單的客戶成本概要與報價，故答案為 (B)。

㉛ Why does Mr. Moore mention his company's ability to produce large batches?

(A) It is a cheaper way to manufacture electronics.

(B) Quality control is easier for large quantities.

(C) There is a big demand for sports headphones.

(D) Only large batches can be shipped worldwide.

為何摩爾先生要提及他的公司有大量生產的能力？

(A) 這是生產電子產品較便宜的方法。

(B) 數量大時品管比較容易。

(C) 運動耳機的需求量大。

(D) 只有大批生產才可以運送到全世界。

正解 (C)

本題詢問摩爾先生為何要提及他的公司有量產的能力。電子郵件的第三句說 There is currently a big market for sports earphones and, as you know, our factories have the capacity to produce large batches that can ship worldwide. ，故知是為了強調他的公司能滿足運動耳機市場的龐大需求量，答案要選 (C)。

㉜ How many units does Mr. Moore give Mr. Greenfield a quote for?

(A) 135,000　　　(B) 13,500

(C) 10,000　　　(D) 20,000

摩爾先生給格林菲爾先生多少數量的報價？

(A) 135,000　　　(B) 12,500

(C) 10,000　　　(D) 20,000

正解 (C)

本題為細節題。詢問摩爾先生給格林菲爾先生的報價是以多少數量計算。由生產成本概要最上方的 Total Units: 10,000 可知答案應為 (C)。

㉝ Which of the following components will not be made in-house at LBJ Group's factories?

(A) Plastic casing

(B) Rubber ear buds

(C) Wire

(D) Electronics

以下哪個零件不會在 LBJ 集團的工廠內部生產？

(A) 塑膠套

(B) 橡膠耳塞

(C) 電線

(D) 電子產品

正解 (D)

本題詢問哪個零件不會在內部生產。電子郵件的第二句說 The proposed new line of in-ear headphones will be comprised of parts made in our own factories, unless stated otherwise.；對照生產成本概要，有另外說明由其他公司供應的項目是電子零件與包裝，所以答案為 (D) Electronics。

㉞ What was the original cost per unit price of the electronic components, before the adjustment?

(A) $5.25　　　(B) $5.00

(C) $3.80　　　(D) $2.00

價格調整之前，每個電子零件原本的價格是多少？

(A) 5.25 元　　　(B) 5 元

(C) 3.8 元　　　(D) 2 元

正解 (A)

本題為整合題，詢問價格調整之前每個電子零件的價格。由電子郵件第二段的 . . . I have lowered the cost per unit for each electronic component. 可知價格有調降，而根據生產成本概要，電子零件是每件五元，得知原本應高於五元，所以答案是 (A)。

Unit 5 Purchasing 採購

P. 156~164

Part 1: Photographs

TRACK 37

❶ (A) The woman is ordering coffee in a café.

(B) The woman is placing an order online.

(C) The woman is signing a contract.

(D) The woman is showing her ID to a staff member.

(A) 那位女子正在咖啡廳點咖啡。

(B) 那位女子正在上網下訂單。

(C) 那位女子正在簽署合約。

(D) 那位女子正在向工作人員出示身分證。

正解 **(B)**

圖中的女子正在電腦前拿著信用卡，因此符合圖片的敘述為 (B)「那位女子正在上網下訂單。」

....

❷ **(A) Many items are stored in a warehouse.**

(B) Some people are working in a factory.

(C) All of the boxes are wrapped in plastic.

(D) The items are being loaded onto a truck.

(A) 許多貨品都儲存在倉庫裡。

(B) 有些人正在工廠工作。

(C) 所有的箱子都用塑膠包裹。

(D) 那些物品正被裝到卡車上。

正解 **(A)**

圖中可見倉庫堆滿了貨品，故正確答案為 (A)。

❸ How do we plan to expand in the region?

(A) We're cutting employees to lower costs.

(B) I plan to pay in one lump sum.

(C) We will partner with local suppliers.

我們如何計畫在該地區擴張？

(A) 我們正在削減員工以降低成本。

(B) 我打算一次付清。

(C) 我們將與當地供應商合作。

正解 **(C)**

本題以 How 詢問計畫在該地區擴張的方式。選項 (C) 回答「我們將與當地供應商合作」，為符合邏輯之可能方法，故為正解。

(A) 和 (B) 與題意無關。

❹ Have you found any vendors yet?

(A) Yes, I'll e-mail you the list later today.

(B) No, I don't think Ray has much potential.

(C) Sorry, I can't give you a refund on this.

你找到任何供應商了嗎？

(A) 有，今天稍晚我會寄名單給你。

(B) 沒有，我不認為雷有什麼潛力。

(C) 抱歉，我無法退款給你。

正解 **(A)**

本題為以 Have 開頭的一般是非問句，詢問對方是否找到任何供應商。合適的回應為 (A)「有，今天稍晚我會寄名單給你。」

(B) 和 (C) 與題意無關。

❺ Is the parcel arriving in the morning or afternoon?

(A) I'll be awake before the sun rises.

(B) They said later this afternoon.

(C) His plane arrives at 9:40 a.m.

包裹是早上還是下午寄到？

(A) 在太陽升起之前我會醒著。

(B) 他們說今天下午晚點會到。

(C) 他的班機在上午九點四十分抵達。

正解 **(B)**

本題為選擇疑問句，詢問對方包裹是早上還是下午送達。合適的回應為選擇其一的 (B)「他們說今天下午晚點會到。」

(A) 與題意無關。

(C) 問包裹卻回答班機抵達時間，答非所問。

❻ Why do we need to count the inventory again?

(A) To check if anything got lost in the transfer.

(B) She's a great inventor because she's creative.

(C) We need to make sure everyone is here.

為什麼我們需要再次盤點庫存？

(A) 檢查運輸中是否遺失了任何東西。

(B) 她是一位偉大的發明家，因為她很有創造力。

(C) 我們需要確保每個人都在這裡。

正解 **(A)**

本題為以 Why 詢問再次盤點庫存的原因，故合適的回應為 (A)「檢查運輸中是否遺失了任何東西。」

(B) 以與題目 inventory 拼法相近的 inventor 企圖混淆作答，但答非所問。

(C) 與題意無關。

Part 3: Short Conversations

Questions 7-9 refer to the following conversation.

W: Hello, this is Melinda Barnes from Kennedy Organic. We're interested in placing a large order for your Platinum desk units. Do you have many in stock?

M: Yes, we currently have an abundance of the Platinum desks. How many were you looking to get hold of?

W: We want 75 units. But first, I'd like to get an estimate for that.

M: No problem. Just leave your e-mail and phone number with me, and I'll get back to you before the end of the day.

W: Great. My e-mail is melinda.barnes@10excel.com, and my number is 0944 893 9393. By the way, what does the estimate include?

M: Estimates include merchandise, packaging, and shipping, as well as any taxes and duty required.

女：您好，我是肯尼迪有機食品公司的梅琳達·巴恩斯。我們有意下大筆訂單購買您的白金鋼辦公桌組。你們的存貨充足嗎？

男：有，我們目前有大量的白金鋼辦公桌。您想要訂幾組？

女：我們要七十五組。但首先我想先取得估價。

男：沒問題。您只需留下您下電子郵件和電話號碼，我會在今天下班之前回覆您。

女：太好了。我的電子郵件是 melinda.barnes@10excel.com，電話是 0944 893 9393。對了，估價包含了什麼？

男：估價包含商品、包裝和運輸費用，以及任何所需的稅金和關稅。

---

❼ Why is the woman contacting the supplier?
(A) To open an account
(B) To clarify payment terms
(C) To request a refund
(D) To ask for an estimate

女子為何聯繫供應商？
(A) 為了開戶
(B) 為了釐清付款條件
(C) 為了要求退款
(D) 為了要求估價

正解 **(D)**
本題詢問女子聯繫供應商的目的。由關鍵句 We're interested in placing a large order for your Platinum desk units. 及 I'd like to get an estimate for that. 可知女子需買辦公桌並尋求估價而聯繫供應商，故答案選 (D)。

---

❽ What is implied about the man's company?
(A) It sells a wide range of food products.
(B) It's currently having some problems.
(C) Their main business is shipping.
(D) They have enough desks for the woman.

關於該名男子的公司，說話者有何暗示？
(A) 它出售各種各樣的食品。
(B) 它目前有一些問題。
(C) 他們主要經營運輸業。
(D) 他們有足夠的辦公桌給那名女子。

正解 **(D)**
本題詢問關於該名男子的公司，說話者有何暗示。由男子所說 we currently have an abundance of the Platinum desks. 可知他們有足夠的辦公桌給那名女子，故選 (D)。

⑨ What does the man mean when he says "get hold of"?

(A) To succeed in getting something

(B) To talk to somebody face to face

(C) To talk to somebody on the phone

(D) To test a product before buying it

當男子說 "get hold of" 時，他的言下之意是？

(A) 成功取得某物

(B) 面對面跟某人談話

(C) 與某人通話

(D) 購買前測試產品

正解 (A)

本題考句意。關鍵句為男子說 we currently have an abundance of the Platinum desks. How many were you looking to get hold of? 可知他是詢問女子要買多少組辦公桌，故答案選 (A)。片語 get a hold of sth. 有「獲得、取得（某物）」之意。另外，get a hold of sb. 則指「找到或聯繫上（某人）」。

Questions 10-12 refer to the following conversation and coupon.

W: Good afternoon, sir. Oh, how sweet. Are all these items for your kids?

M: Yes, they are. I hope they like them! Here, I have this discount coupon.

W: OK, I'll take it, thank you. So, the subtotal comes to 100 dollars. After the discount has been subtracted, your final total is just 90 dollars. Will you be paying by cash or credit card?

M: Card.

W: OK. Please place your card on the reader . . . Excellent. That's gone through. 90 dollars has been credited to your account. Thank you for shopping at Harry's Toys and Merry Christmas to you and your family.

M: Thanks very much! And the same to you, too.

女：先生，午安。哦，真貼心。所有這些商品都要給您的孩子嗎？

男：對，沒錯。我希望他們會喜歡！我這裡有張優惠券。

女：好的，給我吧，謝謝您。那麼，小計為一百美元。折扣後，您最後的金額剛好為九十美元。您要付現還是刷信用卡？

男：信用卡。

女：好的。請把您的卡放在讀卡機上⋯⋯太好了。已經好了。九十美元的消費已記在您的帳戶。感謝您在哈利斯玩具購物，祝您和您的家人聖誕快樂。

男：非常感謝妳！也祝妳聖誕快樂。

HARRY'S TOYS
Dolls — Buy 3 Get 1 Free!
Toy cars — Buy 2 Get 1 Free!
Clothes — 10% off every $100 spent!
Board games — 30% discount!
Offers Expire 12/26!

哈利斯玩具
玩偶 — 買三送一！
玩具車 — 買二送一！
服飾 — 滿百享九折！
桌遊 — 七折！
優惠截至 12 月 26 日止！

SECTION B 試題練習

UNIT **5** Purchasing 採購

10 What is the man buying?

(A) Christmas gifts for his kids

(B) Some gifts for his coworkers

(C) A Christmas tree for his family

(D) A gift for someone called Harry

男子正在買什麼？

(A) 給他孩子的聖誕禮物

(B) 給他同事的一些禮物

(C) 給他家人的聖誕樹

(D) 給哈利的禮物

正解 (A)

本題詢問男子正在買的東西為何。由女子說 Are all these items for your kids? 而男子肯定回應 Yes, they are.，可知他買的是給他孩子的聖誕禮物，故選 (A)。

---

11 How does the man pay?

(A) With coupons only

(B) By credit card and a coupon

(C) With credit card only

(D) By cash and with a coupon

男子如何付款？

(A) 僅使用優惠券

(B) 用信用卡和優惠券

(C) 僅使用信用卡

(D) 用現金和優惠券

正解 (B)

本題詢問男子付款的方式為何。關鍵句為男子說 I have this discount coupon.，而女子結算金額時有給予折扣。又當女子問男子說 Will you be paying by cash or credit card? 時，他回覆說要用信用卡，故選 (B)。

---

12 Look at the graphic. What does the man buy?

(A) Dolls

(B) Toy cars

(C) Clothes

(D) Board games

看圖表。男子購買什麼商品？

(A) 玩偶

(B) 玩具車

(C) 服飾

(D) 棋盤遊戲

正解 (C)

本題詢問男子購買的商品為何。由女子結帳時跟男子說 the subtotal comes to 100 dollars. After the discount has been subtracted, your final total is just 90 dollars.，可知原消費金額一百元，折扣後為九十元，故折扣為 10%。對照圖表，符合該折扣條件的選項為 Clothes「服飾」，因此答案為 (C)。

Part 4: Short Talks

Questions 13-15 refer to the following talk.

Today we're going to be taking a look at customer care, because you can always improve the way you deal with people. First up, customer complaints. Now, every company has to deal with complaints at some point in time, and yours is no different. This particular customer may be especially difficult and, to make matters worse, you are having a really bad day. So how should you respond? Of course, we must always react in the same way: Without emotion, and by representing the company with 100% professionalism at all times. Remember that the job of service staff is to minimize the impact of customer complaints. And never forget the golden rule: the customer is always right.

今天,我們將著眼於顧客服務,因為你們始終可以改善與人打交道的方式。首先是顧客投訴。現在,每間公司都必須在某個時間點處理客訴,而你們公司也是如此。這位特別的顧客可能尤其刁難,更糟的是,你今天過得很不好。那麼你該如何回應?當然,我們必須始終以相同的方式做出反應:不帶情緒,並總是以百分之百的專業精神代表公司。要記得,服務人員的工作就是將客訴的影響降到最低。且永遠不要忘記這個黃金法則:顧客永遠是對的。

SECTION B 試題練習

UNIT 5 Purchasing 採購

---

⑬ What is the purpose of the talk?

(A) To educate staff on medical care procedures

(B) To teach staff about customer care

(C) To prepare actors for a movie about shopping

(D) To discuss methods of managing stress

這段談話的主要目的是?

(A) 對員工進行醫療照護程序的教育

(B) 教導員工顧客服務的相關事宜

(C) 為演員準備一部有關購物的電影

(D) 討論緩解壓力的方法

正解 (B)

本題詢問此獨白的目的。關鍵句為說話者一開始便說道 we're going to be taking a look at customer care「我們將著眼於顧客服務」,故答案選 (B)。

---

⑭ Who is being addressed?

(A) A company's VIP customers

(B) Lawyers and accountants

(C) A company's management team

(D) Service staff

這段談話的對象是誰?

(A) 一間公司的 VIP 顧客

(B) 律師和會計師

(C) 一間公司的經營團隊

(D) 服務人員

正解 (D)

本題詢問這段談話的對象。由關鍵句 Remember that the job of service staff is to minimize the impact of customer complaints「要記得,服務人員的工作就是將客訴的影響降到最低」,且整段獨白都是在講處理客訴的相關事宜,故答案選 (D)。

15 When does the speaker think you may not want to deal with a customer?

(A) **When you are having a bad day**

(B) When the customer is right and you're wrong

(C) When you have problems with your boss

(D) When you have forgotten their name

說話者認為你什麼時候可能會不想跟客戶打交道？

(A) **當你今天過得很不好**

(B) 當顧客是對的而你是錯的

(C) 當你和老闆有問題時

(D) 當你忘記了他們的名字

正解 **(A)**

從關鍵句 This particular customer may be especially difficult and, to make matters worse, you are having a really bad day.「這位特別的顧客可能尤其刁難，更糟的是，你今天過得很不好。」以及後續談到面對顧客應不帶私人情緒並具備專業態度，可推知答案選 (A)。

Questions 16-18 refer to the following voice mail message and price list.

Hello, this is Rita Sullivan from InvestSmart. I tried making a purchase on your website earlier but the form didn't seem to be working. So I'd like to make my order now. It's mostly our usual order, minus the erasers, and with one new thing. So the usual order is for 150 pens; blue, red, and black, 50 of each, as well as the 25 sticky tape boxes that we normally get. However, this time we want to add 10 staplers. I noticed on your website that you have three sizes of staplers. We want the smallest ones, and any color is fine. We can make the payment in advance or upon delivery. If there are any issues, please notify me as soon as possible. Thank you and I hope to hear from you shortly.

你好，我是聰明投資的瑞塔·沙利文。我稍早試著在貴公司網站上進行購買，但表格似乎無法正常運作。所以我想趁現在下訂單。大部分是我們的常規訂單，刪去橡皮擦，然後再添加一件新東西。而常規訂單是一百五十枝筆；藍筆、紅筆和黑筆各五十枝，以及我們通常會買的膠帶盒二十五個。但這次我們要添加十個訂書機。我在你的網站上注意到你有三種尺寸的訂書機。我們想要最小的，任何顏色都可以。我們可以預先或貨到付款。如有任何問題，請盡快通知我。謝謝你，希望很快能收到你的消息。

Items	Price
Calculator	$10
Pen (black/blue/red)	$0.99
Eraser	$0.49
Stapler (small/medium/large)	$3/5/8
Sticky Tape	$1.99

項目	價錢
計算機	10 美元
原子筆（黑／藍／紅）	0.99 美元
橡皮擦	0.49 美元
訂書機（小／中／大）	3/5/8 美元
膠帶盒	1.99 美元

16 What was the problem that caused the woman to make the call?

(A) She couldn't find the right number.

(B) She couldn't make an order online.

(C) She sent an e-mail that was rejected.

(D) She made an order that wasn't delivered.

是什麼原因導致該女子打電話？

(A) 她找不到正確的號碼。

(B) 她無法在線上下訂單。

(C) 她發送的電子郵件被退回。

(D) 她下的訂單商品並未送達。

正解 **(B)**

本題詢問女子打電話的原因為何。女子一開始即說道 I tried making a purchase on your website earlier but the form didn't seem to be working.「我稍早試著在貴公司網站上進行購買，但表格似乎無法正常運作。」，故答案選 (B)。

---

17 How can the woman pay?

(A) Only in advance

(B) Only upon delivery

(C) Neither in advance nor on delivery

(D) Both in advance and on delivery

女子可以如何付款？

(A) 僅能預先付款

(B) 僅能貨到付款

(C) 既無法預先付款也無法貨到付款

(D) 預先付款和貨到付款皆可

正解 **(D)**

本題詢問女子可以付款的方式為何。關鍵句為女子說 We can make the payment in advance or upon delivery.「我們可以預先或貨到付款。」，故答案選 (D)。

---

18 Look at the graphic. What is the subtotal for the staplers?

(A) $10

(B) $30

(C) $50

(D) $80

看圖表。訂書機的小計為何？

(A) 十美元

(B) 三十美元

(C) 五十美元

(D) 八十美元

正解 **(B)**

本題詢問訂書機的小計為何。關鍵句為女子說 this time we want to add 10 staplers . . . We want the smallest ones.，可知她要添購十個最小的訂書機。對照圖表，小的訂書機單價為 3 美元，故 10 個共 30 美元，答案選 (B)。

Part 5: Incomplete Sentences

⑲ Regrettably, we have had to stop offering the _____ account option to all buyers, due to several late and missed payments.
(A) purchase
(B) payment
(C) closed
(D) open

正解 (D)

本題考商用詞彙。open account 表示「記帳交易」，符合句意所說因延遲和未履行付款故要停止記帳交易，因此 (D) 為正確答案。

遺憾的是，由於幾次延遲和未履行付款，我們不得不停止向所有買家提供記帳交易的選擇。
(A) 無 purchase account 之搭配用法。
(B) 無 payment account 之搭配用法。
(C) 無 closed account 之搭配用法。
(D) open account 指「記帳交易」。

⑳ Management feels we can improve our efficiency, so they are considering the _____ of a new software system.
(A) pallet
(B) partner
(C) procurement
(D) parcel

正解 (C)

本題考字義。依照句意可知空格處填入 (C) procurement 指「採購」，表示考慮「採購」新的軟體系統。

管理階層覺得我們可以提高效率，因此他們正在考慮採購新的軟體系統。
(A) 貨板
(B) 合夥人
(C) 採購
(D) 包裹

㉑ The advertised cost of the flight ticket is $419, but that will rise to $449 after _____ are added.
(A) lump sums
(B) invoices
(C) flaws
(D) surcharges

正解 (D)

本題考字義。依照句意費用有增加，可知空格處填入 (D) surcharges 指「額外費用」才合乎句意。

公告刊登的機票費用為四百一十九美元，但再加上額外費用後，該費用會提高至四百四十九美元。
(A) 一次付清
(B) 發票
(C) 瑕疵
(D) 額外費用

㉒ This particular hotel _____ an extra night for you if you choose to stay for three nights or longer.

(A) has thrown in

(B) will throw in

(C) would throw in

(D) would have thrown in

如果您選擇入住三晚或是更久，這家特定的酒店將為您加贈一晚的住宿。

(A) 現在完成式

(B) 未來簡單式

(C) 與現在事實相反的假設

(D) 與過去事實相反的假設

正解 (B)

本題考假設語氣。if 所引導的條件句用現在簡單式（if you choose）表示是未來可能發生的事，因此主要子句用未來簡單式「will + 原形動詞」的句型，故選 (B)。

㉓ Computers bought within the last two years are still under _____ and are therefore eligible for free inspection and repairs if necessary.

(A) warranty　　　(B) rebate

(C) freight　　　(D) net weight

最近兩年內購買的電腦仍處於保固內，因此如果必要的話可進行免費檢查和維修。

(A) 擔保

(B) 折扣；貼現

(C) 貨運

(D) 淨重

正解 (A)

本題考字義。依照後半段句意商品可享有免費檢查和維修，故空格處填入 (A) warranty 合乎句意，under warranty 為常見搭配詞，指「在保固期內」。

Part 6: Text Completion

Questions 24-27 refer to the following e-mail.

To:	174 recipients
From:	paul.franks@mtla.com
Subject:	The 11th Annual Maryville Tech Manufacturing Trade Show (5/25)

Dear Manager/Owner,

Please make space in your calendar now for the tech manufacturing industry event of the year! The 11th Annual Maryville Tech Manufacturing Trade Show ---24--- on Tuesday, May 25th, from 9:30 a.m. – 3:30 p.m. at the Maryville Conference Center, at 49 Lindon Road, Maryville.

Invite employees to gain insightful information on the latest technology and network with major ---25--- in the industry. Expect more than 100 vendors to be on hand, showing off the latest exciting products. Educational sessions on current industry topics will also be offered free of charge during the event. ---26--- Everyone attending the event will be entered automatically into the competitions and has a chance to win. We ---27--- that this is an event you can't miss!

For more information, call Tiana Rhodes of the Maryville Tech Association at 504-334-0816, or e-mail t.rhodes@mtech.com.

Sincerely,

MTLA Tradeshow Committee

收件者：一百七十四位收件者
寄件者：paul.franks@mtla.com
主　旨：第十一屆年度瑪麗維爾科技製造業貿易展（五月二十五號）

敬愛的經理／老闆：

請立即在您的行事曆中為今年的科技製造業活動預留時間！第十一屆年度瑪麗維爾科技製造業貿易展將於五月二十五號星期二上午九點半至下午三點半舉行，地點位於瑪麗維爾市林登路四十九號的瑪麗維爾會議中心。

邀請員工來汲取關於最新科技的深刻洞見，並與業界主要經銷商建立人脈。預計將有一百多家供應商在現場展示令人興奮的最新產品。活動期間還將免費提供以當前產業為主題的教育研討會。此外，還有超過五千元的現金獎勵。出席展覽的每個人都將自動進入抽獎活動並有機會獲勝。我們保證這是您不能錯過的活動！

更多相關資訊，請致電 504-334-0816 洽詢瑪麗維爾科技協會的蒂安娜・羅德斯，或發送電子郵件至 t.rhodes@mtech.com。

謹致，

MTLA 貿易展委員會

㉔ **(A) will be held**
(B) was held
(C) are held
(D) has been held

(A) 將被舉行（未來式的被動語態）
(B) 被舉行（過去式的被動語態）
(C) 被舉行（現在式的被動語態）
(D) 已被舉行（現在完成式的被動語態）

正解 **(A)**

本題考文法。依照句意，可判斷展覽會將於未來某時間舉行，又主詞為一項活動（Trade Show）須用被動語態，因此用未來式被動「will + be + 過去分詞」，故選 (A)。

㉕ (A) catalogs   (B) appliances
(C) dealers   (D) freights

(A) 目錄   (B) 器材
(C) 經銷商   (D) 貨運

正解 **(C)**

本題考字義。原句提到「來汲取關於最新科技的深刻洞見，並與業界主要 ＿＿＿ 建立人脈」，可知符合句意的答案為 (C)。

㉖ (A) Get a first glimpse of technology no one has seen yet.
(B) What's more, there will be over $5,000 in cash prizes.
(C) Send us an e-mail or telephone us to find out more.
(D) But bringing your own lunch won't be necessary.

(A) 首次看見尚未見過的科技。
(B) 此外，還有超過五千美元的現金獎勵。
(C) 發送電子郵件或打電話給我們以了解更多資訊。
(D) 但是不必自己帶午餐。

正解 **(B)**

空格的下一句說「出席展覽的每個人都將自動進入抽獎活動並有機會獲勝。」，因此空格處填入選項 (B) 提及抽獎的獎勵以符合上下文意，故為正選。

㉗ (A) deliver
(B) fluctuate
(C) minimize
(D) guarantee

(A) 傳送
(B) 波動
(C) 使減到最少
(D) 保證

正解 **(D)**

本題考字義。原句提到「我們 ＿＿＿ 這是你們不能錯過的活動！」可知符合句意的答案為 (D)。

Part 7: Reading Comprehension

Questions 28-29 *refer to the following text message chain.*

Cindy Hart   1:35 p.m.
Hey Robert. I'm on my way to the Alpha meeting and I'd like to review the catalog one more time before I arrive. Do you have a copy of that to hand by any chance?

Robert Bates   1:36 p.m.
I don't, but I'll find it as soon as possible. How about I send you a copy through text message, and another one to your e-mail address?

Cindy Hart   1:36 p.m.
That would be great. Thanks.

Robert Bates   1:38 p.m.
I'll do that right away. Let me know if you have any issues.

Cindy Hart   1:40 p.m.
Will do. Thanks, Robert. I knew I could count on you.

Robert Bates   1:40 p.m.
Don't mention it.

辛蒂·哈特   下午 1:35 分
嘿，羅伯特。我正在去阿爾法會議的路上，我想在抵達之前再看一次目錄。你是否剛好有目錄在手邊呢？

羅伯特·貝茲   下午 1:36 分
我沒有，但我會盡快找到。我用簡訊傳一份給妳，也傳一份到妳的電子郵件如何？

辛蒂·哈特   下午 1:36 分
那太好了。謝謝。

羅伯特·貝茲   下午 1:38 分
我會馬上傳。如果妳有任何問題，請告訴我。

辛蒂·哈特   下午 1:40 分
好的。謝謝，羅伯特。我就知道我可以信賴你。

羅伯特·貝茲   下午 1:40 分
不客氣。

28 Where is Ms. Hart at the time of the conversation?
(A) In a meeting room
(B) In her company's office
(C) On the way back to her office
(D) On the way to a meeting

談話時哈特小姐在哪裡？
(A) 在會議室
(B) 在她公司的辦公室
(C) 在回她辦公室的路上
(D) 在前往會議的路上

正解 **(D)**
本題詢問哈特小姐的所在位置。解題關鍵在哈特小姐一開始即說 I'm on my way to the Alpha meeting.，故選 (D)。

29 At 1:40 p.m., what does Ms. Hart mean when she tells Mr. Bates "I knew I could count on you"?
(A) She thinks Mr. Bates is good at math.
(B) She thinks Mr. Bates is easy to find.
(C) She thinks Mr. Bates is always reliable.
(D) She thinks Mr. Bates is very honest.

在下午一點四十分，當哈特小姐跟貝茲先生說 "I knew I could count on you" 是何用意？
(A) 她認為貝茲先生擅長數學。
(B) 她認為貝茲先生很容易找到。
(C) 她認為貝茲先生總是很可靠。
(D) 她認為貝茲先生很誠實。

正解 **(C)**
本題考句意，題目問哈特小姐寫道 "I knew I could count on you" 有何用意。片語 count on 意指「信賴；依靠」，意近選項 (C) 中的形容詞 reliable。而由簡訊對話中可知，哈特小姐請求貝茲先生協助，他就立即為其處理，因此哈特小姐這句話是要表達可以仰賴、信任貝茲先生，故 (C) 為正選。

Questions 30-33 *refer to the following purchase order.*

Yellow Bus Stationery
1234 Main Street, Atlanta, GA

Tax Reg#: ABC 69786

PURCHASE ORDER

Purchase from	Deliver to		P.O.#	YB00010
WorkSmart	**Yellow Bus Stationery**	Date	Aug. 21
PO Box 8446	1234 Main Street	Your ref#	XY1234
Atlanta, GA	Atlanta, GA	Our ref#	YB00010-1234

Attention: Ms. Vanessa Villier

We are pleased to confirm our order of the following items:

	Product ID	Description	Quantity	Unit Price	Amount
1	P1001	Pencils HB	60	$1.00	$60.00
2	P1002	Pencils 2B	15	$1.00	$15.00
3	P1235	Paper – A4 Printer, 70 gram	10 packs	$3.00	$30.00
4	P1040	Paper – A4 Photocopier, 80 gram	15 packs	$3.50	$52.50
5	P2007	Pens – ball point, blue	10 boxes	$10.00	$100.00
6	P2009	Highlighters – 3 colors	8 sets	$6.00	$48.00

Comments:

Total before tax:	$305.50
Tax:	$0.00
Total After tax:	$305.50

TERMS & CONDITIONS
Delivery: All goods to be delivered within 14 days of PO
Condition: We reserve the right to reject goods that are not in good order or condition as determined by our quality control.

黃公車文具
喬治亞州亞特蘭大市，緬因街 1234 號

登記稅號：ABC 69786

訂購單

賣方	運至	採購單號	YB00010
聰明工作	黃公車文具	日期	8 月 21 日
郵政信箱 8446 號	緬因街 1234 號	來案檔號	XY1234
喬治亞州亞特蘭大市	喬治亞州亞特蘭大市	本局檔號	YB00010-1234

此致：凡妮莎‧維利爾斯小姐

我們很樂意確認以下訂購的物品：

	產品編號	描述	數量	單價	總額
1	P1001	HB 鉛筆	60 枝	$1.00	$60.00
2	P1002	2B 鉛筆	50 枝	$1.00	$15.00
3	P1235	紙 – A4 列印紙，每平方公尺重 70 公克	10 包	$3.00	$30.00
4	P1040	紙 – A4 影印紙，每平方公尺重 80 公克	15 包	$3.50	$52.50
5	P2007	原子筆 – 圓頭，藍色	10 盒	$10.00	$100.00
6	P2009	螢光筆 – 三種顏色	8 組	$6.00	$48.00

意見：

扣稅前總額： $305.50

稅： $0.00

扣稅後總額： $305.50

約定條款
運送：所有貨物將在訂單的十四天內送達
條件：依本公司品管的裁決，我們保留拒收狀況不佳的貨物之權利。

30 What is the name of the company placing the order?

(A) Worksmart

(B) Yellow Bus Stationery

(C) Atlanta, GA

(D) Vanessa Villier

下訂單的公司名稱為何？

(A) 聰明工作

(B) 黃公車文具

(C) 喬治亞州

(D) 凡妮莎·維利爾斯

正解 (B)

本題詢問下訂單的公司名稱為何。訂購單顯示商品運送至黃公車文具，故選 (B)。

---

31 How many packs of photocopier paper does the customer order?

(A) 10   **(B) 15**

(C) 30   (D) 60

顧客訂購幾包影印紙？

(A) 10   **(B) 15**

(C) 30   (D) 60

正解 (B)

本題為細節題，詢問訂購數量。在訂購單中找出題目詢問的 photocopier paper，可知為產品編號的第四項，其數量顯示為 15 包，故答案選 (B)。

---

32 The word "determined" in Terms & Conditions is closest in meaning to

(A) decided   (B) resolute

(C) chosen   (D) awarded

約定條款中的 "determined" 意思最接近

(A) 決定了的   (B) 堅決的

(C) 挑選出來的   (D) 被授予獎項的

正解 (A)

本題為字義題。原文中包含 determined 的句子是要表達若品管部門檢視後決定商品狀況不佳，買方將有權拒收。determined 在此指「已決定了的」，因此意思最接近 (A) decided。

---

33 What will the buyer do if items are damaged upon delivery?

(A) They will fix the items on site.

(B) They will keep the items without paying.

(C) They will not accept the items.

(D) They will order replacements items.

如果物品在送達時損壞，買方將如何處理？

(A) 他們將會當場修理這些物品。

(B) 他們將保留這些物品而無需付款。

(C) 他們將不接受這些物品。

(D) 他們將訂購替代品。

正解 (C)

本題詢問若物品在送達時損壞，買方的處理方式為何。根據原文中的約定條件 Condition: We reserve the right to reject goods that are not in good order or condition as determined by our quality control. 可知買方會拒收狀況不佳的貨物，故答案選 (C)。

Finance and Budgeting
金融／預算

P. 177~186

Part 1: Photographs

TRACK 42

 (A) Money is being withdrawn from the ATM.

(B) A card is inserted into the ATM.

(C) A man is entering his PIN into the ATM.

(D) The ATM is inside the bank.

(A) 錢正從自動提款機中被提領出來。

(B) 有張卡片被插入自動提款機中。

(C) 一名男子正將密碼輸入自動提款機。

(D) 自動提款機位於銀行裡面。

正解 **(C)**

圖中可見有人正在將數字輸入到自動提款機中，因此符合圖片的敘述為 (C)。

(B) insert *(v.)* 插入。

 (A) A girl is checking her bankbook.

(B) A girl is receiving her allowance.

(C) A cashier is being paid by a girl.

(D) A check has been written out to the girl.

(A) 一位女孩正在檢查她的銀行存摺。

(B) 一位女孩正在領取零用錢。

(C) 一位女孩正在付錢給收銀員。

(D) 一張支票已經被開給那名女孩。

正解 **(B)**

圖中可見女孩正在拿取別人給予的鈔票，故正確答案為 (B)。

Part 2: Question and Response

❸ We don't seem to have any money in our account.

(A) It seems like we're in the money.

(B) It looks like we are in the red.

(C) I think that we are in the clear.

我們的戶頭裡似乎沒有錢了。

(A) 看來我們發財了。

(B) 看來我們負債累累。

(C) 我想我們沒有問題。

正解 **(B)**

本題為直述句，描述「我們的戶頭裡似乎沒有錢了」。選項中符合邏輯的回答為 (B)「看來我們負債累累。」

(A) in the money 是「發財；突然有錢」的意思，與題意不符。

(C) in the clear 是「沒有問題；清白之身」之意，與題意不符。

---

❹ The market seems bullish right now, doesn't it?

(A) Yes, we should consider selling some shares.

(B) The investment forecast is not good.

(C) No bulls were being sold at the market.

目前市場行情相當樂觀，對吧？

(A) 是的，我們應該考慮釋出更多股票。

(B) 投資預期並不樂觀。

(C) 市場上沒有販售公牛。

正解 **(A)**

本句是附加問句，表「目前市場行情相當樂觀，對吧？」合適的回應是 (A)「是的，我們應該考慮釋出更多股票。」

(B) 與題意相反。

(C) 與題目無關。

---

❺ What's the minimum deposit needed to open an account?

(A) You can withdraw $100 at a time.

(B) You will receive a bankbook tomorrow.

(C) You need at least $100 to open an account.

開戶時的最低存款金額是多少？

(A) 你一次可以提領一百美元。

(B) 你明天會收到一本存摺。

(C) 你至少需要一百美元才能開戶。

正解 **(C)**

本題詢問開戶所需的 minimum deposit「最低存款金額」。(C) 明確回覆開戶所需的金額為「至少一百美元」，故為正解。

(A) 題目與提領的金額無關。

(B) 與題意無關。

6 When will the accountants audit the company?

(A) They will need all of our financial statements.

(B) They will prepare a budget for us in January.

(C) They do it at the end of the fiscal year.

會計師們何時會來公司查帳？

(A) 他們會需要我們所有的財務報表。

(B) 他們會在一月時為我們準備一筆預算。

(C) 他們會在會計年度的尾聲進行。

正解 **(C)**

本題以 When 詢問會計師們何時會來公司查帳，因此回答應包含時間。(C) 指出「他們會在會計年度的尾聲進行。」

(A) 題目問查帳的時間，而非所需的資料。

(B) 並未說明查帳的時間。

Part 3: Short Conversations

TRACK 44

Questions 7-9 refer to the following conversation.

M: I just met with the accountant. He thinks we should diversify our assets.

W: Why is he recommending that?

M: He thinks there could be a global economic downturn, so we shouldn't rely solely on our current investments.

W: So what does he suggest?

M: He thinks we should consider investing in property and moving some money into high-interest accounts.

W: Maybe he's right. We should look into it.

男：我剛剛跟會計師會面完。他認為我們應該要分散我們的資產。

女：他為什麼會如此建議？

男：他覺得可能會出現全球性的經濟衰退，所以我們不應該只仰賴目前的投資項目。

女：所以他的建議是什麼？

男：他認為我們應該考慮投資房地產並把部分資金轉到利息高的帳戶。

女：也許他是對的。我們應該要研究看看。

❼ What are the man and woman talking about?
(A) Their financial assets
(B) The properties they own
(C) The global economic downturn
(D) A meeting they had with an investor

男子和女子正在談論什麼？
(A) 他們的財務資產
(B) 他們擁有的房地產
(C) 全球性的經濟衰退
(D) 一場他們與一名投資人的會議

正解 (A)

本題是主旨題，詢問兩人在談論什麼事情。由男子轉述會計師的建議以及女子的回覆，可知他們主要在討論接下來該如何根據會計師的建議處理資產，答案選 (A)。

---

❽ Why does the accountant think the speakers should diversify their assets?
(A) He wants to make more money from the couple.
(B) Their current house will soon drop in value.
(C) He wants them to open an account at his bank.
(D) The economy is slowing down worldwide.

為什麼會計師認為說話者們應該要分散資產？
(A) 他想要從兩人身上賺到更多錢。
(B) 他們目前房子很快就會貶值。
(C) 他想要兩人在他的銀行開戶。
(D) 全球經濟正在下滑。

正解 (D)

題目詢問會計師為何認為說話者應該分散資產。由男子所說 He thinks there could be a global economic downturn, so we shouldn't rely solely on our current investments. 可知是因為他預測經濟將會衰退，故選 (D)。

---

❾ What will the speakers likely do next?
(A) Visit the accountant for more advice
(B) Go to a real estate agent to sell a property
(C) Consider other ways of investing their money
(D) Sell all of their investment bonds

說話者接下來很有可能會做什麼？
(A) 拜訪會計師尋求更多建議
(B) 去房地產仲介出售一件房產
(C) 考慮其他投資方式
(D) 賣出他們全部的投資債券

正解 (C)

本題是推論題，詢問說話者接下來可能的行為。男子後來轉述會計師的具體建議後（即投資房地產、把資金轉到利息高的帳戶），女子最後說 We should look into it.「我們應該研究看看。」可知他們接下來會考慮其他投資方式，故選 (C)。

Questions 10-12 refer to the following conversation and table.

W: Good afternoon. I would like to know more about savings account options with StarBank.

M: Well, you've come to the right place. We have many different options available. Our savings accounts pay different rates of interest, depending on how **flexible** you want to be with your withdrawal and deposit amounts. Do you have a savings goal?

W: Well, I recently **inherited** $80,000 and I want to **hold on to** it, as I would like to buy a house within the next ten years.

M: Here is an overview of some of our savings accounts for you to take a look at. But as you seem sure you won't be making any withdrawals within the next five years, then I think only one of these would be suitable for you.

W: Great! I think I know which one you mean.

女：午安。我想知道更多有關於恆星銀行存款帳戶的資訊。

男：好的，您來對地方了。我們有多種方案可供選擇。我們的存款帳戶根據您希望的提領資金靈活度與存款的金額提供不同利息。您有存款目標嗎？

女：這個嘛，我最近繼承了八萬美元，我想要存起來，因為我想在未來十年內買一間房子。

男：這裡有一份我們存款帳戶的簡介供您參考。但由於您似乎很確定未來五年內不會進行任何提領，那麼我覺得會適合您的只有其中一種。

女：太好了！我想我知道你指的是哪一種。

- flexible *(adj.)* 有彈性的；可變通的
- inherit *(v.)* 繼承
- hold onto/on to sth. *(phr.)* 保留、保存某物

Account Name	Interest Rate	Restrictions
Savings Deposit Account	0.01%	• Withdrawals limited to 5 per month
Savings Plus Account	0.10%	• Withdrawals limited to 12 per month • Minimum balance of $100,000
Certificate of Deposit Account	0.10%	• No withdrawals permitted for 5 years

帳戶名稱	利息	限制
活期存款帳戶	0.01%	• 每月提領上限五次
加值存款帳戶	0.10%	• 每月提領上限十二次 • 最低餘額十萬元
定期存款帳戶	0.10%	• 五年內不得提領

10 Why does the man ask the woman if she has a savings goal?

(A) To explain why she should save more

(B) To discover how much money she has

(C) To help her find the right account

(D) To discover whether she is ambitious

為什麼男子詢問女子是否有儲蓄目標？

(A) 為了說明她為什麼應該存更多錢

(B) 為了知道她有多少錢

(C) 為了幫她找到合適的帳戶

(D) 為了得知她是否具有野心

正解 (C)

題目問男子為何詢問女子是否有儲蓄目標。男子得知女子的儲蓄目標後，以未來可能的提領次數幫她排除了不適合她的選擇，可推知男子是為了協助她找到合適帳戶，故答案選 (C)。

(D) ambitious *(adj.)* 有野心的。

---

11 Why does the woman have a large amount of money?

(A) A family member left her some money when they died.

(B) She won a lot of money gambling in Las Vegas.

(C) She has saved all of her money for many years.

(D) She made some wise investments in the past.

為什麼女子會有一大筆錢？

(A) 一位家族成員在去世後留給她的。

(B) 她在賭城賭博時贏了許多錢。

(C) 她多年來把錢都存了下來。

(D) 她在過去有幾筆聰明的投資。

正解 (A)

本題詢問女子金錢的來源，由女子所說 I recently inherited $80,000「我最近繼承了八萬美元」，可知正確答案為 (A)。

---

12 Look at the table. Which savings account is the most suitable for the woman?

(A) None of them

(B) Certificate of Deposit Account

(C) Savings Deposit Account

(D) Savings Plus Account

看圖表。女子最適合哪個存款帳戶？

(A) 全部都不適合

(B) 定期存款帳戶

(C) 活期存款帳戶

(D) 加值存款帳戶

正解 (B)

本題須結合對話與圖表作答。關鍵在女子說 I recently inherited $80,000 and I want to hold on to it, as I would like to buy a house within the next ten years.「我最近繼承了八萬美金，我想要存起來，因為我想在未來十年內買一間房子」，故男子表示看來女子未來五年內不會進行提領。對照表格，活期與加值存款帳戶都提供提領次數，但這是女子不需要的，且女子繼承的金額也不達加值存款帳戶的最低餘額（十萬元），排除後可知 (B)「定期存款帳戶」是最適合女子的方案。

Part 4: Short Talks

Questions 13-15 refer to the following telephone message.

Good morning, Mr. Jones. This is Mr. Adams from Capital Credit calling. We wanted to make you aware that our records show that <u>there have been no recent transactions on your account</u>. In fact, you have failed to pay the necessary installments for the past two months. Unfortunately, this means that there is more interest due on your loan. If you are currently experiencing cash flow problems, please get in touch with us as soon as possible so that we can figure out a new repayment plan for you. If this is not the case and you are able to pay the next installment, or the outstanding balance in full, you can do so using a credit card, check, or bank transfer. We look forward to hearing from you.

早安，瓊斯先生。我是首都信用的亞當先生。我們想要通知您我們的記錄顯示<u>您的帳戶並沒有任何近期交易</u>。事實上，您過去兩個月並未繳納必要的分期款項。很遺憾，這表示您貸款的應付利息會增加。如果您正經歷現金周轉的問題，請盡快與我們聯絡，好讓我們為您規劃新的還款方案。如果情況並非如此，而您可以支付下一期的分期款項，或能全額付清未付帳款，您可以透過信用卡、支票或銀行轉帳繳納。我們期待聽到您的消息。

13 What is the purpose of the telephone message?
- (A) To inform someone of a new way that they can repay a loan
- (B) To tell someone that they are eligible for a loan from Capital Credit
- **(C) To notify someone that they have missed some payments**
- (D) To offer support to someone who is having cash flow problems

這則電話留言的目的為何？
- (A) 為了通知某人一個償還貸款的新方式
- (B) 為了告訴某人具備向首都信用申辦貸款的資格
- **(C) 為了通知某人少繳納了一些款項**
- (D) 為了提供幫助給某個有現金周轉問題的人

正解 **(C)**

本題詢問這則留言的目的為何。由關鍵句 you have failed to pay the necessary installments for the past two months 「您過去兩個月並未繳納必要的分期款項」，可知留言主要目的為通知某人少繳納了一些款項，答案選 (C)。

14 Who is Mr. Jones?

(A) Someone who would like to take out a loan

(B) Someone who has a loan with Capital Credit

(C) Someone who would like to make an investment

(D) Someone who would like to open an account

瓊斯先生是誰？

(A) 某個想要申辦貸款的人

(B) 某個向首都信用貸款的人

(C) 某個想要投資的人

(D) 某個想要開戶的人

正解 **(B)**

題目詢問瓊斯先生是誰。由第一句 Good morning, Mr. Jones.「早安，瓊斯先生。」可知瓊斯就是這則電話留言的對象，而從留言中的 you have failed to pay the necessary installments for the past two months，可推知瓊斯先生已向首都信用貸款，但最近沒有定期還款，故選 (B)。

---

15 What does the speaker imply when he says, "there have been no recent transactions on your account"?

(A) There have been no deals closed recently.

(B) There have been no withdrawals.

(C) No new loans have been taken out.

(D) There have been no deposits made.

當說話者說 "there have been no recent transactions on your account" 時，他是何意？

(A) 最近沒有談成的交易。

(B) 沒有款項被提領。

(C) 沒有新的貸款被申辦。

(D) 沒有款項被存入。

正解 **(D)**

此題考句義，說話者說完題目句 "there have been no recent transactions on your account" 後又接著說 In fact, you have failed to pay the necessary installments for the past two months. 以及後續提到 loan「貸款」、repayment plan「還款方案」等關鍵字詞，可知他主要用意是告知對方並未在帳戶存入款項以支付貸款，故答案選 (D)。

Questions 16-18 refer to the following talk and chart.

Thank you for attending our information session. Our goal is to help you make **informed** choices when deciding to invest in the stock market. We all know that wise investments can pay dividends in the long run. Understanding how **investment funds** work, doing your research, and calculating the risks will help you buy shares wisely and build a strong share portfolio. Investing in shares should be a long-term commitment and if you buy different assets, you will keep the overall risk to a minimum. If you diversify your stock investments, you can benefit from the performance of different assets. For example, as you can see in this chart, if company shares are not performing particularly well, property or bonds may be performing better instead.

- informed *(adj.)* 有見識的；消息靈通的
- investment funds *(n.)* 投資基金

感謝各位蒞臨我們的說明會。我們的目標是協助各位在決定投資股市時做出明智的選擇。我們都知道聰明的投資長期下來是可以收取股利的。了解投資基金的運作方式、做好調查並計算風險將有助您聰明買股且建立一個強力的股票投資組合。投資股票應當是一種長期的投入，且如果您購買不同的資產，您可以把整體風險降至最低。如果您分散您的股票投資，您可以從不同資產的表現獲利。舉例來說，如這張圖表所示，如果公司股票表現並不特別理想，房地產和公債的表現反而可能較佳。

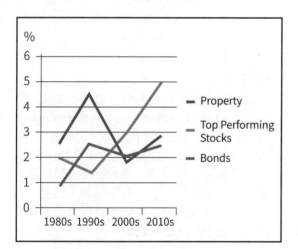

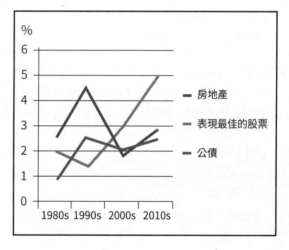

⑯ Who most likely is the speaker?
(A) A bank teller
(B) An accountant
(C) A stock broker
(D) An investor

說話者最有可能是誰？
(A) 一名銀行行員
(B) 一名會計師
(C) 一名股票經紀人
(D) 一名投資人

正解 **(C)**

本題問人物身分，問說話者最有可能是誰。談話一開頭便表明要幫助聽眾做出明智的投資決定，且內容提到許多理財方面的關鍵字詞如 invest in the stock market「投資股市」、investment funds「投資基金」、a strong share portfolio「強力的股票投資組合」、diversify your stock investments「分散股票投資」等，可知他最有可能是一名股票經紀人，答案選 (C)。

⑰ What is the purpose of the talk?
(A) To introduce investment basics
(B) To sell a particular stock
(C) To warn about risky stocks
(D) To entertain some clients

這段談話的目的為何？
(A) 為了介紹投資的基本概念
(B) 為了販售某一支特定股票
(C) 為了針對高風險股票提出警告
(D) 為了娛樂一些客戶

正解 **(A)**

本題詢問該談話的目的為何。由關鍵句 Our goal is to help you make informed choices when deciding to invest in the stock market.「我們的目標是協助各位在投資股市時做出明智的選擇。」及後續解釋關於購買股票與分散股票投資的概念等等，可知是為了說明投資的基本概念，故選 (A)。

⑱ Look at the graphic. Which decade might the speaker be referring to when he gives the example?
(A) 1980s
(B) 1990s
(C) 2000s
(D) 2010s

看圖表。說話者所舉的例子可能是哪個年代？
(A) 一九八〇年代
(B) 一九九〇年代
(C) 二〇〇〇年代
(D) 二〇一〇年代

正解 **(B)**

本題詢問舉例的年代為何。最後一句說 if company shares are not performing particularly well, property or bonds may be performing better instead.「如果公司股票表現並不理想，房地產和公債的表現反而可能較佳。」，對照圖表，可見一九九〇年代房地產和公債表現優於公司股票，故 (B) 為正確答案。

Part 5: Incomplete Sentences

19 If you sign up for paperless bank statements, they will be sent to your e-mail account _____ through the mail.

(A) due to   **(B) instead of**

(C) more than   (D) as well

如果你註冊非紙本的銀行對帳單，它們會被寄到你的電子信箱而非郵寄給你。

(A) 因為   **(B) 而非**

(C) 不僅   (D) 也

正解 (B)

本題考片語。空格的前後是銀行提供對帳單的兩種不同方式，故應選可表達相反或對照的 (B) instead of「而非」。

---

20 When Suzie goes to university, she will need to open a special student checking account, _____ she?

(A) will

(B) won't

(C) does

(D) isn't

當蘇西去念大學時，她會需要開一個特別的學生支票存款帳戶，對嗎？

(A) 將（未來式肯定助動詞）

(B) 將不（未來式否定助動詞）

(C)（現在式第三人稱單數肯定助動詞）

(D) 不是（現在式第三人稱單數否定 be 動詞）

正解 (B)

本題考附加問句。主要子句 she will need to ... 為肯定敘述句，由 will 可知時態為未來式。因此附加問句應選否定，且時態同樣要用未來式，故選 (B) won't。

---

21 People always used to use _____ when they went on vacation, but now people are more likely to use their credit card.

(A) cash flow

(B) down payments

(C) income statements

(D) traveler's checks

人們過去習慣在度假時使用旅行支票，但現在人們更傾向使用信用卡。

(A) 現金流量

(B) 頭期款

(C) 損益表

(D) 旅行支票

正解 (D)

本題考字義。逗點後方有表轉折的連接詞 but，之後提到 credit card「信用卡」，可判斷空格處應為另一種支付工具，故選 (D) 旅行支票。

22 Being in debt is causing Jake a lot of stress and he will be much _____ once he pays off all of his loans.

(A) happiest

(B) happy

(C) happier

(D) the happier

負債累累的情況給傑克帶來許多壓力，當他還清貸款後，他將快樂多了。

(A) 最快樂的（最高級）

(B) 快樂的（形容詞原形）

(C) 較快樂的（比較級）

(D) 無 much the happier 之用法

正解 **(C)**

選項中有形容詞 happy 的原級、最高級與比較級，而空格前為 much，得知本題考修飾比較級的用法。要強調比較的程度時，可在比較級前加上 much、a lot、even、far 等詞來修飾，故答案為 (C)。much happier 強調「快樂多了」。

(D)「the + 比較級」不與 much 連用。「the + 比較級 , the + 比較級」指「越……就越……」，如 The sooner, the better.「越快越好。」

---

23 Travelers are advised to change their _____ before leaving the airport, as they may not find a bank that will change money later.

(A) currency

(B) capital

(C) expenditure

(D) dividend

旅客們被建議要在離開機場之前兌換貨幣，因為他們可能之後找不到提供兌幣的銀行。

(A) 貨幣

(B) 資金

(C) 消費

(D) 股利

正解 **(A)**

本題考字義。change currency 表「兌換貨幣」，等於原句後半段提到的 change money，故正確答案為 (A)。

Part 6: Text Completion

Questions 24-27 refer to the following letter.

Ms. S. Holmes
571 Kenwood Avenue
Boston, MA

FIRST CAPITAL BANK

Dear Ms. Holmes,

Thank you for ---24--- a new checking account with First Capital Bank. We are committed to providing the highest level of service to all of our customers. Please find enclosed your new debit card, bankbook, and a brochure with more information about your account.

Your ---25--- can be activated at any one of our bank's ATM machines around the city or by visiting the service counter at your local branch. Once activated, you will be able to use your card at any ATM, including overseas. Please note that for security reasons, your **temporary** PIN number will be sent separately. ---26---

Now that you have your new account, you will receive monthly ---27--- which will show all of your transactions for the previous month. In addition, we are pleased to be able to send you an annual financial statement. This will give you an overview of your savings and expenditures.

We are very pleased that you have decided to bank with us and hope you will take advantage of our wide variety of savings, investment, and loan products. More detailed information about our products and services can be found on our website at www.firstcapital.com.

Please do not hesitate to contact me should you have any questions.

Yours sincerely,

James Randolph
Branch Manager
First Capital Bank

賽賓娜・福爾摩斯女士
肯伍德大道 571 號
麻薩諸薩州波士頓市

第一首都銀行

親愛的福爾摩斯女士：

感謝您選擇第一首都銀行開設新的支票存款帳戶。我們致力於為我們的顧客提供最高品質的服務。隨函附上您新的簽帳金融卡、存摺以及一本提供您戶頭更多資訊的小冊子。

您的簽帳卡可以在市內任何一台本行的自動提款機進行開卡，亦可造訪您當地分行服務櫃台。一旦完成開卡，您將能在任何自動提款機使用卡片，包括海外提款機。請注意基於安全考量，您臨時的個人身分識別碼會分別寄送。您一收到臨時個人身分識別碼，就可在本行任一台自動提款機進行修改。

既然現在您已經獲得了新的帳戶，您每月都會收到銀行對帳單，上面會顯示前一個月的所有交易記錄。除此之外，我們也很高興能提供年度財務報表，讓您檢視整體的收入和開支。

我們很高興您選擇本行作為往來銀行，希望您善加利用我們多樣化的儲蓄、投資和貸款等商品。您可以在我們的網站 www.firstcapital.com 找到更多相關產品與服務的詳細資訊。

如果有任何問題，請不吝與我聯繫。

謹致，

詹姆斯・蘭道夫
分行經理
第一首都銀行

• temporary *(adj.)* 臨時的

24 (A) logging in　　　(B) finding out
(C) setting up　　　(D) pulling off

(A) 登入
(B) 找出
(C) 設立
(D) 成功；(車輛)開始發動

正解 **(C)**

本題考片語動詞。原句提到，感謝您選擇第一首都銀行 ＿＿＿ 新的支票存款帳戶。故依句意，可知最適合的答案為 (C)。

---

25 (A) bond　　　　**(B) debit card**
(C) transfer　　　(D) budget

(A) 債券　　　**(B) 簽帳金融卡**
(C) 轉帳　　　(D) 預算

正解 **(B)**

此題考字義。空格後是被動的 can be activated，從語意來看可知本句主詞應選 (B)「簽帳金融卡」，表示利用自動提款機為新的卡片進行開卡，故選 (B)。

---

26 (A) It is a good idea to write down your PIN number somewhere where it can easily be found.
(B) You can rest assured that there is tight security at all of our bank branches.
(C) This will be your permanent PIN number, and it's important that you memorize it immediately.
(D) Once you receive your temporary PIN, you will be able to change it at any of our ATM machines.

(A) 將您的個人身分識別碼寫在某個容易被發現的地方是一個好主意。
(B) 您可以放心，我們的所有分行都有嚴謹的保全系統。
(C) 這將是您永久的身分識別碼，馬上背下來是很重要的。
(D) 您一收到臨時個人身分識別碼，就可在本行任一台自動提款機進行修改。

正解 **(D)**

空格前一句說「請注意基於安全考量，您臨時的個人身分識別碼會分別寄送」，而 (D) 說明收到臨時識別碼之後，客戶可以如何處理，承接了空格前的語意故為正確答案。

---

27 (A) allowances
(B) profits
(C) bank statements
(D) down payments

(A) 零用錢
(B) 利潤
(C) 銀行對帳單
(D) 頭期款

正解 **(C)**

本題考字義。該句提到「您每月都會收到 ＿＿＿，上面會顯示前一個月的所有交易紀錄。」選項中 (C)「銀行對帳單」的功能符合空格後的描述（列出前一個月的所有交易記錄），故為正確答案。

Part 7: Reading Comprehension

Questions 28-29 refer to the following text message chain.

 Lisa [1:35 p.m.]
Hey James. What's our budget for our trip to Paris next week?

 James [1:36 p.m.]
Why do you ask?

 Lisa [1:38 p.m.]
I am going to go to the bank today to get some local currency.

James [1:40 p.m.]
Great idea! Our hotel is paid for, but I think we will need at least €500 each for food. So you should exchange the equivalent of €1,000.

 Lisa [1:40 p.m.]
Will do.

James [1:45 p.m.]
Don't forget the bank will deduct a fee for currency exchange, so you will need to calculate how much you need to exchange once you know what the bank charges.

 Lisa [1:46 p.m.]
Oh yeah. I hadn't thought of that!

  麗莎 [1:35 p.m.]
嘿,詹姆士。我們下週到巴黎旅行的預算是多少?

詹姆士 [1:36 p.m.]
妳為什麼問?

麗莎 [1:38 p.m.]
我今天正要去銀行去換點當地的貨幣。

 詹姆士 [1:40 p.m.]
好主意!我們的旅館費用已經付了,但我想我們每人至少需要五百歐元在吃的方面。所以妳應該要換相當於一千歐元的貨幣。

 麗莎 [1:40 p.m.]
沒問題。

 詹姆士 [1:45 p.m.]
不要忘記銀行會扣兌幣的手續費,所以知道銀行收取多少費用後,妳要計算妳需要換多少錢。

麗莎 [1:46 p.m.]
對耶。我之前沒想到!

---

28 Why has Lisa messaged James?
- (A) She wants to know what the equivalent of € 1,000 is.
- (B) She wants to ask him to go to the bank to change money.
- **(C) She wants to know how much money they need for their trip.**
- (D) She wants to know how much the bank charges to change money.

麗莎為什麼傳訊息給詹姆士?
- (A) 她想要知道一千歐元等於多少。
- (B) 她想要請他去銀行換錢。
- **(C) 她想要知道他們旅行需要多少錢。**
- (D) 她想要知道銀行收取多少的兌幣手續費。

正解 **(C)**
麗莎在下午 1:35 時,詢問詹姆士他們下週到巴黎旅行的預算多少,故符合答案的選項為 (C)。

㉙ At 1:40 p.m., what does Lisa mean when she writes "Will do"?

(A) **She will exchange an amount of her own currency equal to € 1,000.**

(B) She will calculate the budget for the trip to Paris next week.

(C) She will transfer € 1,000 to pay for accommodation.

(D) She will calculate how much money she needs to exchange.

在下午 1:40 時，麗莎所說的 "Will do" 是什麼意思？

(A) 她會兌換相當於一千歐元的貨幣。

(B) 她會計算下週到巴黎旅行的預算。

(C) 她會轉帳一千歐元以便支付住宿費用。

(D) 她會計算需要兌換多少錢。

正解 (A)

詹姆士在下午 1:40 說 So you should exchange the equivalent of € 1,000.「所以妳應該要換相當於一千歐元的貨幣」，而接著麗莎回覆 Will do.「沒問題。」，由此可知麗莎會去兌換相當於一千歐元的貨幣，故選 (A)。

Questions 30-34 *refer to the following advertisement, bill, and e-mail.*

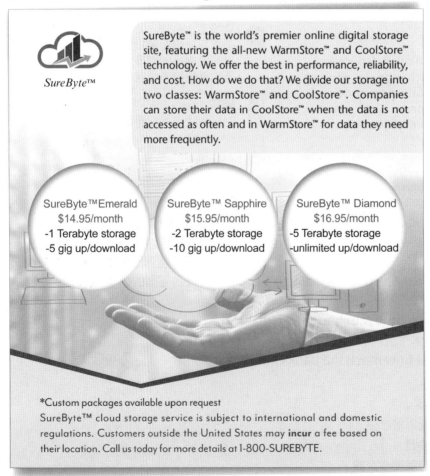

SureByte™ is the world's premier online digital storage site, featuring the all-new WarmStore™ and CoolStore™ technology. We offer the best in performance, reliability, and cost. How do we do that? We divide our storage into two classes: WarmStore™ and CoolStore™. Companies can store their data in CoolStore™ when the data is not accessed as often and in WarmStore™ for data they need more frequently.

SureByte™ Emerald
$14.95/month
-1 Terabyte storage
-5 gig up/download

SureByte™ Sapphire
$15.95/month
-2 Terabyte storage
-10 gig up/download

SureByte™ Diamond
$16.95/month
-5 Terabyte storage
-unlimited up/download

*Custom packages available upon request
SureByte™ cloud storage service is subject to international and domestic regulations. Customers outside the United States may **incur** a fee based on their location. Call us today for more details at 1-800-SUREBYTE.

• incur *(v.)* 招致；帶來

SureByte™

肯信位元是世界首屈一指的雲端數位儲存網站，我們主打全新的暖儲存和冷儲存科技。我們提供最優秀的性能、穩定性和價格。我們如何辦到的？我們將儲存系統區分成兩種類別：暖儲存和冷儲存。公司可以將沒那麼常使用的資料存放在冷儲存，而將較常使用的資料存放在暖儲存。

肯信位元 翡翠方案
每月 14.95 美元
-1TB 儲存空間
-5GB 上傳／下載量

肯信位元 藍寶石方案
每月 15.95 美元
-2TB 儲存空間
-10GB 上傳／下載量

肯信位元 鑽石方案
每月 16.95 美元
-5TB 儲存空間
- 無限上傳／下載量

* 可依需求提供客製方案
肯信位元的雲端儲存服務受限於國際與國內法規。位於美國以外的客戶可能會根據所處地區而產生額外費用。請電洽 1-800-SUREBYTE 獲取更多資訊。

SureByte™
info@surebyte.com

Customer Name: DialonFire Inc.
Account Number: 1029384756

SureByte™ News:

Here at SureByte ™, we we are as dedicated to protecting the planet as we are to protecting your data. In keeping with this, we are offering a $0.50 discount to our monthly subscribers who switch to non-paper e-billing. If you'd like to know more, give us a call at 1-800-SUREBYTE, or e-mail us at ebilling@surebyte.com!

Monthly Statement Summary	
SureByte™ Diamond service	$16.95
Regional surcharge	$10.07
Total New Charges	**$27.02**

Thank you for being a valued SureByte™ customer!

SureByte™
info@surebyte.com

用戶名稱：戴倫費股份有限公司
用戶編號：1029384756

肯信位元最新資訊：

在肯信，我們致力於保護地球，一如我們致力於保護您的資料。為此，我們提供五十美分的折扣給願意轉換為電子帳單的每月訂戶。若想知道更多資訊，請電洽 1-800-SUREBYTE，或寄電子郵件到 ebilling@surebyte.com 給我們！

每月帳單概要	
肯信位元鑽石方案	16.95 美元
區域附加費	10.07 美元
最新總額	**27.02 美元**

感謝您成為肯信位元的重要客戶！

```
●●●
To:       SureByte
From:     David Bright
Subject:  Canceling service
```

To SureByte Customer Service,

This is David Bright at DialonFire. We are looking to cancel our service with you. The issue is not with the service itself, which has been fine for the past ten years we've been with you. However, the extra charge pushes it a little out of our budget. If the total bill were a little cheaper, then I think we could keep the service. We are also not interested in switching to a lower package—we need the unlimited uploads and downloads. Unfortunately, we have no choice but to pursue other options.

Thank you,
David Bright

收件者：肯信位元
寄件者：大衛‧布萊特
主　旨：取消服務

致肯信位元服務部：

我是戴倫費的大衛‧布萊特。我們想要取消向您購買的服務。問題並非服務本身，您所提供的服務在過去我們配合的十年間一直很好。然而，附加費用使我們有點超出預算了。如果整體費用可以更低一點，我想我們可以繼續使用您的服務。我們對於轉換成較低價的方案並不感興趣——我們需要無限上傳與下載量。很遺憾，我們除了尋求其他選擇之外別無他法。

感謝，
大衛‧布萊特

---

30 In the advertisement, the word "premier" in paragraph 1, line 1, is closest in meaning to
(A) earliest   **(B) best**
(C) last   (D) cheapest

在廣告中，第一段第一行的 "premier" 意思最接近何者？
(A) 最早的   **(B) 最棒的**
(C) 最後的   (D) 最便宜的

正解 (B)

本題考字義。由後一句 We offer the best in performance, reliability, and cost.「我們提供最優秀的性能、穩定性和價格」，可推知 premier 意思最接近 (B)「最棒的」。

---

31 What is suggested about DialonFire Inc.?
(A) The company is not in the US.
(B) The company is going out of business.
(C) The company has not been using SureByte™ for long.
(D) The company was previously using SureByte™ Sapphire.

關於戴倫費股份有限公司，本文有何暗示？
(A) 這間公司並不在美國。
(B) 這間公司要倒閉了。
(C) 這間公司使用肯信位元沒有很久。
(D) 這間公司之前使用肯信位元的藍寶石方案。

正解 (A)

本題為整合題。在肯信位元廣告的最底下提到 Customers outside the United States may incur a fee based on their location.「位於美國以外的客戶可能會根據所處地區而產生額外費用」，而戴倫費公司的帳單中有 Regional surcharge「區域附加費」，因此推知該公司並不在美國，故答案選 (A)。

32 How could DialonFire Inc. save some money on its bill?

(A) Switch to a lower-priced package

(B) Switch to electronic billing

(C) Put more data in CoolStore™

(D) Call for a discount

戴倫費股份有限公司可以如何減少帳單上的支出？

(A) 換到更低價的方案

(B) 換成電子帳單

(C) 在冷儲存系裡存入更多資料

(D) 要求打折優惠

正解 (B)

本題詢問戴倫費公司能如何減少帳單上的支出。帳單上提及 . . . we are offering a $0.50 discount to our monthly subscribers who switch to non-paper e-billing「我們提供五十美分的折扣給願意轉換為電子帳單的每月訂戶」，可知 (B) 為減少支出的可行辦法。

(A) 大衛・布萊特在回信的倒數第二句說到 We are also not interested in switching to a lower package . . .「我們對於換到較低價的方案並不感興趣……」，故知 (A) 不在大衛的考慮範圍之內。

---

33 What problem does David mention in his e-mail?

(A) The service is too expensive.

(B) The service is too unreliable.

(C) They have not been using the service much.

(D) They no longer need the service.

大衛在郵件中提及了什麼問題？

(A) 服務太貴了。

(B) 服務太不可靠了。

(C) 他們不常使用該項服務。

(D) 他們不再需要該項服務。

正解 (A)

由郵件第四句 If the total bill were a little cheaper, then I think we could keep the service.「如果整體費用可以更低一點，我想我們可以繼續使用您的服務。」，可知大衛在意的問題是價格，答案選 (A)。

---

34 Which service package does David say he needs?

(A) SureByte™ Emerald

(B) SureByte™ Sapphire

(C) SureByte™ Diamond

(D) A custom package

大衛說他需要哪項服務方案？

(A) 肯信位元翡翠方案

(B) 肯信位元藍寶石方案

(C) 肯信位元鑽石方案

(D) 客製方案

正解 (C)

此題為整合題。郵件倒數第二句說到 . . . we need the unlimited uploads and downloads「我們需要無限上傳和下載量」，對照廣告，提供無限上傳和下載量的方案是鑽石方案，故答案為 (C)。

P. 198~206

Part 1: Photographs

TRACK 47

❶ (A) The display board is in the classroom.
(B) The display board shows plane times.
(C) The display board shows listed companies.
(D) The display board is not working.

(A) 這個告示板是在教室裡。
(B) 這個告示板顯示班機時刻。
(C) 這個告示板顯示上市的公司。
(D) 這個告示板壞掉了

正解 **(C)**
圖中可見告示板顯示了股價，可推測上面皆為上市的公司，故正確答案為 (C)。

❷ (A) A merger contract is being signed.
(B) The man is performing a simulation test.
(C) A new model of car is in the showroom.
(D) The coworkers are discussing a prototype.

(A) 合併契約正被簽署。
(B) 男子正在執行模擬測試。
(C) 一款新車在展示間裡。
(D) 同事們正在討論一個產品原型。

正解 **(D)**
圖中的男子手上正拿著汽車原型樣品，並正和女子在討論，因此符合圖片的敘述為 (D)。

Part 2: Question and Response

❸ Which companies could be possible acquisitions for us this year?

   (A) Thames Tech is a small company that we could look at acquiring.

   (B) The acquisition of language comes naturally to children.

   (C) We can't possibly compromise on that.

   我們今年可能可以收購哪幾間公司呢？

   (A) 泰晤士科技是一間我們可以考慮收購的小公司。

   (B) 語言學習對小孩來說是很自然的。

   (C) 我們不可能在那件事上妥協。

正解 **(A)**

本題以 Which 開頭詢問可能可以收購的公司。(A) 明確表示「泰晤士科技是一間我們可以考慮收購的小公司」，符合語意故為正解。

(B) 企圖以相同字 acquisition 混淆作答，但該字在此是指「獲得；學習」，與題目無關。

(C) 回答與題目無關。

---

❹ This is a highly marketable product.

   (A) Yes, the market is high on a hill.

   (B) Yes, it should prove very popular.

   (C) Yes, we should ask marketing.

   這是非常好賣的產品。

   (A) 是，那個市場在一座小山丘上。

   (B) 是，它應該會非常受歡迎。

   (C) 是，我們應該要問行銷部。

正解 **(B)**

本題為直述句，表該產品非常好賣。最可能的回應為 (B)「是，它應該會非常流行。」表示贊同其想法，合乎邏輯。

(A) 企圖以發音相似字 market 混淆作答，該字在此是指「市場」，且題目與市場的地理位置無關。

(C) 企圖以發音相似字 marketing 混淆作答，該字在此是指「行銷」，與題目無關。

---

❺ Is the company likely to face a hostile takeover?

   (A) Maybe hostilities will cease soon.

   (B) It's possible as the directors don't want to sell.

   (C) The company has taken over the entire building.

   這間公司可能面臨惡意併購嗎？

   (A) 或許惡意很快會停止

   (B) 這是有可能的，因為管理者不想要賣。

   (C) 這間公司會接手這整棟大樓。

正解 **(B)**

本題為以 Is 開頭的一般是非問句，詢問這間公司是否可能面臨惡意併購。(B) 雖未直接以 Yes/No 回答，但表示「這是有可能的，因為管理者不想要賣」，符合邏輯故為正解。

(A) 企圖以發音相似字 hostilities 混淆作答，但該字是名詞指「敵意」，並沒有回答到題目的問題。cease *(v.)* 停止。

(C) 企圖以發音相似字詞 taken over 混淆作答，該詞在此是片語動詞指「接手」，其回答內容與題目矛盾。

SECTION B 試題練習

UNIT 7 Corporate Development 企業發展

⑥ How many calls are the telemarketers expected to make?
(A) It was marketed on television.
(B) They are not expected to arrive soon.
(C) They should make at least 300 calls.

電話行銷員預計要打多少通電話呢？
(A) 它是在電視上推銷的。
(B) 他們預計不會很快到達。
(C) 他們至少得打三百通電話。

正解 **(C)**
本題以 How many 開頭詢問數量。(C) 回答明確說出「他們至少得打三百通電話」，符合語意故為正解。

(A) 企圖以發音相似字 marketed 混淆作答，該字在此是指「行銷；宣傳」，其回答與題目無關。
(B) 回答與題目無關。

Part 3: Short Conversations

TRACK 49

Questions 7-9 refer to the following conversation with three speakers.

W: For the launch of our new Internet subscription package, I think it would be a good idea to set up a strong telemarketing team.

M1: What would be their function?

W: They could cold-call people to see if they would be interested in switching their Internet provider.

M2: Do you think a telemarketing team is necessary, as well as the television and print advertising we are planning?

W: I think so, because well-trained <u>telemarketers are skilled at talking people into things</u>.

M2: That's true. But we need to make sure we target the right demographic before we start making those calls.

女：為了推出我們新的網路訂購方案，我認為組一個強大的電話行銷團隊會是個好主意。

男一：他們的功能會是什麼？

女：他們可以對人們進行陌生電訪，看看是否他們有興趣更換網路供應商。

男二：妳認為除了我們正在計畫的電視和平面廣告，電話行銷團隊也是有必要的嗎？

女：我認為是，因為訓練有素的<u>電話行銷員擅長說服人們</u>。

男二：沒錯。但在我們進行電訪前，必須先確保我們掌握正確的目標族群。

⑦ What type of company do the speakers work for?
(A) A web design company
(B) A telemarketing company
(C) An Internet service provider
(D) An advertising company

說話者在哪種類型的公司上班？
(A) 網頁設計公司　　(B) 電話行銷公司
(C) 網路服務供應商　(D) 廣告公司

正解 **(C)**
本題問人物身分，詢問說話者在哪種類型的公司上班。由女子一開頭說 For the launch of our new Internet subscription package, I think . . . 得知他們公司是網路供應商，答案為 (C)。

8 What does the company NOT want to do?

(A) Have telemarketers make cold calls

(B) Hire a telemarketing team

(C) Spend more money on advertising

(D) Have telemarketers call the existing customers

該公司不想做什麼事情？

(A) 讓電話行銷人員打陌生電話

(B) 雇用電話行銷團隊

(C) 在廣告上花更多錢

(D) 讓電話行銷人員打電話給目前的客戶

正解 **(D)**

題目問該公司不想做的事。由女子所說 They could cold-call people to see if they would be interested in switching their Internet provider. ，得知公司進行陌生電訪的目的是說服人們更換網路供應商，也就是想要開發新的客戶，所以答案選 (D)。選項 (B) 由女子說 it would be a good idea to set up a strong telemarketing team 以及選項 (C) 從男子問 Do you think a telemarketing team is necessary, as well as the television and print advertising we are planning? 而女子給予肯定回應 I think so 可知皆是該公司想進行的事。

---

9 What does the woman mean when she says, "telemarketers are skilled at talking people into things"?

(A) They are good at telling people where to go.

(B) They can convince people to do something.

(C) They are good at getting customer feedback.

(D) They enjoy telling stories to customers.

當女子說 "telemarketers are skilled at talking people into things" 時，是什麼意思？

(A) 他們擅長告訴人們該去哪裡。

(B) 他們可以說服人們去做一些事。

(C) 他們擅於獲取顧客回應。

(D) 他們喜歡向顧客說故事。

正解 **(B)**

本題詢問女子說 "telemarketers are skilled at talking people into things" 的意思。talk sb. into N./V-ing 指「說服（某人）做某事」，選項 (B) 符合此意故為正確答案。

Questions 10-12 *refer to the following conversation and chart.*

M: I just wanted to confirm where we're at with the launch of our new wearable camera.

W: Great. Please **fill me in**.

M: Well, as you know, the concept received a positive response during our brainstorming session, and we are almost ready to do some market research. Market segmentation will allow us to target specific consumers and incorporate certain features.

W: Sounds good. Do we have product designers **lined up** to make a prototype for us?

M: Yes, we've **enlisted** Albany Design to make the prototype.

- fill sb. in *(phr.)* 向某人提供（關於某事物的）詳情
- line sth. up *(phr.)* 安排／準備好某事
- enlist *(v.)* 爭取；謀取（幫助或支援）

男：我只是想要確認我們推行新穿戴式相機的進展。

女：很好。請說吧。

男：嗯，如妳所知，這個概念在我們的腦力激盪會議上收到正面的回應，且我們幾乎準備好要進行一些市場調查。市場區隔會讓我們能夠鎖定特定消費族群並融入某些功能。

女：聽起來很棒。我們有安排產品設計者來幫我們做原型了嗎？

男：有，我們已經請艾爾本尼設計公司來做原型了。

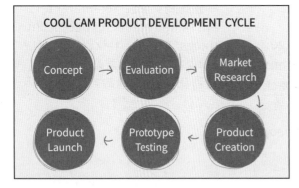

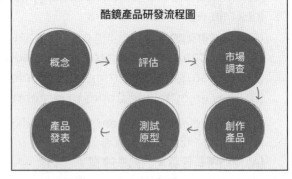

🔟 What is the man doing?
(A) Asking for information
(B) Explaining a concept
(C) Providing an update
(D) Conducting market research

正解 **(C)**

題目問男子正在做的事。由男子說 I just wanted to confirm where we're at with the launch of our new wearable camera. 得知男子想向女子報告公司推行新穿戴式相機的進度，所以答案為 (C)。

男子正在做什麼？
(A) 詢問資訊
(B) 解釋概念
(C) 提供最新訊息
(D) 執行市場調查

⓫ What is implied about the market research?

(A) It will help the company to advertise its new wearable camera.

(B) It will be conducted using Internet surveys of consumers.

(C) The market research will only target certain people.

(D) It will help the company develop the product for particular consumers.

關於市場調查,對話有何暗示?

(A) 它會幫助公司宣傳新的穿戴式相機。

(B) 它會透過消費者的網路調查來進行。

(C) 市場調查只會鎖定特定的人。

(D) 它將有助公司為特定消費者研發產品。

正解 **(D)**

題目問關於市場調查,對話有何暗示。由男子說 . . . ready to do some market research. Market segmentation will allow us to target specific consumers and incorporate certain features. 可知市場調查可將消費者做出區隔,而公司便能針對特定消費者融入其需要的功能,所以答案為 (D)。

⓬ Look at the graphic. At which stage of the product development cycle is the company?

(A) Concept

(B) Prototype Testing

(C) Evaluation

(D) Market Research

看圖表。目前這間公司是在產品研發流程圖中的哪個階段?

(A) 概念

(B) 測試原型

(C) 評估

(D) 市場調查

正解 **(C)**

題目問該公司目前產品研發的階段,須結合圖表與對話作答。男子說 the concept received a positive response during our brainstorming session, and we are almost ready to do some market research. 得知目前介於「概念」與「市場調查」之間,對照流程圖,這中間的階段是「評估」,故答案為 (C)。

Part 4: Short Talks

Questions 13-15 *refer to the following talk.*

Hello, everyone. Thank you for attending this meeting **at short notice**. The reason I have gotten everyone together today is to let you know that our merger with EduTech has now officially gone through. As you know, we have long been looking to branch out into the education sector. While consumer electronics still remains our core business, this merger will allow us to corner the market in education technology. The education sector is evolving and looking to technology to drive innovation. Bringing together the expertise that exists in our two companies is a very exciting development. Over the next few weeks, the directors will be holding meetings with individual departments to discuss these developments. In the meantime, keep up the good work!

大家好。謝謝各位參加這個臨時的會議。我今天把每個人找來的理由是要讓各位知道我們和育科公司的合併已經正式通過了。如大家所知道的,我們一直很想要拓展到教育產業。雖然電子產品的消費者仍然是我們的核心事業,這項合併將讓我們得以壟斷教育科技的市場。教育產業正在進化,且正仰賴科技來推動革新。結合兩間公司既有的專門技術是一項讓人非常興奮的發展。接下來幾週,主管們會和各自的部門開會來討論這些發展。在此期間,請維持目前的好表現!

• at short notice *(phr.)* 在短時間內;一經通知立即

---

⑬ Who is the audience for this talk?
(A) The media   **(B) Employees**
(C) Directors   (D) Teachers

這段談話的聽眾是誰?
(A) 媒體   **(B) 員工**
(C) 主管   (D) 老師

正解 (B)

本題詢問這段話的聽眾。由關鍵句說 The reason I have gotten everyone together today is to let you know that our merger with EduTech has now officially gone through. 得知說話者在向聽眾宣布他們公司和另一家公司合併的消息,可推測聽者應是公司的內部員工,故答案為 (B)。

---

⑭ What does the speaker say about the education sector?
(A) It is changing.
(B) It is profitable.
(C) It's their core business.
(D) It is traditional.

關於教育產業,說話者說了什麼?
(A) 它正在改變。
(B) 它是有利潤的。
(C) 那是該公司的核心事業。
(D) 它是傳統的。

正解 (A)

本題詢問說話者對教育產業的看法。由關鍵句 The education sector is evolving and looking to technology to drive innovation. 可得知教育產業正在改變。evolve 是「進化;演變」之意,故答案為 (A)。

⓯ What will happen next?
(A) The merger will be publicized.
(B) Some employees will be laid off.
(C) Staff expertise will be evaluated.
(D) Smaller meetings will be held.

接下來會發生什麼？
(A) 合併會被公開。
(B) 有些員工會被解雇。
(C) 員工的專業知識會被評估。
(D) 較小型的會議會被召開。

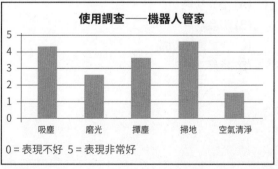正解 (D)

本題為推論題，問接下來會發生什麼事。倒數第二句說 Over the next few weeks, the directors will be holding meetings with individual departments to discuss these developments. 得知接下來幾週各部門主管會和部門人員開會，所以答案為 (D)。

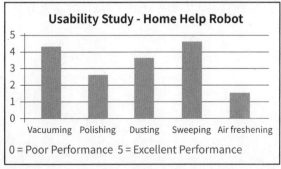SECTION B 試題練習

UNIT 7 Corporate Development 企業發展

Questions 16-18 refer to the following talk and chart.

Hi, everyone. I'd like to start the meeting by reviewing the results of our recent usability study. As you know, we are hoping that this home help robot will represent a breakthrough in affordable domestic cleaning products with its cutting-edge features and improved functionality. During the simulation test, we asked users to rate the robot on several aspects. Well, it looks like all the time and effort we spent on research and development has paid off. As you can see, users were pretty happy with it for the most part, but two functions received less than 3-star averages. Obviously, we need to get to work on this. But the air freshening function will take longer to figure out, so we'll do that second. Over the coming week, I'd like you all to take another look at this area and see if any improvements can be made. Don't get me wrong—overall, the feedback was so good, that I believe if we can fix these things, then we will have a very marketable product.

大家好。會議的一開始我想要檢討我們最近的使用調查結果。如同你們所知道的，我們期望機器人管家隨著它先進的特色與改善過的功能，在價格親民的居家清掃用品中，能象徵一個突破。在模擬測試期間，我們要求使用者就幾個方面為機器人評分。嗯，看來我們在研發上花的所有時間和心力已經得到回報了。各位可以看到，使用者在大部分方面都相當滿意，但有兩個功能平均僅不到三分。顯然我們需要在這方面多下功夫。但空氣清淨功能會需要花較長的時間才能解決，所以我們會其次再進行。在下一週，我想要你們換個角度看看這方面是否有任何地方可以改進。總之不要弄錯我的意思——整體而言，反應非常好，因此我相信如果我們修改這些地方，我們將有一個非常暢銷的產品。

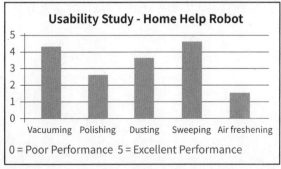

Usability Study - Home Help Robot

(bar chart: Vacuuming, Polishing, Dusting, Sweeping, Air freshening)

0 = Poor Performance 5 = Excellent Performance

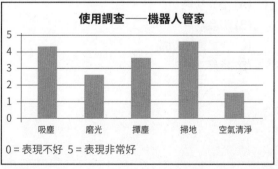

使用調查——機器人管家

(bar chart: 吸塵、磨光、撢塵、掃地、空氣清淨)

0 = 表現不好 5 = 表現非常好

⓰ What is the purpose of this talk?
(A) To launch a marketing campaign
(B) To discuss the results of some product testing
(C) To inform people how to use the home help robot
(D) To ask staff to clean the office

這段談話的目的是什麼？
(A) 推出促銷活動
(B) 討論一些產品測試的結果
(C) 告知人們如何使用機器人管家
(D) 要求員工打掃辦公室

正解 (B)

題目問這段談話的目的。由關鍵句說 During the simulation test, we asked users to rate the robot on several aspects.，且後續提到使用者的滿意程度以及產品在某些方面得到的評分，可知說話者正在說明產品測試的結果，答案為 (B)。

⓱ What does the speaker think about the research and development results?
(A) He thinks they were successful.
(B) He thinks they were a waste of time.
(C) He thinks they were not clear enough.
(D) He thinks they were surprising.

說話者覺得研發結果如何？
(A) 他覺得非常成功。
(B) 他覺得浪費時間。
(C) 他覺得不夠清楚。
(D) 他覺得很驚訝。

正解 (A)

題目問說話者對研發結果的想法。答題關鍵在 Well, it looks like all the time and effort we spent on research and development has paid off.，片語動詞 pay off 指「得到好結果；有正面的回報」，得知他認為研發結果很成功，答案為 (A)。

⓲ Look at the graphic. What problem area is going to be worked on first?
(A) Polishing functionality
(B) Vacuuming functionality
(C) Air freshening functionality
(D) Dusting functionality

看圖表。哪個問題會先被處理？
(A) 磨光功能
(B) 吸塵功能
(C) 空氣清淨功能
(D) 撢塵功能

正解 (A)

本題為圖表題，問說哪個問題會先被處理。說話者提及有兩個功能平均僅不到三分，顯然需要多下功夫，對照圖表可知是「空氣清淨功能」與「磨光功能」。但說話特別提到 . . . the air freshening function will take longer to figure out, so we'll do that second. 可知他們決定先處理另一個不到三分的「磨光功能」，所以答案為 (A)。

Part 5: Incomplete Sentences

19 Please _____ our branch offices know that the prototypes will be delivered as early as next Monday.

(A) get   (B) allow

(C) enable   **(D) let**

請讓我們的分公司知道原型將會盡快在下週一運送。

(A) 讓；使得；得到

(B) 允許

(C) 使能夠

(D) 讓……

正解 (D)

本題考使役動詞。空格後方有原形動詞 know，可知空格處應搭配使役動詞，選項中唯一的使役動詞為 (D) let，後常接「人 + 原形動詞」。

(A) get 可表「使／讓……」，為有使役意味的一般動詞；(B) allow 表「允許」；(C) enable 指「使……能夠」，指的是賦予某種能力。(A)、(B)、(C) 均須在受詞後接不定詞 to V.。

---

20 All of the specs for this computer, as well as the software that comes pre-installed, _____ shown in this brochure.

(A) are   (B) were

(C) be   (D) has

這台電腦的所有規格以及事先安裝好的軟體可以在這本小冊子上看到。

(A) 是（現在式第二人稱或第三人稱複數 be 動詞）

(B) 是（過去式第二人稱或第三人稱複數 be 動詞）

(C) 是（be 動詞原形）

(D)（現在式第三人稱單數助動詞）

正解 (A)

本題考時態。本句欲表「所有規格以及事先安裝好的軟體可以在這本小冊子上被看到」。句意在描述一般事實，故須用現在式，又因主詞為表事物的 specs「產品規格」且是第三人稱複數，因此須用複數 be 動詞，形成現在式的被動語態 are shown，答案為 (A)。

(D) 置入後形成 has shown，為主動語態且單複數與主詞不一致，故不可選。

---

21 There is a _____ on the website where you can read about the history, directors, and recent innovations of the corporation.

(A) preliminary stage

(B) core business

(C) company profile

(D) simulation test

這個網站上有這間公司的概況，你可以在其中讀到這間企業的歷史、管理者和最近的創新作為。

(A) 初步階段

(B) 核心事業

(C) 公司概況

(D) 模擬測試

正解 (C)

本題考字義。依照句意可知空格處填入 (C) company profile，表示網站上有列出「公司概況」供人閱讀。

㉒ Following the _____, it will be interesting to see what passengers think of the new driverless bus.

(A) market capitalization

(B) trial run

(C) intellectual property

(D) market segmentation

試用結束後,看乘客對於新的無人駕駛公車有何想法將會很有趣。

(A) 市價總值

(B) 試用

(C) 智慧財產

(D) 市場區隔

正解 (B)

本題考字義。依照句意可知空格處填入 (B) trial run,描述「試用」結束後使用者的反應。其餘選項均不合語意。

㉓ The training program gives students practical, _____ experience in product development and design.

(A) low-end

(B) hands-off

(C) high-end

(D) hands-on

訓練課程在產品發展和設計方面給予學生實用、親身參與的經驗。

(A) 低階的;廉價的

(B) 不插手的;不干涉的

(C) 高檔的;高價位的

(D) 實際動手做的

正解 (D)

本題考字義。依照句意可知空格處填入 (D) hands-on 指「實際動手做的」,hands-on experience 表「實作經驗」。

Part 6: Text Completion

Questions 24-27 refer to the following article.

Caledine Partners with High Schools for National STEM Week

Caledine Sydney, a ---24--- of The Caledine Group Inc., partnered with high schools in the Sydney area as part of the national STEM (Science Technology Engineering Math) Week. ---25--- Caledine organized tours of its branch offices and hands-on product development activities in its production facilities in the city. "Promoting interest in research and development, and fostering innovation in young people, is something that we take very seriously at Caledine," says Karen Young, Vice President of the ---26---. "We want to see the next generation enter the STEM fields in ---27--- numbers and come up with the cutting-edge designs that will make a difference in the future."

科蘭丁集團有限公司與高中合作推動國際理工週

雪梨科蘭丁是科蘭丁集團有限公司的一個事業部，他們與雪梨地區的高中合作，為國際理工週（科學、科技、工程、數學）獻上一份心力。<u>理工週是一項政府計畫，希望提升學生對這些領域的興趣。</u>科蘭丁規劃其分公司的辦公室導覽以及在其位於市內的生產設施舉辦產品開發實作活動。「促進研發相關的興趣和培養年輕人的創新思維是我們科蘭丁非常認真看待的事。」該企業的副總裁凱倫·楊這麼說。「我們想要看到下個世代有更多人進入理工領域並構想出尖端設計，讓未來變得不同。」

㉔ (A) division
(B) monopoly
(C) resource
(D) demographic

(A) 事業部；部門
(B) 獨占；專賣
(C) 資源
(D) 人口統計資料

正解 **(A)**

本題考字義。原句提到，「雪梨科蘭丁是科蘭丁集團有限公司的一個____，他們與雪梨地區的高中合作 ……」依句意可知最適合的答案為 (A)。

㉕
(A) The idea is that students in high school will stay at home and study for their tests.

(B) The week is forecast to be hot and humid, so people are advised to stay indoors.

(C) The week is a government initiative that hopes to increase students' interest in these areas.

(D) During certain weeks of the year, members of the public can visit Caledine's factory.

(A) 這個主意是高中學生會待在家裡為考試用功念書。

(B) 這週預計會是炎熱潮濕的天氣，所以建議人們待在室內。

(C) 理工週是一項政府計畫，希望提升學生對這些領域的興趣。

(D) 在今年的某幾週，民眾可以參觀科蘭丁的工廠。

正解 **(C)**
空格的前一句說雪梨科蘭丁與雪梨地區的高中合作，參與了國際理工週的活動，而 (C) 進一步介紹「國際理工週」的主辦單位與目標，語意連貫故為正選。

㉖
(A) acquisition
(B) resource
(C) corporation
(D) merger

(A) 收購
(B) 資源
(C) 公司；企業
(D) 合併

正解 **(C)**
本題考字義。空格前是 Vice President of the，可知應選 (C)，表「該企業的副總裁」。其餘選項均不合語意。

㉗
(A) equal
(B) sooner
(C) lesser
(D) higher

(A) 相同的
(B) 較快的
(C) 較少的
(D) 較多的

正解 **(D)**
本題考字義。空格後為 numbers「數字」，可知應選 (D) higher 來修飾 numbers。in higher number 表「較大量的」。原句欲表「想要看到下個世代有更多人進入理工領域」。

Part 7: Reading Comprehension

Questions 28-30 refer to the following invitation.

Invitation for Submission of Proposals
Lea Valley Business Incubation—The Place to Grow your Business

The Lea Valley Enterprise Authority (LVEA) invites suitable manufacturing enterprises or individuals to the Lea Valley Business Incubator. The incubator provides a conducive environment for small to medium enterprises to grow and establish themselves as sustainable and commercially viable manufacturing enterprises. The program is expected to take a maximum period of 2 years, on a 1 year renewable lease.

Selected clients will benefit from the following resources and expertise:

- Research and Development units and office space at **subsidized** rates
- Hands-on business coaching and training
- Technology coaching and support
- **Facilitation** of market access
- Workshops on intellectual property rights
- Administration services such as Internet, photocopying, and printing

REQUIREMENTS

Eligible candidates should submit a business proposal which clearly outlines the following:

1. The core business and concept
2. The product development plan
3. Marketing plan and product line
4. Availability of funds to run the business
5. Historical and projected financials
6. Company documents

Candidates should submit relevant documents to:
The Selection Committee
Lea Valley Business Incubator
Post Office Box #339
Sacramento, CA

敬邀企劃提交

里・維立企業育成機構——
讓您的事業成長茁壯

里・維立企業發展局邀請合適的製造公司或個人來到里・維立企業育成機構。育成機構提供有益中小企業的環境，有助其成長茁壯並確立成為可持續發展且具商業利益的製造公司。此計畫預計為期最多兩年，可續約一年。

被選上的客戶將可受益於以下的資源和專業技術：
- 以補助後的價格租用研發場地與辦公空間
- 實作企業輔導和員工訓練
- 技術指導與支援
- 促進打入市場
- 智慧財產權之專題討論會
- 網際網路、影印和列印等行政服務

需求
具資格的候選人應提交清楚概述以下資訊的商業企劃案：
1. 核心事業和概念
2. 產品發展計畫
3. 行銷計畫和產品系列
4. 公司運作所需資金之可運用性
5. 過往和預計的財務數字
6. 公司文件

候選者應提交相關文件至：
評選委員會
里・維立企業育成機構
加州薩克拉門托郵政信箱 339 號

- subsidize *(v.)* 給……津貼；補助
- facilitation *(n.)* 促進；簡易化

28 What is the purpose of this invitation?
(A) To invite business people to lunch
(B) To ask people to prepare some documents
(C) To ask people to attend a meeting
(D) To invite business proposals

這個邀請函的目的為何？
(A) 邀請商務人士共進午餐
(B) 要求人們準備一些文件
(C) 要求人們參加一場會議
(D) 邀請提出商業企劃案

正解 (D)

本題為主旨題，詢問此邀請函的目的。由標題 Invitation for Submission of Proposals 以及 REQUIREMENTS 中第一句 Eligible candidates should submit a business proposal which clearly outlines the following 可知是要邀請企業提出企劃案，所以答案選 (D)。

29 What is NOT mentioned as a benefit of joining the business incubator?
(A) Receiving coaching
(B) Making use of office space
(C) Receiving funding
(D) Using administration services

哪一項加入企業育成的好處未被提及？
(A) 可接受輔導
(B) 有辦公空間可利用
(C) 可招募到新職員
(D) 可使用行政服務

正解 (C)

本題為除外題，詢問文中沒提到哪一項加入企業育成的好處。(A) 關鍵字可見文中第二段清單中第二、三行的 coaching；(B) 可見第二段清單的第一行，關鍵字為 office space；(D) 可見第二段清單的最後一行 Administration services。唯獨 (C) 未提及故為正選。

30 The word "sustainable" in paragraph 1, line 4, is closest in meaning to
(A) enduring
(B) environmental
(C) temporary
(D) innovative

第一段第四行 "sustainable" 意思最接近何字？
(A) 持久的；長遠的
(B) 環境的
(C) 暫時的；短暫的
(D) 創新的

正解 (A)

本題考同義字，詢問 sustainable 的意思最接近何者。包含該字的原句為 The incubator provides a conducive environment . . . to grow and establish themselves as sustainable and commercially viable manufacturing enterprises.，可知該機構有助於中小企業的發展，sustainable 為「可持續的」之意，因此意思最接近的是 (A)「持久的；長遠的」。

Questions 31-33 refer to the following meeting minutes.

MEETING MINUTES

ITEM #	Description	Status
1.	Acquisition of Innovate Games by computer games conglomerate, InGames.	Talks are ongoing. --[1]-- No decisions have been made yet.
2.	Research and Development of WarQuest game.	Still in preliminary stage. Programmers and designers are still working on specs for new game. --[2]-- Marketing team to initiate market segmentation.
3.	Directors wish to branch out into games for stay-at-home mothers and fathers. They would like us to corner the market in this area.	Marketing looking into whether this is a marketable idea.
4.	A new telemarketing team is being trained by the Marketing Department to target users of the mobile gaming app. --[3]--	Training is due to be completed this week and new team will hopefully start generating new leads. --[4]--
5.	Decision was made to meet again when more is known about the acquisition.	A new meeting date will be sent to you.

會議記錄

項目	描述	狀態
1.	收購隸屬電腦遊戲企業集團之「遊戲中公司」的「創新遊戲」。	持續溝通中。尚未定案。
2.	「求戰」遊戲的研發。	仍在初步階段。 程式工程師和設計師仍在著手設計新遊戲的規格。行銷團隊將開始進行市場區隔。
3.	主管希望將遊戲推廣給在家的父母使用。他們希望我們壟斷這個領域的市場。	行銷部調查這個想法是否有市場性。
4.	行銷部正在訓練新的電話行銷團隊,目標鎖定在手遊軟體使用者。<u>這是為了瞭解他們是否有興趣更新。</u>	訓練會在這週完成,新團隊可望能開發新的客戶。
5.	已決定當收購案有更進一步消息時要再次召開會議。	將寄出新的會議資料給各位。

31 What kind of work is being discussed in the meeting minutes?
(A) Teaching
(B) Telemarketing
(C) Games development
(D) Manufacturing

會議記錄中討論的是哪類的工作？
(A) 教學
(B) 電話行銷
(C) 遊戲研發
(D) 製造業

正解 (C)
本題詢問會議記錄中討論的是哪類的工作。由描述欄第二點的 Research and Development of WarQuest game. 與狀態欄第二點的 Programmers and designers are still working on specs for new game.，得知這是遊戲公司的會議記錄，他們正在研發新的遊戲，所以答案要選 (C)。

32 What type of customer would the company like to target next?
(A) Parents
(B) Kids
(C) Designers
(D) Business people

哪類的顧客是公司下一步的目標族群？
(A) 父母
(B) 小孩
(C) 設計師
(D) 商務人士

正解 (A)
本題為細節題。詢問公司下一步的目標族群。描述欄的第三點提到 Directors wish to branch out into games for stay-at-home mothers and fathers. 得知公司想要讓在家父母也玩遊戲，故答案為 (A)。

33 In which of the positions marked [1], [2], [3], and [4] does the following sentence best belong?
"This is to see if they would be interested in upgrading."
(A) [1]
(B) [2]
(C) [3]
(D) [4]

以下句子最適合放在標示 [1]、[2]、[3]、[4] 的哪個位置？
「這是為了瞭解他們是否有興趣更新。」
(A) [1]
(B) [2]
(C) [3]
(D) [4]

正解 (C)
本題為篇章結構題。根據上下文之意，[3] 的前方提到行銷部正在訓練新的電話行銷團隊，目標鎖定在手機遊戲軟體使用者。下一句銜接題目句「這是為了瞭解他們是否有興趣更新」可形成語意順暢連貫，其中「他們」就是的是前句的手遊軟體使用者，故應選 (C)。

Unit 8 Technical Areas 技術層面

P. 218~226

Part 1: Photographs

TRACK 52

① **(A) The woman is wearing a headset.**
(B) The woman works in a laboratory.
(C) The woman is fixing some hardware.
(D) The woman works in agriculture.

(A) 一名女士戴著頭戴式耳機。
(B) 有張卡片被插入自動提款機中。
(C) 一名女士正在修理一些硬體設備。
(D) 一名女士從事農業方面的工作。

正解 **(A)**
圖中女子頭戴頭戴式耳機，因此符合圖片的敘述為 (A)「一名女士戴著頭戴式耳機。」
(D) agriculture *(n.)* 農業的。

② (A) A printer has been disconnected.
(B) Ink cartridges are in a printer.
(C) A printer is being assembled.
(D) Paper is stuck inside a printer.

(A) 一台印表機的連線被切斷了。
(B) 墨水匣在印表機中。
(C) 一台印表機正在被組裝。
(D) 印表機卡紙了。

正解 **(B)**
圖中可見印表機的墨水匣已經安裝好，故正確答案為 (B)。

Part 2: Question and Response

---

❸ How do I log in to get online?
(A) Press your card on the door's sensor.
(B) Yes, the company has an online system.
(C) Enter your user name and password.

我如何登入來連上網路？
(A) 把卡片按在門上的感應區。
(B) 沒錯，公司有個線上系統。
(C) 輸入你的帳號和密碼。

正解 **(C)**

本句以 How 開頭，詢問登入上網的方式。合適的回應為 (C)「輸入你的帳號和密碼。」

(A) 與題意無關。
(B) 並未回答如何登入。

---

❹ Are the new laptops coming this week?
(A) No, not this week.
(B) At the end of last year.
(C) I bought it online.

新筆電是這禮拜到嗎？
(A) 不是，不是這個禮拜。
(B) 去年年底。
(C) 我上網購買的。

正解 **(A)**

本題為以 Are 開頭的是非問句，詢問對方新筆電是否這個禮拜到。(A) 的答案符合邏輯，故為正解。

(B) 回答為過去的時態與題目不符。
(C) 題目與如何購買無關。

---

❺ Where is the power button?
(A) It's at the top of the monitor.
(B) It charges the phone.
(C) Hold it down for two seconds.

電源開關在哪裡？
(A) 在螢幕的上方。
(B) 它幫手機充電。
(C) 長按兩秒鐘。

正解 **(A)**

此題以 Where 詢問電源開關在哪裡。選項中唯一符合邏輯的回應為 (A)「在螢幕上方。」

(B) 題目與功能無關。
(C) 該動作並未回答題目。

---

❻ My screen keeps crashing.
(A) Yes, it's too cold in here.
(B) You may have a virus.
(C) You should see a doctor.
我的螢幕一直當機。
(A) 沒錯，這裡太冷了。
(B) 你可能中毒了。
(C) 你應該去看醫生。

正解 **(B)**

本題為直述句，描述「我的螢幕一直當機。」選項中 (B)「你可能中毒了。」為符合邏輯之可能理由，故為正解。

(A) 與題意無關。
(C) 並未回應螢幕當機一事。

Part 3: Short Conversations

Questions 7-9 refer to the following conversation with three speakers.

W: Hi, I'm Mary James, calling from Optika Dental. We purchased some 3D printers from you recently, but we've been having a few problems and need some assistance.

M1: OK, hold on a second while I put you through to a technician.

M2: Hello, Technical Support. Derek speaking. How may I help you?

W: Hello. This is Optika Dental. We're having problems using the software for our 3D printer. We've read the instruction manual thoroughly, but we're finding the process very complicated and are wondering if someone from your department could come in to **take** our operators **through** it one more time.

M2: I see. We'll send someone over this afternoon. Expect a visitor between 2 p.m. and 2:30 p.m.

W: OK, I appreciate it. But please don't send the same engineer as last time. We didn't feel he was very good at explaining.

• take sb. through sth. *(phr.)* 對某人說明某事

女：嗨，我是奧蒂卡牙科診所的瑪莉·詹姆斯。我們最近從貴公司購買了一些 3D 印表機，但一直有一些問題因此需要協助。

男一：好的，我幫您轉給我們的技術人員，請稍等。

男二：您好，技術支援部。我是德瑞克。我可以如何幫您呢？

女：您好。這裡是奧蒂卡牙科診所。我們在使用 3D 印表機的軟體上遇到一些問題。我們已經詳讀了說明書，但是覺得流程相當複雜，我們想知道是否貴部門是否有人可以過來再為我們的操作員解釋一遍。

男二：我了解了。我們今天下午會派人過去。預計下午兩點到兩點半之間會到達。

女：沒問題，感謝你們的協助。但是請不要派上次那位工程師了，我們覺得他並不是很擅長講解。

---

7 What does the caller need help with?
(A) An Internet connection
(B) E-commerce
(C) Some software
(D) An operating system

來電者在哪方面需要幫忙？
(A) 網路連線
(B) 電子商務
(C) 軟體部分
(D) 作業系統

正解 **(C)**
本題詢問來電者需要哪方面的協助。由女子所說 We're having problems using the software for our 3D printer.「我們在使用 3D 印表機的軟體上遇到一些問題。」可知正確答案為 (C)。

❽ What does the technician offer to do?

(A) Send someone to explain later

(B) Come and visit the office himself

(C) Send the woman an instruction manual

(D) Provide advice over the phone

技術人員提議要做什麼？

(A) 稍晚派人過去解釋

(B) 親自拜訪公司一趟

(C) 寄給女子一份操作手冊

(D) 透過電話提供建議

正解 (A)

本題詢問技術人員提議會做何事。對話中電話轉接至技術部門後，女子要求對方派人過來再次說明流程，而技術人員回應說 We'll send someone over this afternoon.，故知他會派人過去解釋，正確答案為 (A)。

---

❾ Why didn't the woman like the person that was sent last time?

(A) He arrived later than expected.

(B) He didn't understand the problem.

(C) He didn't appreciate the company.

(D) He wasn't good at explaining.

女子為什麼不喜歡上次派來的人？

(A) 他來得比預期晚。　　(B) 他並不了解問題。

(C) 他不欣賞這家公司。　**(D) 他並不擅長解釋。**

正解 (D)

本題詢問女子不喜歡上次派的人的原因。由女子所說 We didn't feel he was very good at explaining.「我們覺得他並不是很擅長講解」，可知答案應選 (D)。

Questions 10-12 refer to the following conversation and graphic.

M: So Mary, I want to replace the clear glass window between the laboratory and the control room, with one-way glass.

W: That makes sense. The people working in the laboratory don't need to see the people watching them.

M: Exactly. It's an unnecessary distraction. Secondly, I need more space. So let's switch my office with the conference room.

W: OK, neither of those should be too much trouble. And do you still want to move the control room?

M: Actually, I've **had second thoughts** on that. Let's keep it between the laboratory and observation room.

W: OK, sure. I'll check our options for the glass online and hopefully we can start work right away.

• have second thoughts *(phr.)* 重新考慮；改變主意

男：瑪莉，我想要把實驗室跟控制中心之間的透明玻璃窗換成單向玻璃。

女：有道理。實驗室的工作人員並不需要看到注視他們的人。

男：沒錯。那會造成不必要的分心。另外，我需要更多空間。所以我們把我的辦公室跟會議室對調過來吧。

女：好的，這兩件事應該都不會太麻煩。然後，你仍然想要移動控制中心的位置嗎？

男：事實上，我重新考慮了一下。我們還是把它留在實驗室跟觀察室之間好了。

女：好的，沒問題。我會上網查看一下我們的玻璃選擇，希望我們可以馬上動工。

Laboratory	Conference Room
Control Room	Office
Observation Room	Break Room

Window

實驗室	會議室
控制中心	辦公室
觀察室	員工休息室

窗戶

⑩ Why does the man want one-way glass?

(A) Because it will cost less money

(B) To make sure workers are not distracted

(C) Because lab workers have complained

(D) He doesn't want workers to see into his office.

男子為什麼想要單向玻璃？

(A) 因為它所需的經費比較少

(B) 來確保工作人員不會分心

(C) 因為實驗室工作人員有所抱怨

(D) 他不希望工作人員看到他的辦公室內部。

正解 **(B)**

本題詢問男子想換成單向玻璃的原因。由男子所說 It's an unnecessary distraction. 可知男子認為原本的雙向玻璃會讓工作人員分心，故答案選 (B)。

⑪ What will the woman most probably do next?

(A) Contact a glass manufacturer

(B) Buy some tools

(C) Call a staff meeting

(D) Search the Internet

女子接下來最有可能會做什麼事情？

(A) 聯絡玻璃生產商

(B) 購買一些器具

(C) 召開員工會議

(D) 上網搜尋

正解 **(D)**

題目詢問女子接下來會做什麼事情。由女子所說 I'll check our options for the glass online and hopefully we can start work right away. 可知她希望可以馬上動工，因此會先上網查看玻璃的選擇，因此 (D) 為最合適的答案。

⓬ Look at the graphic. Where will the man's office be after the changes have been made?

(A) **Next to the laboratory**
(B) Between the control room and the lab
(C) Next to the observation room
(D) Between the lab and observation room

看圖表。在更動完成後，男子的辦公室會在哪裡？

(A) 在實驗室旁邊
(B) 在控制中心跟實驗室中間
(C) 在觀察室旁邊
(D) 在實驗室跟觀察室中間

正解 **(A)**

此為圖表題。題目詢問男子的辦公室會在哪個位置。由男子所說 So let's switch my office with the conference room.「所以我們把我的辦公室跟會議室對調過來吧」，又對照圖表，目前會議室的位置位於實驗室旁邊，故答案選 (A)。

Part 4: Short Talks

TRACK 55

Questions 13-15 refer to the following talk.

These days it seems like there is an app for everything, so what is so special about DateMarker? Sure, you have the calendar on your phone and there are various apps out there which can apparently help you to organize your life, but the question I want you to ask yourself is "do those things really work, or are they more trouble than they're worth?" With DateMarker, we do the hard work for you, so you don't need to. The app combines a user-friendly interface with interactive features to provide you with the ultimate platform for managing your schedule. There are no annoying pop-ups or advertisements. <u>Using DateMarker really is a walk in the park.</u> No stress. No worries. Just better organization, 24 hours a day, seven days a week.

現今似乎所有事物都有專屬的應用程式，所以日程標註師有什麼特別之處？當然，您的手機裡有行事曆且市場上有諸多其他應用程式顯然都可以協助你規劃生活，然而我有個問題想要請您捫心自問「這些東西真的有用嗎？還是它們製造的麻煩多過所帶來的成效？」有了日程標註師，我們幫您做那些苦差事，這樣一來您就無需費心。這個應用程式結合容易操作的介面以及互動的功能來提供您最好的行程安排平台。沒有惱人的彈出式視窗或廣告。<u>使用日程標註師真的是件輕鬆愉快的事情。</u>沒有壓力。沒有煩惱。只有一週七天、一天二十四小時更妥善的規劃。

13 What is DateMarker?

(A) A TV show about digital media

(B) An app for learning a language

(C) A new online dating app

(D) An app for organizing your schedule

日程標註師是什麼？

(A) 一個有關數位媒體的電視節目

(B) 一個語言學習的應用程式

(C) 一個新的約會應用程式

(D) 一個規劃行程的應用程式

正解 **(D)**

題目詢問日程標註師是什麼。由獨白中的 With DateMarker ... 以及 The app ... provide you with the ultimate platform for managing your schedule. 可知 DateMarker 是一款規劃行程的應用程式，故答案選 (D)。

- -

14 What does the speaker mean when she says, "Using DateMarker really is a walk in the park"?

(A) DateMarker is very portable.

(B) It is easy to use DateMarker.

(C) The app is good for dating.

(D) DateMarker plans activities.

說話者提到 "Using DateMarker really is a walk in the park" 時的言下之意是什麼？

(A) 日程標註師非常便於攜帶。

(B) 日程標註師非常容易操作。

(C) 這個應用程式有利於約會。

(D) 日程標註師可以安排活動。

正解 **(B)**

本題考句意。由題目句的前後文 The app combines a user-friendly interface ...、No stress. No worries. Just better organization ... 可知是在說明此應用程式容易使用的優點，故選項 (B) 為符合上下文意的答案。慣用語 be a walk in the park 用來比喻就像在公園散步一樣，是輕而易舉的事。

- -

15 What is a feature of DateMarker?

(A) Traditional calendar

(B) Interesting pop-ups

(C) User-friendly interface

(D) Advertisements

日程標註師主打什麼特色？

(A) 傳統的行事曆

(B) 有趣的彈出式視窗

(C) 容易操作的介面

(D) 廣告

正解 **(C)**

本題詢問此應用程式主打的特色。由關鍵句 The app combines a user-friendly interface ... 可知易於使用的介面是日程標註師的特色，故答案選 (C)。

Questions 16-18 refer to the following talk and web page.

Hi everyone. A basic version of the new system has gone live, but only some parts are in use, as the system is still being updated. To log on to the server, just click the icon on your desktop then enter your username and password. Your username is a number on the piece of paper you were given yesterday. It's not the company ID number on your swipe card. As mentioned, access at this time is limited. The links at the top of the page are for fully-operational pages, including the home page on which there is another link to instructions for using the system. The three links on the left side of the page are for sections that have basic functions working, but not all functions. And the links at the bottom are currently not accessible. Are there any questions?

大家好。新系統的一個基礎版本已經上線，但是因為系統仍然在更新中，所以只有部分可以使用。只要點擊桌面上的圖示並輸入帳號和密碼就可以登入到伺服器中。你的帳號是你昨天所收到紙張上所寫的數字。並不是公司門禁卡上的員工識別碼。如上所述，這段期間的使用是有限制的。頁面上方的連結所連到的頁面已可全面使用，包括首頁，而首頁上有另一個連結可連至系統操作說明頁面。頁面左側的三個連結是連到有基礎運作功能的區塊，但尚未完成全部的功能。而頁面底部的連結目前無法使用。還有其他問題嗎？

16 What is the main purpose of this talk?

(A) **To introduce a new system to staff**

(B) To help staff fix user problems

(C) To explain how a website was designed

(D) To tell staff how to change their password

這個獨白的目的為何？

(A) **為了介紹新的系統給員工**

(B) 為了協助員工處理使用者問題

(C) 為了解釋網站是如何設計的

(D) 為了告訴員工如何更改密碼

正解 **(A)**

本題詢問主旨。由關鍵句 A basic version of the new system has gone live . . . 以及後續的相關操作說明，可知答案為 (A)「為了介紹新的系統給員工」。

---

17 Where can listeners find their usernames?

(A) In the instructions

(B) In a link

(C) **On a piece of paper**

(D) On their swipe card

聽者可以在何處取得他們的帳號？

(A) 在操作說明中　　(B) 在一個連結裡

(C) **在一張紙上面**　(D) 在他們的門禁卡上

正解 **(C)**

此為細節題。題目詢問聽者可在何處取得帳號。由關鍵句 Your username is a number on the piece of paper you were given yesterday. 可得知帳號在昨天收到的紙張上，正確答案選 (C)。

---

18 Look at the graphic. Which of the following links is not currently accessible?

(A) The "Home" section

(B) The "Upload" section

(C) **The "Help" section**

(D) The "Edit Files" section

看圖表。下列哪個連結目前並不能使用？

(A)「首頁」部分　　(B)「上傳檔案」部分

(C)**「協助」部分**　(D)「編輯檔案」部分

正解 **(C)**

此為圖表題。由關鍵句 And the links at the bottom are currently not accessible. 可知頁面底部的連結目前無法使用。對照圖表，選項中位在頁面底部的連結為 (C)「協助」。

Part 5: Incomplete Sentences

19 The _____ inside the computer was damaged and had to be replaced.

(A) digital　　　　(B) **chip**

(C) serial number　(D) access

電腦中的晶片已受損且必須被更換。

(A) 數位的　　　　(B) **晶片**

(C) 序號　　　　　(D) 使用權限

正解 **(B)**

本題考字義。依照句意可知空格處填入 (B) chip，表示電腦中的「晶片」受損。

⑳ The new computers we're buying _____ top-of-the-line ones, won't they?

(A) will be　　　　(B) have been

(C) must be　　　　(D) are

我們正要購買的新電腦將會是最先進的，對嗎？

(A) 將會是（未來式）

(B) 一直是（現在完成式）

(C) 肯定是（現在式）

(D) 是（現在式）

正解 (A)

此題考附加問句。附加問句為表未來否定的 won't they，故空格處應選擇肯定且時態一致的未來式，因此答案選 (A)。

㉑ The search button can be found _____ the top of the page, beside the help button.

(A) above　　　　(B) in

(C) at　　　　(D) under

你可以在頁面頂端找到搜尋按鍵，就在支援按鍵旁邊。

(A) 在……之上　　(B) 在……內／之中

(C) 在……定點　　(D) 在……下方

正解 (C)

此題考介系詞的搭配用法。at the top of 表示「在……頂端」之意，符合句意，故正確答案為 (C)。無 above/in/under the top of 之用法，故 (A)、(B)、(D) 均不可選。

㉒ The operating system on this computer needs to be _____ because it is too old.

(A) logged on　　　**(B) updated**

(C) browsed　　　　(D) accessed

這台電腦的作業系統需要被更新，因為它太老舊了。

(A) 登入　　　　　**(B) 更新**

(C) 瀏覽　　　　　(D) 授權使用

正解 (B)

本題考字義。空格後段提到做這個行為的原因是因為作業系統老舊，可推知空格處應指 (B) updated「更新」。

㉓ I've _____ the computer several times already, but the problem persists.

(A) been trying to restarted

(B) tried to restarting

(C) restarted to try

(D) tried restarting

我已經試著重新啟動電腦好幾次，但是問題依舊存在。

(A) 無 been trying to restarted 之搭配用法。

(B) 無 tried to restarting 之搭配用法。

(C) 無 restarted to try 之搭配用法。

(D) 試著重新啟動

正解 (D)

此題考文法。從選項可知本句要表達已「嘗試做某事」，其用法為 try + V-ing / to V.，故正確答案選 (D)。選項 (A) 應改為 been trying to restart、選項 (B) 應改為 tried to restart 才符合文法。

Part 6: Text Completion

Questions 24-27 *refer to the following online article.*

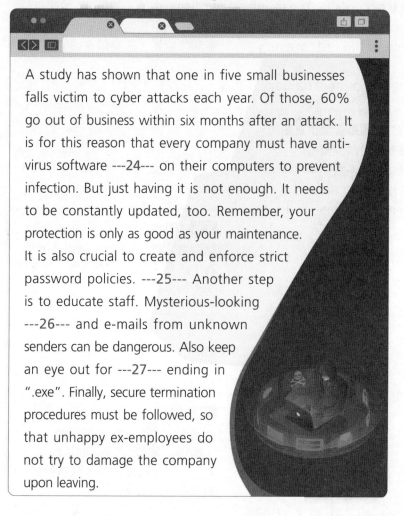

A study has shown that one in five small businesses falls victim to cyber attacks each year. Of those, 60% go out of business within six months after an attack. It is for this reason that every company must have anti-virus software ---24--- on their computers to prevent infection. But just having it is not enough. It needs to be constantly updated, too. Remember, your protection is only as good as your maintenance. It is also crucial to create and enforce strict password policies. ---25--- Another step is to educate staff. Mysterious-looking ---26--- and e-mails from unknown senders can be dangerous. Also keep an eye out for ---27--- ending in ".exe". Finally, secure termination procedures must be followed, so that unhappy ex-employees do not try to damage the company upon leaving.

一則研究顯示每年每五家小型企業中就有一家會淪為網路攻擊的受害者。在這些受害公司中，六成在遭受攻擊後的六個月就會倒閉。正是因為這個原因，每家公司都一定要在電腦上安裝防毒軟體來避免遭受病毒感染。但是光擁有防毒軟體是不夠的。軟體也需要持續更新。切記，您所受到的防護取決於您的維護作業。建立並執行嚴苛的密碼政策也相當重要。良好的、難以猜測的密碼對於電腦安全很重要。另一個步驟是要教育員工。看似神秘的連結和不知名寄件者所寄來的電子郵件可能具有危險性。還有，留意以 .exe 結尾的檔名。最後，一定要遵守安全的解雇程序，這樣心有不滿的前員工才不會在離職時試圖傷害公司。

㉔ (A) installing   (B) installation
   (C) installed   (D) install

(A) 安裝（現在分詞或動名詞）

(B) 安裝（名詞）

(C) 安裝（過去分詞或過去式）

(D) 安裝（原形動詞）

正解 **(C)**

此題考文法。空格前有使役動詞 have 接受詞 anti-virus software，因為受詞防毒軟體是「物」，故空格應選表被動的過去分詞 installed 作為受詞補語，字面上表「每家公司一定要使防毒軟體『被安裝』到他們的電腦上」。have + O. + p.p. 的句型中以過去分詞來呈現受詞被動的狀態，本題答案為 (C)。

㉕ **(A)** **Good, difficult-to-guess passwords are essential to computer security.**

(B) Many companies have strict policies regarding lateness at work.

(C) So don't forget to log out of the system every time you use it.

(D) Viruses can cause a huge amount of damage to a company.

(A) 良好的、難以猜測的密碼對於電腦安全很重要。

(B) 許多公司對於工作遲到都有嚴苛的政策。

(C) 所以不要忘記在每次使用後登出系統。

(D) 病毒可以造成公司的大量損失。

正解 (A)

空格前提到建立並執行嚴苛的密碼政策的重要性，選項 (A) 說明良好的密碼會影響電腦的安全性，使語意前後連貫，故為最合適的答案。

㉖ (A) linked

(B) links

(C) link

(D) linking

(A) 已連結的（過去分詞或過去式）

(B) 連結（名詞）

(C) 連結（動詞）

(D) 連結（現在分詞）

正解 (B)

此題考詞性。keep an eye out for 為「注意；留意」的意思，其後須接名詞，故正確答案為 (B)。

㉗ (A) keyboards

(B) monitors

(C) capacities

(D) filenames

(A) 鍵盤

(B) 螢幕

(C) 容量

(D) 檔名

正解 (D)

此題考字義。由該句所說的「還有，留意以 .exe 結尾的 _____」，可推知符合邏輯的選項為 (D) filenames「檔名」。

Part 7: Reading Comprehension

Questions 28-29 refer to the following e-mail.

To:	all@alleviate.com
From:	palmer.greg@alleviate.com
Subject:	System update

📄 how-to.pdf   📄 System Differences.pdf

Dear Employees,

We are updating our operating system. As has been pointed out, the old one kept crashing. There were two reasons for this. Firstly, it had a lot of bugs. And secondly, it was not compatible with some of our newer software.

The new system will be installed by the technicians this weekend, so employees are hereby instructed to back up their own files to ensure nothing is lost. I've attached a "How to" file outlining the steps for backing up files. Please read through them carefully. Once you have backed everything up, tell Simon Jones, who will come and check that everything has been done correctly.

There are some differences between the new operating system and the old one. The second file I've attached explains these, so please read through these to familiarize yourself with everything. Again, for any questions about backing up files or using the new system, please speak to Simon.

Thank you and have a nice weekend.

Greg Palmer
CEO Alleviate Inc.

收件者：all@alleviate.com
寄件者：palmer.greg@alleviate.com
主　旨：系統升級
📄 說明.pdf　📄 系統差異.pdf

親愛的工作同仁：

我們正在升級我們的作業系統。正如之前被提出的，舊系統不斷當機。主因有兩個。其一，系統有許多瑕疵。其二，它跟我們一些較新的軟體不相容。

新的系統會由技師們在本週末進行安裝，所以在此說明，請員工備份自己的檔案以確保沒有東西遺失。我已附加了一個「說明」的檔案，用以說明備份檔案的步驟。請仔細詳讀。一旦你備份完所有東西，請告知賽門·瓊斯，他會來確認一切都處理妥當。

新的作業系統跟舊系統之間有一些差異。我在第二個附件中進行了說明，所以請詳閱以便使自己全面熟悉新的作業系統。同樣地，如果你有備份檔案或使用新系統的相關疑問，請聯絡賽門。

感謝配合並祝週末愉快。

克雷格·帕爾莫
執行長　艾利維特股份有限公司

28 What most likely is Simon Jones's job?
(A) Software Salesman
(B) Data Entry Assistant
(C) CEO
(D) Technician

賽門‧瓊斯的工作最有可能是什麼？
(A) 軟體業務　　　(B) 資料輸入助理
(C) 執行長　　　　**(D) 技師**

正解 **(D)**
由信件中所提到 Again, for any questions about backing up files or using the new system, please speak to Simon「同樣地，如果你有備份檔案或使用新系統的相關疑問，請聯絡賽門」，可推論賽門‧瓊斯的工作最有可能是技師，故答案選 (D)。

29 What is NOT something that employees are required to do?
(A) Back up files on their computer
(B) Read the attachments in the e-mail
(C) Install the new operating system
(D) Familiarize themselves with the new system

何者並非員工被要求完成的事項？
(A) 備份電腦中的檔案
(B) 閱讀這封電子郵件的附件
(C) 安裝新的作業系統
(D) 熟悉新的作業系統

正解 **(C)**
本題為除外題，詢問下列哪一項並非員工被要求完成的事項。由第二段 The new system will be installed by the technicians this weekend ...「新的系統會由技師們在本週末進行安裝……」，可知員工並未要求要進行新的作業系統安裝，故適合的答案為 (C)。

Questions 30-34 refer to the following flyer and e-mail.

Platinum Cloud

PLATINUM CLOUD STORAGE!

Creating and operating your own server requires time, space, effort, manpower, and most of all—money. And what happens if something goes wrong? Choosing to move your company's data to our server will save you a huge amount of time and money (no more need for backup!), while making your life a whole lot easier.

Why move to the cloud?
-Reduce costs
-Increase security
-Enhance flexibility
-Improve collaboration
-Remove need for daily backup

Why Platinum?
-Free consultation
-Free cancellation and removal
-Free data transfer (first 40TB)
-Only $0.01 per GB (all transfers after 40TB)

Platinum Cloud

白金雲端儲存系統

建立和運作自己的伺服器需要時間、空間、精力、人力和最為重要的──財力。而萬一出錯了怎麼辦？選擇將貴公司的資料儲存至我們的伺服器會為您節省大量的時間和金錢（再也不需要備份！），讓您的生活更為輕鬆容易。

為什麼要移到雲端？
- 節省開銷
- 增加安全性
- 增進彈性
- 提升合作
- 無需日常備份

為什麼選擇白金？
- 免費諮詢
- 免費取消和移除
- 免費資料傳輸（前 40TB）
- 每 GB 只收取一美分（前 40TB 用罄後的每次傳輸）

To: info@platinumcloud.com
From: ATaylor@astarweb.com
Subject: Cloud Storage

Dear Sir/Madam,

My company is going through a period of rapid growth. All our hard drives have reached capacity and we do not possess the resources to run our own server. It is for this reason that I read your flyer with great interest, as I have recently been considering moving my company's data to the cloud.

We are a one-year-old startup and we have 25TB of data that would require immediate transfer. Obviously, we expect that amount to increase over time as the company continues to grow.

I have very little idea of how cloud computing works, so the free meeting was of particular interest to me. What is the deal with this, exactly? Would you send a technician to my office or would I have to pay you guys a visit? Please supply me with as much information as possible and advise me on the next step.

Thank you.

Alan Taylor
(Owner of A-Star Web Design)

收件者：info@platinumcloud.com
寄件者：ATaylor@astarweb.com
主　旨：雲端儲存

敬啟者：

本公司正在經歷一段迅速成長期。我們所有的硬碟都已經到達容量上限，而我們並沒有資源來運作自己的伺服器。正因為如此，我看到了您的傳單時很感興趣，因為我目前正在考慮將本公司資料上傳到雲端。

我們是新創一年的公司，我們有 25TB 的資料需要立即轉存。顯然地，我們預計這個數量會隨著日後公司成長而有所增加。

我不太清楚雲端電腦作業如何運作，所以我對於免費諮詢特別感興趣。這個部分究竟是如何進行的呢？你們會派遣一位技師到我的公司抑或是我要造訪你們呢？請盡可能提供我相關資訊，並且提供我下一步的建議。

謝謝。

艾倫‧泰勒
（首星網頁設計公司所有人）

---

30 According to the flyer, what is the disadvantage of running your own server?

(A) A lot of things often go wrong.

(B) You need specialist knowledge.

(C) It requires a lot of resources.

(D) A personal server has limited capacity.

根據傳單，自己運行伺服器的缺點是什麼？

(A) 許多事情經常出錯。

(B) 你需要專業知識。

(C) 需要很多的資源。

(D) 一個私人的伺服器容量有限。

正解 **(C)**

由傳單第一句 Creating and operating your own server requires time, space, effort, manpower, and most of all—money.「建立和運作自己的伺服器需要時間、空間、精力、人力和最為重要的——財力。」，可知符合的答案為 (C)。

31 What is the purpose of the e-mail?

(A) To apologize for something

(B) To answer a customer's questions

(C) To make a direct order

(D) To state interest in a service

此封電子郵件的主旨為何？

(A) 為了因某事道歉

(B) 為了回答顧客的問題

(C) 為了直接下單

(D) 為了表達對一項服務感興趣

正解 **(D)**

本題詢問此封郵件的目的為何。由郵件的最後一段寄件人對於此項服務表達高度的興趣，並提出有關進一步諮詢的流程相關問題，可知選項 (D) 為郵件主旨。

---

32 What kind of business is Mr. Taylor in?

(A) Internet banking   **(B) Web design**

(C) Online fashion   (D) Cloud storage

泰勒先生從事哪方面的工作？

(A) 網路銀行

(B) 網頁設計

(C) 線上時尚產業

(D) 雲端儲存

正解 **(B)**

由電子郵件末端的屬名 Owner of A-Star Web Design「首星網頁設計公司所有人」，可知泰勒先生的工作領域為網頁設計，故答案選 (B)。

---

33 How much would Mr. Taylor have to pay for the first transfer?

(A) Nothing   (B) $0.01

(C) $0.40   (D) $100.00

泰勒先生需要為他的首次傳輸量支付多少費用？

(A) 無需支付   (B) 一美分

(C) 四十美分   (D) 一百美元

正解 **(A)**

此為整合題，由傳單可知，前 40TB 的傳輸量是無需支付費用的，又從信件第二段第一句得知泰勒先生的公司有 25TB 需要轉存，故正確答案為 (A)。

---

34 Which part of the "Why Platinum?" section in the flyer is most appealing to Mr. Taylor?

(A) Free consultation

(B) Free cancellation and removal

(C) Free data transfer (up to 40TB)

(D) Only $0.01 per GB (after 40TB)

傳單中「為什麼選擇白金？」的哪一部分最吸引泰勒先生？

(A) 免費諮詢

(B) 免費取消和移除

(C) 免費資料傳輸（以 40TB 為上限）

(D) 每 GB 只收取一美分（40TB 以後的傳輸量）

正解 **(A)**

泰勒先生在郵件第三段第一句提及他並不清楚雲端電腦作業如何運作，因此對於免費諮詢特別感興趣，故符合題意的選項為 (A)。

P. 237~246

Part 1: Photographs

TRACK 57

❶ (A) A maintenance worker is fixing an escalator.

(B) A plumber is standing by a leaky pipe.

(C) A plumber is driving his truck to work.

(D) A maintenance worker is standing next to a van.

(A) 一名維修工人正在修理電扶梯。

(B) 一名水管工站在破裂的水管旁。

(C) 一名水管工開著他的卡車去工作。

(D) 一名維修工人站在休旅車旁邊。

正解 **(D)**

由圖中男子身上的工具來看，他的工作可能是水管工或維修工人，而因為他站在休旅車旁邊，所以唯一符合的敘述為 (D)「一位維修工人站在休旅車旁邊。」

❷ **(A) A woman is entering an office building.**

(B) A woman is sitting at her office desk.

(C) The office building is being renovated.

(D) The office building is under construction.

(A) 一名女士正進入大樓。

(B) 一名女士坐在她的辦公桌前。

(C) 這棟辦公大樓正在被裝修。

(D) 這棟辦公大樓正在興建中。

正解 **(A)**

圖中女子正要推開門進入大樓，故正確答案為 (A)。

Part 2: Question and Response

❸ What kind of apartment are you looking for?

(A) For a few weeks already.

(B) It's in an old building.

(C) Preferably somewhere quiet.

你在尋找哪一種公寓？

(A) 已經好幾週了。

(B) 在一棟老舊的建築裡面。

(C) 最好是某處安靜的地方。

正解 **(C)**

題目詢問對方尋找的公寓類型。(C) 表示最好是安靜的地段，為合理的回應方式故為正確答案。

(A) 題目並非在詢問時間。

(B) 題目並非在詢問所在地。

---

❹ Would you like a place near a station?

(A) Yes, I take the train daily.

(B) Yes, go straight and turn left.

(C) Yes, trains are often late.

你是否想要在車站附近的房子？

(A) 是的，我每天搭火車。

(B) 是的，直走並左轉。

(C) 是的，火車經常誤點。

正解 **(A)**

題目以 Would 開頭的是非問句，詢問對方是否想要位於車站附近的房子，(A) 以 Yes 回應後進一步說明理由是因為「我每天搭火車」，故為正確答案。

(B) 題意與問路無關。

(C) 題意與火車是否常誤點無關。

---

❺ Why were you late to work?

(A) He was late by 25 minutes.

(B) My neighbors kept me awake.

(C) OK, I'll call you back later.

你為何上班遲到？

(A) 他遲到二十五分鐘。

(B) 我的鄰居們讓我無法入眠。

(C) 好的，我稍後回電給你。

正解 **(B)**

題目以 Why 詢問對方工作遲到的原因，選項中唯一符合邏輯的回應為 (B)「我的鄰居們讓我無法入眠。」，暗示他是因為睡眠不足才遲到。

(A) 題目在問「你」遲到的原因，卻回答「他」遲到多久，答非所問。

(C) 與題意無關。

---

❻ The average mortgage price in the capital city is almost $100,000.

(A) If we raise enough capital, we can start a company.

(B) Really? I thought the average rent was only $1,000.

(C) That's a lot more than the national average!

首都的平均房貸將近十萬美元。

(A) 如果我們募得足夠的資金，就能創立一間公司。

(B) 真的嗎？我以為平均租金只要一千美元。

(C) 這比全國的平均值高出很多！

正解 **(C)**

此題為直述句，描述首都平均房貸的金額。回答可能針對該金額發表意見或想法。(C) 回答「這比全國平均值高出很多！」，為符合邏輯之回覆，故為正解。

(A) 以 capital 的另一定義混淆作答，實與題意無關。capital 在此指「資本；資金」。

(B) 題目在討論房貸的金額，並非房租的金額。

Part 3: Short Conversations

Questions 7-9 refer to the following conversation.

M: Hey, Sarah. There's a really serious water leak in the men's bathroom.

W: Oh, really? Thanks for telling me. Where is it, exactly?

M: It's coming from the ceiling above the sinks.

W: Right. There is a bathroom on the floor above us, so that sounds like it could be a problem with their sinks.

M: That's what I thought. I've put a bucket there for now to catch the **drips**, but if it continues to get worse, I fear part of the ceiling could **collapse**.

W: OK, thanks, Michael. I'll get a plumber to come round and fix it as soon as possible. <u>For the time being</u>, could you make a sign telling people that the bathroom is out of order?

M: Sure. But we'd better tell the plumber to hurry!

- drip *(n.)* 水滴；滴下之液體
- collapse *(v.)* 倒塌

男：嘿，莎拉。男廁裡有很嚴重的漏水狀況。

女：喔，真的嗎？謝謝你跟我說。明確地說是在哪裡呢？

男：水槽上方的天花板有水漏下來。

女：好的。我們上方的樓層有一間廁所，所以聽起來可能是他們的水槽有問題。

男：我也這麼想。我已經在那裡放了一個水桶來接水，但如果情況持續惡化，我擔心一部分的天花板會垮下來。

女：好的，謝謝你，麥可。我會請水管工盡快來修理。與此同時，可以請你做一個標示告訴人們廁所無法使用嗎？

男：沒問題。但我們最好叫水管工加快腳步！

---

7 How does the man think the woman should feel about the leak?

   (A) She should feel patient and relaxed.

   (B) She should feel extremely angry.

   (C) She should feel guilty and apologetic.

   (D) She should feel a sense of urgency.

男子覺得女子應該要對漏水狀況感到如何？

   (A) 她應該要有耐心且放鬆。

   (B) 她應該要感到極度生氣。

   (C) 她應該要心懷愧疚並懷抱歉意。

   (D) 她應該要感到事態急迫。

正解 **(D)**

此題詢問男子覺得女子應對漏水狀況有何感受。由男子在得知女子會請水管工盡快來處理後，最後又再次強調 But we'd better tell the plumber to hurry! 可知男子覺得事態緊急，故答案選 (D)。

(C) apologetic *(adj.)* 表示愧疚的。

❽ What does the woman mean when she says "for the time being"?

(A) Before they set up a warning sign

(B) Until a plumber comes to fix the leak

(C) While the plumber is fixing the leak

(D) Until the ceiling collapses

女子提到 "for the time being" 時，她指的是什麼？

(A) 在他們設好警告標示之前

(B) 直到水管工來修理漏水之前

(C) 正當水管工修理漏水的時候

(D) 直到天花板垮下來之前

正解 (B)

for the time being 是指「與此同時；目前」，根據上下文，女子指的是當她找水管工來處理漏水的同時，男子去做一個標示放在廁所前，故最接近的答案為 (B)。

---

❾ What does the woman tell the man to do?

(A) Make a sign　　(B) Fix the ceiling

(C) Call a plumber　　(D) Speak to staff

女子請男子做什麼事情？

(A) 做一個標示　　(B) 修理天花板

(C) 打電話給水管工　　(D) 跟員工說

正解 (A)

本題詢問女子請男子做什麼。由女子所說 . . . could you make a sign telling people that the bathroom is out of order? 可知女子請男子做一個標示，答案選 (A)。

Questions 10-12 refer to the following conversation and table.

W: You said on the phone that you were looking for somewhere just inside the city, but not too central.

M: Yes, or even in the suburbs. I can't afford to live downtown.

W: OK. And do you prefer a house or an apartment?

M: I'd prefer a house but I'll consider anything if the price is right.

W: Right. And how about furnishings?

M: I'll be bringing my own bed, couch, and closet. But I do need amenities to be included. Specifically, air conditioning, a shower, a washing machine, a TV, and a dryer.

W: I see. Well, let's take a look through our database and see if we have anything that matches your requirements.

女：您在電話上說您在尋找位於市區內的地段，但不要太靠市中心。

男：是的，甚至郊區也可以。我負擔不起住在市中心。

女：好的。那麼您希望住在獨棟房屋或者是公寓呢？

男：我比較喜歡獨棟房屋，但如果價格合理我都會考慮。

女：好的。那麼配置家具的部分呢？

男：我會帶我自己的床、沙發和衣櫥。但我需要含便利設施。特別是空調、淋浴間、洗衣機、電視和烘衣機。

女：我了解了。嗯，讓我們瀏覽我們的資料庫，看看是否有符合您需求的物件。

	Furniture	Washing Machine	Dryer	Air Conditioner
Property 1	✔	✔	✔	
Property 2		✔	✔	✔
Property 3	✔			✔
Property 4		✔		✔

	家具	洗衣機	烘衣機	冷氣機
房產物件 1	✔	✔	✔	
房產物件 2		✔	✔	✔
房產物件 3	✔			✔
房產物件 4		✔		✔

⑩ What type of home is the man willing to consider?

(A) A house　　　　(B) An apartment

(C) A townhouse　　**(D) Any type**

男子會願意考慮哪一種房子？

(A) 獨棟房屋　　　　(B) 公寓

(C) 多棟聯建住宅　　**(D) 任何種類**

正解 **(D)**

本題詢問男子會考慮的房屋類型。由男子所說 I'll consider anything if the price is right「如果價格合理我都會考慮」，可知答案選 (D)。

- -

⑪ What most likely is the woman's job?

(A) College student advisor

(B) Software programmer

(C) Bank clerk

(D) Estate agent

女子的工作最有可能是什麼？

(A) 大學的學生事務顧問

(B) 軟體工程師

(C) 銀行櫃員

(D) 房地產仲介

正解 **(D)**

本題詢問人物身分。由女子記下男子的租屋需求以及搜尋資料庫的行為，可推知女子最有可能是房地產仲介，答案為 (D)。

⑫ Look at the table. Which property is most suitable for the man?

(A) Property 1   **(B) Property 2**

(C) Property 3   (D) Property 4

看圖表。哪一個房產物件可能會最適合男子？

(A) 房產物件 1   **(B) 房產物件 2**

(C) 房產物件 3   (D) 房產物件 4

正解 **(B)**

本題為圖表題，須結合圖表與對話內容作答。由男子所說 I'll be bringing my own bed, couch, and closet. But I do need amenities to be included. Specifically, air conditioning, a shower, a washing machine, a TV, and a dryer. 可知男子自己有一些家具，但會需要一些家用設施。對照圖表，有提供男子所需設備的是房產物件 2，故答案選 (B)。

Part 4: Short Talks

TRACK 60

Questions 13-15 refer to the following excerpt from a meeting.

Let's go over some important points regarding security for the new building. You all visited yesterday and saw how big and impressive the facility is. These are exciting times here at Warren Trogg, with the company continuing to expand by the day. However, with that expansion comes added responsibility. If private information were to fall into the hands of the wrong people, it could cause severe damage. So security is tighter in the new building. You will be getting new swipe cards for the office, and you'll also be given personal access codes for the gate which lets you into the whole block. Visitors need to be met by a member of staff at reception, and then be signed in upon entry. They must also leave their ID at reception, to be retrieved on departure. Is everything clear so far?

我們來看一些新建築保全系統的相關重點。你們昨天全部都參觀了新建築，也看到了設施是多麼雄偉壯觀。隨著公司規模與日俱增，現在對於沃倫特格企業來說，正是激動人心的時刻。然而，隨著規模壯大，責任也隨之而來。如果私密資料落入錯誤的人手裡，可能會帶來嚴重的損失。因此，新建築的保全更為嚴謹。各位會收到新辦公室的門禁卡，也會收到能讓你進入整個大樓區的個人大門通行碼。訪客須在接待處由員工接待，然後進入時要被記錄姓名。他們也需要將身分證件押在接待處，並於離開時取回。目前一切都清楚嗎？

⑬ Who is being addressed?

(A) Company staff

(B) CEO of a company

(C) Visitors to a company

(D) Security staff

誰是談話的對象？

(A) 公司員工   (B) 一間公司的執行長

(C) 一間公司的訪客   (D) 保全員工

正解 **(A)**

本題詢問談話的對象。獨白一開始表明要看一些新建築保全系統的相關重點。而關鍵句在 You will be getting new swipe cards for the office, and you'll also be given personal access codes for the gate which lets you into the whole block.，故推知聽眾為公司員工，正在聽取進入公司新大樓的注意事項，因此答案應選 (A)。

⓮ Why is the company moving to a new office building?

(A) The old office was badly damaged.

(B) The company is growing larger every day.

(C) It has newer and more impressive facilities.

(D) Access to the old office is temporarily blocked.

為什麼公司要搬遷到新的辦公大樓？

(A) 因為舊的辦公室備嚴重損毀了。

(B) 因為公司規模與日俱增。

(C) 因為有更新更好的設施。

(D) 通往舊公司的道路暫時封閉。

正解 **(B)**

由關鍵句 . . . with the company continuing to expand by the day 得知公司規模正在壯大，故可推論公司因擴張而搬遷到更大更新的大樓，答案是 (B)。

⓯ What is required to get into the main gate for the new office block?

(A) A signature　　(B) A swipe card

(C) An access code　　(D) An ID card

進入新的辦公大樓區需要什麼？

(A) 一個簽名　　(B) 一張門禁卡

(C) 一個通行碼　　(D) 一張身分證件

正解 **(C)**

本題為細節題。由關鍵句 . . . you'll also be given personal access codes for the gate which lets you into the whole block. 可知進入大樓區需要一個大門的通行碼，故正確的答案為 (C)。

Questions 16-18 refer to the following presentation and graphic.

Our website offers businesses the chance to make extra money with **minimal** effort. If you have excess space (which could be anything from an entire office block to a single desk or even, yes, a cupboard), why not consider becoming a landlord? After you sign up, we allow space to be listed on our website completely free of charge! We only charge for priority listings and, once a transaction is finalized, you keep 90% of the monthly rent. Our online forms will make it super easy for you to set terms and conditions for the lease and, once a potential tenant has contacted you, the finalization process couldn't be easier. No paperwork, no stress. So try our service today and find the right tenant or buyer for you!

我們的網站提供企業毫不費力就能賺更多錢的機會。如果你有多餘的空間（可以是整個辦公大樓、一張桌子或甚至是，沒錯，一個櫥櫃），何不考慮成為一個房東呢？在您完成註冊後，我們便讓您把空間刊登在我們的網站上，完全免費！我們只向優先刊登的物件收取費用而且一旦交易完成，您可以保留九成的月租。我們的線上表格讓您輕鬆設定租賃條款和條件，且當有潛在租客聯繫您時，結案的流程再簡單不過了。沒有文書作業，也沒有壓力。所以，今天就試試看我們的服務，並為自己找到合適的租客或買家吧！

• minimal *(adj.)* 最小的；最少的

16 What is being promoted in the presentation?
- (A) A company offering real estate lawyer services
- (B) An online bank's mortgage service
- (C) A furniture removals company promotion
- **(D) A website for renting out office space**

簡報中所推廣的是什麼？
- (A) 一間提供房地產相關法律服務的公司
- (B) 一間網路銀行的房屋貸款服務
- (C) 一間家具清運公司的促銷活動
- **(D) 一個出租辦公室空間的網站**

正解 **(D)**
本題詢問簡報中所推廣的為何？獨白先提到若有多餘的辦公空間，可考慮成為房東。而由關鍵句 After you sign up, we allow space to be listed on our website completely free of charge! 可知該網站為一個辦公空間的租賃平台，故選項 (D) 為正確答案。

17 Look at the graphic. How much money will the website keep from the listing of meeting spaces?
- (A) Nothing. The entire rental fee is kept by the landlord.
- (B) The website will keep $135 per month.
- **(C) The website will keep $15 per month.**
- (D) 100% of the rental fee is kept by the website.

看圖表。這筆會議室空間的刊登資料，網站會收取多少費用？
- (A) 完全免費。房東保有全額的租金。
- (B) 網站每個月會酌收一百三十五美元。
- **(C) 網站每個月會酌收十五美元。**
- (D) 網站會收取全額的租金。

正解 **(C)**
本題是圖表題，須結合圖表與獨白資訊作答。答題關鍵在 you keep 90% of the monthly rent「您可以保留九成的月租」，可知一成的月租會由網站收取。而圖表顯示該會議室的租金是每月一百五十美元，一成則為十五美元，故正確答案為 (C)。

⑱ What do the online forms make it easy for landlords to do?

(A) Set terms and conditions

(B) Buy or sell furniture

(C) Find new spaces to lease

(D) Contact potential tenants

線上表格讓房東輕鬆完成什麼？

(A) 設立條款和條件

(B) 買賣家具

(C) 找到租賃地點

(D) 聯繫潛在客戶

正解 **(A)**

本題為細節題，由關鍵句 Our online forms will make it super easy for you to set terms and conditions for the lease ...「我們的線上表格讓您輕鬆設定租賃條款和條件……」，可知正確選項為 (A)。

Part 5: Incomplete Sentences

⑲ People who live in this _____ say they like it because it's very peaceful but also very convenient.

(A) neighborhood　　(B) soil

(C) renovation　　(D) tile

住在這一帶的人們說他們喜歡這一區，因為這裡相當寧靜但也很方便。

(A) 鄰近地區；住家附近

(B) 土壤

(C) 整修

(D) 磁磚

正解 **(A)**

本題考字義。空格前的動詞是 live，可知應填入 (A) neighborhood「鄰近地區」，表居住在「這一帶」。

UNIT **9** Housing & Corporate Property 房屋／公司地產

⑳ Outside the front of the house is a porch with some chairs _____ you can relax and get some fresh air.

(A) whose　　(B) which

(C) where　　(D) whom

屋子外面在前方有一個門廊，上面有些椅子，你可以在那邊休息和呼吸新鮮的空氣。

(A) 他／她／牠／它（們）的（表人或物的所有格關係代名詞）

(B) 那個；那些（表物的關係代名詞）

(C) 那裡（表地點的關係副詞）

(D) 他（們）；她（們）（表人的受格關係代名詞）

正解 **(C)**

本題測驗關係詞。空格前方為地點 a porch with some chairs「有著椅子的門廊」（其中 with some chairs 是用來修飾 porch 的介系詞片語），而空格後方是結構完整的子句，故知空格處應填入表地點的關係副詞 where，引導形容詞子句修飾先行詞 porch，因此答案為 (C)。

㉑ All workers on this construction site, including the foreman, _____ by law to wear a hard hat.

(A) is requiring

(B) are required

(C) require

(D) required

這個工地的所有工人，包含工頭，都依法被要求戴安全帽。

(A) 要求（現在進行式）

(B) 被要求（現在式的被動語態）

(C) 要求（原形動詞）

(D) 要求（過去式或過去分詞）

正解 **(B)**

本題考文法。本句主詞是 All workers「所有工人」，空格後有 by law，可知本句採被動語態。選項中為被動語態（be 動詞 + p.p.）的只有 (B)，故為正確答案，表示工人「被法規要求」戴安全帽。

....

㉒ We keep extra supplies, such as tissue paper and washing liquid, _____ the cabinet under the kitchen sink.

(A) by

(B) at

(C) on

(D) in

我們把多餘的日用品，如衛生紙和洗潔液等，放在廚房水槽下的櫥櫃裡面。

(A) 在……旁邊

(B) 在……地點

(C) 在……上面

(D) 在……裡面

正解 **(D)**

本題考介系詞。本句句意為「把多餘的日用品放在廚房水槽下的櫥櫃 _____」，選項中 (D) in 可表「在某空間內部」，置入後指把物品放在櫥櫃的「裡面」，符合邏輯故選 (D)。

....

㉓ We still have another four months left on the lease, _____?

(A) don't we

(B) won't we

(C) do we

(D) will we

我們還有四個月的租期，不是嗎？

(A) 不是嗎（don't 為現在式否定助動詞）

(B) 不會嗎（won't 為未來式否定助動詞）

(C) 是嗎（do 為現在式肯定助動詞）

(D) 會嗎（will 為未來式肯定助動詞）

正解 **(A)**

本題考附加問句。主要子句中 We still have . . . 為肯定敘述句，時態為現在式，因此附加問句須為否定、且時態同樣要用現在式，故 (A) 為正解。

Part 6: Text Completion

Questions 24-27 refer to the following notice.

CAUTION!

Dear All,

Due to recent issues with a couple of the elevators, a team of repairmen will be working on them ---24--- the next 2-3 days. ---25--- We understand and apologize for the inconvenience. The escalators from the first to the fifth floor are in perfect working order, so please use these and/or the stairs until the elevator system is up and running again. Please also make sure to stay clear of the areas in front of the elevators in order to ---26--- the repair workers to do their job. Thank you for your ---27--- during this time and we apologize once again for the inconvenience.

Security & Maintenance
The Elden Building

注意！

親愛的大家：

由於有些電梯最近出了點問題，一組維修人員會在接下來的兩、三天內進行處理。<u>因此，所有的電梯在進一步通知之前將無法運作。</u>我們了解所造成的不便並深感抱歉。一樓到五樓的手扶梯運作狀態良好，在電梯系統運作之前，請使用手扶梯以及／或者樓梯。也請務必避開電梯前方的區域以便讓維修人員進行作業。感謝您這段期間的耐心，我們再次為造成的不便表示抱歉。

保全和維修部門
艾爾頓大樓

㉔ (A) over
　　(B) with
　　(C) under
　　(D) by

　　(A) 在……期間（表時間）；在……上方（表空間）
　　(B) 和……一起；有了／隨著……（表工具或特質）
　　(C) 在……下方（表空間）
　　(D) 藉由／透過……（表方法）

正解 (A)

此題考介系詞。空格後為 the next 2-3 days，因此應選表時間的介系詞。選項中僅 (A) 可表時間，置入後指「接下來兩、三天內的這段期間」之意，符合語意與文法故為正確答案。

㉕
(A) Unfortunately, we cannot say exactly when the escalators will be working again.

(B) This is a modern system that has a reputation for never breaking down.

(C) So until tomorrow, please use the stairs and/ or escalators.

(D) As a result of this, all elevators are out of order until further notice.

(A) 很遺憾地，我們無法明確告知何時手扶梯會重新運作。

(B) 這是一個現代化系統，以從不故障享有盛名。

(C) 因此直到明天，請使用樓梯以及／或者手扶梯。

(D) 因此，所有的電梯在進一步通知之前都無法運作。

正解 (D)

文章為篇章結構題。空格前一句提到電梯會在接下來的兩、三天內進行維修，若填入選項 (D)，可繼續說明「電梯（因維修的緣故）在進一步通知前將無法運作」，接著下一句則對此造成的不便表示歉意，因此 (D) 連貫前後文意，為適合的答案。

(C) 前一句提到接下來的兩、三天內都要進行維修，故知維修作業並非只持續到明天為止。

㉖
(A) make

(B) cause

(C) allow

(D) force

(A) 使

(B) 造成

(C) 允許

(D) 強迫

正解 (C)

本題考使役動詞與字義。空格後是受詞 the repair workers 加上不定詞 to do，而 (A) make 為使役動詞，其受詞後須接原形動詞故不可選。(B)、(C)、(D) 在受詞後須接不定詞，但根據語意，僅 (C) 為適合的答案。allow sb. to V 是「允許某人做某事；讓某人得以做某事」之意，故選 (C)。

㉗
(A) patient

(B) patience

(C) patients

(D) patiently

(A) 有耐心的（形容詞）；病人（單數名詞）

(B) 耐心（名詞）

(C) 病人（複數名詞）

(D) 耐心地（副詞）

正解 (B)

本題考詞性。空格前方 your 為所有格，可知空格處應填入名詞，又依句意可知最適合的答案為 (B)。

Part 7: Reading Comprehension

Questions 28-30 refer to the following e-mail.

To: Adam Reynolds <a.reynolds@tmail.com>
From: Patricia Johnson <patricia@corpproperty.com>
Subject: Lionsdown Road

Dear Mr. Reynolds,

Thank you for expressing an interest in the property at 32A Lionsdown Road. ---[1]--- I will do my best to answer your questions as far as possible. First of all, yes, the property is still available at the price quoted. ---[2]--- And no, the property does not currently have a restaurant license but it would make a great venue for a restaurant. There are fire escapes on both floors, which make it legally possible to run a restaurant. ---[3]--- **As far as** the construction of a kitchen **goes**, there is a large area in the basement which may be suitable. As you know, it is located in the heart of a commercial district that is famous for its cuisine. ---[4]---

Give me a call if you have any further questions or would like to arrange a viewing.

Thank you,
Patricia Johnson

收件者：亞當‧雷諾斯
　　　　<a.reynolds@tmail.com>
寄件者：派翠西亞‧瓊森
　　　　<patricia@corpproperty.com>
主　旨：萊士登路

親愛的雷諾斯先生：

感謝您對萊士登路三十二 A 號房產感興趣。我會盡可能回答您的一切問題。首先，是的，該房產的報價依然有效。以及，不，該房產目前並沒有餐廳的執照，但會是經營餐廳的絕佳地點。兩個樓層都有逃生梯，因此依法可以經營餐廳。而關於建造廚房，地下室有很大的空間，也許會很適合。就如您所知道的，它位處一個以美食聞名的商業區中心。因此，當地居民和遊客都習慣在該區域用餐。

如果您有其他疑問或想安排看房請不吝來電。

感謝
派翠西亞‧瓊森

• as far as sth. goes *(phr.)* 就某事而言；談到某事；關於某事

28 What is the purpose of the e-mail?

(A) To answer questions about food health and safety

(B) To persuade someone to open a specific business

(C) To answers questions from a potential buyer

(D) To find out information about a new venue

這封電子郵件的目的為何？

(A) 為了回答食安相關的問題

(B) 為了說服某人創立某種公司

(C) 為了回答潛在買家的問題

(D) 為了獲得新場所的資訊

正解 (C)

由郵件第一至二句 Thank you for expressing an interest in the property at 32A Lionsdown Road. I will do my best to answer your questions . . . 以及接下來以 yes 和 no 明確回覆關於某房產的相關問題，可知寄件人在針對潛在買家的一些問題進行回覆，因此答案是 (C)。

---

29 What is NOT listed as a reason why the venue would make a good restaurant?

(A) It already has a restaurant license.

(B) It has fire escapes on both floors.

(C) It has a basement that could fit a kitchen.

(D) It is in a good area for this kind of business.

何者並非該地段適合開餐廳所列出的原因？

(A) 已經具有餐廳的執照。

(B) 兩個樓層都有逃生梯。

(C) 地下室的空間可以容納廚房。

(D) 該地段適合經營這類型的生意。

正解 (A)

本題為除外題，詢問何者並非此房產適合開餐廳的原因。根據第四句的 And no, the property does not currently have a restaurant license . . . ，可知該地並沒有餐廳執照，故 (A) 為正確答案。(B) 可見第五句 there are fire escapes on both floors；(C) 可見第六句 As far as the construction of the kitchen goes, there is a large area in the basement which may be suitable；(D) 可見第一段最後一句 It is located in the heart of a commercial district that is famous for its cuisine。

---

30 In which of the positions marked [1], [2], [3], and [4] does the following sentence best belong? "So local residents, as well as tourists, are used to dining out in the area."

(A) [1]   (B) [2]

(C) [3]   **(D) [4]**

下列句子最適合插入在文中標示為 [1]、[2]、[3]、[4] 的哪一個位置？「因此，當地居民和遊客都習慣在該區域用餐。」

(A) [1]   (B) [2]

(C) [3]   **(D) [4]**

正解 (D)

題目句意指「因此，當地的居民和遊客都習慣在該區域用餐」，推測空格前後可能提及與用餐地段有關的說明。位置 [4] 的前一句提到該餐廳位處一個以美食聞名的商業區中心，可知 [4] 為最適合插入本句的位置。

Questions 31-35 refer to the following letter, enclosed map, and e-mail.

To the shareholders of RealGoods Inc.,

I am writing today to inform you of updates regarding the continued expansion of RealGoods Inc. In January's annual meeting, we reported on the wonderful progress being made at our new Beijing location. I'd like to update you on what is happening with our other enterprises: Tokyo and Delhi. Firstly, construction on the new factory and warehouse in Tokyo remains on track and we fully expect to meet our target opening date of November 30th.

With regards to the India project, our Delhi offices are finally up and running. However, we are still researching factory and warehouse sites that **tick the right boxes**, namely transport links and the availability of local skilled workers. Until we have laid the foundations for our own site, we will rent factory space in Delhi. Expansion can be one of the best ways to drive growth, but it is also inherently high-risk, so we are being as thorough as possible in gathering local knowledge for the Indian market.

We remain optimistic that expansion into the Japanese and Indian markets will be productive, and you can expect to see gains reflected in the next financial report. If all goes as well as forecast over the coming year, we will start looking more closely at the other locations on the enclosed map.

Yours faithfully,

Ron Williams
CEO
RealGoods Inc.

致真善美股份有限公司的股東們：

我今天撰寫此信乃是為了告知各位有關真善美股份有限公司持續拓展的最新狀況。在一月的年度會議時，我們報告了有關於北京新據點的驚人進展。我想要為各位更新我們其他拓點計畫的發展：東京和德里。首先，東京新工廠和倉庫的建設正順利進行，我們可以充分期待能按照計畫在十一月三十號開始啟用。

而關於印度的計畫，我們的德里辦公室終於開始運作。然而，我們仍然在尋找可滿足所有需求的工廠與倉庫的地點，即交通要便利，也要能找到熟練的在地工人。在我們建造自己的工廠之前，我們會在德里租用工廠空間。拓點可能是促進成長的最佳方式之一，但是自然也伴隨著高度風險，因此我們會盡可能徹底地蒐集印度市場的當地資料。

我們保持著樂觀態度，認為拓展至日本和印度市場將能帶來成效，您可以期待在下一份財務報告中看到收穫。如果明年的發展如預期般順利，我們會仔細考慮在附件地圖中的其他地方拓點。

您誠摯的，

榮恩‧威廉斯
執行長
真善美股份有限公司

• tick the right boxes / tick all the boxes *(phr.)* 滿足所有需求（字面意思是「將正確／所有的框框打勾」）

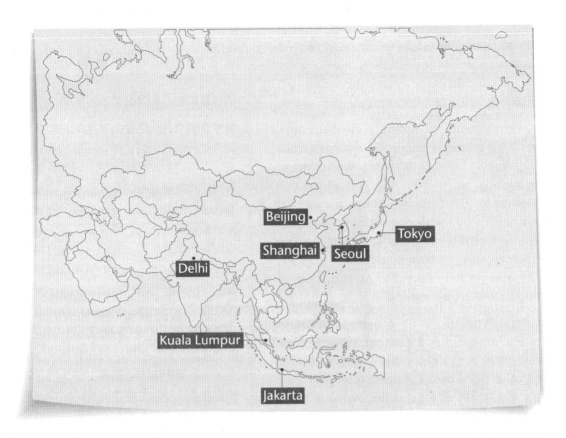

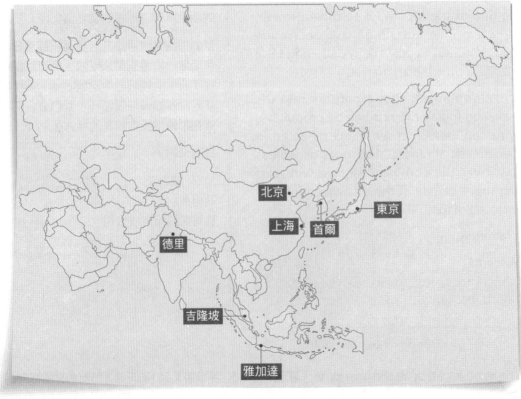

To: Ron Williams <rwilliams@realgoods.com>
From: Raju Singh <rjsingh@imail.com>
Subject: New Asia Locations

Dear Mr. Williams,

I read your recent letter with great interest. Not only have I held shares with RealGoods for almost ten years, but I am also originally from Delhi, India. I understand that good things take time and <u>I am encouraged by your attention to detail in this matter</u>. I think the idea to rent space until this is achieved is a good one, as it is important to get into the market as soon as possible. I do, however, have some concerns. It is always a delight when new buildings complement the local architecture instead of merely adding another "eyesore" to the skyline. So I would like to be forwarded any designs for new buildings when they come about. I also hope that a company as RealGoods would be aiming to continue its care in the community projects. As well as providing jobs and contributing to the economy, it is vitally important to help out local neighborhoods wherever possible. Can you tell me what the plans are with regards to this?

Thank you very much.

Sincerely,
Raju Singh

收件者：榮恩‧威廉斯
　　　　<rwilliams@realgoods.com>
寄件者：拉賈‧辛格
　　　　<rjsingh@imail.com>
主　旨：亞洲新地點

親愛的威廉斯先生：

我帶著極大的興趣讀了您最近的信件。我不僅持有真善美公司的股票將近十年，我也是印度德里出身的。我明白好事多磨，您在這件事情上對細節的關注，也讓我受到了鼓舞。我覺得租用空間直到確認好所有細節的想法很好，因為盡早地投入到市場相當重要。然而，我也的確有一些疑慮。每當新建築物為當地建築增色，而非僅是把另一個「礙眼的東西」加入天際線時，總是令人感到愉悅。因此我想要收到新建築物的每一份設計。我也希望一間如真善美這樣的公司可以將延續社區關懷計畫設為目標。除了提供工作機會以及貢獻經濟，盡可能地幫助當地社區也是極度重要的。可以請您告訴我這部分的規劃嗎？

十分感謝。

誠摯的，
拉賈‧辛格

31 What kinds of projects are being discussed?

(A) Marketing analysis projects
(B) Staff development and training
(C) Financial reports for the previous year
(D) The opening of new overseas locations

什麼類型的計畫正在被討論？

(A) 行銷分析報告　　　(B) 員工發展和訓練
(C) 前一年度的財務報告 **(D) 新海外據點的開拓**

正解 (D)

由信件的第一段第三句 I'd like to update you on what is happening with our other enterprises: Tokyo and Delhi. 「我想要為各位更新我們其他拓點計畫的發展：東京和德里。」，可知主要的討論事項是海外據點的拓展報告，故答案選 (D)。

32 The word "sites" in paragraph 2, line 2 of the letter is closest in meaning to

(A) markets　　　　　**(B) locations**
(C) websites　　　　　(D) properties

信件中第二段第二行的 "sites" 字義與何者最接近？

(A) 市場　　　　　　**(B) 地點**
(C) 網站　　　　　　(D) 財產

正解 (B)

本題考同義字，詢問與 sites 意思最相近的字。site 可指「地點；場所」，在文中指的是「適合用來建造工廠與倉庫的地點」，意近選項中的 (B) location。

㉝ What is NOT mentioned as a consideration for the India project?

(A) Transport links

(B) Availability of local workers

(C) National growth forecast

(D) Local knowledge

何者並非印度計畫所提及的考量？

(A) 交通便利性　　(B) 在地工人的可得性

(C) 國內成長預測　(D) 當地知識

正解 (C)

本題為除外題，詢問何者並非印度計畫所提及的考量。(A) 和 (B) 可見信件第二段第二句 . . . namely transport links and the availability of local skilled workers；(D) 可見信件第二段最後一句 as thorough as possible in gathering local knowledge for the Indian market。唯有選項 (C) 未提及，故為正確答案。

㉞ How many additional cities will RealGoods look at if everything goes well?

(A) 1　　　　　　(B) 2

(C) 3　　　　　　**(D) 4**

如果一切順利，真善美公司考慮還要拓展到幾個城市？

(A) 一個　　　　　(B) 兩個

(C) 三個　　　　　**(D) 四個**

正解 (D)

本題為整合題。信件第一段的第二至三句提及目前正在進行的拓展計畫有北京、東京和德里，對照地圖，除了上述三個地點之外，還有四個被標示的城市，分別是上海、首爾、吉隆坡與雅加達，因此 (D) 選項為正解。

㉟ What is Mr. Raju Singh referring to when he says, "I am encouraged by your attention to detail in this matter"?

(A) The company's investment in transportation

(B) The company's thorough research into locations

(C) The company's commitment to meeting deadlines

(D) The company's consideration of local architecture

拉賈・辛格先生提到 "I am encouraged by your attention to detail in this matter" 時，指的是什麼？

(A) 該公司對於運輸工具的投資

(B) 該公司對於新地點的徹底研究

(C) 該公司對於趕上截止期限的投入

(D) 該公司對於當地建築的關心

正解 (B)

電子郵件中，辛格先生提到自己出身德里，而題目句的後一句說 I think the idea to rent space until this is achieved is a good one . . .「我覺得租用空間直到確認好所有細節的想法很好……」，可知拉賈・辛格先生是在回應執行長於信件第二段第二至三句所提到的，目前該公司在德里的工廠仍是以租用的方式，尚未自己建造工廠，因為 "we are still researching factory and warehouse locations that tick the right boxes . . ."，故知辛格所謂的 your attention to detail in this matter「在這件事情上對細節的關注」，其中的 matter 指的便是真善美公司為了找出最合適的地點而徹底研究的這件事，答案為 (B)。

P. 257~264

Part 1: Photographs

TRACK 62

 (A) The woman is boarding a flight.

(B) Someone is reading an e-mail message.

(C) A flight attendant is checking some documents.

(D) A passport and ticket are being given to an officer.

(A) 那名女子正在登機。

(B) 有人正在讀一篇電子郵件訊息。

(C) 一名空服員正在檢視一些文件。

(D) 有人正將護照和票券拿給移民官。

正解 **(D)**

圖中的人在櫃檯前方，左手拿著護照，右手拿著一張票證，因此符合圖片的敘述為 (D)。

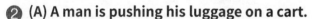 **(A) A man is pushing his luggage on a cart.**

(B) A man is carrying his luggage by hand.

(C) A member of staff is helping the man.

(D) A man is checking in some luggage.

(A) 一名男子正在用推車推行李。

(B) 一名男子正在用手提著行李。

(C) 一位工作人員正在協助那名男子。

(D) 一名男子正在託運一些行李。

正解 **(A)**

圖中可見一名男子正在大廳推著推車，推車上有一些行李，故正確答案為 (A)「一名男子正在用推車推行李。」

Part 2: Question and Response

❸ Hi, could I get a room for tonight, please?
(A) Try calling to see if anything is available.
(B) I'm afraid we don't have any vacancies.
(C) You've booked a room at our discounted rate.

嗨，我今晚想要一間房間，可以嗎？
(A) 試著打電話看看有沒有空房。
(B) 恐怕我們沒有空房了。
(C) 您已用我們的折扣價訂了一間房間。

正解 (B)

本題為以助動詞 could 開頭的是非問句，回應可能為表示肯定、否定或不確定的答案。題目問「嗨，我今晚想要一間房間，可以嗎？」，選項 (B) 的回應「恐怕我們沒有空房了。」為表否定的回應，故為正確答案。

(A)、(C) 均和題意不符。

---

❹ What destination do you have in mind?
(A) I'm thinking about Bali.
(B) We leave from London.
(C) No, I don't mind, thanks.

你想去哪一個目的地？
(A) 我在考慮峇里島。
(B) 我們從倫敦離開。
(C) 不，我不介意，謝謝。

正解 (A)

因為題目問 What destination . . . ?，所以答案應提到某地點、場所，故最適合的選項為 (A)；解題關鍵字為 Bali。

(B) 雖然有提到地點 London，但回答離開的地點與題目要問的目的地不符。

(C) 企圖以題目用到的 mind 一字混淆作答，但該字在此是動詞表「介意」，與題意無關。

---

❺ What time is the next bus arriving?
(A) I arrive in Sydney at five o'clock.
(B) The time right now is half past four.
(C) There's a timetable at the bus stop.

下一班公車何時抵達？
(A) 我五點抵達雪梨。
(B) 現在時間是四點半。
(C) 公車站有時刻表。

正解 (C)

問題以 What time 開頭問「下一班公車何時抵達？」，回答應指出某個時間。(C) 雖未明確指出某個時間，但指出公車站有時刻表，言下之意就是到了公車站看到時刻表就會知道公車抵達的時間，故為正確答案。

(A)、(B) 雖都有提到時間，但均與題意不符，故不選。

---

❻ What kind of room will I have?
(A) There's enough legroom.
(B) A business suite.
(C) The maids are kind.

我會住什麼樣的房間？
(A) 腿部空間很足夠。
(B) 商務套房。
(C) 女服務員很親切。

正解 (B)

本題問 What kind of room . . . ?，詢問住宿的房型，因此適合的選項為 (B)。

(A) 以與題目中 room「房間」發音相近的 legroom「腿部空間」一字試圖影響作答，實為與題意無關的答案。

(C) 企圖以題目用到的 kind 一字混淆作答，但該字在此是形容詞表「親切的」，與題意無關。

Part 3: Short Conversations

Questions 7-9 refer to the following conversation with three speakers.

M: Good afternoon, ladies. How was your flight?

W1: Hello, it's nice to finally be here. It's been a long trip and we're pretty tired.

M: Well, I'm sure you'll have a relaxing stay here. Do you have any suitcases I can help you with?

W2: Sure. Would you mind **grabbing** one of these big ones in the trunk for me?

M: No problem at all, ma'am.

W2: Great. Here you go.

M: OK, please follow me to the check-in counter. Right this way, please.

W1: I can't wait to pick up the keycards and get to our room.

W2: Same here. I'm looking forward to taking a nice long nap before dinner.

• grab *(v.)* 拿

男：女士們午安。旅途還順利嗎？

女一：你好，很高興終於到這裡了。這趟旅程很漫長，我們很累了。

男：嗯，我確定妳們會在這裡住得輕鬆愉快。妳們有行李要我幫忙提的嗎？

女二：當然。你可以幫我拿後車箱裡的其中一個大行李嗎？

男：完全沒問題，女士。

女二：太棒了。拿去吧。

男：好的，請跟我到登記入住的櫃檯。請往這邊走。

女一：我等不及要拿房卡到我們的房間了。

女二：我也一樣。我期待在晚餐前好好睡一下。

---

❼ What are the guests doing?
(A) Leaving their home
(B) Arriving at a hotel
(C) Getting on a plane
(D) Collecting luggage at an airport

這些客人們在做什麼？
(A) 離開家
(B) 到達一間旅館
(C) 上飛機
(D) 在機場拿行李

正解 **(B)**

本題問「這些客人們在做什麼？」。第一位女子一開始表示剛結束一段很長的旅程，之後男子要她們跟著他到櫃檯（check-in counter），接著女子說 I can't wait to pick up the keycards and get to our room. 表示等不及拿房卡到她們的房間了，因此可知這些客人們應是剛到旅館，答案選 (B)。

❽ What most likely is the man's job?

(A) Housekeeper

(B) Receptionist

(C) Concierge

(D) Bellhop

男子的工作最有可能是什麼？

(A) 飯店打掃人員

(B) 接待員

(C) 服務台職員

(D) 行李員

正解 (D)

本題問男子的工作類型。關鍵句是他在第三行所說 Do you have any suitcases I can help you with? 「妳們有行李要我幫忙提的嗎？」因此可知其工作應是 (D)「行李員」。

---

❾ What do the guests say they want to do soon?

(A) They want to have dinner.

(B) They want to relax in the room.

(C) They want to go on a long trip.

(D) They want someone to pick them up.

這些客人們說她們想很快做什麼事？

(A) 她們想要吃晚餐。

(B) 她們想要在房間放鬆。

(C) 她們想要去長途旅行。

(D) 她們想要某人來接她們。

正解 (B)

針對本題所問「這些客人們說她們想很快做什麼事？」，可從最後兩位女子分別說到 I can't wait to pick up the keycards and get to our room.「我等不及要拿房卡到我們的房間了。」以及 I'm looking forward to taking a nice long nap before dinner.「我期待在晚餐前好好睡一下。」得知答案為 (B)「她們想要在房間放鬆。」

(A) 因女子說想在晚餐前睡一下，所以她們想先休息放鬆，而非先吃晚餐。

(C) 她們剛結束一段長途旅行非常疲憊，所以應不會想很快再進行一次長途旅行。

(D) 想以發音相同片語 pick up 混淆作答，但該片語在選項裡是指「接（某人）」，而非對話中的「拿（某物）」。

Questions 10-12 refer to the following conversation and timetable.

M: Good evening. Could you tell me the most **efficient** way of getting into the city?

W: The fastest way is the express train, but the shuttle bus is the cheapest.

M: How fast is the express train and how much does it cost?

W: The next express train from the airport leaves in 10 minutes and the **journey** takes 15 minutes. It costs fifteen dollars and the entrance is right here.

M: OK. It's 6:30 p.m. now. So I would arrive in the city at 6:55 p.m. How about the shuttle bus?

W: That takes 30 minutes and the next one leaves in 30 minutes. It's only five dollars.

M: I can't **afford** to wait that long. I'll just take a ticket for the express train. Thanks.

- efficient *(adj.)* 效率高的
- journey *(n.)* 行程
- afford *(v.)* 承受得起

男：晚安。妳能告訴我進城最有效率的方法嗎？

女：最快的方法是高速列車，但接駁車是最便宜的。

男：高速列車有多快，要花多少錢？

女：下一班從機場出發的高速列車在十分鐘內就會發車，路程會花十五分鐘。這要花十五美元，入口就在這裡。

男：好的。現在是下午六點半。所以我會下午六點五十五分到達城市。那接駁車呢？

女：那會花三十分鐘，下一班接駁車會在三十分鐘內發車。票價只要五美元。

男：我等不了那麼久。那我就買一張高速列車票。謝謝。

Express Train		Shuttle Bus	
Train No.	Leaving Times	Bus No.	Leaving Times
41B	18:10	102	18:00
42A	18:40	104	19:00
43B	19:10	111	20:00
44A	19:40	118	21:00

高速列車		接駁車	
列車號碼	發車時間	接駁車號碼	發車時間
41B	18:10	102	18:00
42A	18:40	104	19:00
43B	19:10	111	20:00
44A	19:40	118	21:00

10 Where most likely is the conversation taking place?

(A) In a restaurant

(B) In an airport

(C) On a train

(D) In a train station

這段對話最有可能在哪裡發生？

(A) 餐廳裡

(B) 機場裡

(C) 火車上

(D) 火車站裡

正解 **(B)**

題目問「這段對話最有可能在哪裡發生？」。男子一開始問進城的方法，女子接下來說了兩個方法，其中談到高速列車時說 The next express train from the airport leaves in 10 minutes and the journey takes 15 minutes.「下一班從機場出發的高速列車在十分鐘內就會發車，路程會花十五分鐘。」，可知他們人在機場，答案選 (B)。

---

11 What is the man's main concern when choosing how to travel?

(A) Convenience

(B) Money

(C) Time

(D) Comfort

當男子選擇旅行的方式時，他主要擔心什麼事？

(A) 方便性

(B) 金錢

(C) 時間

(D) 舒適度

正解 **(C)**

針對此題所問「當男子選擇旅行的方式時，他主要擔心什麼事？」，可從男子最後所說 I can't afford to wait that long.「我等不了那麼久。」得知他在趕時間，答案選 (C)。

---

12 Look at the graphic. Which train number does the man buy a ticket for?

(A) 42A

(B) 43B

(C) 44A

(D) 41B

看圖表。男子買了哪一張列車號碼的票？

(A) 42A

(B) 43B

(C) 44A

(D) 41B

正解 **(A)**

本題問男子買了哪個時間的票，須結合對話與圖表來回答。關鍵為男子最後說會買高速列車票，又女子提到高速列車在十分鐘內就會發車，路程會花十五分鐘。之後男子又說 OK. It's 6:30 p.m. now. So I would arrive in the city at 6:55 p.m.「好的。現在是下午六點半。所以我會下午六點五十五分到達城市。」可推知他買的票的發車時間應是下午六點四十分，再對照圖表，可看到 18:40 這班車的號碼為 42A，故 (A) 為正解。

Part 4: Short Talks

Questions 13-15 refer to the following radio advertisement.

Being **frequent** business flyers ourselves, here at BuzzCase we understand the various issues when dealing with hand luggage. That is why we've designed the ultimate carry-on case. BuzzCase suitcases **allow for** maximum storage, which means you can take all those valuable belongings with you into the cabin. Our cases are fitted with 360 degree rotating wheels that allow you to move easily when getting through the airport; what's more, they can be opened and closed while standing in an **upright** position. Easy side pocket access enables you to speed **effortlessly** through airport security. BuzzCase cases are also extremely light, which means easy access to and **retrieval** from the overhead compartment. For the business traveler, look no further than BuzzCase. Visit our website at www.buzzcase.co.uk to view our full range of products.

- frequent *(adj.)* 頻繁發生的
- allow for *(phr.)* 使……變得有可能
- upright *(adj.)* 直立的
- effortlessly *(adv.)* 輕鬆地
- retrieval *(n.)* 取回

身為經常搭飛機的商務旅客，巴茲皮箱的我們了解手提行李的各種問題。那就是我們設計這只終極隨身皮箱的原因。巴茲皮箱的手提箱能提供最大的儲藏空間，這意味著你可以把所有貴重物品一起帶上機艙。我們的皮箱配有三百六十度旋轉輪，方便你通過機場；更重要的是，它們可以直立開關。側袋容易打開，讓你能輕鬆加速通過機場安檢。巴茲皮箱的手提箱也極度輕巧，這意味著不管是從上方置物櫃放箱子或拿箱子都很容易。對商務旅客來說，巴茲皮箱就是最好的選擇。請上我們的網站 www.buzzcase.co.uk 來看看我們全系列的商品。

---

13 What is being promoted in the advertisement?
(A) Personal security
(B) Travel luggage
(C) Transport rental
(D) Home storage

這則廣告在推銷什麼東西？
(A) 人身安全
(B) 旅行行李箱
(C) 出租交通工具
(D) 家庭儲藏櫃

正解 **(B)**
題目問廣告在推銷什麼。由關鍵句 That is why we've designed the ultimate carry-on case.「那就是我們設計這只終極隨身皮箱的原因。」以及後續針對手提箱特色的描述，可知是在推銷 (B)「旅行行李箱」。

14 What does the speaker mean when he says, "look no further than BuzzCase"?
(A) Don't ask questions about BuzzCase.
(B) Don't consider other options besides BuzzCase.
(C) Don't travel too far without BuzzCase.
(D) It's not difficult to find a BuzzCase.

當說話者提到 "look no further than BuzzCase" 時，他的言下之意是什麼？
(A) 別問關於巴茲皮箱的問題。
(B) 除了巴茲皮箱，不用考慮其他選擇。
(C) 別沒帶巴茲皮箱就到太遠的地方旅行。
(D) 要找到一只巴茲皮箱並不難。

正解 (B)

further 指「更遠的」。look no further 字面意思是「到此為止，不用再找了」，即「眼前的事物就是最佳選擇」的意思。因此與該句意最接近的答案為 (B)。

15 Who is being addressed?
(A) Cabin crew
(B) Business Travelers
(C) Suitcase manufacturers
(D) Vacationers

談話的對象是誰？
(A) 機艙人員　　　**(B) 商務旅客**
(C) 手提箱製造商　(D) 度假者

正解 (B)

本題問「講話的對象是誰？」。從說話者一開始說他們身為經常搭飛機的商務旅客，很了解手提行李的各種問題。倒數第二句又說 For the business traveler, look no further than BuzzCase.「對商務旅客來說，巴茲皮箱就是最好的選擇。」，可推測其對象最有可能是 (B)「商務旅客」。

Questions 16-18 refer to the following welcome speech and itinerary.

Hello and welcome to Avast Tours! I'm your tour guide, Tabatha. Today, we'll see famous landmarks, including stunning architecture and an ancient bridge before taking a stroll through the fascinating **winding** streets of the old town. Then, we'll head over to the dock area for dinner at Captain Jack's Sea Shack. As you have already been notified, Captain Jack's is hosting a private event today, so dinner will be half an hour later than scheduled. Believe me, it'll be worth the wait. Jack's offers a magnificent view of the sun setting over the harbor. And finally, we'll visit the lighthouse. Entry is free but the ferry charges a small fare. At the top, there are telescopes from which we can view the night stars. Sounds great, right? The **coach** will now take us to our first destination, Saint Martin's Church!

您好，歡迎來到艾維斯特旅遊！我是你們的導遊塔芭瑟。今天我們會看到著名的地標，包括美輪美奐的建築以及一座古橋，之後會在古鎮迷人的蜿蜒街道上散步。然後我們將前往碼頭區的傑克船長海洋小屋餐廳用晚餐。正如先前所通知的，傑克船長今天正主辦一場私人活動，所以晚餐會比預定時間晚半小時開始。相信我，等待是值得的。傑克的餐廳提供碼頭壯麗的夕陽景色。最後我們會造訪燈塔。雖然進場免費，但是搭乘渡輪會收取少許費用。塔頂會有望遠鏡，在那裡我們可以觀看夜星。聽起來很棒，對吧？現在巴士會載我們到第一個目的地，聖馬丁教堂！

- winding *(adj.)* 曲折的　　　• coach *(n.)* 巴士

Saint Martin's Church	11:00
Lunch	13:00
Dunphy's Bridge	15:30
The Old Streets	17:30
Dinner	19:30
Farnley's Lighthouse	21:00

聖馬丁教堂	11:00
午餐	13:00
鄧菲橋	15:30
老街	17:30
晚餐	19:30
法恩利燈塔	21:00

⑯ Why should the tour group look forward to visiting the harbor?
(A) Because the food there is delicious
(B) Because it offers a great sunset view
(C) Because they can use telescopes
(D) Because it has fascinating streets

為什麼旅行團應該要對造訪碼頭一事感到期待？
(A) 因為那裡的食物很美味
(B) 因為它提供了很棒的夕陽景色
(C) 因為他們可以使用望遠鏡
(D) 因為它有迷人的街道

正解 **(B)**
題目問旅行團期待造訪碼頭的原因。答題關鍵句為 Believe me, it'll be worth the wait. 以及下一句 Jack's offers a magnificent view of the sun setting over the harbor.，故答案選 (B)「因為它提供了很棒的夕陽景色」。

⑰ What will the speaker do next?
(A) Take the group for a walk around the dock
(B) Show the group how to use a telescope
(C) Tell the group about the dock area
(D) Take the group to Saint Martin's Church

說話者接下來會做什麼事？
(A) 帶團在碼頭附近散步
(B) 向旅遊團展示如何使用望遠鏡
(C) 告訴旅遊團關於碼頭區的事
(D) 帶團到聖馬丁教堂

正解 **(D)**
題目問「說話者接下來會做什麼事？」。答題關鍵在最後一句 The coach will now take us to our first destination, Saint Martin's Church!「現在巴士會載我們到第一個目的地，聖馬丁教堂！」，可見答案是 (D)。

⑱ Look at the itinerary. When will the tour group eat dinner?
(A) 20:00　　　　(B) 19:30
(C) 20:30　　　　(D) 19:00

看行程表。旅遊團何時會吃晚餐？
(A) 20:00　　　　(B) 19:30
(C) 20:30　　　　(D) 19:00

正解 **(A)**
這是圖表題，題目問旅遊團何時會吃晚餐。若單看圖表，晚餐是 19:30 開始。但根據獨白，因為傑克船長餐廳主辦一場私人活動的緣故，晚餐會比預定時間晚半小時開始（dinner will be half an hour later than scheduled），可知 (A) 20:00 才是他們實際用餐的時間。

Part 5: Incomplete Sentences

19 I advised Jason to apply for this sales manager _____ at Thomson Airlines because I think he would be perfect for the job.

(A) captain   (B) landing

(C) vacancy   (D) crew

我建議傑森申請湯姆森航空公司的銷售經理一職，因為我覺得他會很適合這份工作。

(A) 船長   (B) 降落

(C) 缺額   (D) 全體機員

正解 (C)

本題考字義。依照句意可知空格處填入 (C) vacancy 指「缺額」，表示建議傑森申請湯姆森航空公司銷售經理的「職缺」。

---

20 I _____ to over 30 countries, but I would like to go to Africa because I have never been there.

(A) have been

(B) have ever been

(C) haven't been

(D) haven't ever been

我去過超過三十個國家，但我想去非洲，因為我從未去過。

(A) 去過（現在完成式）

(B) ever 通常用於疑問句、否定句以及表示比較和條件的附屬子句，此句為肯定句，故不選

(C) 沒有去過（現在完成式）

(D) 沒有去過（現在完成式）

正解 (A)

本題考文法。由連接詞 but「但是」可以得知空格所在句意應與後面句子相反，因此得知他應「去過」超過三十個國家，但沒去過非洲，答案選 (A)「去過」。

---

21 We will be departing _____ Port McArthur at 8 p.m., and arriving at Gray's Harbor at around 8:45 p.m.

(A) for

(B) from

(C) to

(D) at

我們晚上八點會從麥克阿瑟港出發，然後大約晚上八點四十五分到格雷港。

(A) depart for (+ 地方) 指「前往……」。

(B) depart from (+ 地方) 指「從……出發」。

(C) 無 depart to 之搭配用法。

(D) 無 depart at 之搭配用法。

正解 (B)

本題考片語動詞。depart from (+ 地方) 表示「從……出發」，合乎句意，故 (B) 為正確答案。

㉒ The airline's new baggage _____ service will help travelers cut short waiting times at check-in counters.

(A) duty-free
(B) full-fare
(C) front-desk
(D) drop-off

正解 (D)

本題考字義。依照句意可知空格處填入 (D) drop-off 指「託運的」，表示行李託運服務會幫助旅行者縮短等待的時間。

那間航空公司新的行李託運服務會幫助旅行者縮短在報到櫃檯的等待時間。

(A) 免稅的
(B) 全價的
(C) 櫃檯的
(D) 託運的

㉓ This is an announcement by Southwest Trains: Please let passengers _____ off the train first before boarding.

(A) to get
(B) getting
(C) get
(D) gotten

正解 (C)

本題考文法。空格前有使役動詞 let，得知受詞 passengers 後面的空格應填入原形動詞，適合的答案為 (C) get。

• get off *(phr.)* 下車；離開

這裡是西南火車廣播：請各位在上車之前先讓車上乘客下車。

(A) （不定詞）
(B) （動名詞或現在分詞）
(C) （原形動詞）
(D) （過去分詞）

Part 6: Text Completion

Questions 24-27 refer to the following travel notice.

CONSULATE GENERAL OF INDIA
<u>Travel **Advisory** Notice</u>
<u>For Indian Nationals Visiting Hong Kong</u>

Please note that Indian nationals visiting Hong Kong are required to complete a Visitor Registration Card (VRC) before ---24--- flights. If VRC application is unsuccessful, applicants must apply for a VISA from the Hong Kong Immigration department at least two months prior to travel. ---25--- may be made on the Internet via the official Hong Kong Immigration website, or over the telephone, **and are subject to** a fee. If calling from overseas, please note that individuals may be subject to a higher rate. ---26---

<u>For Indian Nationals Transiting through Hong Kong</u>

Indian passport holders passing through Hong Kong for extensive periods of transit should note that ---27--- may not be permitted to leave Hong Kong airport and enter the city **in absence of** a valid Hong Kong VISA or VRC.

印度總領事館
旅遊警示
針對造訪香港的印度公民

請注意，造訪香港的印度公民必須在預訂航班之前，填妥訪客登記證（VRC）。如果訪客登記證的申請不成功，申請人必須在至少旅行兩個月之前，向香港入境事務處申請簽證。您可以透過香港入境事務處的官方網站線上申請，或是用電話申請，且會產生費用。若是海外的來電，請注意所產生的費用會比較高。<u>關於電話費用以及申請費用的詳情均可在網上找到。</u>

針對過境香港的印度公民

會在香港長時間停留過境的印度護照持有人應注意，未具有效香港簽證或是訪客登記證的旅客不可離開香港機場進到城市裡。

- advisory *(n.)* 警告
- be subject to . . . *(phr.)* 易受……影響；易遭……
- in absence of . . . *(phr.)* 在缺乏……時

㉔ (A) landing
  (B) booking
  (C) docking
  (D) claiming

  (A) 降落
  (B) 預訂
  (C) 停靠
  (D) 要求……的所有權

正解 **(B)**
本題考字義。原句提到造訪香港的印度公必須在＿＿＿航班之前，填妥訪客登記證，故依句意可知最適合的答案為 (B)。

㉕ (A) **Applications**
(B) Applicant
(C) Applicable
(D) Apply

(A) 申請（名詞）
(B) 申請人（名詞）
(C) 適用的（形容詞）
(D) 申請（原形動詞）

正解 **(A)**

本題考詞性與字義。由句構可知空格處為本句主詞，推知空格內應填名詞，故 (C)、(D) 不選；又由空格後方的句意 may be made on the Internet via the official Hong Kong Immigration website 可以得知空格內應填 Applications，表示可在官方網站進行線上「申請」，因此正確答案為 (A)。

㉖ (A) Upon completion of VRC, please make your way to the Immigration department.
(B) All foreign nationals entering Hong Kong will be subject to a search upon arrival.
(C) It is not possible to submit applications via the Hong Kong Immigration official website.
(D) Further information regarding call fees and application fees can be found online.

(A) 完成填寫訪客登記證後，請前往入境事務處。
(B) 所有進入香港的外國公民在到達後會接受搜查。
(C) 透過香港入境事務處的官方網站遞交申請是不可能的。
(D) 關於電話費用以及申請費用的詳情均可在網上找到。

正解 **(D)**

空格的前兩句說 . . . and are subject to a fee. If calling from overseas, please note that individuals may be subject to a higher rate.，指出申請 VRC 會產生費用，且從海外致電申請時費用會比較高，故選項 (D) Further information regarding call fees and application fees can be found online.「關於電話費用以及申請費用的詳情均可在網上找到。」與前文語意連貫，故為正解。

(A) make one's way to . . . (phr.) 前進到⋯⋯。

㉗ (A) we
(B) it
(C) they
(D) she

(A) 我們
(B) 它
(C) 他們
(D) 她

正解 **(C)**

本題考代名詞。原句為 Indian passport holders passing through Hong Kong for extensive periods of transit should note that _____ may not be permitted to . . . ，依句意可知空格內的代名詞是指前面提及的印度護照持有人，在此要表達他們不被允許⋯⋯，因此答案為 (C)。

Part 7: Reading Comprehension

Questions 28-30 refer to the following apartment rental listing.

California Apartment ($150 per night)

2 Bedrooms - PRIME LOCATION!
Apartment Listing by Jon Sanders

Entire apartment:
x5 guests
x2 bedrooms (3 beds)
x1 living room
x1 bathroom

A spacious apartment for rent, within five minutes' walk of the nearest subway station. Downtown location provides easy access to the city center, parks, restaurants, and plenty of art and culture. Apartment is suitable for all types of travelers, from couples, to solo adventurers, business travelers, families, and groups.

The space
A newly renovated space, fully furnished with new furniture, TV (100+ satellite stations + YouTube feature), and Wi-Fi access. Our space fits three people comfortably, and can sleep up to five people.

The services
A 24-hour security guard occupies the front desk in the lobby and housekeeping is included free of charge, once per day. There is a laundromat one block down from the apartment (2-3 minutes' walk).

** 加州公寓 ** (每晚一百五十元)

兩間臥室 - 位在最佳地段！
公寓刊登者：喬恩‧桑德斯

整間公寓：
可容納五位客人
含兩間臥房（三張床）
含一間客廳
含一間浴室

寬敞公寓出租，離最近的地鐵站走路不用五分鐘。市區地段讓您不論到市中心、公園、餐廳或是要接觸許多藝術文化都很方便。公寓適合各種類型的旅行者，從夫妻到單獨的冒險家、商務旅行者、家庭以及團體都很合適。

空間
全新翻修的空間，配備齊全新家具、電視（有超過一百台的衛星頻道，可看 YouTube）並提供 Wi-Fi。我們的空間能舒適地容納三個人，可睡多達五人。

服務
一天二十四小時都有警衛在大廳櫃檯，一天會有一次免費的房間清潔。還有一間自助洗衣店就在一個街區外（走路要兩到三分鐘的路程）。

28 What is implied about the apartment?

(A) It is not suitable for some travelers.

(B) It is in a new building.

(C) It is conveniently located.

(D) It is in a quiet and peaceful area.

關於這間公寓，文中有何暗示？

(A) 對某些旅行者來說並不合適。

(B) 它在一棟新建築物裡。

(C) 它的位置很方便。

(D) 它位在靜謐祥和的區域中。

正解 **(C)**

本題為推論題，詢問該廣告的公寓狀況。解題關鍵在標題下方的 PRIME LOCATION! 與第一段第二句的 Downtown location provides easy access to the city center, parks, restaurants, and plenty of art and culture. ，可知這間公寓的地段很方便，答案選 (C)。

29 What is the maximum number of people that can stay in the apartment?

(A) 2

(B) 3

(C) 5

(D) 6

最多能有多少人住在這間公寓裡？

(A) 二

(B) 三

(C) 五

(D) 六

正解 **(C)**

本題為細節題，詢問最多能有多少人住在這間公寓裡。由廣告上「空間」段落的最後一句 Our space fits three people comfortably, and can sleep up to five people. 可知公寓最多可以住五個人，答案選 (C)。

30 Which service is NOT included in the apartment?

(A) Security

(B) Laundry

(C) Housekeeping

(D) Internet

下列哪一項服務沒有包括在這間公寓裡？

(A) 警衛

(B) 洗衣店

(C) 房間清潔

(D) 網路

正解 **(B)**

本題為除外題，詢問哪一項服務沒有包括在這間公寓裡，解題關鍵在第二段第一句的 . . . and Wi-Fi access. 可知有網路，以及最後一段 A 24-hour security guard occupies the front desk in the lobby and housekeeping is included free of charge, once per day. There is a laundromat one block down from the apartment (2-3 minutes' walk). 可知有警衛和房間清潔服務，但當中提到的自助洗衣店並不在公寓裡，因此答案選 (B)。

SECTION B 試題練習

UNIT **10** Travel 旅遊

Questions 31-34 refer to the following passage.

Visit the beating heart of Kansai, known as Osaka. ---[1]--- Second only to Tokyo in terms of population, and home to Japan's main port, the city is famous for its friendly citizens, laid-back vibe, and delicious cuisine. Here, you will find cultural and historical sites mixed with all the urban **phenomena** of a modern Japanese metropolis.

It is at night when Osaka really comes alive. Indeed, the Dotonbori district offers **futuristic** nightscapes, the likes of which you might expect to see in a science fiction movie— its flashing **neon** lights and **audacious** fashions providing a visual treat for the **onlooker**. ---[2]---

Of course, like everything the Japanese do, the food is **exquisitely** prepared. In addition to culinary delights, further highlights include Osaka Castle and its surrounding **moats**; Osaka Aquarium, famous for its giant whale shark; and a distinctive Open-Air Museum of Japanese Farmhouses. ---[3]--- It is a city to experience in its **totality**, and leisurely strolls through **backstreets** can be more rewarding than following the route map of an organized tour. ---[4]---

造訪關西的心臟地帶,這裡被稱為大阪。其人口僅次於東京,並且是日本主要港口的所在地,該市以其友善市民、悠閒的氣氛與美食而聞名。在這裡,你會發現融合著現代日本大都市現象的文化與歷史遺跡。

到了晚上,大阪才真正開始熱鬧起來。的確,道頓堀區提供了具未來風格的夜景,像這樣的景色你也許只會期待在科幻電影裡看到——它那閃爍的霓虹燈光以及大膽的時尚都為圍觀者提供了視覺的饗宴。

當然,就像日本人所做的每件事情一樣,這裡的食物都經過精心準備。除了美食外,更為精彩的部分包括了大阪城與其周圍的護城河;以其大鯨鯊聞名的大阪水族館;以及一間特殊的日本民家集落博物館。然而,大阪就像東京一樣,除了遺址外還有更多可以逛的地方。這是一座要整體去體驗的城市,而悠閒地漫步在舊城區會比按照跟團旅遊的路線圖走還要令人滿足。

- phenomenon *(n.)* 現象(複數為 phenomena)
- neon *(n.)* 霓虹燈
- onlooker *(n.)* 旁觀者
- moat *(n.)* 護城河
- backstreets *(n.)* (城鎮中的)舊區
- futuristic *(adj.)* 未來派的;超前新奇的
- audacious *(adj.)* 大膽的
- exquisitely *(adv.)* 精緻地
- totality *(n.)* 全部

31 Where would this passage most likely appear?
(A) On a newspaper front page
(B) In a science-fiction novel
(C) In a travel brochure
(D) In a history book

這篇文章最有可能在哪裡出現?
(A) 在一份報紙的頭版　　(B) 在一本科幻小說裡
(C) 在旅遊指南裡　　(D) 在一本歷史書裡

正解 **(C)**

本題為推論題,詢問這篇文章最有可能在哪裡出現。本篇文章主要在介紹大阪這座城市的特色和值得遊玩的地方,可以推論出這篇文章最有可能出現在旅遊指南裡,提供到大阪旅遊的資訊,故答案選 (C)。

32 The word "vibe" in paragraph 1, line 3, is closest in meaning to

(A) discussions

(B) atmosphere

(C) views

(D) appearance

第一段第三行的單字 "vibe" 意思最接近

(A) 討論

(B) 氣氛

(C) 景色

(D) 出現

正解 **(B)**

本題為字義題。原文中 laid-back vibe 的 vibe 指的是「氣氛」，在此是在描述大阪這個城市的氣氛令人感到悠閒放鬆，含義最接近的選項為 (B) atmosphere。

---

33 What is NOT listed as a reason to visit Osaka?

(A) The nightlife

(B) Osaka Castle

(C) A unique museum

(D) An organized tour

下列何者不是被列為造訪大阪的理由？

(A) 夜生活

(B) 大阪城

(C) 特殊的博物館

(D) 跟團旅行

正解 **(D)**

本題為除外題，詢問何者不是被列為造訪大阪的理由。(A) 由第二段第一句 It is at night when Osaka really comes alive . . . 可知大阪的夜生活很熱鬧；(B)、(C) 由第三段第二句 . . . further highlights include Osaka Castle and its surrounding moats . . . and a distinctive Open-Air Museum of Japanese Farmhouses. 可知大阪城和特殊的日本民家集落博物館都是造訪大阪的賣點。唯獨 (D)「跟團旅行」沒有被列為造訪大阪的理由，故答案選 (D)。

---

34 In which of the positions marked [1], [2], [3], and [4] does the following sentence best belong?

"However, like Tokyo, Osaka has more to offer than just its sites."

(A) [1]   (B) [2]

(C) [3]   (D) [4]

下列句子最適合插入在文中標示為 [1]、[2]、[3]、[4] 的哪一個位置？

「然而，大阪就像東京一樣，除了遺址外還有更多可以逛的地方。」

(A) [1]   (B) [2]

(C) [3]   (D) [4]

正解 **(C)**

題目句指出大阪除了遺址外還有更多可以逛的地方。位置 [3] 的前面列舉大阪值得一看的景點，後一句則提到大阪是一座要整體去體驗的城市，而悠閒地漫步在舊城區會很令人滿足，因此題目句最適合置於此以銜接上下文意，故答案選 (C)。

Unit 11 — Dining Out 外食

P. 276~284

Part 1: Photographs

1 (A) A man has a napkin.
(B) A waiter is delivering food.
(C) A man has a glass of wine.
(D) A man's checking a menu.

(A) 男子有一張紙巾。
(B) 服務生正在送餐。
(C) 男子有一杯紅酒。
(D) 男子正在看菜單。

正解 **(D)**

圖中男子手上正拿著菜單在看，因此符合圖片的敘述為 (D)「男子正在看菜單」。

(B) 圖中未見食物且服務生是在準備接受點餐。
(C) 圖中的杯子是空的。

2 (A) The beef is in the refrigerator.
(B) Meat is being grilled on a barbecue.
(C) Two steaks have just been eaten.
(D) Barbecue sauce is being placed on a dining table.

(A) 牛肉在冰箱裡。
(B) 肉正在烤肉架上燒烤。
(C) 兩份牛排剛被吃掉。
(D) 烤肉醬被放在餐桌上。

正解 **(B)**

圖中可見有肉在烤肉架上烤，故正確答案為 (B)。

Part 2: Question and Response

❸ Hi, I'd like to order the lemon salmon.
  (A) I love fish with pepper, too.
  (B) Sure, and anything for dessert?
  (C) Yes, everything is in working order.

  嗨，我想要點檸檬鮭魚。
  (A) 我也喜歡魚搭配胡椒。
  (B) 沒問題，要點什麼當甜點嗎？
  (C) 是，一切都正常運作。

正解 (B)

本題為直述句，說「我想要點檸檬鮭魚。」。選項中唯一合理之回應為 (B)「沒問題，要點什麼當甜點嗎？」

(A) 回答內容與題目無關。
(C) 企圖以題目中用到的 order 一字混淆作答；片語 in working order 表「（機器等）正常運作中」。

---

❹ What kind of turnout do we expect for the banquet?
  (A) From 6 p.m. till 8 p.m.
  (B) Three dishes each.
  (C) At least 100.

  宴會預計有多少人出席？
  (A) 從下午六點到晚上八點。
  (B) 每人三道菜。
  (C) 至少一百人。

正解 (C)

本題詢問宴會的出席人數，回答應說明數量。(C) 回覆「至少一百人」，為符合邏輯之理由，故為正解。

(A) 和 (B) 回答內容皆與題目無關。

---

❺ I really fancy a curry tonight.
  (A) Oh, I had that last night.
  (B) Oh really, how was it?
  (C) Italian is my favorite.

  我今晚很想吃咖哩。
  (A) 喔，我昨晚吃了。
  (B) 喔，真的嗎，吃起來如何？
  (C) 義大利菜是我最喜歡的。

正解 (A)

本題為直述句，fancy 在此作動詞表「想要；愛好」。題目說「我今晚想要吃咖哩。」，選項中唯一符合邏輯之回應為 (A)「喔，我昨晚吃了。」

(B) 題目說想吃咖哩表示還沒吃，回答卻問吃了後覺得如何，與題目時態不符。
(C) 回答內容並未回應到題目。

---

❻ Please let the chef know we loved the meal.
  (A) The chef recommends the meal.
  (B) I'll tell him you're looking forward to it.
  (C) I'd be happy to pass on the message.

  請讓主廚知道我們喜歡這道餐點。
  (A) 主廚建議這道餐點。
  (B) 我會告訴他你很期待。
  (C) 我很樂意傳達這個訊息。

正解 (C)

題目說「請讓主廚知道我們喜歡這個餐點。」，選項中唯一符合邏輯之回應為 (C)「我很樂意傳達這個訊息。」

(A) 題目內容發生於用完餐後，回答卻以現在式描述主廚會推薦的餐點，答非所問。
(B) 回答內容與題意無關。

Part 3: Short Conversations

Questions 7-9 refer to the following conversation.

W: Hey, Mike, shall we make a decision on the restaurant for Allison's fortieth birthday?

M: Yes, we should. It's only a week away, right?

W: Exactly. <u>I've been leaning towards the gourmet option.</u> What are your thoughts?

M: The French restaurant? Count me in! Although I know Nick and Sara were a little concerned about the price.

W: Well, it's a special occasion, so how about we just book it anyway? We can always cancel later if we can't persuade them.

M: Sure thing. Allison's a great boss and she deserves a proper celebration.

W: She does. And she's a real foodie so she'll appreciate it.

女：嘿，麥克，我們是不是應該要決定在哪間餐廳幫愛莉森慶祝四十歲生日了？

男：對，應該要。只剩一週了，對嗎？

女：沒錯。<u>我傾向於選擇美食。</u>你的想法是什麼？

男：那間法國餐廳嗎？算我一份！雖然我知道尼克和莎拉有點在意價錢。

女：嗯，這是特別的場合，所以我們就直接訂位如何？如果不能說服他們，我們之後可以隨時取消。

男：當然。愛莉森是一位很棒的老闆，值得好好幫她慶祝。

女：她是。而且她是個真正的美食家，所以會感謝我們的安排。

❼ When is Allison's birthday?
(A) In 14 days from now
(B) On the 14th day of this month
(C) 7 days from now
(D) In 40 days from now

愛莉森的生日是哪一天？
(A) 現在起十四天內
(B) 這個月的十四號
(C) 現在起七天後
(D) 現在起四十天內

正解 (C)
本題詢問愛莉森的生日。開頭女子說要決定在哪間餐廳幫愛莉森慶生，而男子回覆說 It's only a week away, right? 後，女子回答 Exactly.，可知生日離現在只剩一週，所以答案選 (C)。

8 What does the woman mean when she says, "I've been leaning towards the gourmet option"?

(A) She's been calling a number of gourmet restaurants.

(B) She thinks gourmet food would be the best choice.

(C) She'd prefer a restaurant with lean meats.

(D) She is not considering the gourmet food option.

當女子說 "I've been leaning towards the gourmet option" 時是什麼意思？

(A) 她一直在打電話給許多間美食餐廳。

(B) 她認為美食是最好的選擇。

(C) 她偏好供應瘦肉的餐廳。

(D) 她沒考慮要選擇美食。

正解 (B)

本題詢問女子說 I've been leaning towards the gourmet option 的意思。lean toward sth. 表「傾向於……」，因此本句是在說她傾向於選擇美食，合乎意思的選項為 (B)。

---

9 How does the woman most probably feel about making the reservation?

(A) Bored

(B) Amused

(C) Annoyed

(D) Hurried

關於訂餐廳女子最可能有何感受？

(A) 無聊的

(B) 愉快的

(C) 生氣的

(D) 匆忙的

正解 (D)

本題詢問女子對於訂餐廳的感覺。由男子說 It's only a week away, right? 且稍後女子又說 . . . so how about we just book it anyway? 可得知距離愛莉森生日時間很近，女子想趕快訂位，所以答案選 (D)。

Questions 10-12 refer to the following conversation and menu.

M: That meal was absolutely exquisite. My steak was delicious, the seafood spring rolls were packed with flavor and I thought the ingredients seemed super fresh.

W: Agreed about the spring rolls! I'm glad I could give you a hand in sharing them. They probably get their fish delivered from that canal we passed earlier. Having said that, though, my vegetable pasta dish was nothing special.

M: Really? That surprises me. Everything I had **was of the highest order**.

W: Well, I guess pasta isn't their strong point. Anyway, the decor in here is beautiful. I love what they've done with the rugs and candles. Also, the service was top-notch. They definitely make an effort to make sure you have a pleasurable dining experience.

M: Agreed. And if we're ever in town again you know what to order, right?

W: Yep. Seafood!

• be of the highest order *(phr.)* 最優等的；最棒的

男：那餐點精緻無比。我的牛排很美味，海鮮春捲包著香料，我覺得食材似乎超級新鮮。

女：關於海鮮春捲我同意！我很高興我可以跟你一起享用它們。他們的魚很可能是從我們稍早經過的運河那裡運送過來的。不過，我的鮮蔬義大利麵倒是沒什麼特別的。

男：真的嗎？我很驚訝。我吃到的每一道菜都是最棒的。

女：嗯，我猜義大利麵不是他們的強項。不管怎樣，這裡裝飾得很美。我喜歡他們擺設的地毯和蠟燭。而且，服務是一流的。他們肯定下了一番功夫讓你有愉快的用餐經驗。

男：同意。如果我們再來鎮上一次，妳知道要點什麼了，對吧？

女：知道。海鮮！

Hua Binh Restaurant

Seafood Spring Rolls
$10
Rice Noodles
$8

Steak
$20
Grilled Chicken
$15

Chicken Pasta
$12
Vegetable Pasta
$10

和平餐廳

海鮮春捲
$10
米線
$8

牛排
$20
烤雞
$15

雞肉義大利麵
$12
鮮蔬義大利麵
$10

⑩ Why does the woman think the spring rolls were good?

(A) They had a high amount of fish in them.

(B) They seemed like they were handmade.

(C) The ingredients complemented each other well.

(D) The ingredients were most likely locally sourced.

為何女子認為春捲很棒？

(A) 裡面有很多魚。

(B) 看起來像是手工的。

(C) 食材彼此搭配得很好。

(D) 食材很可能來自當地。

正解 (D)

本題詢問女子認為春捲很棒的原因。當男子說到海鮮春捲的食材 "seemed super fresh" 時，女子回應說 Agreed about the spring rolls . . . They probably get their fish delivered from that canal we passed earlier. 得知女子認為春捲用到的新鮮食材可能來自當地的運河，所以答案為 (D)。

(C) complement (v.) 補足；與……相配。

---

⑪ Which of the following is the woman not impressed with?

(A) The pasta

(B) The decor

(C) The rugs and candles

(D) The service

女子並未對以下何者印象深刻？

(A) 義大利麵

(B) 裝潢

(C) 地毯和蠟燭

(D) 服務

正解 (A)

題目問女子對餐廳的哪方面並未感到印象深刻。由女子說 Having said that, though, my vegetable pasta dish was nothing special. 得知她認為義大利麵沒什麼特別，其餘選項皆得到女子的正面評價，故答案為 (A)。

---

⑫ Look at the graphic. What was the total cost of the meal?

(A) $30

(B) $40

(C) $47

(D) $52

看菜單。餐點總價是多少？

(A) 30 元

(B) 40 元

(C) 47 元

(D) 52 元

正解 (B)

本題為圖表題，問餐點的總價。由開頭男子說 My steak was delicious, the seafood spring rolls were . . . 以及女子回說 . . . my vegetable pasta dish was nothing special. 得知他們點了牛排、海鮮春捲和鮮蔬義大利麵，對照菜單可算出三樣加總為 40 元，故答案為 (B)。

Part 4: Short Talks

Questions 13-15 refer to the following welcome speech.

At Helen's Table, we work closely with local food producers to ensure delivery of the highest quality, most nutritious recipes possible, in a way that protects our health and environment. This means, for example, developing seasonal menus to take advantage of in-season fruits and vegetables. So, if one of our guests inquires about the peach pie, it is your duty to inform them that our peaches have been locally and organically grown this season, on ethical farms within 100 miles of the restaurant. This commitment to quality and the customer experience is what make Helen's Table special, and it is vital that everyone be familiar with such details. The head chef and I have prepared leaflets, which you must memorize before the Soft Opening. Thanks to everyone for your hard work so far. I'll see you **bright and early** on Saturday morning.

在海倫餐廳，我們和當地食品供應商密切合作以確保我們收到的是最高品質的食材，推出的是盡可能營養的食譜，且是以一種維護我們的健康和環境的方式。舉例來說，這意味著要研發季節性菜單以便善加利用當季蔬果。所以，如果有客人問起桃子派，各位就有責任告知他們我們的桃子是當季在本地有機栽種的，就栽種於距離餐廳一百英里內的道德農場。對於品質與顧客經驗的承諾正是海倫餐廳的獨特之處，而各位熟悉這樣的細節是至關重要的。主廚和我已準備了宣傳單，各位一定要在試營運之前熟記。謝謝大家目前為止的努力。我們週六一大早見。

- bright and early *(phr.)* 一大早

⑬ Who most likely is the speaker?
 (A) The head chef
 (B) The restaurant manager
 (C) A waiter
 (D) A customer

誰最有可能是說話者？
 (A) 主廚
 (B) 餐廳經理
 (C) 服務生
 (D) 顧客

正解 (B)

本題詢問說話者的身分。關鍵句是 The head chef and I have prepared leaflets, which you must memorize before the Soft Opening. 可推測說話者最有可能為餐廳經理，正對員工發表談話，所以答案為 (B)。

14 How does Helen's Table guarantee the quality of its food?

(A) It works closely with local food producers.

(B) It inquires with guests about their experiences.

(C) It educates staff on the details of its policies.

(D) It imports quality produce from abroad.

海倫餐廳如何保證食物的品質？

(A) 和當地食品供應商密切合作。

(B) 詢問客戶的經驗。

(C) 教育員工公司政策的細節。

(D) 從國外進口高品質的食品。

正解 **(A)**

題目問海倫餐廳如何保證食物品質。由開頭第一句說 . . . we work closely with local food producers to ensure delivery of the highest quality . . . 得知是和當地食品供應商密切合作，答案為 (A)。

---

15 What will the listeners do before Saturday?

(A) Develop a plan

(B) Visit local farms

(C) Read leaflets

(D) Make a peach pie

星期六之前，這段談話的聽眾會做什麼？

(A) 制定計畫

(B) 拜訪當地農場

(C) 閱讀宣傳單

(D) 做桃子派

正解 **(C)**

本題是推論題，詢問聽這段話的人週六之前會做什麼。由關鍵句 The head chef and I have prepared leaflets, which you must memorize before the Soft Opening. 得知聽這段話的人必須在試營運前牢記所有宣傳單上刊載的細節，又從最後一句 I'll see you bright and early on Saturday morning. 可推斷試營運的日期應該就是週六，所以答案選 (C)。

Questions 16-18 refer to the following training talk and menu.

If you invite someone to lunch, this makes you the host, meaning <u>you foot the bill</u>. It also means that you are the one responsible for tipping. If you're just on a one-hour lunch break, tell the restaurant host that you don't wish to order appetizers or desserts and aim to keep things short. You can come back another day for that blueberry cheesecake! Oh, and note the word "meeting." It's important to strike the right balance between the relaxation of lunch, and sticking to your professional agenda. And of course, in a semi-formal atmosphere such as this, you should refrain from talking with your mouth full or leaning across the table. You are the host and guests will follow your lead, so set a good example with your etiquette.

若你邀請某人吃午餐,你就成了主人,意思就是<u>你要付帳</u>。這也意味著你就是那位負責付小費的人。若只是一小時的午休時間,告訴餐廳的接待員你不想要點前菜或點心,用餐想要從簡。你可以改天再回來吃藍莓起士蛋糕!喔,要留意「會議」這個詞。在放鬆的午餐與遵照專業議程間取得適當的平衡是很重要的。當然在這種半正式的氣氛下,你應該避免嘴巴滿是食物時說話或是身體越過桌面。你是主人,客人會有樣學樣,所以要做好禮節的好榜樣。

The Savoy Restaurant

Appetizers
Lamb Kebab w/ Cucumber Salad | Salmon Tartare | Nicoise Vegetables

Main Courses
Crispy Sea Bass | Beef Burgundy | Mushroom Risotto | Smoked Chicken Pasta

Desserts
Crème Brûlée | Iced Passion Fruit Mousse | Warm Banana Crumble

Drinks
Sparkling Water | Fresh Juice | English Tea | Americano Coffee | Espresso

Alcohol
Bottled Beer | Cocktails

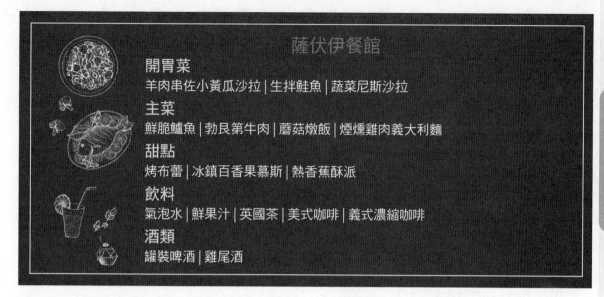

16 What does the woman mean when she says, "you foot the bill" in the first sentence?

(A) You have to tip the staff.

(B) You have to pay for the meal.

(C) You should eat quickly.

(D) You collect everyone's money.

當女子在第一句說 "you foot the bill" 時是什麼意思？

(A) 你必須給員工小費。

(B) 你必須付餐點的錢。

(C) 你應該要快點吃。

(D) 你要跟每個人收錢。

正解 **(B)**

本題問女子在第一句說 you foot the bill 的意思。foot 在此作動詞指「付款」，慣用語 foot the bill 是「付帳單」的意思。因此答案要選 (B)。

17 Look at the graphic. What does the speaker suggest avoiding on a short business lunch?

(A) Smoked Chicken Pasta

(B) Iced Passion Fruit Mousse

(C) Beef Burgundy

(D) Sparkling Water

看圖表。說話者建議短暫的商業午餐要避免點什麼？

(A) 煙燻雞肉義大利麵

(B) 冰鎮百香果慕斯

(C) 勃艮第牛肉

(D) 氣泡水

正解 **(B)**

本題為圖表題，須結合圖表與獨白回答。題目問說話者建議短暫商業的午餐應要避免點什麼。獨白中的關鍵句是 If you're just on a one-hour lunch break, tell the restaurant host that you don't wish to order appetizers or desserts . . .，可知要避免開胃菜和甜點，對照菜單，(B)「冰鎮百香果慕斯」屬於甜點類故應避免，答案是 (B)。

⑱ Why should the host set a good example with his/her etiquette?
(A) Because it will help guests feel more relaxed
(B) Because it is required by the restaurant
(C) Because business lunches are very formal
(D) Because guests will be influenced by the host's actions

為何主人要做好禮節的好榜樣？
(A) 因為會有助客人感到較為放鬆
(B) 因為餐廳要求
(C) 因為商業午餐非常正式
(D) 因為主人的行為會影響客人

正解 **(D)**
本題問為何主人要做好禮節的好榜樣。由最後一句 You are the host and guests will follow your lead, so set a good example with your etiquette. 得知客人會有樣學樣，因此答案要選 (D)。

Part 5: Incomplete Sentences

⑲ Seeing as I don't eat meat, could you please tell me about your _____ options?
(A) tender
(B) lean
(C) vegetarian
(D) alcoholic

由於我不吃肉，可以請你告訴我你們素食的選項嗎？
(A) 嫩的（形容詞）
(B)（肉）無脂肪的（形容詞）；傾向（動詞）
(C) 素菜的（形容詞）；素食主義者（名詞）
(D) 含酒精的（形容詞）；酒經中毒的人（名詞）

正解 **(C)**
本題考字義。本句一開頭表明「不吃肉」，故依語意可知空格應填入 (C) vegetarian「素菜的」，表示「素食選項」。

⑳ I've reserved a table _____ eight at 7:30 tonight, so make sure you're on time.
(A) for   (B) to
(C) about   (D) aside

我訂今晚七點半八位，所以務必要準時到。
(A) 為了……（介系詞）
(B) 向／往……（介系詞）
(C) 關於……（介系詞）
(D) 在旁邊（副詞）

正解 **(A)**
本題考介系詞。空格前的 I've reserved a table 表「訂位」，空格後為數字 eight 加時間 at 7:30，可推測數字 eight 應是指人數，故應選 (A)，置入後表「我訂了八個人的位子」。

㉑ This restaurant's menu contains a _____ of Thai and Cantonese cuisine.

(A) mixing　　　(B) mixture
(C) mixes　　　(D) mixed

這間餐廳的菜單包含泰式和廣式的混合菜餚。

(A) 使混合（動名詞）
(B) 混合物（名詞）
(C) 使混合（現在式第三人稱單數動詞）
(D) 使混合（過去式或過去分詞）

正解 **(B)**
本題考詞性和字義。看到空格前方有冠詞 a、後有介系詞 of 得知應要填入名詞，依照句意可知空格處填入 (B) mixture「混合物」，表示泰式和廣式料理的「混合」菜餚。

㉒ Recently, the city's harbor area _____, and it now features a number of gourmet restaurants where you can experience fine dining.

(A) is going to develop
(B) was going to develop
(C) develops
(D) has been developed

最近，這座城市的港口區已經發展起來了，現在它有好幾間美食餐廳，你可以在那裡獲得美好的用餐體驗。

(A) 將要發展（未來進行式）
(B) 過去正在發展（過去進行式）
(C) 發展（現在式）
(D) 已經發展（現在完成式）

正解 **(D)**
本題考文法。句首的時間副詞 Recently 表「近來」，常與完成式連用，且依照句意得知應是要表達「城市的港口區已經發展起來了」，故答案為 (D)。

㉓ You're on a diet, so you're not allowed to eat chocolate, _____ you?

(A) are
(B) aren't
(C) do
(D) don't

你正在節食，所以你不能吃巧克力，對嗎？

(A) 是（第二人稱單複數／第三人稱複數肯定 be 動詞）
(B) 不是（第二人稱單複數／第三人稱複數否定 be 動詞）
(C) （第二人稱單複數／第三人稱複數現在式肯定助動詞）
(D) （第二人稱單複數／第三人稱複數現在式否定助動詞）

正解 **(A)**
本題考附加問句。空格前的子句以否定表示 you're not allowed to ...，故附加問句應用肯定的第二人稱現在式 be 動詞，答案應為 (A) are。

Part 6: Text Completion

Questions 24-27 refer to the following e-mail.

To:	jfarmar@tmail.com
From:	terrypritchard@mandalin.com
Re:	About our banquet hall

Dear Mrs. Farmar,

In response to your e-mail with regard to our Banquet Hall, please be ---24-- as to the following:

The Banquet Hall hosts up to 200 seated guests, and has a standing ---25-- of 400 with the tables and chairs removed.

As per your inquiry regarding the possibility of utilizing the banquet hall for both a dinner function and a party function, the answer is yes. However, there is a more suitable option for this occasion.

The problems with using the same space for the after party are **twofold**. Firstly, the time it would take to remove the tables and chairs from the hall. Secondly, the issue of cleaning. --26-- It is next to the Banquet Hall and boasts the following advantages:

-Large space (up to 600 guests)
-Performance stage
-State-of-the-art lighting and sound
-A beautiful art deco style cocktail bar

I can give you a 50% discount on the use of the Grand Hall, ---27--- that you are already booking the Banquet Hall. Please see the attached PDF file for more information.

Thank you for your interest in the Mandalin Hotel.

Yours sincerely,

Terry Pritchard
Senior Events Coordinator
The Mandalin Hotel Group

收件者：jfarmar@tmail.com
寄件者：terrypritchard@mandalin.com
主　旨：關於我們宴會廳

親愛的法默女士，

回覆您關於我們宴會廳的電子郵件，謹告知如下：

宴會廳可容納多達兩百位貴賓入席，桌椅撤掉則有四百個站位。

關於您詢問有關利用宴會廳舉辦晚宴及派對的可能性，答案是可以的。不過這樣的活動有一個更適合的選擇。

使用同樣空間舉辦餐後派對有兩個問題。首先是將桌椅撤離宴會廳所需耗費的時間。第二是清潔問題。<u>正是基於這些理由我們建議使用我們的格蘭廳來舉辦您的餐後派對。</u>它在宴會廳的隔壁，且有以下優點：

- 空間寬敞（容納多達六百位賓客）
- 表演舞台
- 先進的燈光聲效
- 優美裝飾藝術風格的雞尾酒吧台

鑒於您已經要訂宴會廳了，使用格蘭廳我可以為您打五折。更多詳情請看附件的 PDF 檔。

感謝您對於瑪黛麗飯店的喜愛。

謹致，

泰瑞・彼特查德
資深活動統籌專員
瑪黛麗飯店集團

• twofold *(adj.)* 雙重的

24
(A) advise
(B) advised
(C) advisable
(D) adviser

(A) 告知（原形動詞）
(B) 告知（過去式及過去分詞）
(C) 明智的（形容詞）
(D) 顧問（名詞）

正解 **(B)**

本題考詞性。動詞 advise 表「建議；告知」。空格前有 be，可知此處應填過去分詞，答案為 (B) advised。 "please be advised as to the following" 是商務書信中常見的固定用法，禮貌性地表達「謹告知／注意如下」，後面帶出要提供給對方的資訊。若欲請對方提供建議或訊息，則常用主動語態 "please advise if . . ."。

25
(A) **capacity**   (B) quality
(C) specialty   (D) durability

(A) **容量**   (B) 品質
(C) 專業   (D) 耐用

正解 **(A)**

本題考字義。空格前提到「宴會廳可容納多達兩百位貴賓入席，桌椅撤掉則⋯⋯」，可知此處在持續說明該空間的容納人數，符合句意的答案為 (A) capacity「容量」。

26
(A) It takes about fifteen minutes to remove all of the tables and chairs.
(B) So when you finish having dinner, the staff will clean up the hall.
(C) It is for these reasons that we advise using our Grand Hall for your after party.
(D) We do, however, have a small hall that may be able to accommodate your party.

(A) 撤掉所有桌椅要花十五分鐘。
(B) 所以當您用完晚餐，工作人員會清掃宴會廳。
(C) 正是基於這些理由我們建議使用我們的格蘭廳來舉辦您的餐後派對。
(D) 不過我們確實有小廳也許可以容納您的派對。

正解 **(C)**

空格前說「使用同樣空間舉辦餐後派對有兩個問題。首先是將桌椅撤離宴會廳所需耗費的時間。第二是清潔問題。」而 (C) 說「正是基於這些理由」而建議使用格蘭廳，其中的 these reasons 指的就是空格前提出的時間與清掃方面的兩大問題，故 (C) 為正選。

(D) accommodate *(v.)* 容納。

27
(A) **given**   (B) allowed
(C) including   (D) saying

(A) **鑒於；考慮到**   (B) 允許
(C) 包含   (D) 說

正解 **(A)**

本題考字義。原句提到「＿＿＿您已經要訂宴會廳了，使用格蘭廳我可以為您打五折」，可知符合句意的答案為 (A)。 given that + S. + V. 指「有鑒於⋯⋯；考慮到⋯⋯」。

Part 7: Reading Comprehension

Questions 28-30 refer to the following website review.

"A Perfect Introduction to Afternoon Tea!" - *By Karen Roper*

5 / 5 stars ★ ★ ★ ★ ★

My husband and I are American and this was our first visit to London. Of course, we just had to indulge in one of the great British traditions: afternoon tea. And I can happily say, after dining at The Regency Hotel, that I now know what all the fuss is about! Of course, I don't have anything to compare it to, but to me, the experience was absolutely perfect. The scones were **to die for**. I wish I could eat them every day and not get fat! There was a wide range of teas, and plenty of food between the sandwiches, scones, and desserts. The displays were very nice, and we even received a free refill as part of a special offer. It'll set you back 50 pounds for two people (that's around 70USD, I believe) but it's totally worth it. The vintage decor is beautiful as well.

www.vacationadviser.com

• to die for *(phr.)* 特別棒的;非常誘人的

「完美的下午茶初體驗!」——*凱倫·羅佩*

五／五顆星 ★ ★ ★ ★ ★

我和我先生是美國人,這是我們第一次造訪倫敦。當然,我們一定要縱情享受英國一個很棒的傳統:下午茶。我很高興地說,在瑞珍希飯店用餐後,我現在知道它到底在紅什麼了!當然,我沒有任何可以比較的對象,但對我來說,這個經驗完美極了。司康好吃得要命。我希望我可以每天吃而不會變胖!有很多種茶,以及很多三明治、司康和甜點等食物。擺盤很漂亮,而且我們甚至獲得一次免費續杯,那是特別優惠的一部分。兩人要花掉五十英鎊(我想大概是七十美元)但是非常值得。復古的裝潢也很漂亮。

www.vacationadviser.com

28 Why did the woman decide to try afternoon tea?

(A) Because she won't come to London again

(B) Because she'd heard it was good value for money

(C) Because she'd never tried it before

(D) Because she'd heard about a special offer

為何女子決定要去嘗試下午茶？

(A) 因為她不會再去倫敦

(B) 因為她聽說它很超值

(C) 因為她從未嘗試過

(D) 因為她聽說有特別的優惠

正解 **(C)**

本題詢問女子為何要去嘗試下午茶。由評論的開頭說 . . . this was our first visit to London. Of course, we just had to indulge in one of the great British traditions: afternoon tea. 可知這是女子第一次造訪倫敦，所以想要嘗試英國的傳統，答案為 (C)。

---

29 The word "fuss" in line 4 is closest in meaning to

(A) argument

(B) relaxation

(C) anger

(D) excitement

第四行的 "fuss" 一字意思最接近

(A) 爭論

(B) 放鬆

(C) 生氣

(D) 激動；興奮

正解 **(D)**

本題考同義字。詢問 fuss 意思相近於何者。從原句 And I can happily say, after dining at The Regency Hotel, that I now know what all the fuss is about! 及後續筆者對飯店下午茶的正面評價，可知 fuss 在此指「過分激動；大驚小怪」，意思最接近 (D)「激動；興奮」。也就是筆者親身品嚐後，能理解那裡的下午茶為何如此令人興奮。

---

30 What does the writer mean when she says, "It'll set you back 50 pounds"?

(A) It's fairly cheap.

(B) It's a little expensive.

(C) It saves you fifty pounds.

(D) It's extremely heavy.

當作者說 "It'll set you back 50 pounds" 時是什麼意思？

(A) 它很便宜。

(B) 它有點貴。

(C) 它幫你省下五十英鎊。

(D) 它非常地重。

正解 **(B)**

本題為句意題，問 It'll set you back 50 pounds 的意思。set sb. back 指「花去某人一筆錢」，原句後面接著說 but it's totally worth it.，可知作者認為花五十英鎊雖然不便宜但很值得，所以答案選 (B)。

Questions 31-34 *refer to the following online chat discussion.*

Kristina [10:42 A.M.]
Hey all. I was thinking it might be nice to order takeout for lunch today. Would anyone like to join me?

Jamie [10:48 A.M.]
Great idea, Kristina. I was going to get seafood but I'm flexible.

Cathy [10:49 A.M.]
Me too. Did you have anything in mind, Kristina? I'm starving.

Kristina [10:50 A.M.]
I haven't had Mexican for ages. Are you guys into that?

Cathy [10:51 A.M.]
I love Mexican. And Jamie does, too. There are a few cool Mexican restaurants on the food app I use, DeliverU.

Jamie [10:53 A.M.]
I'm **down for** Mexican, although Cathy, the one you and I tried the other week from DeliverU wasn't all that. Shall we try another one this time?

Cathy [10:54 A.M.]
Agreed. The meat seemed old and wasn't tender at all. I'm just looking now. There's one called Jorge's Tex Mex. They have a nice mix of dishes and they even have some vegan options **by the looks of** it.

Kristina [10:55 A.M.]
Great! Could you order me a vegetarian burrito and I'll pay you the cash later?

Jamie [10:55 A.M.]
And I'll get the chicken tacos!

Cathy [10:55 A.M.]
Sure, I'll order for all three of us. We can go and sit in the break room. Speak soon!

- be down for sth. *(phr.)* 加入（某活動等）
- by the looks of . . . *(phr.)* 看樣子；從⋯⋯的外表看來

克里斯汀娜 [10:42 A.M.]
嘿，各位。我想今天午餐來叫外賣應該會不錯。有誰想要和我一起嗎？

傑米 [10:48 A.M.]
這是個好主意，克里斯汀娜。我原本要去吃海鮮不過我可以改。

凱西 [10:49 A.M.]
我也是。克里斯汀娜，妳有想吃什麼嗎？我餓扁了。

克里斯汀娜 [10:50 A.M.]
我很久沒有吃墨西哥料理了。你們喜歡墨西哥菜嗎？

凱西 [10:51 A.M.]
我愛墨西哥料理。傑米也是。我用的一個食物外送應用程式 DeliverU 上有一些不錯的墨西哥餐廳。

傑米 [10:53 A.M.]
我也要吃墨西哥料理，不過凱西，你和我前幾週嘗試從 Deliver U 訂餐的那間餐廳沒那麼好吃。我們這次要換別間嗎？

凱西 [10:54 A.M.]
同意。那次的肉似乎過老一點也不嫩。我現在正在找。有一間叫做喬治德墨餐廳。他們有很不錯的餐點搭配，看起來甚至還有素食餐。

克里斯汀娜 [10:55 A.M.]
太棒了！妳可以幫我訂一個素捲餅，然後我待會給妳錢嗎？

傑米 [10:55 A.M.]
我要雞肉夾餅！

凱西 [10:55 A.M.]
沒問題，我會幫我們三個人點餐。我們可以去坐在員工休息室用餐。待會聊！

31 What is the purpose of the conversation?

(A) To review a bad experience ordering online

(B) To arrange a restaurant visit for lunch

(C) To order food for a group lunch at work

(D) To discuss working part-time as a waitress

這段對話的目的是什麼？

(A) 評論一次網路購物的負面經驗

(B) 安排午餐要去的餐廳

(C) 幫工作場所的午餐聚會訂餐

(D) 討論兼差當女服務生

正解 **(C)**

本題為主旨題，詢問這段對話的目的。由開頭克里斯汀娜寫 I was thinking it might be nice to order takeout for lunch today. Would anyone like to join me? 以及最後凱西寫 We can go and sit in the break room. 可知他們想訂午餐外送並在員工休息室一起用餐，所以答案是 (C)。

㉜ What will likely happen next?

    (A) Cathy will order using the DeliverU app.

    (B) Jamie will go to Jorge's Tex Mex.

    (C) Kristina will make a call to order food.

    (D) Cathy and Jamie will buy seafood.

接下來可能會發生什麼？

(A) 凱西會用應用程式 DeliverU 訂餐。

(B) 傑米會去喬治德墨餐廳。

(C) 克里斯汀娜會打電話訂餐。

(D) 凱西和傑米會買海鮮。

正解 **(A)**

本題為推論題，詢問接下來可能會發生的事。由對話最後凱西寫 Sure, I'll order for all three of us. 得知會由凱西幫大家訂餐，所以答案選 (A)。

㉝ What is Jamie going to eat for lunch?

    (A) Seafood   **(B) Tacos**

    (C) A burrito   (D) He is undecided.

傑米午餐要吃什麼？

(A) 海鮮   **(B) 墨西哥夾餅**

(C) 墨西哥捲餅   (D) 他還沒決定。

正解 **(B)**

本題為細節題，詢問傑米午餐要吃什麼。由傑米在早上 10:55 寫 And I'll get the chicken tacos! 可知傑米要吃的是雞肉夾餅，答案為 (B)。

㉞ At 10:53 a.m., what does Jamie mean when he writes "the one you and I tried the other week from DeliverU wasn't all that"?

    (A) He can't remember the name of the last place they went.

    (B) The restaurant they bought from previously wasn't good.

    (C) The place they went to before did not accept online orders.

    (D) The Mexican food that they ate last time was delicious.

早上 10:53 傑米寫 "the one you and I tried the other week from DeliverU wasn't all that" 時，是什麼意思？

(A) 他不記得他們上次去的餐廳的名字。

(B) 他們之前買過的那間餐廳東西不好吃。

(C) 他們之前去過的那間餐廳不接受線上訂餐。

(D) 他們上次吃的墨西哥料理很美味。

正解 **(B)**

本題考句意。詢問傑米寫 the one you and I tried the other week from DeliverU wasn't all that" 的意思。傑米在本句後面提議想換另一間餐廳，而凱西接著也同意那間餐廳的肉過老一點也不嫩，可推知他們對之前那間餐廳並不滿意，所以答案選 (B)。(sb./sth.) is not all that 指「（某人／某事）沒那麼吸引人」，也就是說他們認為之前訂餐的那間餐廳，食物沒那麼好吃。

P. 297~306

Part 1: Photographs

TRACK 72

❶ **(A) Some sculptures are in a museum.**
(B) Some paintings are in an art gallery.
(C) People are queueing to enter a gallery.
(D) An artist is painting on a canvas.

(A) 博物館裡有一些雕像。
(B) 美術館裡有一些畫。
(C) 人們正排隊要進入畫廊。
(D) 一名藝術家正在油畫布上作畫。

正解 **(A)**
圖中有一些雕像在博物館裡，因此符合圖片的敘述為 (A)。

....

❷ (A) A musician is writing lyrics for a song.
(B) People are watching ballet at the theater.
(C) An audience is watching a musical performance.
(D) Musicians are rehearsing in a room.

(A) 一位音樂家正在為一首歌寫歌詞。
(B) 人們正在劇院看芭蕾舞。
(C) 一位觀眾正在觀看音樂表演。
(D) 音樂家們正在一個房間裡排練。

正解 **(D)**
圖中有多位樂團的團員正在一個房間裡排練，因此符合圖片的敘述為 (D)。

Part 2: Question and Response

❸ Do you want tickets standing near the stage?
(A) I tend to get nervous on stage.
(B) I can collect my tickets at the box office.
(C) I'd rather sit on a chair further back.

你是否想要舞台附近的站票席？
(A) 我在舞台上往往會緊張。
(B) 我可以在售票處取票。
(C) 我比較想坐後面一點的座位。

正解 (C)

題目詢問是否想要位於舞台附近的票，合理的回應為 (C)「我比較想坐後面一點的座位。」

(A)、(B) 答非所問。

---

❹ This TV show is really boring.
(A) I think it's shown at 7 p.m.
(B) OK, let's change the channel.
(C) Yeah, it has some great characters.

這個電視節目真無聊。
(A) 我想它是晚上七點播映。
(B) 好的，我們轉台吧。
(C) 是的，它有一些很棒的角色。

正解 (B)

本題以直敘句表達電視節目很無聊，有可能的回應為 (B)「好的，我們轉台吧。」

(A) 題目並非在詢問節目播映的時間。
(C) 語意與題目矛盾。

---

❺ There's an independent French cinema opening near my house soon.
(A) Oh, I hope they have subtitles.
(B) I also prefer going to the cinema alone.
(C) Right, I've been there a few times already.

我家附近即將開一家法國獨立電影的戲院。
(A) 哦，希望它們的電影有字幕。
(B) 我也偏好獨自去看電影。
(C) 是的，我已經去過幾次了。

正解 (A)

本題以直敘句說明有一家法國獨立電影的戲院即將開幕，故合適的回應為 (A)「哦，希望它們的電影有字幕。」

(C) 題目說電影院「即將」開幕，此處卻回應「已經去過」，不合邏輯。

---

❻ Streaming TV series' online is better than watching TV, isn't it?
(A) I have never heard of that show.
(B) Yes, but don't get addicted.
(C) I like to download music.

在網路上在線收看電視連續劇比看電視更好，不是嗎？
(A) 我從未聽說過那個節目。
(B) 是啊，但別上癮囉。
(C) 我喜歡下載音樂。

正解 (B)

本題以附加問句詢問對方「在網路上在線收看電視連續劇比看電視更好，不是嗎？」，實在詢問對方是否也有同感，合適的回應為 (B)「是啊，但別上癮囉」。addicted *(adj.)* 沉迷的；上癮的。

(A) 和 (C) 答非所問。

Part 3: Short Conversations

Questions 7-9 refer to the following conversation with three speakers.

W: What kind of entertainment are we going to choose for the party? <u>We've got a thousand dollars to play with.</u>

M1: I think live music is special and we could get a great band for that price.

M2: It depends on the band, though. What if people don't like their style?

W: True. The employees with kids at home may leave shortly after the dinner, and the younger employees who stay may prefer a DJ.

M1: Hmmm . . . But a DJ just isn't really interactive enough. How about some close-up magic?

M2: That could be good. My brother had a magician for his 40th. He just walked around chatting casually to guests and no one knew he was a magician. Then all of a sudden he surprised them with a cool trick!

W: That sounds great. Let's do that.

女：我們要為派對選擇哪種娛樂方式？我們有一千美元可以花。

男一：我認為現場演出很特別，我們以這個價格可以請到出色的樂團。

男二：不過，這取決於樂團。如果大家不喜歡他們的風格怎麼辦？

女：的確。家裡有小孩的員工晚飯後不久就會離開，而留下來的較年輕的員工可能比較喜歡 DJ。

男一：嗯……但 DJ 的互動性沒那麼高。近距離的魔術怎麼樣？

男二：那可能不錯。我哥哥四十歲生日時請了一個魔術師。他只是四處走動，與客人閒聊，沒人知道他是魔術師。然後突然間，他用一個很酷的把戲把他們嚇了一跳！

女：聽起來很棒。就這麼做吧。

❼ What does the woman mean when she says, "we've got a thousand dollars to play with"?

(A) The company has a budget of 1,000 dollars.

(B) They'll have a competition to win 1,000 dollars.

(C) They will still have 1,000 dollars extra after this.

(D) The boss doesn't mind if they spend more than 1,000 dollars.

當女子說 "we've got a thousand dollars to play with" 時，她的意思是什麼？

(A) 公司有一千美元的預算。

(B) 他們將參加一場比賽以便贏得一千美元。

(C) 此後，他們仍會有一千美元的額外收入。

(D) 老闆不介意他們花超過一千美元。

正解 (A)

本題為句意題，詢問該名女子說 "we've got a thousand dollars to play with" 的意思為何。男一在下一句回應說 we could . . . for that price，也就是有了這筆錢他們就能……，可知這是一筆可運用的預算；再從對話中提到的 employees 一字可知此段對話是同事們在規劃公司的派對，因此答案選 (A)「公司有一千美元的預算。」片語 have sth. to play with 指「有（……時間／金錢）可供支配」。

❽ Who may leave shortly after the dinner?

(A) The DJ　　　　　(B) The woman

(C) People with kids (D) Younger employees

誰晚飯後不久就會離開？

(A) 播放音樂的 DJ　　(B) 該名女子

(C) 有小孩的人　　(D) 較年輕的員工

正解 (C)

本題為細節題，問晚飯後不久就會離開的人是誰。由女子提及 The employees with kids at home may leave shortly after the dinner . . . ，可知答案為 (C)。

---

❾ Why do the speakers decide to hire a magician?

(A) It will be more interactive.

(B) It will be cheaper.

(C) It's suitable for children.

(D) It will be expected.

說話者為何決定聘請魔術師？

(A) 會更有互動性。　(B) 會便宜一些。

(C) 適合兒童。　　　　(D) 會被期待。

正解 (A)

本題詢問說話者決定聘請魔術師的原因。男一提到「DJ 的互動性沒那麼高」並提議選擇近距離的魔術表演，而後男二描述自己的哥哥曾在生日宴會上雇請魔術師，且當時的魔術師與客人互動後以出奇不意的表演廣獲好評，接著女子就採納了這個建議，可知「互動性」便是說話者們最後決定雇用魔術師的原因，答案選 (A)。

Questions 10-12 refer to the following conversation and set of magazine coupons.

M: Look, this leaflet has coupons with special offers for some of the city's top museums.

W: But tomorrow we're doing that sightseeing tour before lunch, and then we need to leave for the airport around seven o'clock.

M: Let's just choose one. The Blenheim Museum looks good . . . oh, but that offer is only good on weekdays.

W: Oh, what a pity. We should have gone yesterday. Never mind!

M: There's also one for 25% off exhibitions at The Ancient Art Gallery. But that was only available from November to January. We just missed it! There's also a free tour at the Aboriginal Museum, but I'm not **keen** on that.

W: Oh look, the Museum of Illustration opens from 1 p.m. to 8 p.m., daily! Why don't we do that?

M: Deal.

• keen *(adj.)* 熱衷的；渴望的 （+ on sth.）

男：妳看，傳單上有一些優惠券，上面有市區一些頂尖博物館的特別優惠。

女：但我們明天午餐前要進行觀光旅遊，然後我們要在七點左右出發去機場。

男：我們就選一個吧。布蘭尼姆博物館看起來不錯……喔，但這優惠只在平日提供。

女：喔，真可惜。我們應該昨天去的。算了！

男：古代藝廊的展覽可以打七五折。但只在十一月到一月之間有效。我們剛好錯過了！原住民博物館也有免費導覽，但我沒有很想去。

女：喔你看，插畫博物館每天下午一點至八點開放！我們為何不選這個呢？

男：就這麼決定。

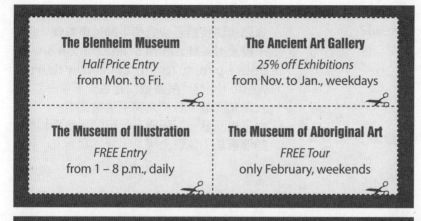

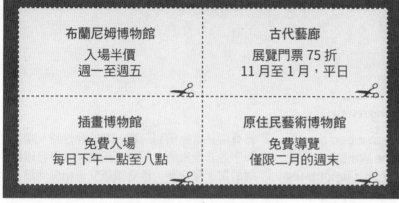

⑩ Why can't they go to a museum in the morning?

(A) They're not open in the morning.

(B) There aren't any special deals.

(C) The deals will have expired.

(D) They've planned a sightseeing tour.

為什麼他們早上不能去博物館？

(A) 它們早上還沒開。

(B) 沒有特別的優惠。

(C) 優惠將會過期。

(D) 他們已安排觀光旅遊。

正解 **(D)**

本題詢問說話者早上不能去博物館的原因。由女子提及 But tomorrow we're doing that sightseeing tour before lunch ...「我們明天午餐前要進行觀光旅遊」，可知答案為 (D)。

⑪ Which month is it now?

(A) February　　(B) January

(C) December　　(D) November

現在是幾月？

(A) 二月　　(B) 一月

(C) 十二月　　(D) 十一月

正解 **(A)**

本題詢問現在是幾月。由男子提及優惠券 ... only available from November to January. We just missed it!「只在十一月到一月之間有效。我們剛好錯過了」，可知此時剛過一月，答案為 (A)。

⑫ Look at the graphic. Which offer do the speakers decide to make use of?
(A) Half Price Entry
(B) FREE Tour
(C) 25% off Exhibitions
(D) FREE Entry

看圖表。說話者決定使用哪項優惠？
(A) 入場半價
(B) 免費導覽
(C) 展覽門票七五折
(D) 免費入場

正解 **(D)**

本題詢問說話者決定使用的優惠為何。男子提及 the Museum of Illustration opens from 1 p.m. to 8 p.m., daily! Why don't we do that?「插畫博物館每天下午一點至八點開開放！我們為何不選這個呢」，而女子也同意。對照圖表，可知插畫博物館的優惠是「免費入場」，故答案為 (D)。

Part 4: Short Talks

TRACK 75

Questions 13-15 refer to the following review.

Things are not quite as they seem when a new family moves in next door to The Watsons. And, after little Johnny uncovers his neighbors' shocking secret, he must persuade his parents of the unlikely discovery. If not, he may have to take matters into his own hands. *The Visitors* boasts a fascinating plot, constant action, and witty dialogue. A unique aspect of the movie is the soundtrack, which features pieces by Mary Ann-Gould that **evoke** the ancient chamber music of Austrian composer, Joseph Haydn—a decision that works extremely well. Mostly, the cast members excel in their roles, although Darius Moore was less than convincing as Mr. Watson. Nevertheless, *The Visitors* is a very watchable horror movie which I'm predicting to be a summer hit that will enjoy plenty of success at the box office.

• evoke *(v.)* 引起；喚起（記憶或感情）

當有個新家庭搬到沃森一家的隔壁時，事情似乎並非像表面上那樣。而當小強尼發現鄰居的驚人秘密後，他必須讓父母相信他那令人難以置信的發現。如果做不到，他可能就得自己處理問題了。《訪客》以擁有引人入勝的情節、頻繁的動作場景和機智的對話而自豪。電影的獨特之處在於配樂，其中瑪麗·安·古爾德的作品讓人聯想起奧地利作曲家約瑟夫·海頓的古典室內樂，收錄古爾德作品的這個決定了帶來絕佳的效果。多半演員都將角色詮釋得十分到位，雖然達瑞斯·摩爾並不像沃森先生那樣令人信服。然而，《訪客》還是一部非常值得看的恐怖電影，我預測這部電影會成為暑期大片，且將在票房上大獲成功。

13 What does the speaker infer about what Johnny may have to do?

(A) **Deal with a problem by himself**

(B) Make sure to keep a secret

(C) Find someone else to help him

(D) Become friends with his neighbors

說話者對強尼可能要做的事情有何推斷？

(A) **自己解決問題**

(B) 確保守密

(C) 找其他人幫助他

(D) 和他的鄰居變成朋友

正解 **(A)**

本題詢問說話者對強尼可能要做的事情有何推斷。關鍵句在男子說如果強尼無法讓父母相信他那令人難以置信的發現，他「可能就得自己處理問題了」，可知答案為 (A)。

---

14 What is the name of the movie?

(A) *The Watsons*

(B) ***The Visitors***

(C) *An Unlikely Discovery*

(D) *The New Neighbors*

這部電影叫什麼名字？

(A)《沃森一家人》

(B)**《訪客》**

(C)《難以置信的發現》

(D)《新鄰居》

正解 **(B)**

本題詢問這部電影的名字為何。由說話者提及 *The Visitors* boasts a fascinating plot, constant action, and witty dialogue.「《訪客》擁有引人入勝的情節、頻繁的動作場景和機智的對話」，可知答案為 (B)。

---

15 Who most likely is the audience for this talk?

(A) Fans of family movies

(B) Fans of classic music

(C) **Fans of horror movies**

(D) Fans of historical movies

此談話最有可能的聽眾是誰？

(A) 家庭電影迷

(B) 古典音樂迷

(C) **恐怖電影迷**

(D) 歷史電影迷

正解 **(C)**

本題詢問誰最有可能是此談話的聽眾。由說話者提及 *The Visitors* is a very watchable horror movie . . .「《訪客》還是一部非常值得看的恐怖電影」，可知答案為 (C)。

Questions 16-18 *refer to the following talk and show ticket.*

Over to your left, we have the Queen Alexandria Opera House. One of the city's oldest and most famous buildings, it was **commissioned** at the beginning of the 18th century by a queen who viewed opera as her primary source of relaxation. That was the reason for this marvelous building that still stands today. Now, the Opera House provides the stage for a variety of shows, from classical music concerts to ballet. Tickets are not cheap, going for a minimum of 100 dollars for a regular seat toward the back of the lower deck, to 2,000 dollars for boxes in the upper deck. This is due in part to the quality of the world class performers that the Opera House hosts, but also for the **upkeep** of this ancient building, which requires constant maintenance. Now, let's move on to our next attraction.

- commission *(v.)* 委任／委託（製作）
- upkeep *(n.)* 維修費；保養費

在各位左邊的是亞歷山大女王歌劇院。它是這座城市最古老、最著名的建築之一，在十八世紀初由一位女王委託建造，她將歌劇視為放鬆的主要來源。這就是興建這座至今仍屹立不搖的非凡建築的原因。現今，歌劇院為各種表演提供舞台，從古典音樂會到芭蕾舞都有。門票價格不菲，下層後方的普通座位最低票價為一百美元，上層包廂的票價則為二千美元。這一部分是由於歌劇院邀請的是世界一流的表演者，也由於須支付這座古建築的維修費用，這棟建築需要持續維修。現在，我們繼續去下一個景點吧。

16 What is the speaker's occupation?
(A) Artist
(B) Taxi Driver
(C) Theater Attendant
(D) Tour Guide

說話者的職業是什麼？
(A) 藝術家
(B) 計程車司機
(C) 劇院服務員
(D) 導遊

正解 **(D)**
本題詢問說話者的職業為何。說話者一開始提及 Over to your left, we have the Queen Alexandria Opera House.「在各位左邊的是亞歷山大女王歌劇院」，之後詳述這座建築的歷史，最後說 Now, let's move on to our next attraction.「我們繼續去下一個景點吧」，故最有可能的答案為 (D)。

17 What was Queen Alexandria's main reason for building the Opera House?

(A) To make money

(B) To impress people

(C) To provide relaxation

(D) To host a variety of shows

亞歷山大女王建造歌劇院的主要原因是什麼？

(A) 為了賺錢

(B) 為了打動人心

(C) 為了提供娛樂

(D) 為了舉辦各種表演

正解 **(C)**

本題問亞歷山大女王建造歌劇院的主要原因為何。關鍵句是 it was commissioned . . . by a queen who viewed opera as her primary source of relaxation.「……由一位女王委託建造，她將歌劇視為放鬆的主要來源。」，故答案為 (C)。

---

18 Look at the graphic. What kind of seat has the ticket holder bought?

(A) A lower deck regular seat

(B) A lower deck box seat

(C) An upper deck regular seat

(D) An upper deck box seat

看圖表。持票者買了哪種座位？

(A) 下層的普通座位

(B) 下層的包廂座位

(C) 上層的普通座位

(D) 上層的包廂座位

正解 **(A)**

本題詢問持票者買了哪種座位。說話者提及 . . . going for a minimum of 100 dollars for a regular seat toward the back of the lower deck, to 2,000 dollars for boxes in the upper deck.「下層後方的普通座位最低票價為一百美元，上層包廂的票價則為二千美元」，對照圖表即可從「票價一百美元」得知此票卷為下層普通座位，答案為 (A)。

Part 5: Incomplete Sentences

19 The band's last _____ went straight to number one in the charts.

(A) canvas

(B) album

(C) literature

(D) illustration

該樂團的上一張專輯在排行榜上躍升第一。

(A) 帆布

(B) 唱片專輯

(C) 文學

(D) 圖解

正解 **(B)**

本題考字義。依照句意可知空格應填入 (B) album 指「唱片專輯」，表示該樂團的上一張「專輯」。

⑳ I've just _____ two tickets to the premiere of the new Quentin Cornelese movie!

(A) winner
(B) winning
(C) win
(D) won

我剛贏得了兩張昆廷‧康奈爾絲新電影首映會的門票！

(A) 獲勝者（名詞）
(B) 贏（現在分詞或動名詞）
(C) 贏（原形動詞）
(D) 贏（過去式或過去分詞）

正解 (D)

本題考時態。由空格前的 I've 可知應選過去分詞形成現在完成式（have won），表「剛贏得了」電影首映會的門票，答案為 (D)。

㉑ The judges felt that Judy's performance had been the most impressive _____ the nine finalists.

(A) of
(B) at
(C) for
(D) in

裁判們認為朱蒂的表現是九位決賽選手中最令人印象深刻的。

(A) ⋯⋯之中
(B) 在⋯⋯地點
(C) 為了⋯⋯
(D) 在⋯⋯內部／廣大區域

正解 (A)

本題考最高級的用法。從空格前的最高級 the most impressive，與空格後的 the nine finalists，可知空格要填入 (A) of。最高級的用法中，若欲利用數字描述比較對象的範圍，其前方應用介系詞 of，即「最高級 + of the three/four/five … + 名詞」的句型。本句以 of nine finalists 表示「在九位決賽選手中」最令人印象深刻，答案為 (A)。

㉒ Do you agree that sequels are often not as _____ as the original?

(A) well
(B) better
(C) good
(D) best

你是否同意續集通常不如原作好？

(A) 很好地（副詞）
(B) 更好的（形容詞 good 的比較級）
(C) 好的（形容詞原級）
(D) 最好的（形容詞 good 的最高級）

正解 (C)

看到空格前後有 as，可知本題考原級的比較。as + 原級形容詞／副詞 + as，表示「和⋯⋯一樣」。因空格所在之 that 子句的動詞為 be 動詞，故應選原級形容詞，答案是 (C)，not as good as … 表「不如⋯⋯好」。

㉓ 1889 was the year _____ Dutch artist Vincent Van Gogh created his masterpiece, *Starry Night*.

(A) who   (B) where

(C) which   **(D) when**

一八八九年是荷蘭藝術家文森‧梵谷創作傑作《星夜》的那一年。

(A) 他／她（們）（表人的主格關係代名詞）

(B) 在……地方（表地點的關係副詞）

(C) 它／牠（們）（表物的主格或受格關係代名詞）

(D) 在……時（表時間的關係副詞）

正解 (D)

本題考關係詞。空格前是表時間的名詞（先行詞）the year，空格後為結構完整的子句，可判斷應選 (D)，以表時間的關係副詞 when 引導形容詞子句，修飾前面的 the year。

Part 6: Text Completion

Questions 24-27 refer to the following letter.

April 12

Dear Parents and Students,

Our year at Stratham Elementary School is drawing to a close. However, I am pleased to remind you that we do still have the annual talent ---24--- to look forward to, which will be held on the morning of May 27ᵗʰ.

Students are welcome to perform alone, or with a group of friends. I just need to know in advance. Talent acts must be tasteful, appropriate, and in line with school rules and expectations. Performances can be anything ---25--- singing, dancing, or playing an instrument, to magic tricks, juggling, karate, stand-up comedy, or anything else they are good at. I will be holding auditions over the next few weeks during music class. ---26---

There are a lot of talented kids at Stratham and I look forward to seeing what they can do! More details ---27--- provided at a later date.

Please let me know if you have any questions.

Sincerely,
Katherine Taylor
Music Teacher

四月十二號

敬愛的家長和學生：

我們在斯特拉姆小學的學年即將結束。不過我很樂意提醒大家，我們仍然有一年一度的才藝比賽可以期待，該比賽將於五月二十七日上午舉行。

歡迎學生獨自或與一群朋友一起表演。我只需要事先知道。才藝節目必須有品味、適當並且符合學校的規定和期待。表演可以是任何形式，從唱歌、跳舞、彈奏樂器，到表演魔術、雜耍、空手道、單人脫口秀等任何其他孩子們擅長的項目。接下來的幾週，我會在音樂課上進行試鏡。我將利用這段時間來決定最適合的節目。

斯特拉姆有很多很有天賦的孩子，我很期待看到他們能帶來什麼樣的表演！更多詳細資訊將於稍後提供。

如果有任何問題，請讓我知道。

謹致，
凱薩林‧泰勒
音樂老師

❷❹ (A) literature
(B) orchestra
(C) sitcom
(D) contest

(A) 文學
(B) 管弦樂隊
(C) 情境喜劇
(D) 比賽

本題考字義。原句提到,我們仍然有一年一度的才藝____可以期待,可知符合句意的答案為 (D)。

---

❷❺ (A) with
(B) from
(C) over
(D) for

(A) 和……
(B) 從……起
(C) 在……之上
(D) 為了……

正解 **(B)**
本題考介系詞。空格前有 anything,空格後開始列舉一連串不同的表演形式,且中間有介系詞 to,因此可知應選 (B) from,形成 anything from A to B 的句型。此句型常用來強調從 A 到 B 的範圍內有多樣化的內容或選擇。

---

❷❻ (A) Let me take a moment to congratulate you on being chosen.
(B) I'll use this time to decide which acts are most suitable.
(C) Some light refreshments will be served between rounds.
(D) Your daughter was one of the most outstanding contestants.

(A) 讓我花一點時間祝賀你被選中。
(B) 我將利用這段時間來決定最適合的節目。
(C) 兩場表演之間將提供一些輕食。
(D) 你的女兒是最傑出的選手之一。

正解 **(B)**
作者在空格之前說她將在接下來的幾週利用音樂課進行試鏡,而 (B) 進一步說「我將利用這段時間來決定最適合的節目」語意連貫故為最合適的答案。其中 this time「這段時間」即前一句說的 over the next few weeks「接下來的幾週」。

---

❷❼ **(A) will be**
(B) would be
(C) have been
(D) had been

(A) 將會(未來式)
(B) 也許會(would 為 will 的過去式)
(C) 已經會(現在完成式)
(D) 已經會(過去完成式)

正解 **(A)**
本題考時態。本句的時間副詞 at a later date 表未來的時間,可判斷本句應採未來式。由於主詞是 More details,故要用未來式的被動語態,即「will + be + 過去分詞」的句型,因此選 (A)。

Part 7: Reading Comprehension

Questions 28-30 refer to the following website article.

TOP PICKS ▶

The streaming giant, MotionPix, is gearing up for one of its biggest ever weeks. Returning are series favorites including Season 3 of *The Unexplained*, as well as drama *Court & Order*, sitcom *Bob & Jane* and the cartoon series, *The Magic Playground*. On the movie front, the pick of the bunch could be new MotionPix original, *The Stuntman*. This action movie is absolutely loaded with superstar talent, such as Jett Middler, Zoey Platt, Gwyneth Farlow and even performances from Christopher Dawkins, as well as basketball superstar, Magic Jordan. Yes, they've really **pulled out the big guns** and I, **for one**, can't wait to find out if *The Stuntman* is really worth the hype. After forming just four years ago, MotionPix cannot afford to take a backward step, with reports that rival services VidSnap and LightReel plan on spending big bucks to compete. Not to mention other established players in the industry desperate to claim **a piece of the pie**. What all this means, of course, is more choice for us, the audience! So which shows are you looking forward to this week? Leave a comment in the section below to let us know now.

影音串流龍頭 MotionPix 正準備迎接有史以來最盛大的一週。眾多高人氣系列節目回歸，包括《不明原因》第三季，以及戲劇《法庭與秩序》、情境喜劇《鮑伯與珍》和動畫系列《魔法遊樂場》。在電影方面，箇中之選可能是 MotionPix 的原創作品《替身》。這部動作片肯定能讓你一睹超級巨星的才華，例如傑特‧米德勒、柔伊‧普拉特、葛妮絲‧法洛，甚至還有克里斯托弗‧道金斯的表演，以及籃球巨星馬吉克‧喬丹。是的，他們真的全都傾盡全力，至少對我來說，我就迫不及待地想知道《替身》是否真的值得這樣大肆宣傳。成立僅不到四年的 MotionPix 禁不起退步，據報導，競爭平台 VidSnap 和 LightReel 計畫斥資與之抗衡。更不用說業界中其他著名的對手也迫切地想在市場中分一杯羹。當然，這一切意味著對我們觀眾來說將有更多選擇！那麼，你期待本週哪些節目呢？在下方留言，現在就告訴我們吧。

- pull out the big guns *(phr.)* 使出最有利的武器；全力以赴
- for one *(phr.)* 起碼對……來說（用來帶出本身觀點或行為，即使他人不這樣認為）
- a piece/slice/share of the pie *(phr.)* 可以得到的一份（盈利或福利）

28 What is the purpose of this article?

(A) To compare different streaming services

(B) To compare different kinds of shows

(C) To generate interest in MotionPix shows

(D) To explain why streaming TV is successful

本文的目的是什麼？

(A) 為了比較不同的串流服務

(B) 為了比較不同種類的節目

(C) 為了引起對 MotionPix 節目的興趣

(D) 為了解釋為什麼串流電視很成功

正解 **(C)**

本題為主旨題，詢問此文章的目的。文章開頭便說影音串流龍頭 MotionPix 將有眾多高人氣節目回歸，之後便開始介紹各節目，最後還邀請讀者留言分享最有興趣的節目，可知其目的是為了引起興趣，故應選 (C)。

---

29 What type of show is *The Magic Playground*?

(A) An animation

(B) A sitcom

(C) A talent show

(D) A drama

《魔法遊樂場》的節目類型是什麼？

(A) 動畫

(B) 情境喜劇

(C) 才藝節目

(D) 戲劇

正解 **(A)**

本題為細節題，詢問《魔法遊樂場》的節目類型為何。文章第二句最後提及 the cartoon series, *The Magic Playground*，故答案為 (A)。

---

30 What is implied about MotionPix's competitors, VidSnap and LightReel?

(A) They provide more shows for their audiences.

(B) They are not very popular among audiences.

(C) They are more established in the industry.

(D) They're going to invest a lot of money.

關於 MotionPix 的競爭對手 VidSnap 和 LightReel，文中有何暗示？

(A) 它們為觀眾提供更多節目。

(B) 它們不是很受觀眾歡迎。

(C) 它們在此行業中更著名。

(D) 它們將投入大量資金。

正解 **(D)**

本題詢問關於 MotionPix 的競爭對手 VidSnap 和 LightReel 有何暗示。解題關鍵在 ... with reports that rival services VidSnap and LightReel plan on spending big bucks to compete.，指出競爭平台 VidSnap 和 LightReel 計畫斥資與 MotionPix 競爭，故答案為 (D)。文中指出 MotionPix 為影音串流龍頭，故依常理其節目選擇應該是最多的，而競爭平台 VidSnap 和 LightReel 等是會讓觀眾有更多平台的選擇，而非它們本身能為觀眾提供更多節目選擇，故 (A) 不選。

Director of Photography Wanted!

Volunteer work (expenses covered)

A chance to join an exciting film project by an independent crew of recent college graduates. The film is a thriller with a strong script which will be provided upon request. The candidate will be working with a talented set of very driven and passionate individuals taking their first steps in the industry. This is a two-week project and the short film will be 30 minutes long. It will be entered into a number of prestigious competitions, including the Royal Film Academy Shorts Competition later this year, so we expect it to get a lot of exposure within the industry. As stated, this is volunteer work, but we do cover all transport, food, and accommodation costs.

Ideal candidates will have:

- *Attention to detail and a commitment to excellence (required)*

- *Experience with the Canon C300 camera (preferred)*

- *Ability to record audio (preferred)*

- *Experience with editing software (preferred)*

- *Ability to thrive in a demanding, fast-paced environment (required)*

- *A flexible schedule including nights and weekends (required)*

Please forward a résumé and covering letter to janhawks954@vrzn.net.

* If you do not have one or more of the skills listed as *"required"* then please do not apply, as these are essential for the position.

招募攝影總監！

無償工作（涵蓋開銷）

現在有一個機會讓您能參與一個令人興奮的電影計畫，其製作團隊乃由一群大學應屆畢業生所組成。這部電影是一部驚悚片，劇本震撼人心，可應要求提供。應徵者將與一群剛入行且才華洋溢、非常積極熱情的人合作。這是一個為期兩週的企劃，短片的總長是三十分鐘。它將競逐許多頗具聲望的比賽，包括今年稍晚的皇家電影學院短片競賽，因此我們期待它能在業界獲得大量的曝光。如前所述，這是一份無償工作，但我們確實會支付交通、餐飲和住宿等所有費用。

理想的應徵者須具有：
- 對細節的專注力並追求卓越（必備）
- 使用佳能 C300 相機的經驗（尤佳）
- 錄音能力（尤佳）
- 使用編輯軟體的經驗（尤佳）
- 在苛刻、快節奏的環境中成長的能力（必備）
- 彈性的時間表，包括晚上和週末（必備）

請發送簡歷和求職信至 janhawks954@vrzn.net.。

* 如果您沒有一個或多個「必備」技能，請不要申請，因為這些對於該職位至關重要。

To: janhawks954@vrzn.net
From: harrymyers@tmail.com
Subject: **Applying for Director of Photography**

Dear Jan,

I read your ad with enthusiasm, as I am keen to build up my experience, and the chance to be entered into the RFA Shorts Competition appealed to me. I graduated from the Marsden School of Arts three years ago and have been working on a number of projects as a DP since then.

As such, please accept this e-mail as a statement of my interest in the position of DP as advertised on jobs4everyone.com.

I take great pride in my work and am extremely thorough. I have extensive software editing experience, as well as a complete understanding of sound recording. I excel in a dynamic environment and currently have a schedule which is open during the period specified. Working late is not a problem for me.

With regard to the equipment side of things, the bulk of my experience is with Sony cameras such as Sony A6600. I do have some experience with the camera brand specified, but not that exact model. However, if awarded the position I would of course familiarize myself with this before shooting began.

Thank you and I hope to hear from you shortly.

Yours Sincerely,

Harry Myers

收件者：janhawks954@vrzn.net
寄件者：harrymyers@tmail.com
主　旨：應徵攝影總監

敬愛的簡：

我帶著熱忱讀了您的應徵廣告，而由於我渴望累積經驗，有機會參加皇家電影學院短片競賽對我來說充滿吸引力。我三年前從馬斯登藝術學院畢業，此後曾致力多項專案擔任攝影總監。

因此，請將電子郵件視為我對 jobs4everyone.com 上刊登的攝影總監職位感興趣的聲明。

我為自己的作品感到自豪，而且我極度細心。我擁有豐富的軟體編輯經驗，且對錄音有完整的了解。我在多變的環境中表現出色，目前的行程可配合指定的時間。工作到很晚對我來說不是問題。

關於設備方面，我大部分經驗是使用索尼相機，例如索尼 A6600。我確實對指定的相機品牌有一些經驗，但並非明確提到的那個型號。然而，如果獲得這個職位，我當然會在開拍之前讓自己熟悉操作。

謝謝您，但願很快能收到您的聯絡。

謹致，

哈利·邁爾斯

31 Why would someone apply for this job?

(A) To receive a highly competitive salary

(B) To work with experienced professionals

(C) To have work be seen by important people

(D) To be given a free camera

為什麼有人要申請這份工作？

(A) 為了獲得高競爭力的薪水

(B) 為了與經驗豐富的專家合作

(C) 為了讓重要人士看到作品

(D) 為了獲贈免費相機

正解 **(C)**

本題詢問有人要申請這份工作的原因。徵人廣告提及電影企劃的短片「將競逐許多頗具聲望的比賽，包括今年稍晚的皇家電影學院短片競賽，因此我們期待它能在業界獲得大量的曝光」，故答案為 (C)「為了讓重要人士看到作品」。

(A) 從廣告標題下方的附註可知此為無償工作。

(B) 從廣告第一句可知團隊由應屆畢業生組成。

(D) 文中未題及。

---

32 How long will the job last?

(A) Two days

(B) Two weeks

(C) 30 days

(D) 30 weeks

這份工作將持續多久？

(A) 兩天

(B) 兩週

(C) 三十天

(D) 三十週

正解 **(B)**

本題為細節題，詢問這份工作將持續多久。廣告第四句提及 This is a two-week project「這是一個為期兩週的企劃」，故答案為 (B)。

---

33 Which of the following is true of Harry's ability to meet the job requirements?

(A) He meets none of the essential requirements.

(B) He meets some essential requirements but not all.

(C) He meets most of the essential requirements.

(D) He meets all of the essential requirements.

關於哈利符合工作需求的能力，下列敘述何者為真？

(A) 他沒有符合任何必備需求。

(B) 他符合一些必備需求，但並非全部。

(C) 他符合大部分的必備需求。

(D) 他符合所有的必備需求。

正解 **(D)**

本題為整合題，詢問關於哈利符合工作需求的能力，下列描述何者為真。哈利在電子郵件中的第三段陸續提及自己「極度細心、在多變的環境中表現出色、行程可配合指定的時間」，對照廣告，以上這些涵蓋了需求清單的標註為 required「必備」的所有項目，故答案為 (D)。

34 In the e-mail, the word "bulk" in paragraph 4, line 1, is closest in meaning to

(A) Majority

(B) Collection

(C) Audience

(D) Trailer

在電子郵件中,第四段第一行中的 "bulk" 意思最接近何者

(A) 大多數

(B) 收集

(C) 觀眾

(D) 電影預告片

正解 **(A)**

本題為字義題,詢問電子郵件第四段中的 bulk 是什麼意思。名詞 bulk 意指「大部分;大量」,和選項 (A) Majority「大多數」意思最接近,故選 (A)。從原文可知,作者欲表達自己設備使用經驗大多是 Sony 相機,而非廣告中提及的品牌和型號。

---

35 What does Harry not have experience with?

(A) The Canon C300

(B) The Sony A6600

(C) Working as a DP

(D) Editing Software

哈利沒有什麼經驗?

(A) 佳能 C300 相機

(B) 索尼 A6600 相機

(C) 當攝影總監

(D) 編輯軟體

正解 **(A)**

本題為整合題,詢問哈利對於什麼不具經驗。哈利在電子郵件中提及「我確實對指定的相機品牌有一些經驗,但並非明確提到的那個型號」。對照廣告中需求清單的第二項可知指定的相機型號是 Canon C300,故答案為 (A)。

Unit 13 Health 保健

P. 318~326

Part 1: Photographs

TRACK 77

1 (A) Prescription glasses are being fitted.
(B) Eye drops have been given to a man.
(C) A man is having his ears cleaned.
(D) An optician is checking a man's eyes.

(A) 矯正眼鏡正在被配戴。
(B) 有人給男人眼藥水。
(C) 男人的耳朵正在被清潔。
(D) 一位驗光師正在檢查男人的眼睛。

正解 **(D)**
圖中的女子正在拿著檢查眼睛的工具靠近男子的眼睛並仔細觀察,因此符合圖片的敘述為 (D)「一位驗光師正在檢查男子的眼睛。」

(A) prescription glasses *(n.)* 矯正眼鏡。

---

2 (A) A woman is carrying a first-aid kit.
(B) A woman is holding a glass of water and a tablet.
(C) A woman's temperature is being checked.
(D) A woman is applying some ointment to her skin.

(A) 女子帶著一個急救箱。
(B) 女子拿著一杯水以及一顆藥錠。
(C) 女子的體溫正在被測量。
(D) 女子將一些軟膏塗抹在皮膚上。

正解 **(B)**
圖中可見女子手上拿著一杯水和一顆藥錠,故正確答案為 (B)。

Part 2: Question and Response

❸ Hello, I would like to make an appointment to see a doctor.

(A) I'm sorry. The dentist you are looking for is off today.

(B) Can I see your national health insurance card, please?

(C) You need to take these pills three times a day, after meals.

你好，我想要預約看診。

(A) 很抱歉。您想要看的牙醫今天休診。

(B) 我可以看您的健保卡嗎？

(C) 你飯後要吃這些藥丸，一天三次。

正解 **(B)**

本句為直述句，說明想要預約看診。合適的回應為 (B)「我可以看您的健保卡嗎？」

(A) 題目並未說明要預約哪一位醫生。

(C) 與題意無關。

---

❹ Does this medicine have any side effects?

(A) Yes, you should start feeling better soon.

(B) No, you don't need to take it after eating.

(C) You may feel a little sleepy, so don't drive.

這種藥有任何副作用嗎？

(A) 是的，你應該不久後就會覺得好多了。

(B) 不，你不需要在飯後吃。

(C) 你可能會覺得有點嗜睡，所以不要開車。

正解 **(C)**

此題為以 Does 開頭的是非問句，詢問對方特定藥品是否有任何副作用。(C) 雖未直接以 Yes/No 回答，但說明了可能的副作用是嗜睡，符合邏輯故為正解。

(A) 藥效與題意無關。

(B) 吃藥時間與題意無關。

---

❺ Could you tell me what your symptoms are, Janet?

(A) My eyes feel sore.

(B) Yes, I feel great.

(C) I exercise regularly.

珍妮特，可以告訴我妳的症狀是什麼嗎？

(A) 我的眼睛很痠。

(B) 對，我覺得好極了。

(C) 我定期運動。

正解 **(A)**

本題為以 Could 開頭的是非問句，詢問對方是否可以告知症狀。(A) 雖未直接以 Yes/No 回答，但說明了症狀為何，符合邏輯故為正解。

(B) 並未回應症狀為何。

(C) 運動與題意無關。

6 Is my temperature too high?

(A) No, I think the weather is perfect.

(B) 40 degrees is above average, yes.

(C) 178 centimeters is average height.

我的體溫過高嗎？

(A) 沒有，我覺得天氣完美。

(B) 四十度高於平均，沒錯。

(C) 一百七十八公分是平均身高。

正解 **(B)**

題目為以 Is 開頭的是非問句，詢問對方自己的體溫是不是過高。(B) 回應對方他的體溫超過平均值，為正確的選項。

(A) 天氣與題意無關。

(C) 身高與題意無關。

Part 3: Short Conversations

TRACK 79

Questions 7-9 refer to the following conversation.

M: I've been getting stomachaches regularly for the past few weeks.

W: OK. Do you also feel heartburn?

M: Yes, I also get heartburn.

W: When do you normally feel pain?

M: In the morning it's usually OK, but it's most intense just after eating, and is sometimes fairly strong when I lie down at night.

W: It's possible that you could have either an ulcer, acid reflux, or both. These are not dangerous if treated. I'll prescribe you some medicine first to ease the pain, and book you in for an X-ray appointment next week.

M: OK, thank you.

男：過去幾週我經常胃痛。

女：好的。你是否也有感到胸腔灼熱感嗎？

男：有的，我也有胸腔灼熱的感覺。

女：你通常什麼時候會覺得疼痛？

男：早上通常還好，剛吃飽後通常最為強烈，而晚上躺下來有時會有強烈的疼痛感。

女：你可能不是胃潰瘍就是胃酸逆流，或者兩者都有。只要接受治療就不危險。我會先給你開處方藥來緩解疼痛，然後幫你預約下個禮拜 X 光檢查。

男：好的，謝謝。

....

7 What are the speakers mainly discussing?

(A) A patient's medical history

(B) A patient's eating habits

(C) How to overcome heartburn

(D) A current medical issue

說話者主要在討論什麼？

(A) 一位病患的用藥史

(B) 一位病患的飲食習慣

(C) 如何克服胸腔灼熱感

(D) 一個目前的醫療問題

正解 **(D)**

由對話可知，說話者正在釐清病人的病症以及開處方藥和安排檢查，故正確答案為 (D)。

8 When has the patient felt the strongest pain?
(A) A few weeks ago　(B) In the morning
(C) After eating　(D) When sleeping

病人何時會感到最強烈的疼痛？
(A) 幾週之前　(B) 早上
(C) 飯後　(D) 睡覺時

正解 (C)

由男子所說 . . . it's most intense just after eating . . . 可知男子在剛剛吃飽飯後最為疼痛，故選 (C)。

9 What will the patient most likely do next?
(A) Nothing
(B) Take medicine
(C) Eat something
(D) Have a scan

病患接下來最有可能會做什麼？
(A) 什麼都不做
(B) 吃藥
(C) 吃點東西
(D) 掃描檢查

正解 (B)

由女子所說 I'll prescribe you some medicine first, to ease the pain, and book you in for an X-ray appointment next week. 可知男子目前可以取得緩解疼痛的處方藥，因此推論男子會先服用止痛藥物，因此 (B) 為符合邏輯的答案。

Questions 10-12 refer to the following conversation and table.

M: How's everything going with your new baby, Wendy?

W: It's OK so far. I'm looking forward to getting some time off soon, though.

M: I bet. So you wanted to talk about your insurance plan?

W: Yes, I'm currently just on that "Self" plan, as my husband has a separate plan with his company. But I was wondering if I could switch plans to include my baby in the coverage.

M: Yes, we do offer a **premium** for that. The contribution for a child is only a few dollars more per month.

W: OK, that's great news. Thank you. Do you have something I can take home and show my husband?

M: Yes, here. Take this.

• premium (n.) 保險類；津貼；獎金

男：溫蒂，新生寶寶一切如何？

女：目前還好。但是我很期待不久之後可以休假。

男：我想也是。那麼，妳說想討論妳的保險方案？

女：對，我目前是在「本人」的方案，因為我的先生自己有所屬公司的方案。但我在想是否可以換成包含我的寶寶的方案。

男：可以，我們有提供那樣的保險方案。為小孩支付的金額每個月只要多幾塊錢而已。

女：這真是好消息。謝謝你。你有沒有可以讓我帶回家給我先生看的資料？

男：有的，這裡。拿去吧。

Monthly Plan Premiums	Rate (in dollars)
Self	9.50
Self + Spouse	19.50
Self + Child(ren)	12.50
Family	23.50

保險費月繳方案	費用（美金）
本人	9.50
本人 + 配偶	19.50
本人 + 子女	12.50
家庭	23.50

❿ What was the woman's original plan?

(A) Self

(B) Self + Spouse

(C) Self + Child(ren)

(D) Family

女子原本的方案是什麼？

(A) 本人

(B) 本人 + 配偶

(C) 本人 + 子女

(D) 家庭

正解 (A)

由女子所說 I'm currently just on the "Self" plan . . . 可知女子原本的方案為 (A) Self 「本人」。

⓫ Why does the woman want to change her private medical insurance plan?

(A) She is planning to retire.

(B) She has had a baby.

(C) She has recently gotten married.

(D) She can't afford her old plan.

女子為什麼想要更換她的個人醫療保險方案？

(A) 她計畫要退休。

(B) 她有了一個寶寶。

(C) 她最近結婚了。

(D) 她沒有辦法負擔舊的方案。

正解 (B)

由女子所說 But I was wondering if I could switch plans to include my baby in the coverage. 再加上前述所提及新生寶寶，可知女子想要更換到新方案的原因是想要幫寶寶加保，因此符合邏輯的答案為 (B)。

⓬ Look at the graphic. How much more will the woman pay per month on her new plan?

(A) $3   (B) $7

(C) $9.50   (D) $12.50

看圖表。女子換到新方案後，每個月需要額外支付多少美元？

(A) 三塊美元   (B) 七塊美元

(C) 九點五美元   (D) 十二點五美元

正解 (A)

本題為圖表題，須結合圖表與對話內容回答。從對話中可知女子想由「本人」換到「本人 + 子女」的方案，對照圖表，「本人」的方案為 9.50 美元，而「本人 + 子女」的方案為 12.50 美元，故知價差為三美元，答案選 (A)。

Part 4: Short Talks

Questions 13-15 refer to the following advertisement.

Are you constantly on the go? Do you wish there were more hours in the day? Modern life can be stressful enough to make you nauseous, and it can be hard to find time to eat properly. <u>That's where we come in.</u> At EatWise, we are dedicated to delivering delicious, healthy meals, direct to your door! We make everything from chicken salads, to smoked salmon and **turmeric** rice, **beef stroganoff**, and rich sausage **casseroles**. Or try our trademark vegan **fajitas**! With EatWise, you also have the ability to customize your meals by the month, week, or even day! You can even consult one of our leading nutritionists for free advice! And whichever plan you choose, it'll come complete with all the nutrition required to power your body, so that you'll be left **feeling** not only **on top of** your schedule, but **the world** too!

您是否經常忙個不停呢？您是否希望一天不只二十四小時呢？現代生活的壓力大到讓人噁心想吐，而且也很難找到時間好好吃飯。<u>這就是我們登場的時候。</u>在聰明飲食，我們致力於將美味健康的餐點送到您的家門口！我們製作各種料裡，從雞肉沙拉、煙燻鮭魚、薑黃飯、俄式酸奶牛肉到濃郁的砂鍋香腸等等。或者試試看我們的獨門料理素食墨西哥法士達捲餅！有了聰明飲食，您可以按月、按週甚至按天客製化您的餐點！您甚至可以請教我們其中一位頂尖營養師尋求建議！而不論您選擇什麼計畫，餐點都完整涵蓋您身體所需的所有營養，因此您不僅會感到進度超前，也會感到幸福至極！

- turmeric *(n.)* 薑黃
- beef stroganoff *(n.)* 俄式酸奶牛肉
- casserole *(n.)* 砂鍋
- fajita *(n.)* 墨西哥烤肉；法士達
- feel on top of the world *(phr.)* 感到極度幸福

---

⑬ What is being advertised?
(A) A website about nutrition
(B) A new health food restaurant
(C) A food delivery service
(D) An ice cream delivery service

獨白是在為什麼打廣告？
(A) 一個營養相關的網站
(B) 一間新的健康飲食餐廳
(C) 一個餐點外送服務
(D) 一個冰淇淋的外送服務

正解 **(C)**

由關鍵句 At EatWise, we are dedicated to delivering delicious, healthy meals, direct to your door! 可知內容主打健康美食的外送服務，因此答案為 (C)。

⓮ What does the speaker mean when he says, "That's where we come in"?

(A) EatWise makes you nauseous.

(B) EatWise helps organize your schedule.

(C) EatWise helps you switch to a vegan diet.

(D) EatWise helps you eat properly.

說話者提到 "That's where we come in" 時是什麼意思？

(A) 聰明飲食讓你噁心想吐。

(B) 聰明飲食幫你規劃行程。

(C) 聰明飲食幫你轉換成素食。

(D) 聰明飲食幫你適當飲食。

正解 (D)

由題目句的前一句提到 . . . it can be hard to find time to eat properly. 以及後面提到 At EatWise, we are dedicated to delivering delicious, healthy meals . . . ，故知答案為 (D)。

. . . .

⓯ Who is the intended audience for this advertisement?

(A) People who don't have much free time

(B) People who enjoy cooking at home

(C) People who like eating "on the go"

(D) People who do a lot of exercise

何者是這則廣告的預期客戶？

(A) 沒有太多空閒時間的人們

(B) 喜歡在家煮飯的人們

(C) 喜歡在外奔波用餐的人們

(D) 做很多運動的人們

正解 (A)

由開頭說道 Are you constantly on the go? Do you wish there were more hours in the day? . . . it can be hard to find time to eat properly. 可知這則廣告是以繁忙、時間不夠用的人們做為目標客戶，故最合適的選項為 (A)。

Questions 16-18 refer to the following podcast and graph.

The US Department for Health and Human Services states that 80% of Americans do not exercise enough. With one third of American adults living with obesity, many companies are investing in employee wellness. This could include either yoga, aerobics classes, massages, or sessions with a therapist. Exercise has been shown to improve general fitness, as well as boosting weight loss, heart health, energy levels, recovery time after injury, and concentration abilities. It also reduces stress and has been shown to help diabetics. These days, many of us are stuck staring at computer screens for prolonged periods, but this is unnatural because thousands of years of biological programming has made the body dependent on physical activity. Even one daily workout session is unnatural if you are **dormant** for the rest of the day. Ideally, we should be working out before, during, and after work in order to **optimize** our health.

美國的衛生及公共服務部表示有八成的美國人缺乏運動。隨著三分之一的美國成人有肥胖問題，許多公司正在投入改善員工的健康。其中包含瑜珈、有氧運動課程、按摩或者與治療師的療程。運動被證實可以改善整體的健康並促進減重、心臟健康、能量、傷後復健以及專注度。它也可以減少壓力並顯示能有助糖尿病患者。近來，我們之中許多人已經被迫長時間盯著電腦螢幕，但這樣相當不正常，因為數千年的生物工程已經讓人體仰賴身體活動。如果你一天之中的其他時間都保持靜態，就算每天有一個運動時段也是不正常的。理想狀況下，我們應該要在工作前、中、後都運動，以便讓我們的健康達到最佳狀態。

- dormant *(adj.)* 靜態的
- optimize *(v.)* 使完美；最佳化

BMI of Adults Aged 20 and Older

BMI	Classification
18.5 to 24.9	Normal weight
25 to 29.9	Overweight
30+	Obesity
40+	Extreme obesity

二十歲以上成人之身體質量指數

身體質量指數	分類
18.5 至 24.9	一般體重
25 至 29.9	過重
30 以上	肥胖
40 以上	極度肥胖

⑯ Look at the graphic. Which is most likely the BMI figure for one third of American adults aged 20 and older?

(A) under 18.5   (B) 18.5-24.9

(C) 25-29.9   **(D) above 30**

看圖表。何者最有可能是三分之一二十歲（含）以上的美國成人之身體質量指數？

(A) 低於 18.5

(B) 介於 18.5 和 24.9 之間

(C) 介於 25 和 29.9 之間

(D) 高於 30

正解 (D)

由關鍵句 With one third of American adults living with obesity . . .「有三分之一的美國人患有肥胖問題……」，又根據圖表，肥胖問題的身體質量指數是高於 30，因此選項 (D) 為正解。

---

⑰ What is the purpose of this podcast?

(A) To promote exercise

(B) To sell health products

(C) To sell fitness equipment

(D) To compare health in different countries

這則線上有聲節目的目的為何？

(A) 推廣運動

(B) 販售健康產品

(C) 販售健身器材

(D) 比較不同國家的健康

正解 (A)

本題詢問這則線上有聲節目的目的。

由關鍵句 Exercise has been shown to improve general fitness . . . 以及 Ideally, we should be working out before, during, and after work in order to optimize our health. 可知內容主要提及運動的諸多益處並鼓勵大家要多運動，故答案選 (A)。

---

⑱ Why is it good for employees to be physically active?

(A) Because they can make more money

(B) Because they enjoy it more than sitting down

(C) Because they can do less work this way

(D) Because it is natural for the human body

為什麼員工保持體能上的活動是良好的？

(A) 因為他們可以賺更多錢

(B) 因為他們比起坐下來更能享受其中

(C) 因為如此一來他們可以做更少的工作

(D) 因為這對人體來說是正常的

正解 (D)

由關鍵句 These days, many of us are stuck staring at computer screens for prolonged periods, but this is unnatural because thousands of years of biological programming has made the body dependent on physical activity. 可知對於人體來說長時間緊盯電腦螢幕並不正常，而是應該要常有身體活動，因此答案選 (D)。

Part 5: Incomplete Sentences

⑲ Jenny's rash started _____ a few hours after she had applied ointment to it.
(A) to disappear   (B) disappear
(C) will disappear   (D) disappeared

珍妮的皮疹在塗抹藥膏後的幾個小時開始消退。
(A) 消退（不定詞）
(B) 消退（原形動詞）
(C) 會消退（未來式）
(D) 消退（過去式）

正解 **(A)**

本題考文法。空格前方 started「開始」其後須以不定詞或動名詞表示「開始進行某動作」，故選 (A) to disappear。

---

⑳ In this first-aid kit, there are some _____ which can be used to treat cuts.
(A) thermometers   (B) pharmacies
(C) bandages   (D) eye drops

在這個急救箱中，有一些可以用來處理傷口的繃帶。
(A) 溫度計   (B) 藥房
(C) 繃帶   (D) 眼藥水

正解 **(C)**

本題考字義。空格前方提到在急救箱中，又符合空格後可治療傷口（treat cuts）條件之物品為 (C) bandages「繃帶」。

㉑ A sudden drop in blood pressure caused Karen to start feeling _____.
(A) allergic   **(B) dizzy**
(C) optic   (D) clinical

血壓突然下降讓凱倫開始覺得暈眩。
(A) 過敏的   **(B) 頭暈的**
(C) 眼睛的   (D) 診所的

正解 **(B)**

本題考字義。空格前方提到凱倫的血壓突然下降（drop in blood pressure），可推測空格處應填入血壓下降所造成的症狀，故合適的答案為 (B)。

㉒ He's going to give himself indigestion if he keeps eating that quickly, _____?
(A) isn't he   (B) is he
(C) won't he   (D) doesn't he

如果他繼續吃那麼快，他會害自己消化不良，不是嗎？
(A) 不是嗎（isn't 為現在式否定 be 動詞）
(B) 是嗎（is 為現在式肯定 be 動詞）
(C) 不會嗎（won't 為未來式否定助動詞）
(D) 不是嗎（doesn't 為現在式否定助動詞）

正解 **(A)**

本題考附加問句。主要子句 He's going to ... 為肯定敘述句，由 is 可知時態為現在式。因此附加問句應選否定，且時態一致的 isn't，故選 (A)。

㉓ _____ the surgeon is, I hope he or she is very well-qualified and experienced.

(A) Whenever (B) Whatever
(C) Whichever (D) Whoever

無論外科醫生是誰，我希望他或她極具資格且經驗豐富。

(A) 無論何時 (B) 無論什麼
(C) 無論哪個 (D) 無論是誰

正解 (D)

選項均為複合關係詞，而由於空格之後提到希望外科醫生極具資格且經驗豐富，可知空格中應填入與人相關的複合關係詞，故正確答案為 (D)，表示「不論是誰」。

Part 6: Text Completion

Questions 24-27 refer to the following website article.

Eating healthy foods has always been the best medicine, and one of the ultimate "superfoods" is beans. Take pinto beans, for example, which are often used in Mexican cuisine. They have a nutty kind of earthy flavor, are very easy to prepare, and are most commonly eaten whole or mashed. Pinto beans are full of vitamins and minerals and provide a great source of ---24---. Additionally, recent research has suggested that the pinto may offer even more health benefits than was first thought. ---25--- The bean may also improve blood sugar regulation, prevent ---26---, aid heart health, and boost weight loss. So ---27--- you want to spend less time in the drugstore and emergency room, try adding some beans to your diet.

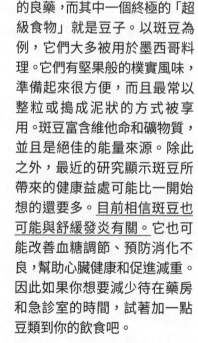

攝取健康的食物一直都是最佳的良藥，而其中一個終極的「超級食物」就是豆子。以斑豆為例，它們大多被用於墨西哥料理。它們有堅果般的樸實風味，準備起來很方便，而且最常以整粒或搗成泥狀的方式被享用。斑豆富含維他命和礦物質，並且是絕佳的能量來源。除此之外，最近的研究顯示斑豆所帶來的健康益處可能比一開始想的還要多。<u>目前相信斑豆也可能與舒緩發炎有關。</u>它也可能改善血糖調節、預防消化不良，幫助心臟健康和促進減重。因此如果你想要減少待在藥房和急診室的時間，試著加一點豆類到你的飲食吧。

㉔ (A) energy
(B) energize
(C) energetic
(D) energetically

(A) 能量；活力（不可數名詞）
(B) 使精力充沛（動詞）
(C) 精力充沛的（形容詞）
(D) 精力充沛地（副詞）

正解 **(A)**

本題考詞性。由空格處前的 a great source of「絕佳的＿＿來源」，可知空格處應填入名詞。故答案為 (A) energy「能量；活力」。

㉕ (A) One of the ways that pinto beans can be prepared is by mashing them into a paste.
(B) It is now believed that they may be associated with reduced inflammation.
(C) Indeed, pinto beans are the most popular type of bean eaten in the United States.
(D) Unfortunately, beans can lead to stomach cramping and flatulence.

(A) 其中一個料理斑豆的方式是將他們搗成泥狀。
(B) 目前相信斑豆也可能與舒緩發炎有關。
(C) 確實，斑豆是美國最受歡迎的食用豆種。
(D) 很遺憾地，豆子會導致胃痙攣和脹氣。

正解 **(B)**

空格的前一句提到 Additionally, recent research has suggested that the pinto may offer even more health benefits than was first thought.，後一句則說 The bean may also improve blood sugar regulation . . .，可知這裡在講斑豆所帶來的健康益處以及可能對哪些病徵有幫助，因此選項 (B) 說到斑豆可能舒緩發炎，與前後文語意連貫，故為正解。

㉖ (A) stethoscopes
(B) painkillers
(C) hygiene
(D) indigestion

(A) 聽診器
(B) 止痛藥
(C) 衛生
(D) 消化不良

正解 **(D)**

本題考字義。本句列舉出幾種斑豆所帶來的健康益處，空格前為動詞 prevent「預防」，可知空格處應填 indigestion，指預防「消化不良」，故正確答案選 (D)。

㉗ (A) if
(B) until
(C) though
(D) while

(A) 如果
(B) 直到
(C) 雖然
(D) 正當

正解 **(A)**

本題考從屬連接詞。空格後方的子句 . . . you want to spend less time in the drugstore and emergency room 表示希望少在藥房和急診室花時間，而主要句 try adding some beans to your diet. 提出建議的作法，因此要用引導「條件」的連接詞 if，故答案選 (A)。

Part 7: Reading Comprehension

Questions 28-29 *refer to the following text message chain.*

Thompson, Janice	14:38
Hey darling, how's Johnny?	
Thompson, Mike	14:41
He's doing well. The doctors gave him some painkilling gas through a mask, and something to stop him feeling dizzy. Now they're doing an X-Ray to assess the fracture.	
Thompson, Janice	14:42
So he's definitely got a broken leg?	
Thompson, Mike	14:43
Yes. They just need to find out exactly where it's broken and how bad it is. They're going to put a plaster cast on him.	
Thompson, Janice	14:43
Will he need a full cast?	
Thompson, Mike	14:44
He'll probably need to come back in a few days to have one fitted.	
Thompson, Janice	14:45
OK. Make sure they give him some extra painkillers to take home. I can't believe he broke his leg, the poor thing.	
Thompson, Mike	14:47
Don't worry too much. <u>He's in good hands.</u>	

珍妮絲·湯普森　　　14:38
嘿，親愛的，強尼狀況如何？

麥可·湯普森　　　14:41
他還不錯。醫生們用面罩為他輸送了止痛氣體，也給了讓他舒緩頭暈的東西。現在在做 X 光掃描檢查斷裂處。

珍妮絲·湯普森　　　14:42
所以他的腿確定是斷了？

麥可·湯普森　　　14:43
是的，他們現在只須找出到底斷在哪裡以及情況有多嚴重。他們要幫他上石膏模型。

珍妮絲·湯普森　　　14:43
他需要全腿上石膏嗎？

麥可·湯普森　　　14:44
幾天後他應該要回來全腿上石膏。

珍妮絲·湯普森　　　14:45
好的。確認他們有給他額外的止痛藥他帶回家。我不敢相信他弄斷了他的腿，真可憐。

麥可·湯普森　　　14:47
別太擔心。<u>他受到良好的照顧。</u>

28 How did the doctors make Johnny feel better?

(A) They did an X-Ray on him.

(B) They gave him special gas.

(C) They put a cast on him.

(D) They gave him some pills.

醫生們做了什麼來舒緩強尼的不適？

(A) 他們幫他做 X 光檢查。

(B) 他們給他特殊氣體。

(C) 他們幫他上石膏。

(D) 他們給他一些藥丸。

正解 **(B)**

解題關鍵是麥可在 14:41 提到 The doctors gave him some painkilling gas through a mask . . . 可知醫生有給強尼止痛氣體，故正確答案為 (B)。

---

29 At 14:47, what does Mike Thompson mean when he writes, "He's in good hands"?

(A) His son has good parents who support him.

(B) His son doesn't feel any pain in his hands.

(C) The doctors taking care of his son are reliable.

(D) The doctors think his son is healthy.

在 14:47 時，麥可‧湯普森提到 "He's in good hands" 的意思為何？

(A) 他的兒子有支持他的好家長。

(B) 他的兒子感受不到手部的任何疼痛。

(C) 照顧他兒子的醫生很值得信賴。

(D) 醫生認為他的兒子很健康。

正解 **(C)**

本題考句意。由整段對話麥可說明強尼接受到的治療以及最後讓太太珍妮絲別太擔心推論，他要表達他們的孩子受到醫生很好的照顧，因此太太可以信賴醫生的診療，故答案選 (C)。

Flu Outbreak Sweeps Across North

An outbreak of the flu has occurred in the north of the country. As many as 2,000 people are already believed to have contracted the virus since the first case was identified last week. It is looking as if this epidemic could rival the last major outbreak that swept through the country in 2004. Over 1,000 of the cases identified so far have been in Morgrove County, with further outbreaks in Sheptan and Hollinsdale. Ann Wilson, of Morgrove, was in bed for four days after contracting the virus last week and has yet to make a full recovery, even after returning to work.

"I had this awful **chesty** cough and I had it so badly I had to sleep sitting upright," she said.

"I can't remember feeling this bad before," the forty-two-year-old mother of three was quoted as saying. "Fortunately, the symptoms started to subside after my local doctor prescribed me some antiviral medication. But I am still wearing a mask to make sure no one around me catches this thing. I wouldn't wish it on my worst enemy!"

The virus may have already spread to surrounding areas such as Murton-On-Sea, so members of the general public are advised to proceed with caution. For individuals experiencing flu-like symptoms, such as fever, coughing, sneezing, vomiting or diarrhea, it is strongly recommended that you contact your local doctor immediately. Those wishing to be **immunized** may receive a vaccine at their local health clinic.

大規模流感席捲北部

我國北部爆發大規模流感。自上週首例被診斷出來後,已有多達兩千人確診。看來,這場流行病可能與上一次在二〇〇四年肆虐全國的大型流行病匹敵。目前超過一千名確診的個案都在莫古郡,還有個案是分布在薛普坦和霍林斯戴。莫古郡的安·威爾遜在上週染疫之後在床上躺了四天,甚至在重回工作崗位之後都還沒完全康復。

她說:「我有很嚴重帶痰的咳嗽,嚴重到晚上我要坐立著睡覺。」

「我不記得以前有過如此糟糕的感受,」這位有著三個孩子的四十二歲媽媽如是說。「幸好,當地的醫生給我開了一些抗病毒的用藥後症狀開始趨緩。但我還是戴著口罩確保我身邊的人不會被我感染。我甚至不希望傳染給我最糟糕的敵人!」

這個病毒可能已經傳播到像是鄰海的穆頓鎮等鄰近區域,所以建議一般大眾須謹慎行事。對於有類流感症狀如發燒、咳嗽、打噴嚏、嘔吐或腹瀉等症狀的人,強烈建議你立刻聯繫你當地的醫生。想要免疫的人們可以在當地的醫療診所注射疫苗。

- chesty *(adj.)* 多痰的;有肺炎症狀的
- immunize *(v.)* (通常指透過注射)使免疫

Memo

Date: December 4th

Dear employees of Harwood Inc.,

As some of you may already be aware, in today's local news there is a report about a serious outbreak of the flu, with our area being the most at risk. It is for this reason that I am bringing forward the date of our annual Flu Vaccination Day. Normally, we hold vaccinations at the office somewhere around the middle of December but, with recent news in mind, I have deemed it necessary to take precautions earlier than scheduled.

I have attached a booking schedule to this memo for those wishing to get vaccinated on Wednesday. Vaccination times are grouped **alphabetically** according to surname. Please **make a note**. I will definitely be getting vaccinated myself and I strongly recommend all employees do the same.

For any questions, please contact Cathy Riley (wellness@harwoodinc.com).

Thank you,

Brian Harwood
Head of Human Resources

公告

日期：十二月四號

親愛的哈伍德股份有限公司的工作同仁：

正如你們當中有些人可能已經注意到，在今天的當地新聞中有一則爆發嚴重流感的相關報導，而我們所處的區域面臨最高的風險。正因為如此，我要將我們每年的流感疫苗注射日期提前。通常我們公司的注射疫苗時間是在十二月中，然而考慮到目前的新聞，我覺得有必要將預防措施提前。

這則公告中已附加了一張預約單給想要在週三注射疫苗的人。注射疫苗的時間依照姓氏的字母順序分組。請牢記。我自己一定會接受疫苗注射，而我強烈建議所有的員工也如此。

如有任何疑問，請聯繫凱西・萊利 (wellness@harwoodinc.com)。

感謝，

布萊恩・哈伍德
人力資源部主任

- alphabetically *(adv.)* 照字母順序排列地
- make a note *(phr.)* 牢記

VACCINATION BOOKING SCHEDULE

I wish to be vaccinated on Wednesday, December 6th.

Group A (A-G) ☐   Group B (H-P) ☐   Group C (Q-Z) ☐

09:30-11:00   11:30-13:00   14:00-15:30

Employee Name (Print): _____

Employee ID Number: _____

Employee Signature: _____

疫苗注射預約單

我希望在十二月六日星期三接受疫苗注射。

A 組 (A-G) ☐   B 組 (H-P) ☐   C 組 (Q-Z) ☐
09:30-11:00   11:30-13:00   14:00-15:30

員工姓名（請以正楷書寫）: _____

員工識別碼: _____

員工簽名: _____

---

30 What is the main purpose of the memo?
  (A) To update staff on company news
  (B) To tell staff when to visit a local health clinic
  (C) To inform shareholders of a virus
  (D) To inform staff of vaccinationsa

這則公告的主要目的為何？
  (A) 為了告訴員工公司的最新消息
  (B) 為了告訴員工何時要造訪當地的醫療診所
  (C) 為了通知股東病毒的消息
  (D) 為了通知員工有關疫苗注射的消息

正解 **(D)**

由公告第一段第二句 It is for this reason that I am bringing forward the date of our annual Flu Vaccination Day. 及之後所提及的皆為疫苗注射的相關事項，可知主要目的為通知員工有關疫苗注射的消息，答案選 (D)。

---

31 When was the current virus first detected?
  (A) December 4th   (B) December 6th
  (C) Last week   (D) Two days ago

目前的病毒最開始在何時被診斷出來？
  (A) 十二月四日   (B) 十二月六日
  (C) 上禮拜   (D) 兩天前

正解 **(C)**

由第一篇新聞的第二句 ...since the first case was identified last week 「……自上週首例被診斷出來後……」，可知目前的病毒最早在該則報導的一週前被檢測出來，故正確答案為 (C)。

㉜ Where is Harwood Inc. located?

(A) **Morgrove**

(B) Sheptan

(C) Hollinsdale

(D) Murton-On-Sea

哈伍德公司位於何處？

(A) **莫古郡**

(B) 薛普坦

(C) 霍林斯戴

(D) 穆頓鎮

正解 **(A)**

本題為整合題。由第二篇公告的第一句 . . . with our area being the most at risk「……我們所處的區域面臨最高的風險……」；又根據第一篇新聞第一段提到已有兩千人確診，而後面又說到 Over 1,000 of the cases identified so far have been in Morgrove County . . .「目前超過一千名確診的個案都在莫古郡」，可知超過半數的確診病例都在莫古郡，因此最為危險，故答案選 (A)。

㉝ In the second sentence of the memo, what does the phrase "bringing forward" mean?

(A) Changing to a later date

(B) **Changing to an earlier date**

(C) Drawing attention to something

(D) Analyzing something in more detail

公告的第二句提到 "bringing forward" 的意思為何？

(A) 將日期延後

(B) **將日期提前**

(C) 將大家的注意力引導到某事

(D) 更仔細地分析某事

正解 **(B)**

本題考字義。由原文 . . . I am bringing forward the date of our annual Flu Vaccination Day. 以及後一句 Normally, we hold vaccinations at the office somewhere around the middle of December but, with recent news in mind, I have deemed it necessary to take precautions earlier than scheduled. 可知公司想將注射疫苗的時間提前，因此可推知答案為 (B)。

㉞ What could be a possible time for the Head of Human Resources to get vaccinated?

(A) 10:45 (B) **11:45**

(C) 13:45 (D) 14:45

何者可能是人力資源部主任接受疫苗的時間？

(A) 10:45 (B) **11:45**

(C) 13:45 (D) 14:45

正解 **(B)**

本題為整合題。由公告的第二段提到 Vaccination times are grouped alphabetically according to surname.「注射疫苗的時間依照姓氏的字母順序分組」，而公告最後的屬名得知人力資源部主任的姓氏開頭為 H；又根據疫苗注射預約單，姓氏開頭為字母 H 到 P 的被歸類在 B 組，施打疫苗時間為 11:30 到 13:00，因此選項中符合此時段的答案為 (B)。

Section C

多益全真模擬測驗

P. 328~345 **Listening Test** TRACK 81

Part 1: Photographs

1 **(A) The woman is in an art gallery.**
(B) The woman is making art.
(C) The woman is posing for a photo.
(D) A camera is being bought.

(A) 女子正在一間畫廊裡。　　(B) 女子正在創作藝術作品。
(C) 女子正在為拍照擺姿勢。　　(D) 一台相機正被買下。

正解 **(A)**

圖中可見女子身處的空間有許多正在展示的畫作，故最符合圖片之敘述為 (A)。

- -

2 (A) A woman is wearing glasses.
(B) The women are using laptops.
(C) A TV screen is positioned on the wall.
(D) Some coworkers are having a meeting.

(A) 一名女子戴著眼鏡。
(B) 那些女子正在用筆記型電腦。
(C) 一台電視螢幕被置於牆上。
(D) 一些同事正在開會。

正解 **(D)**

圖中可見數人圍坐一桌討論，且桌上有圖表資料等，可判斷其為同事，故符合圖片之敘述為 (D)。

(B) 其中一名女子是在使用平板電腦（tablet），並非筆記型電腦。

- -

3 (A) A warehouse is being constructed.
(B) The men are inspecting a factory.
(C) A tape measure is being used.
(D) People have roped off a building.

(A) 一間倉庫正在興建中。
(B) 那些男子正在檢查一間工廠。
(C) 一個捲尺正被使用中。
(D) 人們已用繩子把一棟建築物圍起來。

正解 **(B)**

圖中可見有兩名男子在工廠裡，手上拿著紙筆，正看著工廠某處在討論，可判斷他們正在檢查工廠的狀況，故符合圖片之敘述為 (B)。

(C) tape measure *(n.)* 捲尺。
(D) rope off *(phr.)* 用繩索隔開。

④ (A) Some meals have been given to the men.
(B) The woman is talking to the waitress.
(C) The people are dining in a restaurant.
(D) Everyone is drinking in a bar.

(A) 一些餐點已經給了男子們。
(B) 女子正在和服務生說話。
(C) 人們在餐廳裡用餐。
(D) 大家都在酒吧喝酒。

正解 **(C)**

圖中可見數人正坐在餐廳位子上聊天，女子的餐點已經在桌上，故最符合圖片之敘述為 (C)。

(A) 圖中男子桌前還沒有餐點。
(B) 圖中女子並沒有對著服務生說話。
(D) 圖中未見有人正在喝酒。

---

⑤ (A) Luggage is being taken off the carousel.
(B) The pedestrians are carrying refreshments.
(C) Passengers are stepping out of a building.
(D) People are lining up in an airport.

(A) 行李正從行李輸送帶上被拿下來。
(B) 行人們正帶著茶點。
(C) 旅客正在走出一棟建築物。
(D) 人們正在機場排隊。

正解 **(D)**

圖中可看到一群人在櫃檯前排著隊，大家腳邊都有行李，從照片中的場景可推測他們應該是在機場，故最符合圖片之敘述為 (D)。

---

⑥ (A) Some folders have been opened.
(B) A notepad has been left on a chair.
(C) A monitor is located on a desk.
(D) A telephone cord is hanging off a shelf.

(A) 一些資料夾已被打開。
(B) 一本筆記本已被留在椅子上。
(C) 有台螢幕被置於桌上。
(D) 一條電話線懸掛在書架上。

正解 **(C)**

圖中可看到桌上有一台螢幕，故最符合圖片之敘述為 (C)。

(B) 圖中的筆記本是放在桌上而非椅子上。

Part 2: Question and Response

7 When will the museum add the painting to its gallery?
(A) The director of fine arts.
(B) In the Museum of Modern Art.
(C) By the end of this spring.

這間博物館什麼時候會將這幅畫作放到畫廊？
(A) 美術總監。
(B) 在現代藝術博物館裡。
(C) 今年春天結束前。

正解 **(C)**

本題以 When 開頭，詢問博物館什麼時候會將畫作放到畫廊。回答應為特定的時間，故選 (C) By the end of this spring。

---

8 Do we still have any paper cups in stock?
(A) Yes, they are on sale.
(B) No, you didn't bring cups.
(C) I think we need to order more.

我們的紙杯還有庫存嗎？
(A) 是的，它們正在特價中。
(B) 沒有，你並沒有攜帶杯子。
(C) 我覺得我們需要再訂一點。

正解 **(C)**

題目為以 Do 開頭的是非問句，詢問對方紙杯是否有庫存。(C) 雖未直接以 Yes/No 回答，但表示我們要再訂一些，言下之意就是庫存已不多，符合邏輯故為正解。

(A) 回答紙杯為特價商品並未直接回應題目。

---

9 What should I put in the subject line?
(A) You can write an e-mail to everyone.
(B) You should make it clear that this is urgent.
(C) Yes, you should always write something there.

我在主旨欄應該寫什麼？
(A) 你可以寫一封電子郵件給大家。
(B) 你應該要註明這很急迫。
(C) 是的，你每次都應該要在該欄位寫東西。

正解 **(B)**

本題詢問對方主旨欄位應當寫什麼，回答應說明此封郵件的相關訊息。(B) 回答「你應該要註明這很急迫」符合邏輯故為正解。

---

10 How many people do we need to fire?
(A) I don't know how many people were caught in the fire.
(B) We need to lay off at least ten percent of our staff.
(C) I haven't looked at the statistics of this fire yet.

我們需要資遣多少人？
(A) 我不知道有多少人困在火中。
(B) 我們需要資遣至少一成的員工。
(C) 我還沒看這場大火的統計資料。

正解 **(B)**

本題為以 How many 開頭的疑問句，詢問要資遣多少員工，回答應說明要資遣的員工人數。(B) 回答「我們需要資遣至少一成的員工」符合邏輯，因此為適合的答案。

11 Are you looking to branch out?

    (A) Yes, we hope to expand into the Asian market.

    (B) No, this isn't one of our biggest branches.

    (C) Yes, we hope to stay in the local market.

你們想要拓展業務嗎？

(A) 是的，我們希望可以拓展到亞洲市場。

(B) 不是，這並非我們最大的分公司之一。

(C) 是的，我們希望可以留在當地市場。

正解 **(A)**

本題為以 Are 開頭的是非問句，詢問對方是否想要拓展。(A) 肯定回應並提供了更多相應的資訊，故為正解。

(C) 前段表示同意，但後段卻說要留在當地市場，前後矛盾。

---

12 Do you like your suburb?

    (A) It's one of the best schools in the city.

    (B) Yes, my neighbors are lovely.

    (C) No, we don't usually go there.

你喜歡你的郊區嗎？

(A) 它是市內最好的學校之一。

(B) 喜歡，我的鄰居人很好。

(C) 不，我們不常去那裡。

正解 **(B)**

本題為以 Do 開頭的一般是非問句，詢問對方是否喜歡所住的郊區。(B) 回答喜歡，並進一步說明喜歡的原因，合乎題意故為正解。

---

13 Why does the manager want to see you?

    (A) I made a few mistakes recently.

    (B) The meeting lasted half an hour.

    (C) I can deliver the package for you.

經理為什麼想要見你？

(A) 我最近犯了一些錯。

(B) 那場會議持續了半小時。

(C) 我可以幫你送包裹。

正解 **(A)**

本題有疑問詞 why 詢問原因，可知應選一個適當的理由，故 (A)「我最近犯了一些錯。」為最適當的答案。

---

14 Can you give me an estimate on the number of guests for the party?

    (A) I'm afraid we cannot calculate the cost yet.

    (B) I think there will be about 30 people.

    (C) We can have the party next week.

你可以給我派對賓客的預估人數嗎？

(A) 我們現在恐怕還不能計算成本。

(B) 我覺得應該會有大約三十人。

(C) 我們可以在下個禮拜開派對。

正解 **(B)**

題目以 Can 開頭，詢問對方是否可以預估派對的來賓人數。(B) 回應賓客大約有三十人，為最合適的答案。

⓯ Where did you see the job advertisement?

(A) The proposal needs a few changes.

(B) I work in a convenience store.

(C) It was in today's newspaper.

你是在哪裡看到那則招聘廣告？

(A) 這份提案需要一些修改。

(B) 我在一間便利商店工作。

(C) 就在今天的報紙上。

正解 (C)

題目以 Where 開頭詢問對方是在哪裡看到招聘廣告，回答應指出廣告刊登的地方，故最適合的選項為 (C)。

⓰ Who is the best person to lead the project?

(A) I'm not sure who the current leader is.

(B) I would recommend Nancy or Sid.

(C) It took a week to finally complete it.

誰是帶領這項專案的最佳人選？

(A) 我不確定目前的領導者是誰。

(B) 我會推薦南茜或是席德。

(C) 花了一星期終於完成了。

正解 (B)

題目以 Who 開頭詢問帶領專案的最佳人選，應回答某特定人物。(B) 明確指出了南茜或是席德，故為正確答案。

(A) 題目不是問目前的領導者是誰。

⓱ Can I get a refund on this printer?

(A) Sorry, we don't exchange items.

(B) What seems to be the problem?

(C) We can't lower the price on the printer.

我可以拿到這台印表機的退款嗎？

(A) 很抱歉。我們不提供換貨。

(B) 問題出在哪裡呢？

(C) 我們不能降低印表機的售價。

正解 (B)

本題為以 Can 開頭的一般是非問句，詢問對方是否可以退款。(B) 詢問對方問題出在哪裡，表示想了解顧客退款的原因為何，合乎題意，故為正解。

⓲ My mortgage was approved!

(A) Now you can get your dream house!

(B) You will be very happy at that job!

(C) I'm sure you'll learn a lot!

我的房貸通過核可了！

(A) 現在你可以買你理想中的房子了！

(B) 你做那份工作會非常開心！

(C) 我確信你會學到很多！

正解 (A)

本題為直述句，描述申辦的房貸通過核可了，最可能的回應為 (A)，表示對方可以購屋了，合乎邏輯故為正解。

19 Would you prefer the 10 a.m.-4 p.m. shift or the 4-10 p.m. shift?

(A) Terry works both shifts tomorrow.

(B) The evening one is better for me.

(C) Yes, the cram school closes at 10 o'clock.

你比較喜歡早上十點到下午四點這個輪班時間，還是下午四點到晚上十點這個時段的輪班？

(A) 泰瑞明天這兩班都會上。

(B) 晚班對我來說比較好。

(C) 是的，補習班十點關門。

正解 (B)

題目以助動詞 Would 開頭，但後有關鍵字 or，可知為「選擇疑問句」題型。題目問比喜歡哪一個時段的輪班時間，(B) 回答「晚班對我來說比較好。」，符合題目中 4-10 p.m. shift 的這個時段，故為適當的回應。

---

20 Can you believe so many people showed up?

(A) Sorry, I don't know many people.

(B) I wasn't expecting such a big turnout.

(C) Sure, we can invite more people.

你能相信有這麼多人出席嗎？

(A) 抱歉，我不認識太多人。

(B) 我沒有預期到出席人數這麼多。

(C) 當然，我們可以邀請更多人。

正解 (B)

本題為以 Can 開頭的一般是非問句，詢問對方是否能相信如此多人出席。最合乎邏輯的回應為 (B)「我沒有預期到出席人數這麼多」，表示也贊同對方對於這麼多的出席人數感到驚訝，故為正解。

---

21 How about having a family meeting this evening?

(A) That's fine with me, but Max will be busy.

(B) Yes, my wife and I want to start a family.

(C) Sure, I often tell my family about work issues.

今晚我們舉行一場家庭會議如何？

(A) 我沒問題，但麥克斯會很忙。

(B) 是的，我太太和我想生個孩子。

(C) 當然，我常告訴我家人關於工作上的問題。

正解 (A)

聽到題目中的 How about + V-ing 便知道是在提出邀請或提議。題目是在跟對方提議要「舉行家庭會議」，最適合的回應為 (A)「我沒問題，但麥克斯會很忙。」，表示自己可以參加，但其他家庭成員可能會因忙碌而無法出席。

---

22 Should I make an appointment for your dental checkup?

(A) My eyes are really sore.

(B) No, I don't have a sore throat.

(C) Yes, I should probably make sure everything is OK.

我是否應該幫你預約牙科檢查？

(A) 我的眼睛真的很痠。

(B) 不，我並沒有喉嚨痛。

(C) 好的，我應該要確認一切都正常。

正解 (C)

題目以 Should 開頭詢問是否應該要幫對方預約牙科檢查。本題的解題關鍵字為 dental「牙齒的；牙科的」，故唯一合乎邏輯的選項為 (C)「好的，我應該要確認一切都正常。」，也就是說要確認牙齒健康沒有出問題。

㉓ Would you like a receipt for the cake you purchased?

(A) No, I don't need one.

(B) Actually I have a recipe for that cake.

(C) Sorry, I don't really like cake.

您是否想要一張購買蛋糕的收據？

(A) 不用，我並不需要。

(B) 事實上，我有那個蛋糕的食譜。

(C) 抱歉，我沒有很喜歡蛋糕。

正解 **(A)**

本題目為以助動詞 Would 開頭的一般是非問句，詢問對方購買蛋糕是否需要拿收據。回應應明確說出要或不要，因此正確的答案為 (A)。

(B) 企圖以拼法相似的單字 recipe 混淆作答，但該字是表「食譜」，與題意無關。

㉔ Where is the conference room in this building?

(A) It is forbidden to cook in our facility.

(B) It is available at the front desk.

(C) It is located on the third floor.

會議室位在這棟建築的何處？

(A) 在我們設施裡禁止烹煮。

(B) 櫃檯有提供。

(C) 就在三樓。

正解 **(C)**

題目以 Where 開頭問會議室位在這棟建築的位置，回答應指出某個地方。(C) 指出就在三樓，故為正解。

(B) 雖有提到地點，但題目是問會議室的位置，與櫃檯提供什麼東西無關，故不選。

㉕ The training is quite tough, isn't it?

(A) I'm well-qualified for the position.

(B) You need to fill out an application.

(C) Don't worry; we'll get through it.

這場訓練還滿艱難的，對吧？

(A) 我能勝任這個職位。

(B) 你需要填寫一份申請表。

(C) 別擔心；我們會撐過去的。

正解 **(C)**

本句為「附加問句」題型，意思是「這場訓練還滿艱難的，對吧？」，適當的回應為 (C)「別擔心；我們會撐過去的。」，表示雖然艱難但應該可以順利通過考驗。

㉖ Who's the new girl over there?

(A) We need more staff.

(B) She'll be here soon.

(C) She's replacing Alan.

那邊那個新來的女孩是誰？

(A) 我們需要更多人手。

(B) 她很快就會來這裡。

(C) 她是來接替艾倫的位置。

正解 **(C)**

本題以 Who 開頭詢問新來的女孩是誰，回答應說明女孩的姓名或身分，(C) 指出「她是來接替艾倫的位置。」，說明了她在這裡的身分，故為正選。

27 I suddenly feel very dizzy and tired.
(A) I'm glad to hear you're feeling better.
(B) It could be a side effect of your pills.
(C) Maybe you should go to the dentist.

我突然覺得又暈又累。
(A) 我很高興聽到你好轉了。
(B) 可能是你的藥丸的副作用。
(C) 也許你應該去看牙醫。

正解 **(B)**

本題為直述句，表示自己有暈眩和疲憊的症狀。回答應針對這兩個症狀作回應，選項 (B)「可能是你的藥丸的副作用。」為符合邏輯的回應，故為正解。

(A) 回答內容與題目矛盾。
(C) 暈眩和疲憊的症狀與牙科範疇無關。

---

28 It must be a special occasion because you look amazing.
(A) Oh no, I didn't know we had to dress up.
(B) Thanks, it's Jason's graduation ceremony.
(C) Wow, they do look amazing today!

今天一定是個特殊日子，因為你看起來美極了。
(A) 喔不，我之前不知道我們要盛裝打扮。
(B) 謝謝，今天是傑森的畢業典禮。
(C) 哇，他們今天的確看起來很棒！

正解 **(B)**

本題為直述句，稱讚對方看起來很美。適當的回應為選項 (B)「謝謝，今天是傑森的畢業典禮。」，表示感謝對方的讚美並說明盛裝打扮的原因，故為正解。

---

29 Would you like to pay for this in installments?
(A) No, you don't have to pay for this.
(B) Yes, we can do six payments.
(C) Yes, we can pay the full amount now.

您是否想要用分期付款？
(A) 不，你不需要為這個付錢。
(B) 是的，我們可以分六期付款。
(C) 是的，我們現在可以全額付款。

正解 **(B)**

本題詢問對方是否要分期付款。回答應以是否分期或分幾期回應，故最符合邏輯的答案為 (B)「是的，我們可以分六期付款」。

(C) 回應先是以肯定回覆表示要分期，後面又說可以全額支付，互相矛盾。

---

30 What do you like to do in your leisure time?
(A) I don't have time to go, sorry.
(B) I enjoy doing yoga and going swimming.
(C) I have time, if you want to do something.

你在閒暇時間喜歡做什麼？
(A) 我沒空過去，抱歉。
(B) 我喜歡做瑜珈和去游泳。
(C) 我有空，如果你有想做的事情的話。

正解 **(B)**

本題詢問對方閒暇時間喜歡做什麼，回答應說明喜歡的休閒活動。唯一符合邏輯的答案為 (B)「我喜歡做瑜珈和去游泳」，故為正解。

31 What kind of food do you like?

(A) I love Italian cuisine.

(B) I don't like to cook.

(C) The food is bad.

你喜歡哪一種食物？

(A) 我喜歡義式菜餚。

(B) 我不喜歡下廚。

(C) 這個食物壞掉了。

正解 **(A)**

本題以 What kind . . . 詢問對方喜歡的食物類型。回答應以喜歡哪種食物作為回應，因此合乎題意的選項為 (A)「我喜歡義式菜餚。」

Part 3: Short Conversations

Questions 32-34 refer to the following conversation.

W: Good afternoon. I'd like to make an appointment with Dr. Goodwin. I missed my follow-up appointment last week.

M: That's not a problem. We can schedule a new appointment for you. What time and day would you like to come in?

W: Do you have an opening around 2 p.m. tomorrow afternoon? Or do you have one at 3 p.m. the day after tomorrow?

M: We do have an opening on Friday at 3 p.m. I will schedule the appointment for 3 p.m. Please come half an hour before to do the pre-consultation with our nurse.

女：午安。我要和古德溫醫師預約時間。我錯過了上週的回診。

男：沒問題。我們可以幫妳重新預約。妳想要在哪天的哪個時間過來？

女：你們明天下午兩點有時間嗎？或是後天下午三點？

男：我們星期五下午三點有時間。我幫妳預約下午三點。請提早半個小時到以便讓我們的護士進行就診前的諮詢。

32 Why does the woman have to schedule a new appointment?

(A) She has to make an appointment for her son.

(B) She missed her appointment last week.

(C) She has new symptoms that concern her.

(D) Dr. Goodwin asked her to schedule a new one.

女子為何要重新預約？

(A) 她要幫她兒子預約。

(B) 她錯過了上週的預約。

(C) 她有新的症狀讓她很擔心。

(D) 古德溫醫師要求她預約新的時間。

正解 **(B)**

題目問女子為何要重新預約。由女子開頭說 I missed my follow-up appointment last week. 得知她錯過了上週的回診，所以答案為 (B)。

33 What day is the woman calling on?
(A) Friday   **(B) Wednesday**
(C) Thursday   (D) Monday

女子是哪天打電話？
(A) 星期五   **(B) 星期三**
(C) 星期四   (D) 星期一

正解 (B)

題目問女子打電話的時間。由女子問說 Or do you have one at 3 p.m. the day after tomorrow? 而男子回說 We do have an opening on Friday at 3 p.m. 可得知後天為星期五，所以女子打電話的時間是 (B) 星期三。

---

34 What most likely is the man's job?
(A) A doctor   (B) A nurse
(C) A receptionist   (D) A dentist

男子的職業最可能是？
(A) 醫師   (B) 護理師
(C) 接待員   (D) 牙醫師

正解 (C)

本題詢問男子的職業。對話中男子協助女子預約醫師時間，且最後男子又說 Please come half an hour before to do the pre-consultation with our nurse. 由此得知男子並非醫師或護理師，故按照邏輯推測其為 (C) 接待員。

Questions 35-37 refer to the following conversation.

M: Sarah, have you sent the latest quotes for the marble and **granite countertops** to Mr. Davies?

W: Yes, I sent them yesterday. He says he wants the granite. I told him marble would last longer, and will be protected from all the hot pans and pots, but he still wants the granite.

M: You're right. The marble would be better. Do you think you could find a cheaper quote to convince him? Or, better yet, what if we use a combination of marble and granite?

W: I don't know if combining the two is a good option. But let me call the manufacturer to find out.

• granite *(n.)* 花崗岩
• countertop *(n.)* 操作檯；料理檯

男：莎拉，妳把大理石和花崗岩料理台的最新報價給戴菲斯先生了嗎？

女：是，我昨天寄了。他說他想要花崗岩。我跟他說大理石可以用比較久，且可以耐受熱鍋和熱壺，但他還是想用花崗岩的材質。

男：妳說得沒錯。大理石會比較好。妳認為妳能想辦法用更便宜的報價來說服他嗎？或者，更好的是，如果我們結合大理石和花崗岩怎麼樣？

女：我不知道結合這兩種是不是好的選擇。但讓我打給製造商問問看。

模擬測驗

35 What project are the speakers most likely talking about?

(A) Constructing a new bedroom

(B) Constructing a new bathroom

(C) Making marble statues

(D) Making new kitchen counters

說話者最有可能在討論什麼專案計畫？

(A) 建造新的臥室

(B) 建造新的浴室

(C) 製作大理石的雕像

(D) 製作新的廚房料理台

正解 **(D)**

本題詢問對話中的說話者可能討論的專案計畫為何。由開頭男子問 ... quotes for the marble and granite countertops to Mr. Davies? 以及女子提到 ... marble would last longer, and will be protected from all the hot pans and pots ... ，從當中的關鍵字詞 countertops、hot pans and pots 等可得知此專案計畫為製作廚房料理台，答案為 (D)。

36 What does the man want the woman to do?

(A) Choose new materials

(B) Use granite countertops

(C) Call the manufacturer

(D) Find a cheaper quote

男子想要女子去做什麼？

(A) 選擇新的材料

(B) 使用花崗岩料理台

(C) 打電話給製造商

(D) 想辦法提供更便宜的報價

正解 **(D)**

題目問男子想要女子做的事。由男子說 Do you think you could find a cheaper quote to convince him? 可以得知男子希望女子想辦法提供更便宜的報價來說服戴菲斯先生，答案為 (D)。

37 What does the man suggest would be a better option for the client?

(A) Using granite only

(B) Combining granite and marble

(C) Canceling the order

(D) Putting the price up

男子建議對客戶而言更好的選擇是什麼？

(A) 只用花崗岩

(B) 結合花崗岩和大理石

(C) 取消訂單

(D) 提高價錢

正解 **(B)**

題目問男子建議對客戶而言更好的選擇為何。由男子說 Or, better yet, what if we use a combination of marble and granite? 可以得知男子建議使用結合大理石和花崗岩的料理台，故答案為 (B)。

Questions 38-40 refer to the following conversation.

M: I don't mind working overtime sometimes, but this is the third time in two weeks.

W: I know! It's getting out of hand. They really need to hire someone new.

M: They shouldn't even have agreed to so many new orders before hiring someone new. We were barely keeping up before.

W: That's true. And the money they're spending on our overtime is probably equal to a new employee's salary.

男：我不介意有時候加班，但這次是這兩週裡第三次了。

女：我知道！情況無法控制了。他們真的需要聘雇新人。

男：而且他們甚至不該在找到新人之前同意接下這麼多新的訂單。我們之前幾乎趕不上進度。

女：沒錯。而且他們花在我們加班上的費用可能等同於一位新員工的薪水。

---

38 What are the speakers concerned about?

(A) They don't like working with a coworker.

(B) They have been working overtime too often.

(C) They haven't been paid for working overtime.

(D) They don't want to train a new employee.

說話者的憂慮為何？

(A) 他們不喜歡和一位同事一起工作。

(B) 他們太常加班。

(C) 他們加班沒有得到加班費。

(D) 他們不想要訓練新員工。

正解 (B)

題目問說話者在擔心什麼。由男子開頭說 I don't mind working overtime sometimes, but this is the third time in two weeks. 以及接著皆在討論有關加班的問題，故可得知答案為 (B)。

---

39 What does the woman think about working overtime again?

(A) She feels like quitting.

(B) The situation is out of control.

(C) The company is acting illegally.

(D) It's a good way to make extra money.

女子對於再度加班看法如何？

(A) 她想要辭職。

(B) 情況已經失控。

(C) 公司不合法。

(D) 這是多賺點錢的好方式。

正解 (B)

本題詢問女子對於再度加班的看法。由女子回答說 It's getting out of hand. 可得知她認為情況失去控制。片語 get out of hand 即為「失去控制」之意。答案為 (B)。

40 Why have the speakers been so busy recently?

(A) The company fired a lot of employees.

(B) The company accepted a lot of new orders.

(C) They haven't been working efficiently.

(D) They have been taking a lot of leave.

說話者為何最近這麼忙碌？

(A) 公司資遣了很多員工。

(B) 公司接受很多新的訂單。

(C) 他們工作沒有效率。

(D) 他們請很多天假。

正解 **(B)**

題目問說話者最近忙碌的原因。由男子說 They shouldn't even have agreed to so many new orders before hiring someone new. 可以得知公司同意接很多新訂單，導致他們幾乎趕不上進度（barely keeping up），答案為 (B)。

Questions 41-43 refer to the following conversation.

M: I would like to inquire about the freight charge on my latest order of **utensils**. It was much higher than usual, and it still hasn't arrived.

W: Let me take a look at your account. It seems the latest order was sent from Los Angeles to Sydney, Australia, and is due to arrive on March 23.

M: There must be a mistake. I always place the same order twice a year for my restaurant in Sydney, Nova Scotia. That's Canada. Please check your records to see where the mistake came in.

W: On our records it shows that this was a rush order placed on the 23rd of March and confirmed by you, Mr. Jones.

M: Oh no, that's my bad. I was also trying to place a rush order of napkins for my restaurant in Australia. I must have mixed up the orders.

W: According to our records, 100 boxes of napkins will be delivered to your restaurant in Canada tomorrow. And 10 sets of utensils will be delivered to your restaurant in Australia next week.

M: OK, that will have to do. But let me place an order for utensils and napkins to go to the right restaurants.

男：我想要詢問有關我廚房器具最新訂單的運費。它比平常貴很多，而且還沒有送達。

女：讓我看一下您的帳戶。看起來最新的訂單是從洛杉磯運送到澳洲雪梨，預計會在三月二十三日送達。

男：一定是出錯了。我一直以來每年會幫我在新斯科舍省雪梨市的餐廳下兩次同樣的訂單。那是在加拿大。請查詢妳的記錄看看是哪裡出問題。

女：我們的記錄上顯示這是在三月二十三日下的緊急訂單，且經瓊斯先生您確認過了。

男：喔不，那是我的錯。我也為我在澳洲的餐廳下了餐巾紙的緊急訂單。我一定是把訂單搞混了。

女：根據我們的記錄，一百盒的餐巾紙明天會送達您在加拿大的餐廳。然後十組的廚房器具會在下週送到您在澳洲的餐廳。

男：好，那也只能這樣。但讓我下單將廚房器具和餐巾紙送到正確的餐廳。

• utensil *(n.)* （廚房或家用的）器皿；器具

41 Why were the man's shipping costs higher?

(A) **He accidentally shipped the products to the wrong country.**

(B) He forgot to write an address when he made the order.

(C) He shipped more items than usual to Australia.

(D) He shipped fewer items to Canada than before.

為何男子的運費比較貴？

(A) 他不小心把貨物運送到錯誤的國家。

(B) 他下訂單時忘記寫地址。

(C) 他比平時運送更多的品項到澳洲。

(D) 他比之前運送較少的品項到加拿大。

正解 **(A)**

題目詢問為何男子的運費比較貴。由 Oh no, that's my bad. I was also trying to place a rush order of napkins for my restaurant in Australia. I must have mixed up the orders. 得知男子把兩份訂單搞錯，把要送到加拿大的訂單送到澳洲了，所以答案為 (A)。

---

42 What does the man mean when he says, "that's my bad"?

(A) It's a bad order.

(B) He's having a bad day.

(C) **He made a mistake.**

(D) The products are bad.

男子說 "that's my bad" 是什麼意思？

(A) 這訂單很糟糕。

(B) 他這一天過得很糟糕。

(C) 他犯了一個錯誤。

(D) 這產品不好。

正解 **(C)**

本題詢問男子說 that's my bad 的意思。that's my bad 為「那是我的錯」之意，且由後面又說 I must have mixed up the orders. 得知男子承認是自己搞錯訂單了，所以答案為 (C)。

---

43 Where is the utensils order being sent to?

(A) Canada

(B) **Australia**

(C) The USA

(D) The UK

廚房器具的訂單被送到哪裡？

(A) 加拿大

(B) 澳洲

(C) 美國

(D) 英國

正解 **(B)**

題目問廚房器具的訂單會被送到的地方。女子在對話的最後說 And 10 sets of utensils will be delivered to your restaurant in Australia next week. 所以得知廚房器具會被送到澳洲，答案是 (B)。

Questions 44-46 refer to the following conversation.

M: Hi, Stephanie. It's Mark from CB Concepts. I am calling to offer you the position of IT Assistant. Congratulations!

W: Thank you, Mark. I am so happy and honored to hear that. I mentioned my travel plans for later in the year during the interview. Will this be a problem?

M: It won't be. Just give the dates to the HR manager next week. And you will need to use your week of annual leave. So we will start you off at $30,000 per month with health insurance and retirement benefits.

W: That all seems in order. And there is a three-month probationary period, right?

M: That's correct. During the three months you will receive some on-the-job training to help you **find your feet**. After that we will sit down and discuss your performance and future role with the company.

W: That sounds good to me, thank you. I would like to formally accept the offer. And I will hand in my 30-days' notice at my current company tomorrow.

M: That's good to hear. We look forward to having you on board!

男：嗨，史蒂芬妮。我是 CB 概念公司的馬克。我打給妳是要提供妳資訊科技助理的職位。恭喜妳！

女：謝謝你，馬克。我非常開心且很榮幸聽到這個消息。我在面試時提到我今年稍晚有旅遊計畫。這會有問題嗎？

男：不會。只要下週給人事部經理日期就行了。並且妳得用妳一週的年假。所以我們將提供妳每個月三萬元的起薪，含健保和退休福利金。

女：那聽起來很完善。有三個月的試用期，對嗎？

男：沒錯。這三個月期間妳會接受一些在職訓練來幫助妳適應。在那之後我們會坐下來討論妳的表現以及未來在公司的職責。

女：那聽起來不錯，謝謝你。我想要正式接受這份職務。我會明天會向我目前的公司提出三十天前的離職通知。

男：很高興聽到妳這麼說。我們期待妳到職！

• find one's feet (phr.) 習慣於新環境；（在新環境）立足；站穩腳跟

⓸⓸ What is the woman concerned about?
(A) The salary
(B) The benefits
(C) Taking leave
(D) The job description

女子擔心什麼？
(A) 薪水
(B) 福利
(C) 請假
(D) 職務說明

正解 **(C)**

題目詢問女子擔心的事。由女子說 I mentioned my travel plans for later in the year during the interview. Will this be a problem? 可得知女子擔心請假會不會有問題，所以答案為 (C)。

45 What will happen during the first three months of her employment?

(A) She will receive some training.
(B) She will go on a business trip.
(C) She will be training other employees.
(D) She will not be paid.

在她被雇用的前三個月期間會發生什麼？

(A) 她將會接受一些訓練。
(B) 她將會去出差。
(C) 她將要訓練其他員工。
(D) 她將沒有薪水。

正解 **(A)**

題目詢問女子被雇用的前三個月期間會發生的事。女子詢問 And there is a three-month probationary period, right? 而男子回答中說 During the three months you will receive some on-the-job training . . . 可得知女子會接受在職訓練課程，答案為 (A)。

---

46 When will the woman be able to start at the new company?

(A) Right away   **(B) In a month**
(C) Next week   (D) Tomorrow

女子何時會開始在新公司工作？

(A) 馬上   **(B) 一個月後**
(C) 下週   (D) 明天

正解 **(B)**

本題詢問女子何時會開始在新公司工作。由女子說 And I will hand in my 30-days' notice at my current company tomorrow. 可得知女子明天會向目前公司提出三十天前的離職通知，一個月後再到新公司任職，所以答案為 (B)。

Questions 47-49 refer to the following conversation.

W: Mr. Jeffreys, could I talk to you for a minute? I need to take a few days off next week, please.

M: Janice, you just came back from a two-week holiday. You actually don't have any more annual leave days left.

W: I know. I actually need to take bereavement leave. My grandmother died last night, and I would like to go to the funeral next week.

M: Oh, I apologize for my earlier response and I'm so sorry to hear that. Unfortunately, I do have to ask you to give HR the proper documentation to get the three days off.

W: Of course, it's not a problem. Thank you for your **condolences**. Would it be possible for me to take an extra day of personal leave? The funeral will be in Florida so I have to add extra days for traveling.

M: That's asking a lot. But I do understand the situation. I will approve it but I'm afraid that's the last leave day I can approve for this quarter.

女：傑佛里斯先生，我可以和你談一下嗎？麻煩一下，我下週需要請幾天假。

男：珍妮絲，妳才剛放完兩週的假。事實上妳沒有剩任何年假了。

女：我知道。我實際上是要請喪假。我祖母昨晚過世了，我下週想去參加葬禮。

男：喔，我對我剛才的反應道歉，我很遺憾聽到那個消息。不過我還是必須要求妳提供適當的文件給人力資源部來取得三天休假。

女：當然，這不是問題。謝謝你的慰問。有可能再讓我多請一天事假嗎？葬禮在佛羅里達州，所以我需要多幾天往返。

男：那樣請太多假了。但我確實了解這個情況。我會核准，但恐怕那是這一季我能核准的最後一次休假了。

• condolence *(n.)* 慰問；弔唁（常用複數）

251

47 How many days does Janice want to take off?

(A) Two weeks   (B) Three days

(C) One day   **(D) Four days**

珍妮絲想要休幾天假？

(A) 兩週   (B) 三天

(C) 一天   **(D) 四天**

正解 **(D)**

本題詢問珍妮絲想要休假的天數。由傑佛里斯先生說 . . . give HR the proper documentation to get the three days off. 得知珍妮絲會有三天喪假，珍妮絲後來又詢問 Would it be possible for me to take an extra day of personal leave? 可知她想再多休一天假，而傑佛里斯先生最後有答應會核准，故知總計是四天，答案為 (D)。

---

48 Why can Mr. Jeffreys not approve more leave days?

(A) Janice has already taken too many days this quarter.

(B) The company doesn't allow employees to take leave.

(C) The company doesn't give bereavement leave.

(D) Janice doesn't qualify for annual leave days.

為何傑佛里斯先生不能再核准更多的休假？

(A) 珍妮絲這一季已經休太多天假了。

(B) 公司不准員工請假。

(C) 公司不給予喪假。

(D) 珍妮絲不符合資格休年假。

正解 **(A)**

題目問傑佛里斯先生不核准更多休假的原因。由一開始傑佛里斯先生說 Janice, you just came back from a two-week holiday. 以及最後說到 . . . I'm afraid that's the last leave day I can approve for this quarter. 得知珍妮絲這一季已經休太多天假了，所以答案是 (A)。

---

49 Which of the following does the woman most likely have to give HR?

(A) Her condolences

(B) An job application

(C) A death certificate

(D) An airplane ticket

女子最有可能需要提供下列何者給人力資源部？

(A) 她的弔唁詞

(B) 工作申請書

(C) 死亡證明書

(D) 機票

正解 **(C)**

本題詢問珍妮絲請喪假要給人力資源部什麼。珍妮絲提出要請喪假後，傑佛里斯先生回應說 Unfortunately, I do have to ask you to give HR the proper documentation to get the three days off. 得知須提供適當文件給人力資源部，按照邏輯喪假的證明文件應為 (C)「死亡證明書」。

M: Ms. Grey, I'm James Harris. I just wanted to introduce myself and welcome you on board.

W: Thank you, James. It's a pleasure to be here. I look forward to helping all of you improve the standards of the QC department.

M: That's great. We're looking forward to having someone with your experience lead us. We definitely need to improve.

W: I'm happy to hear that. I will be having a one-on-one meeting with all of you to hear your ideas and concerns.

男：格瑞女士，我是詹姆士‧海瑞斯。我只是要自我介紹並歡迎妳到職。

女：謝謝你，詹姆士。我很榮幸來到這裡。我期待幫助你們所有人改進品管部門的水準。

男：那太棒了。我們很期待能有像妳這樣經驗豐富的人來領導我們。我們確實需要改進。

女：我很高興聽你這麼說。我會和你們所有人一對一開會來聽聽你們的想法和顧慮。

---

50 What position is the woman most likely starting?

(A) Quality Control Assistant

(B) Head of Quality Control

(C) HR Manager

(D) Personal Assistant

女子最可能由什麼職位開始任職？

(A) 品管助理　　　　(B) 品管部長

(C) 人力資源經理　　(D) 私人助理

正解 (B)

題目詢問女子最可能任職的職位。由女子說 ... helping all of you improve the standards of the QC department. 得知女子要來幫助品管部門改善水準，而男子接著又說 ... someone with your experience lead us.，可知女子是要來帶領品管部門人員，所以可以推斷答案為 (B) 品管部長。

---

51 Who most likely is James Harris?

(A) The CEO of the company

(B) The HR manager

(C) Head of Quality Control

(D) An employee in the QC department

誰最可能是詹姆士‧海瑞斯？

(A) 公司的執行長　　(B) 人力資源經理

(C) 品管部長　　　　(D) 品管部的職員

正解 (D)

題目問詹姆士‧海瑞斯最可能的職位。當格瑞女士說要來幫助品管部改善水準，詹姆士‧海瑞斯便說 ... someone with your experience lead us. 可知詹姆士期待格瑞女士的領導，推測其應為品管部的職員，答案為 (D)。

---

52 Why is James excited to have Ms. Grey on board?

(A) She will make a lot of money.

(B) She is very experienced.

(C) She'll impress board members.

(D) She might give him a raise.

為何詹姆士對於格瑞女士到職感到興奮？

(A) 她會賺很多錢。

(B) 她很有經驗。

(C) 她會讓董事會成員印象深刻。

(D) 她可能會幫他加薪。

正解 (B)

題目問詹姆士對於格瑞女士到職感到興奮的原因。由詹姆士說 We're looking forward to having someone with your experience lead us. 得知他期待格瑞女士以其豐富的經驗來帶領他們，所以答案是 (B)。

SECTION C

模擬測驗

Questions 53-55 refer to the following conversation.

M: Hey, Mary. When is your lunch hour at work? And do you have plans during lunch tomorrow? I'm going to see a client around 11 a.m.

W: Hi, John. I usually take lunch around 1 p.m. but it's flexible here. I can change the time if you're going to be **in my neck of the woods**.

M: I think it should work, but maybe we should make it 1:30 just in case. Do you have any suggestions for lunch? I'm dying for a good pizza!

W: In that case, we have to go to Mr. Toni's. It's about 10 minutes from my office. I will send you the address and I can meet you there. In fact, check out their menu and let me know what you want. Then I can order ahead of time.

男：嘿，瑪莉。妳上班的午休時間是什麼時候？妳明天午餐時間有什麼計畫嗎？我大約早上十一點要去見客戶。

女：嗨，約翰。我通常下午一點左右吃午餐，不過在這裡很有彈性。如果你要到我公司附近我可以改時間。

男：我想這樣可行，但以防萬一，或許我們應該要約一點半。妳對於午餐有什麼建議嗎？我很想要吃好吃的披薩！

女：那樣的話，我們得去湯尼先生餐廳。它離我辦公室大約十分鐘的路程。我會傳地址給你，然後和你在那裡碰面。事實上，先看看他們的菜單讓我知道你想要吃什麼。那樣我可以事先點餐。

• in this/one's neck of the woods *(phr.)* 在這／某人所處的這一帶

---

53 When does John want to meet Mary?

(A) At 11 a.m.　　　(B) At 1 p.m.

(C) **At 1:30 p.m.**　(D) In 10 minutes

約翰想要什麼時間跟瑪莉碰面？

(A) 上午十一點　　(B) 下午一點

(C) 下午一點半　　(D) 十分鐘內

正解 (C)

本題為細節題。題目問約翰想要跟瑪莉碰面的時間。由約翰說 I think it should work, but maybe we should make it 1:30 just in case. 可得知他想要約下午一點半，答案為 (C)。

---

54 What can be inferred about the woman's job?

(A) She has strict office hours.

(B) Everyone takes lunch at the same time.

(C) The office closes during lunch.

(D) **She can decide when to have lunch.**

關於女子的工作可以推斷出什麼？

(A) 她的上班時間很嚴格。

(B) 每個人在同一時間吃午餐。

(C) 辦公室午休時間會關閉。

(D) **她可以決定哪個時間吃午餐。**

正解 (D)

本題問關於女子的工作可以推斷出什麼。由女子說 I usually take lunch around 1 p.m. but it's flexible here.，形容詞 flexible 是「可變動的；有彈性的」之意，所以答案為 (D)。

55 What type of restaurant is Mr. Toni's most likely?

(A) A pizzeria

(B) A fast-food place

(C) A Chinese restaurant

(D) A vegetarian restaurant

湯尼先生最可能是哪個類型的餐廳？

(A) 披薩店　　　(B) 速食店

(C) 中式餐廳　　　(D) 素食餐廳

正解 (A)

題目問湯尼先生是哪一種餐廳。由於約翰說 I'm dying for a good pizza! 而瑪莉馬上回應說 In that case, we have to go to Mr. Toni's.，故得知應為披薩店，答案為 (A)。

Questions 56-58 refer to the following conversation.

W: I've been looking at your portfolio and I think you should diversify your assets more. Currently, most of your investments are in real estate. Although that is a good investment, it might be worth the risk to invest in the stock market.

M: I've thought about it, but it just seems too **speculative** to me. I'm not sure if I could handle the stress. I've been researching **cryptocurrency** as well, but that seems even riskier to me! As far as I know, you guys only started investing in that last year, am I right?

W: That's right. The firm decided to start a separate division to solely focus on that. I'd be happy to set up an appointment, if you are interested. For now, though, I think we should start small. Let's move some of your interest into the stock market. That way, you won't lose any capital.

女：我一直在看你的投資組合，我想你應該讓你的資產更多樣化。目前你大部分的投資都在房地產。雖然那是好的投資，但應該值得冒險去投資股票。

男：我有想過，但這對我來講太過投機。我不確定我是否能承受這種壓力。我也一直在研究加密貨幣，但對我來說那看起來似乎更冒險！就我所知，你們去年才剛開始投資那個對嗎？

女：沒錯。公司決定成立一個獨立的部門專門處理那方面的投資。若你有興趣，我很樂意安排會面。然而以目前來說，我認為我們應該從小額投資開始。讓我們運用你的一些利息投入股票市場。那樣一來你就不會損失任何資本。

• speculative *(adj.)* 投機性的；猜測的
• cryptocurrency *(n.)* 加密貨幣

---

56 What most likely is the woman's job?

(A) A store manager

(B) A real estate agent

(C) An office receptionist

(D) A financial advisor

女子最有可能的職業為何？

(A) 店經理　　　(B) 房地產經紀人

(C) 辦公室接待員　　　**(D) 財務顧問**

正解 (D)

題目詢問女子的職業。由開頭女子說 I've been looking at your portfolio and I think you should diversify your assets more. 得知女子在幫男子看投資組合，並建議他要讓資產多樣化，且之後亦給予投資建議，故推知女子為 (D)「財務顧問」。

57 What is the man's concern about investing in new things?

(A) **He doesn't trust the stock market.**

(B) He prefers cryptocurrency.

(C) He thinks it's too boring.

(D) He doesn't have enough money.

關於新的投資男子的顧慮是什麼？

(A) 他不相信股票市場。 (B) 他偏好加密貨幣。

(C) 他認為太無聊。　　(D) 他沒有足夠的錢。

正解 (A)

本題問男子對於新投資的顧慮。開頭女子建議男子投資股票，而男子回答說 I've thought about it, but it just seems too speculative to me. 得知男子認為股票太過投機，因此不敢嘗試，故答案選 (A)。

---

58 What did the woman's firm do last year?

(A) They started investing in the stock market.

(B) **They opened a department for cryptocurrency.**

(C) They created their own cryptocurrency.

(D) They started advising the man.

女子的公司去年做了什麼？

(A) 他們開始投資股票。

(B) **他們成立了加密貨幣的部門。**

(C) 他們創立自己的加密貨幣。

(D) 他們開始給男子意見。

正解 (B)

本題詢問女子的公司去年做的事。由男子說 I've been researching cryptocurrency . . . you guys only started investing in that last year, am I right? 而女子回應 That's right. The firm decided to start a separate division . . .，可以得知女子的公司去年剛成立了加密貨幣的部門，故答案為 (B)。

Questions 59-61 refer to the following conversation with three speakers.

W1: I think we need to give our sales teams in the new cities more tools to track trends and customers.

M: Why would they need more than the other teams?

W2: Because these are new markets that we are trying to break into. Without these tools they might not be able to reach the market.

M: I'm not sure I follow. Why not just stick with current strategies? They're working fine.

W1: It may look like that but we only have limited information. If we had more information we might be able to perform better, so I think it would be a good idea to track the campaigns more closely.

W2: Good call. We should also have them report back sooner than with other campaigns.

女一：我想我們需要提供我們新城市的業務團隊更多工具來追蹤市場動向和顧客。

男：為什麼他們比其他團隊需要更多工具呢？

女二：因為這裡是我們要打入的新市場。沒有這些工具他們可能無法了解市場。

男：我不太懂妳的意思。為何不就使用目前的策略？它們運作得很好。

女一：看起來可能是這樣，但我們只能得到有限的資訊。如果我們有更多資訊我們可能可以表現得更好，所以我認為更密切追蹤宣傳活動會是個好主意。

女二：我贊同。我們應該也要讓他們比其他宣傳活動更快回報。

59 What are the speakers mainly discussing?

(A) New products for potential customers

(B) Necessary tools for a new product line

(C) Marketing strategies for a new market

(D) Marketing campaigns for a new product

說話者主要在討論什麼？

(A) 提供給潛在客戶的新產品

(B) 提供給新產品系列的必要工具

(C) 新市場的行銷策略

(D) 新產品的行銷活動

正解 (C)

題目詢問說話者在討論的主要內容。關鍵句為女一開頭說 I think we need to give our sales teams in the new cities more tools . . . 以及女二說 Because these are new markets that we are trying to break into. 得知公司將要打入新的市場，而男子回應說 Why not just stick with current strategies? 所以知道是在討論要打入新市場的策略，答案為 (C)。

---

60 What does the man mean when he says, "I'm not sure I follow"?

(A) He doesn't want to follow someone.

(B) He can't see where someone is going.

(C) He's not sure he understands something.

(D) He is lost and not sure where to go.

男子說 "I'm not sure I follow" 是什麼意思？

(A) 他不想要跟隨某人。

(B) 他不知道某人要去哪裡。

(C) 他不確定他理解某件事。

(D) 他迷路了不確定該去哪裡。

正解 (C)

題目問 "I'm not sure I follow" 的意思。開頭女一和女二皆建議可以增加工具來幫助新團隊更了解市場，而男子回答說 I'm not sure I follow. Why not just stick with current strategies? They're working fine. 得知男子認為目前策略運作得很好，因此推測此句意思是 (C)「他不確定他理解某件事。」

---

61 Why shouldn't they stay with current market strategies?

(A) New strategies will definitely work in the new markets.

(B) They definitely won't work in the new markets.

(C) They may be lacking in important information.

(D) Employees have complained about the old strategies.

為什麼他們不應該沿用目前的行銷策略？

(A) 新策略絕對能在新市場奏效。

(B) 目前的策略絕對無法在新市場奏效。

(C) 他們可能會缺少重要資訊。

(D) 員工在抱怨舊的策略。

正解 (C)

題目詢問他們不應該沿用現有行銷策略的原因。當男子問說 Why not just stick with current strategies? They're working fine.，女一回應說 It may look like that but we only have limited information.，得知使用目前策略所獲得的資訊有限，所以答案選 (C)。

Questions 62-64 *refer to the following conversation and coupon.*

W: I love how you've arranged the whole store according to seasons. Even the fitting rooms are temperature-controlled to make trying on clothes more comfortable.

M: We're pleased to hear that. We've been working very hard to create the best environment for our customers to find items that will work for them.

W: Well, you've succeeded! Here are the things I want, and could I have this necklace as the free accessory with this coupon?

M: You are **entitled** to a free accessory, but unfortunately that necklace is from the summer collection and isn't included in the promotion anymore. The accessories included in the current promotion are over there in the fall collection.

• entitle *(v.)* 給……權力（或資格）

女：我喜歡你整間店按照季節擺放商品。即使試衣間也有溫度控管讓試穿衣服時更加舒適。

男：我們很開心聽您這麼說。我們一直很努力創造最好的環境讓顧客找到適合他們的商品。

女：嗯，你成功了！這裡是我要的東西，我可以使用這張折價券得到這條項鍊作為免費的配件嗎？

男：妳可以享有一樣免費的配件，不過可惜的是那條項鍊屬於夏季商品，不再包含在促銷裡。目前促銷所涵蓋的配件是在那裡的秋季商品。

Nouveau Fashion

SPECIAL PROMOTION
➢ Buy 4 items from our Fall Collection and get a matching accessory free!
➢ Buy 3 items get 15% off
➢ Buy 2 items get 10% off

Only valid until 10th September

新潮流

特別促銷
➢ 買四樣秋季商品贈送一樣配件！
➢ 買三樣商品打八五折
➢ 買兩樣商品打九折

只到九月十日前有效

62 What is special about this store?
(A) They have just opened recently.
(B) Their bathrooms have air conditioning.
(C) The items are organized by season.
(D) They are environmentally friendly.

這間店有什麼特別的？
(A) 他們最近才剛開幕。
(B) 他們的廁所有空調。
(C) 商品依季節有條理地擺放。
(D) 他們很環保。

正解 **(C)**
題目詢問這間店特別之處。由開頭女子說 I love how you've arranged the whole store according to seasons. 得知這間店按照季節擺放商品，所以答案為 (C)。

63 Look at the graphic. How many items does the woman buy?

(A) 1   (B) 2

(C) 3   **(D) 4**

看圖表。女子買了多少樣商品？

(A) 一樣   (B) 兩樣

(C) 三樣   **(D) 四樣**

正解 (D)

本題為圖表題，須結合對話與圖表作答。題目詢問女子購買幾項商品。由女子問是否可使用折價券得到免費配件，而男子肯定回答說 You are entitled to a free accessory。對照折價券得知要獲得免費配件須購買四樣商品，所以答案為 (D)。

----

64 Where can the woman find a free item?

(A) In the winter section

(B) In the summer section

(C) In the fall section

(D) In the spring section

女子在哪可以找到免費的商品？

(A) 在冬季商品區

(B) 在夏季商品

(C) 在秋季商品區

(D) 在春季商品區

正解 (C)

題目問女子可以找到免費商品的地方。關鍵句為男子提到女子可享有免費配件（free accessory），最後又說 The accessories included in the current promotion are over there in the fall collection. 得知免費商品在秋季商品區，所以答案是 (C)。

Questions 65-67 refer to the following conversation and departure board.

W: Hi, I'm worried that I might have missed my train. Could you help me?

M: I see. What time was the train scheduled to depart?

W: 8:15 from Platform 3.

M: Ah, yes. It was delayed, so you might just make it if you rush. If not, come back and we can switch your ticket to the next one that leaves.

W: OK, thanks very much for your help. Wish me luck!

M: Good luck!

女：嗨，我擔心我可能錯過我的火車班次了。你可以幫我嗎？

男：了解。火車預計幾點發車？

女：八點十五分從第三月台

男：嗯，好。它延遲了，所以妳如果快一點應該剛好可以搭上。如果沒搭上，回來這裡我們可以幫妳換成下一班的車票。

女：好，感謝你的幫忙。祝我好運！

男：祝妳好運！

Due	Destination	Status	Platform
08:09	Stratford (London)	On time	1
08:10	Bishop's Stortford	On time	4
08:13	London Liverpool Street via Seven Sisters	On time	2
08:15	Hertford East	08:18 3 mins late	3
08:18	London Liverpool Street	On time	2

預定時間	目的地	狀態	月台
八點九分	斯特拉特福（倫敦）	準點	第一月台
八點十分	彼謝普斯託福	準點	第四月台
八點十三分	倫敦利物浦街 行經七姊妹巖	準點	第二月台
八點十五分	赫特福德火車東站	八點十八分 延遲三分鐘	第三月台
八點十八分	倫敦利物浦街	準點	第二月台

65 Where most likely are the speakers?

(A) The MRT

(B) A bus station

(C) A train station

(D) A ferry terminal

說話者最有可能在哪裡？

(A) 捷運站

(B) 公車站

(C) 火車站

(D) 渡船碼頭

正解 (C)

題目詢問說話者最有可能的所在地點。關鍵句為開頭女子說 Hi, I'm worried that I might have missed my train. 由此可知他們在火車站。答案選 (C)。

---

66 Look at the graphic. Where is the woman trying to go?

(A) Stratford (London)

(B) Bishop's Stortford

(C) Hertford East

(D) London Liverpool Street

看圖表。該名女子要去哪裡？

(A) 斯特拉特福（倫敦）

(B) 彼謝普斯託福

(C) 赫特福德火車東站

(D) 倫敦利物浦街

正解 (C)

本題為圖表題，詢問該名女子要去的地方。由男子問說 What time was the train scheduled to depart? 而女子回說 8:15 from Platform 3.。對照圖表第三月台所顯示的目的地為 Hertford East，故答案選 (C)。

---

67 What will the woman most likely do next?

(A) Call the police

(B) Buy a new ticket

(C) Run to a platform

(D) Choose another destination

該名女子接下來最有可能會做什麼？

(A) 打電話給警察

(B) 買一張新的票

(C) 跑去月台

(D) 改去其他目的地

正解 (C)

題目問該名女子接下來最有可能會做的事，關鍵句為男子說 It was delayed, so you might just make it if you rush. 由此可知女子接下來應該會趕緊跑到月台搭車，答案選 (C)。

Questions 68-70 refer to the following conversation and chart.

M: Hi, this is Marlon Denning from Eight-Star. I'm calling to ask how production is coming along.

W: We're ahead of schedule. I've shot all the principal **footage**, sent the actors home for the week, and now we're moving into post-production. My script has really **come to life**!

M: Have you **settled on** a title yet? Also, you'd better be under 40 million. I care about my money more than anything.

W: Yes, we have a title, and yes, of course we're still under budget. **Editing** is underway as we speak, and I believe everything will look great.

男：妳好，我是八星公司的馬龍・丹寧。我打電話來詢問製片的進度。

女：我們的進度超前。我已經拍完所有主要的片段，打發演員回家休息一週，現在我們正要準備後製。我的劇本都活了起來！

男：妳決定好片名了嗎？還有，妳最好沒有花超過四千萬。我在乎我的錢勝過一切。

女：是的，我們有片名了，而且我們當然還是在預算之內。在我們講話的同時，剪輯正在進行中，我相信一切都會看起來很棒的。

- footage *(n.)* 影片；影片片段
- come to life *(phr.)* 變得栩栩如生、生動有趣；活躍起來
- settle on/upon *(phr.)* 決定
- edit *(v.)* 剪輯

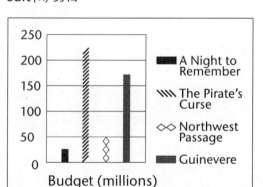

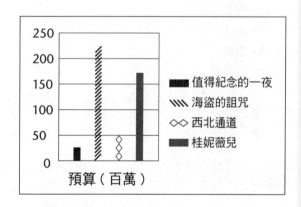

••

68 What is Marlon Denning most concerned about?

(A) The cast of the film

(B) The cost of the film

(C) The title of the film

(D) The script of the film

馬龍・丹寧最關心什麼？

(A) 電影的演員陣容

(B) 電影的成本

(C) 電影的片名

(D) 電影的劇本

正解 (B)

題目問馬龍・丹寧最關心的事。關鍵句為馬龍・丹寧說 Also, you'd better be under 40 million. I care about my money more than anything. 得知他最在乎的是錢，所以答案選 (B)「電影的成本」。

69 Look at the graphic. What is the title of the woman's film?

(A) Guinevere
(B) The Pirate's Curse
(C) Northwest Passage
(D) A Night to Remember

看圖表。女子的電影名稱是什麼？

(A) 桂妮薇兒
(B) 海盜的詛咒
(C) 西北通道
(D) 值得紀念的一夜

正解 (D)

本題為圖表題，詢問女子的電影名稱。答題關鍵是男子提到 Also, you'd better be under 40 million. 之後女子回答 yes, of course we're still under budget.，得知電影預算為四千萬以下，對照圖表預算沒有超過四千萬的電影只有 (D)。

70 Which most likely is Marlon Denning's profession?

(A) A film editor
(B) An actor
(C) A director
(D) An investor

馬龍‧丹寧的職業最有可能是什麼？

(A) 電影剪接師
(B) 演員
(C) 導演
(D) 投資者

正解 (D)

題目問馬龍‧丹寧最有可能的職業。由馬龍‧丹寧詢問了電影的進度、片名、預算且說 I care about my money more than anything. 可判斷他是投資者，答案選 (D)。

Part 4: Short Talks

Questions 71-73 *refer to the following talk.*

I'm Julie Brown and I'm the founder and inventor of the fitness vest. This is a **patent-pending** universal resistance band vest. It can be used for all forms of therapy and at all fitness levels. It has over 30 full body exercises that allow the user the convenience of working out in the comfort of their home. More than 61 million Americans are currently paying health club fees and another 75 million Americans are doing some form of physical fitness therapy **rehab**. That's what inspired myself and my team to invent something new. So please consider investing in my company in exchange for 30% **equity**. I am looking for $300,000 in investment to take this product to market.

- patent-pending *(adj.)* 正在申請專利的；專利申請中的
- rehab *(n.)* 復健 （= rehabilitation）
- equity *(n.)* 普通股；股票

我是茱莉・布朗，是健身背心的創始人和發明者。這是一件正在申請專利的多功能阻力訓練彈力帶背心。它可以用於所有形式的治療，並適合所有健身程度。它具有三十多種全身鍛煉功能，使用者可以在家中舒適地鍛煉身體。目前，有超過六千一百萬名美國人正在支付健身俱樂部費用，另有七千五百萬名美國人正在進行某種形式的體適能治療復健。這就是激發我自己和我的團隊發明新商品的原因。因此，請考慮投資我的公司以換取百分之三十的股票。我正在尋找三十萬美元的投資，以將該產品推向市場。

71 Who is Julie Brown most likely speaking to?
(A) Potential customers
(B) Fitness models
(C) Potential investors
(D) The bank loan manager

朱莉・布朗最有可能在對誰說話？
(A) 潛在客戶　　　(B) 健身模特兒
(C) 潛在投資者　　(D) 銀行借貸經理

正解 **(C)**
本題詢問「朱莉・布朗最有可能在對誰說話？」。由她最後提及 I am looking for $300,000 in investment to take this product to market.「我正在尋找三十萬美元的投資，以將該產品推向市場。」，可知答案為 (C)。

72 Why did the speaker and her team invent this vest?
(A) There are many people who need to lose weight.
(B) There are millions of people who want to exercise.
(C) There are many people who can't leave the house.
(D) There are many people who want to save money.

為什麼說話者和她的團隊要發明這個背心？
(A) 有很多人需要減重。
(B) 有數百萬人想運動。
(C) 有很多人不能離開家。
(D) 有很多人想要存錢。

正解 **(B)**
本題詢問說話者和她的團隊要發明這個背心的原因。由她提及「有超過六千一百萬名美國人正在支付健身俱樂部費用，另有七千五百萬名美國人正在進行某種形式的體適能治療復健。」並接著說 That's what inspired myself and my team . . . ，可知答案為 (B)。

73 What is Julie Brown offering investors in return for their investment?

(A) A guaranteed 30% interest

(B) A 30% share in the company

(C) 30% of the profits she makes

(D) $300,000 per year

朱莉‧布朗為投資者提供什麼作為交換？

(A) 保證百分之三十的利息

(B) 百分之三十的公司股票

(C) 她所賺取利潤的百分之三十

(D) 每年三十萬美元

正解 (B)

本題詢問朱莉‧布朗為投資者提供什麼以換得他們的投資。由她提及 please consider investing in my company in exchange for 30% equity.「請考慮投資我的公司以換取百分之三十的股票。」，可知答案為 (B)。

Questions 74-76 refer to the following meeting excerpt.

In short, ElecCorp can offer you top-of-the-line electronics with flexible payment terms. After your first order, which has to be a minimum of $20,000, we can also extend you a **credit line** of up to $10,000. On top of that, we can negotiate the payment method. Paying in advance would be the most beneficial for you, as we offer a 10 percent discount. On the other hand, if you decide to pay on delivery, then we can't offer any discount. If you put down a 50 percent deposit on your order and pay the rest upon delivery, we could offer a 5 percent discount. We offer payment plans of up to six months if none of these are possible with your current cash flow.

• credit line *(n.)* 信用額度

簡而言之，伊萊克公司可以為您提供具有彈性付款條件的頂級電子產品。在您完成第一筆訂單且金額在兩萬元以上之後，我們還可以將您的信用額度提升至高達一萬元。除此之外，我們可以協商付款方式。預先付款對您最有利，因為我們提供百分之十的折扣。另一方面，如果您決定貨到付款，我們則無法提供任何折扣。如果您支付訂單百分之五十的訂金，並在貨到時付清餘款，我們可以提供百分之五的折扣。如果您目前的現金流量不適用以上任何一種方式，我們將提供最長六個月的付款計畫。

---

74 What most likely is the speaker's job?

(A) A delivery man

(B) A bank manager

(C) A sales representative

(D) A technician

說話者的工作最有可能是什麼？

(A) 送貨員

(B) 銀行經理

(C) 業務代表

(D) 技師

正解 (C)

本題詢問「說話者的工作最有可能是什麼」。由說話者開頭說 ElecCorp can offer you top-of-the-line electronics with flexible payment terms. 得知說話者在推銷產品，且後面又接著說明各種付款方式及所能提供的折扣，因此可推測說話者的工作為 (C)「業務代表」。

75 What would the listener have to do first to start ordering from ElecCorp?

(A) Pay for their full order in advance

(B) Order products worth at least $20,000

(C) Open a line of credit for $10,000

(D) Pay a 50% deposit and the rest upon delivery

聽眾首先必須做什麼才能開始向伊萊克公司訂購？

(A) 預先支付全額訂單

(B) 訂購價值至少兩萬元的產品

(C) 開設一萬元的信用額度

(D) 支付百分之五十的訂金，並在貨到時付清餘款

正解 **(B)**

本題詢問「聽眾首先必須做什麼才能開始向伊萊克公司訂購？」。由說話者提及 After your first order, which has to be a minimum of $20,000, we can also …「在您完成第一筆訂單且金額在兩萬元以上之後，我們還可以……」，可知第一筆訂單的消費須達到兩萬元的門檻，故答案為 (B)。

---

76 What would be the cheapest option to order from ElecCorp?

(A) To pay over six months

(B) To pay with a credit card

(C) To pay in advance

(D) To pay on delivery

向伊萊克公司訂購時最便宜的付款選項是什麼？

(A) 分六個月支付   (B) 信用卡付款

(C) 預先付款   (D) 貨到付款

正解 **(C)**

本題詢問向伊萊克公司訂購時最便宜的付款選項。由說話者提及 Paying in advance would be the most beneficial for you, as we offer a 10 percent discount.「預先付款對您最有利，因為我們提供百分之十的折扣。」，可知答案為 (C)。

(D) 貨到付清餘款的折扣僅百分之五。

Questions 77-79 *refer to the following news report.*

The Board of Directors of ABC Inc. announced today that John Matthews will be appointed as the company's new President and CEO at the end of the month. At the same time, Dave Smith, CEO since 2006 and Chairman, and who had been the President since 2016, will become the Executive Chairman. We are pleased to be welcoming John and Dave to their newly elected positions. Dave Smith will continue to lead the Board of Directors, working closely with Matthews and the senior management team. Matthews is the current President and CEO of LiveNow and also serves on its Board of Directors. He is also Chairman of Fair Holdings and previously served as President and CEO of eDev; a position which he held between 2008 and 2015. Dave earned his bachelor's degree in economics from Dartmouth and his MBA from Stanford.

ABC公司董事會今天宣布，約翰·馬修斯將在本月底被任命為公司的新總裁兼執行長。同時，自二○○六年起擔任執行長兼主席且自二○一六年起擔任總裁的戴夫·史密斯將擔任執行董事。我們很高興歡迎約翰和戴夫擔任新當選的職位。戴夫·史密斯將繼續領導董事會，並與馬修斯和資深管理團隊密切合作。馬修斯是現活公司的現任總裁兼執行長，同時也是其董事會成員。他還是飛爾控股公司的董事長，且之前曾於二○○八年至二○一五年之間曾擔任伊戴夫的總裁兼執行長。戴夫在達特茅斯學院獲得了經濟學學士學位且在史丹佛大學取得了企業管理碩士學位。

77 When did Dave Smith become the CEO at ABC Inc.?

(A) In 2006

(B) In 2016

(C) In 2015

(D) In 2008

戴夫・史密斯何時成為 ABC 公司的執行長？

(A) 二〇〇六年

(B) 二〇一六年

(C) 二〇一五年

(D) 二〇〇八年

正解 **(A)**

本題為細節題。詢問「戴夫・史密斯何時成為 ABC 公司的執行長？」。由說話者一開始宣布 ABC 公司的新總裁兼執行長為約翰・馬修斯後，接著又說 Dave Smith, CEO since 2006 可知戴夫・史密斯乃自二〇〇六年起擔任執行長，故答案為 (A)。

---

78 What does the speaker imply about Dave and John?

(A) They are long-term friends.

(B) They are rivals in the industry.

(C) They will lead ABC Inc.

(D) They went to the same college.

說話者對戴夫和約翰有何暗示？

(A) 他們是多年的好友。

(B) 他們在業界是競爭對手。

(C) 他們將會領導 ABC 公司。

(D) 他們上同一所大學。

正解 **(C)**

本題詢問「說話者對戴夫和約翰有何暗示？」。獨白一開始便宣布 ABC 公司的新總裁兼執行長是約翰・馬修斯，後面又提到 Dave Smith will continue to lead the Board of Directors, working closely with Matthews and the senior management team. ，可知他們兩人都是公司的領導階層，故答案為 (C)。

---

79 What is John Matthews' current position?

(A) CEO of ABC Inc.

(B) CEO of LiveNow

(C) President and CEO of eDev

(D) President at Dartmouth

戴夫・史密斯的目前職位是什麼？

(A) ABC 公司的執行長

(B) 現活公司的執行長

(C) 伊戴芙的總裁兼執行長

(D) 達特茅斯學院的校長

正解 **(B)**

本題詢問「戴夫・史密斯的目前職位是什麼？」。由關鍵句 Matthews is the current President and CEO of LiveNow「馬修斯是現活公司的現任總裁兼執行長」，可知答案為 (B)。

Questions 80-82 refer to the following weather report.

Winter is returning **with a vengeance** to the Greater Chicago Area this weekend. A low-pressure system is expected to bring heavy snowfall and strong winds. The city is preparing for at least two feet of snow. Officials have recommended motorists stay off the road on Friday when the worst of it will hit. Schools are probably going to stay open—sorry kids—but stay tuned on Thursday just in case. Highs for most of this week will stay around a chilly -10°C; however, expect it to feel much colder. With wind chill, temperatures will feel like -20°C. The good news is by Sunday storms should subside and temperatures should return to seasonal averages with highs of -5°C and lows of -12°C. That's all from me. Back to you, Jack.

• with a vengeance *(phr.)* 猛烈地；極度地

冬天將在這個週末猛烈地回到大芝加哥地區。預測低壓系統會帶來大雪和強風。該城市正在為至少兩英尺的積雪作準備。官方建議駕駛人週五勿上路，當天是影響最劇的時候。學校可能會保持開放——抱歉，孩子們——但請在週四等候消息，以防萬一。本週大部分時候最高溫將維持在寒冷的攝氏負十度左右；然而，可預期感覺上會更冷。伴隨著寒風，溫度感覺起來會像是攝氏負二十度。好消息是，暴風雨在週日前將減弱，氣溫應會恢復至季節性的平均值，最高為攝氏負五度，最低為攝氏負十二度。以上是我的報導。交還給你，傑克。

---

80 What has the government asked people to do?
(A) Not go to school
(B) Avoid driving on Friday
(C) Use public transportation
(D) Watch out for heavy winds

政府要求人們做什麼？
(A) 不要到校　　　　(B) 請勿在週五駕駛
(C) 使用大眾運輸　　(D) 當心強風

正解 **(B)**

本題詢問「政府要求人們做什麼？」。由關鍵句 Officials have recommended motorists stay off the road on Friday when the worst of it will hit. 可知官方建議駕駛人週五請勿開車上路，故答案選 (B)。

---

81 What most likely will highs on Friday be?
(A) -5° C　　　　　　**(B) -10° C**
(D) -12° C　　　　　(A) -20° C

週五的最高溫最有可能是？
(A) 攝氏負五度　　　(B) 攝氏負十度
(C) 攝氏負十二度　　(D) 攝氏負二十度

正解 **(B)**

本題詢問「週五的最高溫最有可能是？」。關鍵句為 Highs for most of this week will stay around a chilly -10°C 可知本週大部分時候的最高溫為攝氏負十度左右，故答案為 (B)。

---

82 What is suggested about the weather?
(A) Winter is ending.
(B) It will likely force schools to close.
(C) Things will return to normal next week.
(D) Heavy snowfalls are expected on Sunday.

關於天氣文中有何暗示？
(A) 冬天將結束。　　(B) 有可能會迫使學校關閉。
(C) 下週一切將恢復正常。　(D) 預測週日會降大雪。

正解 **(C)**

本題詢問「關於天氣文中有何暗示？」。由說話者提及 The good news is by Sunday storms should subside and temperatures should return to seasonal averages ... 可知週日前暴風雨將減弱，氣溫應會恢復至季節性的平均值，故推斷下週一開始天氣會恢復正常，因此答案選 (C)。

Questions 83-85 *refer to the following lecture.*

Today, I'd like to give you an update on some key developments in e-commerce in **agriculture**. First, Farm United announced that it's developing and testing an online platform where retailers and farmers can interact. Also, Barrels recently won a food and agriculture technology award. Barrels is an app that **facilitates** the interactions and record-keeping between farmers and companies that buy **grain**. This shows that there are new developments in the grain industry as well. Both of these developments show that there is still a place for traditional links in the supply chain, namely retailers and originators. Retailers need to create the same experience across all their channels to add value to the suppliers and consumers. This will help retailers and originators to succeed.

今天，我想提供您農業電子貿易中一些最新的重要發展資訊。首先，聯合農場宣布正在開發和測試一個供零售商和農民互動的線上平台。另外，貝若斯最近獲得了糧食農業科技獎。貝若斯是一款應用程式，可促進農民與購買穀物的公司之間的互動以及記錄的保存。這顯示穀物產業也有新的發展。這兩項發展均顯示在供應鏈中傳統的關係仍占有一席之地，也就是零售商和原產者。零售商需要在所有的交易管道上創造相同的經驗，才能對供應商和消費者有所幫助。這將幫助零售商和原產者成功。

- agriculture *(n.)* 農業
- facilitate *(v.)* 促進；幫助；使便利
- grain *(n.)* 穀物

---

83 What two developments does the speaker mention?
(A) An online platform and an app
(B) A retail platform and a facilities app
(C) A technology award and supply chain
(D) New technology and traditional links

說話者提及哪兩項發展？
(A) 一個線上平台和一款應用程式
(B) 一個供應商平台和一款設備應用程式
(C) 一項科技獎和供應鏈
(D) 新科技和傳統關係

正解 (A)

本題詢問「說話者提及哪兩項發展？」。關鍵句為 Farm United announced that it's developing and testing an online platform ... 以及 Barrels is an app that facilitates ...，後面又說到 Both of these developments show that ...，故可知這裡說的兩項發展就是指前面提到的 online platform 和 app，因此答案為 (A)。

---

84 What does the speaker think the two developments show?
(A) That retailers need to improve their channels
(B) That the original supply chain still applies
(C) That retailers need to help originators
(D) That the grain industry has changed completely

說話者認為這兩項發展顯示什麼？
(A) 零售商需要改善他們的交易管道
(B) 原本的供應鏈仍適用
(C) 零售商需要幫助原產者
(D) 穀物產業已完全改變

正解 (B)

本題詢問「說話者認為這兩項發展顯示什麼？」。由說話者提及 Both of the developments show that there is still a place for traditional links in the supply chain ...「兩項發展均顯示在供應鏈中傳統的關係仍占有一席之地……」，可知答案為 (B)。

85 What does the speaker suggest retailers do?

(A) Create a lot of channels to sell their products

(B) Pay suppliers more for their products

(C) Sell more products to consumers

(D) Use the same strategy on all their platforms

說話者建議零售商做什麼？

(A) 創造更多的交易管道以銷售他們的產品

(B) 向供應商支付更多產品費用

(C) 向消費者銷售更多產品

(D) 在所有平台上使用相同的策略

正解 **(D)**

本題詢問「說話者建議零售商做什麼？」。關鍵句為 Retailers need to create the same experience across all their channels to add value to the suppliers and consumers. 「零售商需要在所有的交易管道上創造相同的經驗，才能對供應商和消費者有所幫助」，可知答案為 (D)。

Questions 86-88 refer to the following radio advertisement.

Come by Parkview Avenue Automotive this weekend and pick up your dream car at an **outrageously** low price. Saturday and Sunday only, customers will get employee pricing on all sports utility vehicles. That's right. All SUVs are available at discounted prices for this weekend only. Enjoy the same privileges as our workers do and get your new **off-roader** for 15 percent off. On top of that, all customers will be entered in a **raffle** and one lucky customer will walk away with their SUV, minivan, coupe, or convertible of choice at half price! Don't hold off. Cars will be driving themselves off the lot this weekend. Make sure to visit us first thing this Saturday to guarantee you get what you are looking for before someone else does. Parkview Avenue Automotive is more than just the number one rated dealership in the Tri-state area—we're where dreams become reality.

本週末到園景大道汽車，以低得離譜的價格入主您的夢想車。僅在星期六和星期日，顧客才能獲得所有運動型休旅車的員工價。沒錯。所有運動型休旅車僅在本週末以折扣價出售。享有與我們員工相同的優待，並獲得新型越野車八五折的優惠。此外，所有顧客都可參加抽獎活動，一名幸運兒將以半價帶走所選購的運動型休旅車、小客車、雙門小轎車或敞篷車！不要拖延。這個週末，很多汽車將會被開走。請務必在本週六先光顧我們，以確保您在別人之前得到您正在找的汽車。園景大道汽車不僅是三州地區排名第一的經銷商——我們是讓您夢想成真的地方。

- outrageously *(adv.)* 不尋常地；驚人地
- off-roader *(n.)* 越野車
- raffle *(n.)* 抽獎（活動）

---

86 What kind of car will be discounted this weekend?

(A) SUVs   (B) All cars

(C) Minivans   (D) Convertibles

這個週末什麼樣的車有打折？

(A) 運動型休旅車   (B) 所有汽車

(C) 小客車   (D) 敞篷車

正解 **(A)**

本題詢問「這個週末什麼樣的車有打折？」。由關鍵句 All SUVs are available at discounted prices for this weekend only. 可知答案為 (A)。

87 What does the speaker suggest listeners do on Saturday?

(A) Bring a car to exchange

(B) Pick up a coupon

(C) Visit early in the morning

(D) Use their employee discount

說話者建議聽者在週六做什麼？

(A) 帶車來交換　　(B) 領取優惠券

(C) 一早就去光顧　(D) 使用他們的員工折扣

正解 (C)

本題詢問「說話者建議聽者在週六做什麼？」。關鍵句為 Make sure to visit us first thing this Saturday to guarantee you get what you are looking for before someone else does. 可知說話者建議大家將光顧他們當作週六的第一要務，以確保能先找到想要的汽車，故答案選 (C)。

---

88 What does the speaker imply when he says, "cars will be driving themselves off the lot"?

(A) They're moving the cars.

(B) They're selling self-driving cars.

(C) Cars in stock will be sold quickly.

(D) They'll get a new shipment of cars.

當說話者說 "cars will be driving themselves off the lot"，他意味著什麼？

(A) 他們將移動車輛。

(B) 他們將賣自動駕駛汽車。

(C) 庫存的汽車將很快售出。

(D) 他們將獲得新一批的汽車。

正解 (C)

本題詢問 "cars will be driving themselves off the lot" 的意思。drive off 是「把車開走」之意，lot 在此指停車場，因此本句意思是說「車子將會從這個場地被開走」。依前後文可知說話者欲表達由於有促銷折扣活動，很多車子將會很快地被賣掉，故答案選 (C)。

Questions 89-91 refer to the following announcement.

Hello, everyone. This is your captain speaking. This is some of the best weather I've ever experienced taking off from Vancouver, Canada. The weather's warm, and there's not a cloud in the sky. You may now walk around the cabin. However, when you are seated, I recommend that you keep your seat belt fastened. Remember that your belongings in the overhead compartments may have shifted during takeoff, so be careful when opening them. The crew will shortly be giving out complimentary refreshments. You can choose soda, water, juice, tea, or coffee. Wine and beer can be purchased for $8.00. We only accept debit and credit cards. We should be landing at Berlin International Airport at 5:15 p.m. Berlin time. As always, we know that you have many options when choosing an airline to fly with, and we thank you for choosing Los Angeles Air.

大家好。我是機長。這是我從加拿大溫哥華起飛所遇過最棒的天氣之一。天氣很暖和，天空萬里無雲。您現在可在機艙內四處走動。然而，當您坐下時，我建議您將安全帶繫上。記得，您在頭頂置物櫃裡的行李在起飛時可能有移動，所以將置物櫃打開時要小心。機組人員隨即將發送免費的點心與飲料。您可選擇汽水、水、果汁、茶或咖啡。葡萄酒與啤酒的售價為八美元。我們只接受簽帳金融卡與信用卡。我們將於柏林時間下午五點十五分抵達柏林國際機場。如同以往，我們明白您有許多可選擇搭乘的航空公司，我們感謝您選擇洛杉磯航空。

89 Who is being addressed?

(A) A captain in a plane

(B) Flight attendants

(C) Passengers in a plane

(D) Travelers at an airport

說話者的對象是誰？

(A) 飛機上的機長　　　(B) 空服員

(C) 飛機上的乘客　　(D) 機場的旅客

正解 **(C)**

本題詢問獨白者說話的對象。由開頭 This is your captain speaking. 得之說話者為機長，之後又提到坐著時要繫安全帶，且空服員將會發送點心飲料，故可得知答案為 (C)「飛機上的乘客」。

---

90 What beverage is available for purchase only?

(A) Tea　　　　　　　(B) Soda

(C) Wine　　　　　 (D) Coffee

什麼飲料須購買才能取得？

(A) 茶　　　　　　　　(B) 汽水

(C) 葡萄酒　　　　　(D) 咖啡

正解 **(C)**

本題詢問什麼飲料須購買才能取得。由關鍵句 Wine and beer can be purchased for $8.00.「葡萄酒與啤酒的售價為八美元。」可知答案為 (C)。

---

91 When is the plane expected to land?

(A) 5:15 a.m.　　　　**(B) 5:15 p.m.**

(C) 8:00 a.m.　　　　(D) 8:00 p.m.

飛機預計何時降落？

(A) 上午五點十五分　　**(B) 下午五點十五分**

(C) 上午八點　　　　　(D) 下午八點

正解 **(B)**

本題為細節題，詢問「飛機預計何時降落？」。關鍵句為 We should be landing at Berlin International Airport at 5:15 p.m. Berlin time.「我們將於柏林時間下午五點十五分抵達柏林國際機場。」，故知答案為 (B)。

Questions 92-94 refer to the following voice message.

Hi, Patrick, it's Jane from Interpret. I'm happy to inform you that we would like to offer you the job! We would like for you to start on March 2ⁿᵈ. Since you are not a resident, we will need to apply for a work permit for you. Given your business qualifications and management experience, we can apply for the **platinum** work permit that will be **valid** for four years. However, you have to pay half of the permit fee, which is $200. This is according to government regulations. The salary package will be $5,000 per month with ten days' paid leave and a year-end bonus. If this sounds in order, please officially accept the job offer no later than Monday. You can contact me on 02-555-7890. We look forward to having you on board!

• platinum *(n.)* 白金

• valid *(adj.)* 有效的

嗨，派翠克，我是詮譯公司的珍。很高興通知你，我們想提供你這份工作！我們希望你能在三月二日到職。由於你不是居民，我們將需要為你申請工作許可證。有鑑於你的商業資格和管理經驗，我們可以申請有效期為四年的白金工作許可證。然而，你必須支付一半的許可證費，即兩百美元。這是根據政府規定。薪酬待遇為每月五千美元，另有十天有薪假期和年終獎金。如果這樣聽起來妥當的話，請在星期一之前正式接受工作邀請。你可以致電 02-555-7890 與我聯繫。我們期待您的加入！

92 Why does Patrick have to pay $200?

(A) He has to pay the headhunter.

(B) He has to pay a penalty.

(C) He has to pay to work legally.

(D) He has to pay to get a one-year license.

為什麼派翠克必須付兩百美元？

(A) 他必須付費給獵才公司。

(B) 他必須支付罰款。

(C) 他必須付費以便合法工作。

(D) 他必須付費才能取得一年的許可證。

正解 (C)

本題詢問「為什麼派翠克必須付兩百美元？」。由說話者提及許可證期限為四年且又說 However, you have to pay half of the permit fee, which is $200. This is according to government regulations. 得知政府規定他須付一半的許可證費用，所以答案為 (C)。

---

93 What position is Jane's company most likely offering Patrick?

(A) An interpreter

(B) An accountant

(C) A management position

(D) A government position

珍的公司最有可能給派翠克什麼職位？

(A) 翻譯人員

(B) 會計人員

(C) 管理職位

(D) 政府職位

正解 (C)

本題詢問「珍的公司最有可能給予派翠克什麼職位？」。由說話者提及 Given your business qualifications and management experience . . .「鑑於你的商業資格和管理經驗……」，可推測應會給予 (C)「管理職位」。

---

94 What should Patrick do next if he wants the job?

(A) He should pay them $200.

(B) He should go to the office on Tuesday.

(C) He should call Jane before Monday.

(D) He should quit his current job.

如果派翠克想要這份工作，下一步該怎麼做？

(A) 他應該付給他們兩百美元。

(B) 他應該在星期二到辦公室。

(C) 他應該在星期一之前致電給珍。

(D) 他應該辭掉他目前的工作。

正解 (C)

本題詢問「如果派翠克想要這份工作，下一步該怎麼做？」。由關鍵句 If this sounds in order, please officially accept the job offer no later than Monday. You can contact me on 02-555-7890. 可知他須於星期一之前打電話給珍正式接受工作邀請，故答案選 (C)。

Questions 95-97 *refer to the following announcement and floor directory.*

Good morning shoppers! To all the kids who were here yesterday but didn't get to meet Santa, you will be placed first in line between 10 and 11 a.m. Please take your ticket from yesterday to the information center and take a number. Afterwards, make your way up the escalators to Santa's Work Station. Here, kids can make their own Christmas decorations while parents enjoy brunch at one of the restaurants on the same floor. For those doing last-minute shopping, don't miss out on the great bargains at Electronics Jam or PC Hub. If you still need a few ingredients for your family dinner, then stop by at Green Grocer's or avoid the queue by buying the delicious pre-made meals at Granny's Bakery. Thank you for shopping at Sunfish Mall. We wish you all a happy holiday!

早安，各位購物的顧客！對於昨天在這裡但沒能見到聖誕老人的所有孩子們，你們將在上午十點至十一點之間被排在隊伍的最前面。請攜帶你們昨天的票券至服務中心並取得號碼牌。然後，沿著手扶梯上到聖誕老人工作站。在這裡，孩子們可以製作自己的聖誕節裝飾品，而父母則可以在同一樓層的其中一間餐廳享用早午餐。對於那些在最後一刻購物的人，不要錯過電子擺台或電腦房的超值優惠。如果你全家人的晚餐仍需要一些食材，那麼可以光顧綠超市，或者在古早味烘焙坊購買美味的現成餐點以避免排隊。感謝您光顧陽光魚購物中心。祝各位有個愉快的假期！

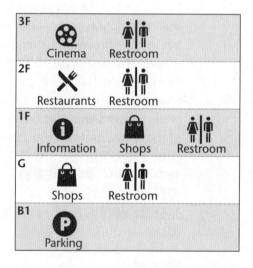

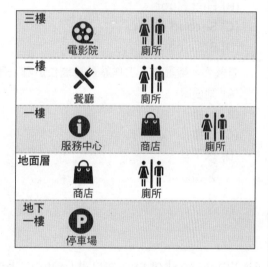

95 What will happen between 10 and 11 a.m.?

(A) All the kids will get to meet Santa Claus.

(B) Kids who missed their chance yesterday will meet Santa.

(C) Kids who get there first will make their own Christmas decorations.

(D) Kids who missed Santa will get a delicious meal.

上午十點至十一點之間會發生什麼事？

(A) 所有的孩子都有機會見到聖誕老人。

(B) 昨天錯過機會的孩子將與聖誕老人見面。

(C) 首先到達那裡的孩子將製作自己的聖誕節裝飾品。

(D) 錯過聖誕老人的孩子們將獲得美味的一餐。

正解 (B)

本題詢問「上午十點至十一點之間會發生什麼事？」。由說話者提及 To all the kids who were here yesterday but didn't get to meet Santa, you will be placed first in line between 10 and 11 a.m.，可知答案為 (B)。

96 Look at the graphic. On which floor is Santa's Work Station most likely located?

(A) Ground Floor

(B) First Floor

(C) Second Floor

(D) Basement

看圖表。聖誕老人工作站最可能位於哪一層樓？

(A) 地面層

(B) 一樓

(C) 二樓

(D) 地下室

正解 (C)

本題為圖表題，詢問聖誕老人工作站所在的樓層。關鍵句為 Please take your ticket from yesterday to the information center and take a number. Afterwards, make your way up the escalators to Santa's Work Station. Here, kids can make their own Christmas decorations while parents enjoy brunch at one of the restaurants on the same floor，可知聖誕老人工作站在服務中心往上的樓層且有餐廳。對照圖表可得知服務中心在 1F，往上有餐廳的樓層則為 2F，故答案選 (C)。

97 What can shoppers buy at Granny's Bakery?

(A) Ingredients for their dinner

(B) Ready-to-eat meals for dinner

(C) A delicious brunch

(D) Electronic devices

顧客可以在古早味烘焙坊購買什麼？

(A) 晚餐的食材

(B) 即食晚餐餐點

(C) 美味的早午餐

(D) 電子裝置

正解 (B)

本題詢問「顧客可以在古早味烘焙坊購買什麼？」。由說話者提及 . . . or avoid the queue by buying the delicious pre-made meals at Granny's Bakery 得知可在古早味烘焙坊購買美味的現成餐點，故答案為 (B)。

Questions 98-100 refer to the following revenue report and pie chart.

So here's the annual revenue report, which confirms that our main source of income remains on the Internet. This includes website design and maintenance, as well as advertisements and banners. Overall, web work accounted for 60% of overall revenue this year. However, if we look closer and compare this chart to last year's chart, we'll notice something very encouraging. Yes, I'm pleased to be able to stand here today as the bearer of good news. We've managed to achieve our primary objective for the year, which is expanding into other areas of design for print, and increasing the overall revenue share of those non-web related services. Additionally, even though web revenue decreased from 64% to 60%, the total revenue earned for web work actually rose by 215,000 dollars. An outstanding performance, meaning our expansion has gone even better than planned, especially clothing which doubled its share of overall revenue this year. <u>We're over the moon</u> with the way things have gone, so please join me in a round of applause for this tremendous team effort.

那麼，這是年度營收報告，報告中確認了我們的主要收入仍然來自於網路。這包括網頁設計和維護，以及網路廣告和橫幅廣告。總體而言，網路工作占今年總收入的百分之六十。然而，如果我們仔細觀察該圖表並將其與去年的圖表進行比較，將會發現一些令人鼓舞的事。是的，我很高興今天能夠帶來好消息而站在這裡。我們設法實現了今年的主要目標，正在擴展到平面設計的其他領域，並增加了非網路相關服務的總收入比例。此外，即使網路收入從百分之六十四下降到百分之六十，網路工作總收入實際上成長了二十一萬五千元。出色的業績意味著我們的擴張甚至比計畫的要好，尤其是服飾，其今年總收入的比例增加了一倍。對於事情的發展我們非常高興，所以讓我們為這個十分努力的團隊鼓掌。

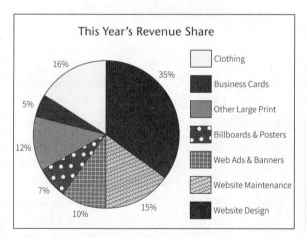

This Year's Revenue Share

- 35% — Clothing
- 16% — Business Cards
- 5% — Other Large Print
- 12% — Billboards & Posters
- 7% — Web Ads & Banners
- 10% — Website Maintenance
- 15% — Website Design

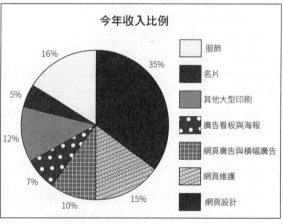

今年收入比例

- 35% — 服飾
- 16% — 名片
- 5% — 其他大型印刷
- 12% — 廣告看板與海報
- 7% — 網頁廣告與橫幅廣告
- 10% — 網頁維護
- 15% — 網頁設計

98 What was the company's main goal at the beginning of the year?

(A) Increase web revenue as a share of total revenue

(B) Decrease total revenue generated from web work

(C) Expand into other areas of design for print

(D) Design more web-related graphics and media

該公司在年初的主要目標是什麼？

(A) 增加網路收入占總收入的比例

(B) 減少網路工作產生的總收入

(C) 擴展到平面設計的其他領域

(D) 設計更多與網路相關的圖象和媒體

正解 (C)

本題詢問「該公司在年初的主要目標是什麼？」。由說話者提及 We've managed to achieve our primary objective for the year, which is expanding into other areas of design for print ...「我們設法實現了今年的主要目標，該目標正在擴展到平面設計的其他領域……」，可知答案為 (C)。

---

99 What does the speaker mean when he says "We're over the moon"?

(A) Management is very happy.

(B) Management is surprised.

(C) A difficult period has ended.

(D) The year has come to an end.

當說話者說 "We're over the moon"，他意味著什麼？

(A) 管理階層非常高興。

(B) 管理階層感到驚訝。

(C) 艱難時期已經結束。

(D) 這一年結束了。

正解 (A)

本題詢問 "We're over the moon" 的意思。由本句前面說話者提及業績的好表現，可推斷此語意思乃正面的評價，片語 be over the moon 是表「欣喜若狂；非常高興」之意。而本句後方說到讓我們為團隊的努力鼓掌，可推測這裡的 We 指的是管理階層，因此答案選 (A)。

---

100 Look at the graphic. What percentage of revenue came from clothing designs in the year before this one?

(A) 7%   **(B) 8%**

(C) 10.5%   (D) 32%

看圖表。在前一年中，服飾設計收入的百分比是多少？

(A) 百分之七   **(B) 百分之八**

(C) 百分之十點五   (D) 百分之三十二

正解 (B)

本題為圖表題，詢問在前一年服飾設計收入的百分比。由說話者提及 especially clothing which doubled its share of overall revenue this year「尤其是服飾，其今年總收入的比例增加了一倍」，對照圖表今年服飾設計收入為百分之十六，故知前一年為百分之十六的一半，答案為 (B)。

Part 5: Incomplete Sentences

101 The _____ department can't get all the products to the clients on time.

(A) **distribution**
(B) distributor
(C) distribute
(D) distributing

配銷部門無法將所有產品準時交付給客戶。

(A) 配銷;分配(名詞)
(B) 銷售者;批發商(名詞)
(C) 分發;配送(原形動詞)
(D) 分發;配送(現在分詞或動名詞)

正解 (A)

空格前方為 The,空格後為 department,可判斷空格應填入 (A),形成 distribution department「配銷部門」的固定用法;空格後方的 get all the products to the clients 即為「配銷部門」的主要職責。

102 In many cultures, it is important to _____ eye contact when speaking to another person.

(A) refrain
(B) remain
(C) explain
(D) **maintain**

在許多文化中,跟別人說話時保持目光的接觸都是很重要的。

(A) 抑制
(B) 餘留;維持
(C) 解釋
(D) **保持**

正解 (D)

本題考字義。依照句意可知空格處填入 (D),maintain eye contact 為常見搭配用法,表示「保持目光的接觸」。

103 The person _____ donated this money prefers to remain anonymous.

(A) **who**
(B) which
(C) whom
(D) whose

捐這筆錢的人想要維持匿名。

(A) 他/她(們)(表人的主格關係代名詞)
(B) 它/牠(們)(表物的關係代名詞)
(C) 他/她(們)(表人的受格關係代名詞)
(D) 他/她/它/牠(們)的(表人或物的所有格關係代名詞)

正解 (A)

本題考關係代名詞。The person 是主詞,且空格後直接接動詞 donated,因此要選可替代 The person 的主格關係代名詞,答案為 (A) who。

• anonymous *(adj.)* 匿名的

SECTION C 模擬測驗

104 Customer service representatives are always available to handle your concerns _____ your choice of e-mail, live chat, or social media.

(A) above   **(B) through**

(C) since   (D) until

您可以選擇透過電子郵件、線上即時交談或是社交軟體找到客服代表來解決您的問題。

(A) 在……上面   **(B) 透過**

(C) 自……以來   (D) 直到……時

正解 (B)

本題考介系詞。根據句意,有電話、電子郵件、線上即時交談或是社交軟體等不同方式可聯繫到客服代表,故最適合答案為 (B) through「透過」。

---

105 Louis said he _____ hiking on Yangmingshan last weekend with friends.

(A) went   (B) will go

(C) is going   (D) will have gone

路易斯說他上週末和朋友一起去陽明山健行。

(A) 走(過去式)   (B) 走(未來式)

(C) 走(現在進行式)   (D) 走(未來完成式)

正解 (A)

本題考時態。從時間副詞 last weekend 可知此句的動作發生於上週末,動詞應用過去式,故選 (A)。

---

106 We have been in the _____ for three months; we'll have to close soon.

(A) trouble   (B) green

(C) red   (D) rise

我們已經負債三個月了;我們必須盡快歇業。

(A) 麻煩   (B) 綠色

(C) 紅色   (D) 上升

正解 (C)

本題考片語。由後半句「必須盡快歇業」可知前半句欲表達已經「負債」三個月,故要用 in the red 這個片語,答案選 (C)。

(A) 要表達「處於困境」,要用 in trouble,而非 in the trouble。

---

107 Please _____ that you will need the booking reservation number to complete the transaction.

(A) vary   (B) affect

(C) rent   **(D) note**

請注意,您將會需要您的訂單號碼方能完成這筆交易。

(A) 變化   (B) 影響

(C) 出租   **(D) 注意**

正解 (D)

本題考字義。依照句意可知空格處填入 (D) note,表示請「注意」。Please note that . . . 為提醒注意事項時的常見句型。

---

108 The company _____ a new policy to ensure equal treatment of all its employees.

(A) initiative   **(B) initiated**

(C) initiator   (D) initial

公司開始實施了一項新政策,以確保全體員工受到平等待遇。

(A) 倡議(名詞);初步的(形容詞)

(B) 開始實施(動詞過去式)

(C) 創始者(名詞)

(D) 開始的(形容詞)

正解 (B)

本題考詞性。分析句構可知主詞是 The company,受詞是 a new policy,而空格處為本句主要動詞,故應選 (B) initiated「開始實施」。

109 Up next, we'll discuss the best marketing strategies with a leading _____ in the field.

(A) directory　　　　(B) catalog

(C) expert　　　　(D) period

接下來，我們將與一名該領域的頂級專家討論最佳行銷策略。

(A)（工商）名錄；指南　(B)（商品）的目錄

(C) 專家　　　　(D) 時期

正解 (C)

本題考字義。依照句意可知空格處填入 (C) expert，表示與該領域的頂級「專家」商討最佳行銷策略。

---

110 The boss was not satisfied with her employees'_____ for the last month.

(A) procedure　　　　(B) patent

(C) output　　　　(D) extension

老闆對她員工上個月的產量不滿意。

(A) 步驟　　　　(B) 專利權

(C) 產量　　　　(D) 延伸

正解 (C)

本題考字義。依照句意可知空格處填入 (C) output，表示員工的「產量」不佳使老闆感到不滿。

---

111 The amount of time worked by the typical European each week is, on average, _____ that worked by the typical American.

(A) less　　　　(B) least

(C) far less　　　　**(D) less than**

平均來說，典型歐洲人每週的工作時間比典型美國人來得少。

(A) 較少的　　　　(B) 最少的

(C) 遠不及　　　　**(D) 比……較少**

正解 (D)

本題考比較級用法。要比較典型歐洲人和典型美國人一週工作時間（The amount of time）的多寡，句型為 A + be 動詞 + 形容詞比較級 + than + B。故空格處應填入 (D) less than。less 為 little 的比較級，表「（數量）較少的」。

---

112 With his _____ headset, Tim could continue the conversation anywhere in the house.

(A) wireless　　　　(B) surrounding

(C) relative　　　　(D) securing

有了無線耳機，提姆可以在家裡的任何地方繼續交談。

(A) 無線的　　　　(B) 周圍的

(C) 相對的　　　　(D) 獲得安全的

正解 (A)

本題考字義。依照句意可知空格處填入 (A) wireless，wireless headset 即「無線耳機」。

---

113 The CEO was not worried about the sales figures, _____ they fluctuated during the last year.

(A) as though　　　　(B) but also

(C) even though　　　　(D) so that

執行長並不擔心銷售數字，即使在過去一年中波動很大。

(A) 好像　　　　(B) 而且

(C) 即使　　　　(D) 以致於

正解 (C)

本題考連接詞。空格前提到執行長不擔心銷售數字，但空格後卻說數字波動很大，故從語意推斷應選可用來表達轉折語氣的從屬連接詞 even though「雖然」，用來引導逗點後的副詞子句，答案選 (C)。

114 You can welcome your family members home at the arrivals _____ of the airport.

(A) departure   (B) nation

(C) terminal   (D) citizen

你可以在機場的入境航廈歡迎你的家人回家。

(A) 離開   (B) 國家

(C) 航廈   (D) 市民

正解 (C)

本題考字義。從空格前後的關鍵字 arrivals 與 airport 可知空格處填入 (C) terminal「航廈」。arrivals terminal 即「入境航廈」。

---

115 Unfortunately, they could not publish the book because they felt it was not _____.

(A) market   **(B) marketable**

(C) marketing   (D) marketed

不幸的是,他們無法出版這本書,因為他們覺得這本書沒有銷路。

(A) 行銷(原形動詞)

(B) 有銷路的(形容詞)

(C) 行銷(現在分詞或動名詞)

(D) 行銷(過去分詞或過去式)

正解 (B)

本題考詞性。從連接詞 because 可知空格處為書籍無法被出版的原因,可判斷此處應在否定 be 動詞 was not 後應填入形容詞 marketable「有銷路的」,故答案選 (B)。

---

116 Many companies have had to downsize _____ the failing economy.

(A) because   (B) apart from

(C) due to   (D) except for

由於經濟衰退,許多公司不得不縮減規模。

(A) 因為   (B) 除……之外

(C) 由於   (D) 除了……以外

正解 (C)

本題考片語。由句意判斷,經濟衰退是公司縮減規模的「原因」,故答案要選 (C) due to「由於」。

(A) because 後須接子句,但空格後是名詞片語 the failing economy,故不可選。

---

117 Mike is relieved that he made it through his _____ period.

(A) frequent   (B) indicative

(C) probationary   (D) comprehensive

邁克對他度過了試用期感到放心。

(A) 慣常的   (B) 指示的

(C) 試用的   (D) 全面的

正解 (C)

本題考字義。依照句意可知空格處填入 (C) probationary「試用的」。probationary period 即為「試用期」。

---

118 Employees are _____ asked to work overtime and will be appropriately compensated according to the law.

(A) exactly   (B) extremely

(C) particularly   **(D) occasionally**

員工偶爾會被要求加班,並將依法給予適當補償。

(A) 確切地   (B) 非常地

(C) 特別地   **(D) 偶爾地**

正解 (D)

本題考字義。依照句意可知選項中最適合的答案是 (D) occasionally,表示「偶爾」會要求員工加班。

119 Sales tax and services charges ＿＿＿＿ in the "new charges" section of each monthly bill.

(A) includes   (B) included

(C) are included   (D) are including

銷售稅跟服務費在每個月帳單上是被計入「新增費用」的部分。

(A) 包括（現在式第三人稱單數動詞）

(B) 包括（過去式或過去分詞）

(C) 包括（現在式的被動語態）

(D) 包括（現在進行式）

正解 (C)

本題考被動語態。本句主詞 Sales tax and services charges 為「事物」，而選項中的動詞是 include，故知應用被動語態（be 動詞＋過去分詞），答案為 (C)。

---

120 As the ＿＿＿＿ shareholder, Mr. Musk is the primary decision-maker for the company.

(A) former   **(B) majority**

(C) minority   (D) minimum

馬斯克先生作為大股東，是該公司的主要決策者。

(A) 前者   **(B) 大多數**

(C) 少數   (D) 最小量

正解 (B)

本題考字義。依照後半段句意「是該公司的主要決策者」可知空格處填入 (B) majority「大多數」；majority shareholder 指的是「控有多數股權的大股東」。

---

121 Our last campaign did not ＿＿＿＿ our target demographic, so we changed tack.

(A) carry out   **(B) appeal to**

(C) tend to   (D) set up

我們上次的競選活動沒有吸引到我們的目標族群，所以我們改變了策略。

(A) 實行   **(B) 對……產生吸引力**

(C) 傾向   (D) 建立

正解 (B)

本題考片語動詞。依照句意可知空格處填入 (B) appeal to 指「對……產生吸引力」，也就是並未「吸引到」目標族群。

• tack (n.) 方針；行動步驟

---

122 The end goal of the production process is to ＿＿＿＿ sufficient goods and services to satisfy consumer demand.

(A) manufacture   (B) manufacturing

(C) manufactured   (D) manufacturer

這個生產流程的終極目標是要製造足夠的商品與服務來滿足顧客需求。

(A) 製造（原形動詞）

(B) 製造業（動名詞或現在分詞）

(C) 製造（過去式或過去分詞）

(D) 製造商（名詞）

正解 (A)

本題考詞性。空格前為 to，且空格後描述的內容乃是遵行該「生產流程」的目標，可判斷應填入原形動詞以便形成不定詞（表目的），故選 (A) manufacture。

123 Enclosed you will find train tickets and a tentative _____ for your upcoming trip.

(A) candidate   (B) franchise

(C) billboard   **(D) itinerary**

隨函為你附上火車票和你即將到來旅行的暫定行程。

(A) 候選人   (B) 特許經銷權

(C) 廣告招牌   **(D) 行程計畫**

正解 (D)

本題考字義。從句中關鍵字 train tickets 與 upcoming trip 可知依句意應在空格處填入 (D) itinerary，表示旅行的暫定「行程」。

- tentative *(adj.)* 暫時性的；試驗性的

---

124 The airline will give you a _____ meal voucher if you book your tickets today.

(A) compliment

(B) complimentary

(C) complimenting

(D) complimented

如果您今天預訂機票，航空公司將會給您一張免費的餐券。

(A) 讚揚（原形動詞）

(B)【美】贈送的（形容詞）

(C) 讚揚（現在分詞或動名詞）

(D) 讚揚（過去分詞或過去式）

正解 (B)

本題考詞性。空格前為冠詞 a，後為名詞片語 meal voucher，可判斷應填入形容詞加以修飾，故選 (B) complimentary。

---

125 Many people believe it's better not to _____, but to focus on one task at a time.

(A) multitask   (B) distinguish

(C) influence   (D) expose

許多人認為最好不要同時做多件事情，而應一次只專注於一件事。

(A) 同時做多件事情   (B) 區別

(C) 影響   (D) 使暴露於

正解 (A)

本題考字義。由題目中的 it's better not to ... but to ... 可推斷空格處與後面描述的 focus on one task at a time 為相反的概念，故知空格處應填入 (A) multitask「同時做多件事情」。

---

126 Mr. Cage had the mechanic _____ the car to find out what was making that horrible noise.

(A) customize   (B) strike

(C) diagnose   **(D) inspect**

凱奇先生讓技師檢查汽車，以找出造成這種可怕聲音的原因。

(A) 訂做   (B) 撞擊

(C) 診斷   **(D) 檢查**

正解 (D)

本題考字義。依照句意可知空格處填入 (D) inspect，表示「檢查」汽車。

(C) diagnose 一字用在醫師「診斷」病人患有某疾病。

127 Please inform all candidates that they are expected to show up early for _____ group interview.

(A) they　　　　　　　**(B) their**

(C) them　　　　　　　(D) themselves

請告知所有候選人，他們應該為其團體面試提早抵達。

(A) 他們（主格）　　　**(B) 他們的（所有格）**

(C) 他們（受格）　　　(D) 他們自己（反身代名詞）

正解 **(B)**

本題考人稱代名詞。空格後的名詞片語 group interview 為名詞 all candidates 的所有物，可判斷應填入複數代名詞 they 的所有格，故選 (B) their，表「他們的」團體面試。

---

128 The scientists received a Nobel Prize for their _____ in the medical field.

(A) estimate　　　　　**(B) breakthrough**

(C) hesitation　　　　 (D) renovation

這群科學家因在醫學領域的突破而獲頒諾貝爾獎。

(A) 估計　　　　　　　**(B) 突破**

(C) 猶豫　　　　　　　(D) 翻修

正解 **(B)**

本題考字義。依照句意可知空格處填入 (B) breakthrough，表示因在醫學領域達到「突破」而獲頒獎項。

---

129 Your agreement with us is comprised of your filled-in and signed membership agreement form, these terms and conditions, and the terms of club use as outlined _____.

(A) below　　　　　(B) besides

(C) behind　　　　　　(D) between

您與我們的協議包括您填寫並簽署的會員協議表格、這些條款和條件，以及下述的俱樂部使用條款。

(A) 在下方　　　　　(B) 此外

(C) 在……後方　　　　(D) 在（兩者）中間

正解 **(A)**

本題考副詞。依照句意可知空格處填入 (A) below 指「在下方」，表示如下所述的俱樂部使用條款。

---

130 _____ you arrive more than 10 minutes after your booking time without informing us of the delay, you may lose your table to another group.

(A) May　　　　　　　(B) Have

(C) Should　　　　　(D) Could

若您未事先通知我們您將延遲，而在晚於預訂時間十分鐘後才抵達，您所預訂的座位可能會被轉讓給其他客人。

(A) 也許　　　　　　　(B) 已經

(C) 萬一　　　　　　(D) 可能

正解 **(C)**

本題考假設語氣的倒裝。逗點後的主要子句（you may . . .）是逗點前所描述的動作一旦發生時，將可能導致的結果，故應用假設法的未來式，句型為 If + S. + should + V., S. + 助動詞 + V.，倒裝時省略 If 並將 should 置於句首，表示「萬一……」，故選 (C)。

SECTION C

模擬測驗

Part 6: Text Completion

Questions 131-134 refer to the following website announcement.

Dear Valued Customers,

At Big Bucks Bank, not only do we aspire to help you achieve your financial goals, we pride ourselves on our solid track record of customer ---131---.

That's why we want to apologize for any difficulties you ---132--- during the launch of our new digital and mobile banking app yesterday. Please know that we designed our new platform with your convenience in mind, offering enhanced security, navigation, tools, and a modern look and feel. Unfortunately, we ran into some technical difficulties along the way, ---133--- we worked around the clock to resolve.

The last thing we want to do is disappoint you. That's why we're committed to making things right. If you have any questions about our new online banking experience or would like to see a video message, visit us <u>here</u>.

Thank you for being a part of the Big Bucks family. ---134---

Sincerely,
Sal Smitherson, Customer Service Director

敬愛的顧客們：

鉅富銀行不只熱切希望幫助您達成財務目標，我們也對本身穩健的客戶滿意度紀錄感到自豪。

那就是為什麼我們想為昨天在新的數位行動銀行應用程式推出期間，您在使用過程中所遭遇的任何困難致上歉意。請您知悉，我們是以您的方便為考量來設計此新平台，提供經強化的安全防護措施、功能導覽與小工具，以及現代化的外觀與感受。很遺憾地，過程中我們遇到一些技術上的困難，而我們也已日以繼夜地趕工解決問題。

讓您失望是我們最不希望見到的事。正因如此我們會致力呈現完美的服務。若您對於我們全新的網路銀行體驗還有任何問題，或是想再看看影片訊息，可以到<u>這裡</u>參訪我們。

感謝您成為鉅富家族的一份子。<u>我們感激您持續的惠顧。</u>

謹致，
客戶服務部經理 薩爾・史密德森

131 (A) satisfy
(B) satisfied
(C) satisfactory
(D) satisfaction

(A) 使滿足（原形動詞）
(B) 感到滿意的（形容詞）
(C) 令人滿意的（形容詞）
(D) 滿足（名詞）

正解 **(D)**

本題考詞性。空格前方為名詞 customer，可知這裡要選名詞形成名詞片語 customer satisfaction 指「客戶滿意度」，故答案為 (D)。

---

132 (A) encounter
(B) encountered
(C) will encounter
(D) will be encountering

(A) 遭遇（原形動詞）
(B) 遭遇（過去式）
(C) 遭遇（未來式）
(D) 遭遇（未來進行式）

正解 **(B)**

本題考時態。由句點前的時間副詞 yesterday 可知此句的動作發生於昨天，動詞應用過去式，故選 (B)。

---

133 (A) that
(B) what
(C) which
(D) how

(A) 他／她／它／牠（們）（表人或物的關係代名詞）
(B) 所……的事物（或人）（複合關係代名詞）
(C) 它／牠（們）（表物的關係代名詞）
(D) 如何（疑問詞）

正解 **(C)**

本題考關係詞。空格後方為形容詞子句，用來修飾前方的先行詞 technical difficulties，選項中表物的關係代名詞有 (A) that 及 (C) which，但 that 前不可有逗點，故選 (C) which。

---

134 (A) We are sorry you closed your account.
(B) We will close early due to the holidays.
(C) We will no longer offer online banking.
(D) We are grateful for your continued loyalty.

(A) 很遺憾您終止了帳戶。
(B) 由於假期，我們將提早打烊。
(C) 我們將不再提供線上銀行業務。
(D) 我們感激您持續的惠顧。

正解 **(D)**

空格之前執行長提到感謝客戶成為鉅富家族的一份子，故推知最符合邏輯的答案為 (D)，表達對於客戶持續忠誠惠顧的感謝，與前文語意連貫，故為正解。

Questions 135-138 refer to the following e-mail.

To:	macey@yaho.com
From:	res@hh.com
Subject:	Confirmation

Dear Macey,

---**135**--- We look forward to receiving you from October 28th to November 2nd. Please take note of the following:

1. Check-in time is at 2 p.m. and check-out time is at 11 a.m.
2. You can order breakfast the day before and enjoy it from 7 a.m. to 9 a.m.
3. There is a communal kitchen where you can cook your own lunch or dinner. ---**136**---, we can suggest some wonderful places very close to the hostel.
4. The **communal** living room has many books, board games, DVDs, etc. for you to enjoy with other guests.
5. Please keep the noise level down after 10 p.m. and be considerate of your fellow guests.
6. You can rent a towel and buy toiletries from our staff ---**137**--- you check in.
7. There is a self-service laundromat very close to the hostel.
8. Your 50% deposit is ---**138**--- until two weeks before your arrival date. After that, we will only refund 25% until two days before your trip. If you cancel two days before your trip, we will not refund your deposit.

Please let us know if you have any questions. We trust you will enjoy your stay with us!

Best,

HH

- communal *(adj.)* 共有的；公共的

收件者：macey@yaho.com

寄件者：res@hh.com

主　旨：訂房確認

敬愛的梅西：

感謝您最近在奧斯陸快樂旅舍的訂房。我們期待在十月二十八日至十一月二日接待您。請注意以下幾點：

1. 入住時間為下午二點，退房時間為上午十一點。
2. 您可以在前一天預訂早餐，便能在早上七點至九點享用。
3. 有一個公共廚房，您可以在那裡準備午餐或晚餐。或者，我們可以建議一些非常接近旅舍的好地方。
4. 公共客廳配有許多書籍、桌遊、DVD 等，您可以與其他客人一起使用。
5. 請在晚上十點後降低音量，並為其他客人著想。
6. 您可以在登記入住時向我們的員工租用毛巾和購買盥洗用品。
7. 距離旅舍非常近的地方有一家自助洗衣店。
8. 您入住日期的兩週前可退一半的押金。兩週之後到您來旅行的兩天前，我們只會退款四分之一。如果您在旅行前兩天取消，我們將不退還您的押金。

如果您有任何問題，請讓我們知道。我們相信您會在我們這裡過得愉快！

祝福您，

HH

135 (A) Thank you for enquiring about our rooms.

(B) **Thank you for your recent booking at Happy Hostel in Oslo.**

(C) We apologize for the incorrect booking on our site.

(D) We would like to offer you a discounted room.

(A) 感謝您詢問我們的房間。

(B) **感謝您最近在奧斯陸快樂旅舍的訂房。**

(C) 對於我們網站上錯誤的預訂，我們深感抱歉。

(D) 我們想為您提供優惠的房間。

正解 **(B)**

由信件標題的 Confirmation 與空格後方說期待接待對方，並由接下來的入住規定可以推測此為訂房後收到的確認信件，故答案為 (B)。

---

136 (A) Impossibly

(B) Initially

(C) **Alternatively**

(D) Defectively

(A) 不可能地

(B) 最初地

(C) **或者**

(D) 有缺陷地

正解 **(C)**

本題考字義。空格前提到「您可以在這裡準備午餐或晚餐」，空格後則又列出另一種選擇，即「我們可以建議一些非常接近旅舍的好地方」，可知應填入 (C) Alternatively「或者」。

---

137 (A) who

(B) **when**

(C) which

(D) whose

(A) 誰（疑問詞）；他／她（們）（表人的主格關係代名詞）

(B) **當……時（表時間的連接詞）**

(C) 它／牠（們）（表物的關係代名詞）

(D) 他／她／它／牠（們）的（表人或物的所有格關係代名詞）

正解 **(B)**

本題考連接詞。空格前後都是結構完整的子句，故應填入連接詞。選項中僅 (B) when 為引導時間副詞子句的連接詞，置入後表「您登記入住時」，故答案為 (B)。

---

138 (A) abundant　　(B) commercial

(C) optical　　(D) **refundable**

(A) 大量的　　(B) 商業的

(C) 光學的　　(D) **可退還的**

正解 **(D)**

本題考字義。從空格後兩句的關鍵字 refund 可知這裡在解釋於不同的時間點取消訂房時，各可退回多少押金，故知符合句意的答案為 (D)。

Questions 139-142 refer to the following notice.

Attention Members!

We would like to take this opportunity to express our gratitude to you, our valued customers, for your years of loyal patronage. As a **token** of our thanks, all frequent-flier members with at least one year **under their belts** will be awarded a bonus of 5,000 miles. Those with five to ten years will receive an additional 5,000 miles, ---**139**--- those with over ten years will see an additional 10,000 miles. They are valid from the time of this announcement and must be **redeemed** within the next two years. As always, they cannot be used **in conjunction with** any other ongoing airline ---**140**---.

Additionally, from now until this time next year, any miles accumulated through our domestic and international flights will be doubled. ---**141**--- As long as they are properly reported to our mileage program and received by midnight on this day a year from now, they ---**142**--- to your account. We hope you take full advantage of these free miles and continue to fly with us.

會員們注意！

我們想藉此機會向我們各位貴賓多年來的忠實惠顧表達感激。為了致上謝意，我們將向所有入會至少一年的飛行常客會員授予五千英里的獎勵。入會五至十年的人將再另外獲得五千英里，而十年以上者則將另外再獲得一萬英里。它們自本公告發布日起有效，且必須在未來兩年內兌換。與往常一樣，它們不能與任何其他正在進行的航空公司促銷結合使用。

此外，從現在起到明年此時，累積自我們國內和國際航班的任何里程數都將加倍。您可以收集的里程數沒有上限。從現在起至明年今天的午夜之前，只要將它們正確地回報給我們的里程計畫，讓里程計畫確實收到，它們就會記入您的帳戶。我們希望您能充分利用這些免費里程，並繼續搭乘我們的航班。

- token *(n.)* 表示；標誌
- (have/with sth.) under one's belt *(phr.)* 已經獲得……；已經掌握……（技能等）
- redeem *(v.)* 贖回；買回
- in conjunction with *(phr.)* 與……一起

139 (A) hence
(B) because
(C) while
(D) nor

(A) 因此（副詞）
(B) 因為（連接詞）
(C) 而；然而（連接詞）
(D) 也不（連接詞，常與 neither 連用）

正解 **(C)**

本題考連接詞。空格前說入會五到十年的會員將再另外獲得五千英里，而空格後又繼續說入會十年以上者則將另外再獲得一萬英里，從句意可知須選可表「對照；對比」的連接詞，故選 (C) while「而；然而」。

---

140 (A) resignation　　**(B) promotion**
(C) depression　　(D) malfunction

(A) 辭職　　**(B) 促銷**
(C) 沮喪　　(D) 故障

正解 **(B)**

本題考字義。原句提到「它們不能與任何其他正在進行的航空公司＿＿＿＿結合使用」，故符合句意的答案為 (B)。

---

141 (A) They will stay frozen for an indefinite period of time.
(B) There is no limit to the number of miles you can collect.
(C) Once that happens, you will no longer be an active member.
(D) After that, they will be halved again and again until nothing is left.

(A) 它們將無限期凍結。
(B) 您可以收集的里程數沒有上限。
(C) 一旦發生這種情況，您將不再是有效會員。
(D) 在那之後，它們將被一再減半，直到耗盡。

正解 **(B)**

空格的前句提及累積自國內和國際航班的任何里程（any miles accumulated）都會加倍，而選項 (B) 接著說明「可以收集的里程數（miles you can collect）沒有上限」，其後可順利接續接下來關於回報里程數方式的說明，語意連貫故答案為 (B)。下一句的主詞 They 指的就是選項中與前一句都有提到的 miles。

(A) indefinite *(adj.)* 不確定的；無限的。
(D) halve *(v.)* 將……減半／對分。

---

142 (A) credit
(B) is crediting
(C) will be credited
(D) have been credited

(A) 把……記入（現在式）
(B) 把……記入（現在進行式）
(C) 把……記入（未來式被動）
(D) 把……記入（完成式被動）

正解 **(C)**

本題考文法。as long as 引導表「條件」的副詞子句，本句欲表「只要將點數正確地回報給……，點數就會被存入」。這屬於「只要現在或未來某條件成立時，主要子句描述的情形就會成立」的情況，此時副詞子句要用現在式（they are properly reported . . .），主要子句則用未來式。因里程數是被記入，所以此處應用未來式的被動語態，答案選 (C)。

模擬測驗

Questions 143-146 refer to the following advertisement.

Seeking Savvy Self-Starter!

Do you want to feel as ---**143**--- as you look? Are you seeking new opportunities for excellence? Contact me for a chance to work for yourself, as much or as little as you want. **Leverage** your networks and start making big money today!

Clary May Cosmetics beauty consultants buy their inventory from the Clary May wholesale division and sell it directly to customers at in-home parties and through personal websites. Similar to brick-and-mortar stores, consultants keep the difference ---**144**--- wholesale and market price.

Consultants desiring to earn a more full-time salary are encouraged to ---**145**---, manage and support a sales team of new consultants. We believe that encouraging consultants to form their own sales teams and rewarding them for sharing in each other's success builds a stronger sales force than one formed via more traditional management approaches. As your network grows, so does your business.

What are you waiting for? Seize this opportunity to become financially successful, and create new standards of personal excellence! ---**146**---

徵求精明且自動自發的人才！

您想要感受到自己成功嗎？您是否在尋求卓越的新契機？請聯繫我，讓您有機會為自己工作，自己掌握工作量。利用您的人際網絡，立刻開始賺大錢！

克萊瑞美化妝品的美容顧問會從克萊瑞美的批發部門購買庫存，並透過產品派對或個人網站直接銷售給顧客。與實體店類似的是，顧問會保有批發價和市場價的價差。

我們鼓勵想要賺取全職薪水的顧問去招募、管理和組織一支新顧問銷售團隊。我們相信，鼓勵顧問組成自己的銷售團隊並獎勵他們分享彼此的成功，比起透過較傳統的管理方法組成的銷售團隊將更為強大。隨著您的人脈發展，您的業務也在增長。

您還在等什麼？抓住這個機會，在財務上取得成功，創造個人卓越的新標準！今天就聯繫我們，開始過您應得的生活吧！

• leverage *(v.)* 借助現有的條件實現新目標（leverage 作名詞時指「槓桿作用」）

143 (A) success

(B) succeed

(C) successful

(D) successfully

(A) 成功（名詞）

(B) 成功（動詞）

(C) 成功的（形容詞）

(D) 成功地（副詞）

正解 **(C)**

本題考詞性。按照句意要表達「和……一樣……」應要用「as + 原級 adj./adv. + as」的句型，又此句的動詞為連綴動詞 feel，表示「感到」，其後與 be 動詞一樣要接形容詞，故選 (C)。

---

144 **(A) between**

(B) among

(C) besides

(D) despite

(A) 在（兩者）之間

(B) 在（三者或以上）之中

(C) 除……之外

(D) 儘管

正解 **(A)**

本題考介系詞。依照句意及空格後方有 and，可知這裡要用 between A and B 表「在（兩者）之間」。本句是要表示介於批發價和市場價「之間」的價差。

---

145 (A) retire

(B) recruit

(C) recall

(D) restock

(A) 退休

(B) 招募

(C) 回想

(D) 重新進貨

正解 **(B)**

空格的前句提及累積自國內和國本題考字義。依照句意可知空格處應填入 (B) recruit 表示「招募」、管理和組織一支新顧問銷售團隊。

---

146 (A) No purchase necessary to enter or win!

(B) Helps control dandruff symptoms with regular use!

(C) Special sales price available for a limited time only!

(D) Contact us today and start living the life you deserve!

(A) 無需購買即可登錄或中獎！

(B) 經常使用有助於控制頭皮屑症狀！

(C) 特惠價僅限時提供！

(D) 今天就聯繫我們，開始過您應得的生活吧！

正解 **(D)**

空格的前句提及盡早把握此次徵才的機會，才能在財務上取得成功。因此最後應會鼓勵盡快聯繫此公司，以便達到廣告中所標榜能賺大錢的目標並擁有更好的生活，推知最符合邏輯的答案為 (D)。

(B) dandruff *(n.)* 頭皮屑。

Part 7: Reading Comprehension

Questions 147-148 refer to the following website announcement.

DATA ANALYST WANTED

BizGov is looking for a data analyst to join our team next year. We are a fast-growing, award-winning tech company, looking to expand into social media. But instead of copying or joining existing platforms, we want to create one that focuses on social awareness. We need your expertise to help us find our audience, reach them, and create the next trend in well-being. If you have proven experience in social media and references, we want to hear from you! We offer a competitive salary, remote work days, double the standard amount of paid leave, company trips, a great office environment, and skills development. Send your résumé to hr@bizgov.ca. We will send a short data test, followed by a short phone interview if you pass the test. After that, we'll set up an on-site interview and trial week.

誠徵資料分析師

比茲鉅正在尋找明年加入我們團隊的資料分析師。我們是一間成長迅速的獲獎科技公司，目前想要拓展到社群媒體產業。然而，比起複製或加入現存的平台，我們更想要創造一個聚焦社會關注度的平台。我們需要你的專業技能來幫我們尋找客群、跟他們取得聯繫並且創造下一個幸福趨勢。如果你有參與社群媒體的相關經驗證明，我們想要收到你的消息！我們提供具競爭力的薪水、在家工作日、比標準多兩倍的帶薪休假、員工旅遊、絕佳的工作環境以及技能進修。請將你的履歷寄到 hr@bizgov.ca。我們會寄送一個簡單的資料分析測試，如果你通過測試，接下來你會收到一個簡短的電話面試。在那之後，我們會安排現場面試以及一週試用期。

147 What project is BizGov most likely working on currently?

(A) Winning awards for technology

(B) Copying a social media platform

(C) Joining a social media platform

(D) Trying to create social awareness

比茲鉅目前最有可能在進行什麼計畫？

(A) 獲得科技類獎項

(B) 複製一個社群媒體平台

(C) 加入一個社群媒體平台

(D) 試圖創造社會關注度

正解 (D)

本題詢問比茲鉅目前最有可能進行的計畫為何。由第三句 But instead of copying or joining existing platforms, we want to create one that focuses on social awareness.「然而，比起複製或加入現存的平台，我們更想要創造一個聚焦社會關注度的平台」，可知正確答案應選 (D)。

......

148 Which is NOT a benefit for employees at BizGov?

(A) Well-being program

(B) Working from home

(C) Paid holidays

(D) Company trips

何者並非比茲鉅員工的福利？

(A) 幸福計畫

(B) 在家工作

(C) 帶薪休假

(D) 員工旅遊

正解 (A)

此題為除外題，詢問何者並非比茲鉅的員工福利。(B)、(C)、(D) 皆可在倒數第四句中 ... remote work days, double the standard amount of paid leave, company trips ...「……在家工作日、比標準多兩倍的帶薪休假、員工旅遊……」中得知。唯獨 (A) 未提及，故為答案。

SECTION C

模擬測驗

Questions 149-150 refer to the following text message chain.

ABLE, TRAVEL REP 10:28 a.m.
Hi, Mark. Can I help you to book your next trip?

MARK JACKSON 10:30 a.m.
Yeah, sure. I want to go to Greece in June or July with my wife and kids.

ABLE, TRAVEL REP 10:32 a.m.
Wonderful idea! We have several tour packages for Greece. Here are the links:
http://www.travelgo.com/packages/greece-ruins/family
http://www.travelgo.com/packages/greece-athens/family
http://www.travelgo.com/packages/greece-islands/family

MARK JACKSON 10:35 a.m.
Thanks, but my kids are actually grown adults. I had a brief skim through your packages. Unfortunately, nothing quite fits our needs. We want a combination of your **pensioner's** package and the young backpacker's packages, if that's possible.

ABLE, TRAVEL REP 10:37 a.m.
Of course! Let me see what we can do for you. Could you give me your preferred dates and budget, please? Also an e-mail address for us to send the tailored packages to.

Aa | Send

艾波，旅遊代辦人 [上午 10:28]
嗨，馬克。我可以協助您預訂您的下一趟旅程嗎？

馬克・傑克遜 [上午 10:30]
好呀，當然。我想要跟我的妻子及孩子們在六月或七月時去一趟希臘。

艾波，旅遊代辦人 [上午 10:32]
好主意！我們有幾個希臘旅遊的套裝行程。連結如下：
http://www.travelgo.com/packages/greece-ruins/family
http://www.travelgo.com/packages/greece-athens/family
http://www.travelgo.com/packages/greece-islands/family

馬克・傑克遜 [上午 10:35]
謝了，但我的孩子們其實已經成年。我迅速瀏覽了你的套裝行程。很遺憾，似乎都不太符合我們的需求。如果可以的話，我們想要你們銀髮族行程跟年輕背包客行程的結合。

艾波，旅遊代辦人 [上午 10:37]
當然！讓我看看我們可以幫您做什麼？可以麻煩您給我您想要的旅遊日期以及預算嗎？還有一個電子郵件地址來寄送量身打造的行程。

- pensioner *(n.)* 退休人士；領養老金者

149 At 10:35, what does Mark Jackson mean when he writes "I had a brief skim through your packages"?

(A) He looked very carefully at some vacations.

(B) He discussed some ideas with the agent.

(C) He hasn't had the chance to go traveling.

(D) He looked very quickly at some trips.

在上午 10:35 時，馬克・傑克遜寫道 "I had a brief skim through your packages" 的意思為何？

(A) 他仔細查看了一些假期。

(B) 他跟代辦人討論了一些想法。

(C) 他沒有機會去旅行。

(D) 他迅速看了一些旅程。

正解 (D)

本題為句意題，詢問 "I had a brief skim through your packages" 的意思。brief skim 是是指「短暫快速瀏覽」，因此答案選 (D)。由本句的前後文可知，馬克欲表達已迅速瀏覽了艾波所提供的幾個套裝行程，但覺得都不符合需求。

---

150 What would Mark like Able to do?

(A) Send quotes for the packages

(B) Create a new package for them

(C) Give suggestions of locations

(D) Send him an e-mail about Greece

馬克希望艾波做什麼？

(A) 寄送行程的報價

(B) 為他們創造一個新的旅遊行程

(C) 給他關於地點的建議

(D) 寄送一封有關希臘的電子郵件

正解 (B)

由馬克在 10:35 所提及 Unfortunately, nothing quite fits our needs. We want a combination of your pensioner's package and the young backpacker's packages, if that's possible，可知現有行程都不符合他們的需求，馬克想要的是結合兩種行程的新行程，因此 (B) 為正解。

Questions 151-152 refer to the following instructions.

Bernkitz Furniture Assembly Instructions

Pine Coffee Table

IMPORTANT

- Read the instructions carefully before starting assembly

Health and Safety

- DO NOT use this table if any parts are missing or broken
- DO NOT use this table if all fixings are not secure
- Only use on a level, even surface
- Recommended for two people to use and assemble

Care and Maintenance

- Do not place item in direct sunlight or next to a radiator. Heat could change the shape of the table.
- Do not place very cold or hot items directly on surface
- Use a duster or slightly damp cloth to clean
- Do not use soap and water or detergents
- You can treat the surface using fragrance-free block wax
- Check all screws and fixings regularly
- Keep sharp objects away from table

伯恩基茲家具組裝說明

松木咖啡桌

重要

- 組裝前請詳閱說明

健康和安全

- 如果缺少零件,切勿使用桌子
- 如果固定零件不牢固,切勿使用桌子
- 只在水平、平坦的表面上使用
- 建議由兩個人組裝使用

照顧和保養

- 請勿讓陽光直射或放在暖器旁邊。高溫可能導致桌子變形。
- 請勿將極低溫或極高溫的物品直接放在表面上
- 用除塵撢或微濕的布清潔
- 請勿使用肥皂、水或清潔劑
- 您可以在表面塗抹無香精的固體蠟
- 定期檢查所有螺絲釘和固定零件
- 讓尖銳物品遠離桌子

151 What is described in these instructions?

(A) How to assemble the table

(B) How to build a table

(C) How to take care of the table

(D) How to purchase a new table

這些說明寫了什麼？

(A) 如何組裝桌子

(B) 如何建造桌子

(C) 如何保養桌子

(D) 如何購買一張新的桌子

正解 **(C)**

本題為主旨題，詢問說明書上的內容。由照顧和保養部分明確提到清潔方式以及上何種蠟等的保養細節，可知正確選項為 (C)「如何保養桌子」。

---

152 Why should the user not put the table in sunlight?

(A) It could change shape.

(B) It will get stained in the sun.

(C) It will break.

(D) It will get too hot to touch.

為什麼使用者不該將桌子放在陽光下？

(A) 可能會導致變形。

(B) 陽光下會染上汙漬。

(C) 它會破掉。

(D) 會變得太燙，不能觸摸。

正解 **(A)**

本題詢問使用者不該將桌子放在陽光下的原因。由照顧和保養的第一項說 Do not place item in direct sunlight or next to a radiator. Heat could change the shape of the table. 得知在陽光的高溫下桌子會變形，答案為 (A)。

SECTION C

模擬測驗

Questions 153-154 refer to the following memo.

MEMO

Date: June 21

There have been a number of complaints recently about late deliveries and subsequent poor treatment from our representatives. We know that delivery delays are out of our control, but our treatment of clients is not.

Please keep the following tips in mind when dealing with a customer complaint:

• Stay calm and acknowledge the client's complaint. Even if the client is complaining about something that is outside of your control, still acknowledge that you understand their problem.

• Explain carefully that you do not have control over the deliveries as they go through a third party. But don't stop there! Offer to help the client follow up with the delivery company. You have two options to help them do this. The first option is to give them the contact details and necessary information regarding their order. The second option is to conference call the delivery company in on your current call with the client. This will take longer and may not be ideal, but it is an option especially when dealing with a difficult client.

• Don't promise to send the order again unless there's no way of getting the original order to the client.

• Don't get angry or hang up the phone. Clients can be difficult and demanding, but becoming angry yourself will only escalate the problem. If the call goes beyond five minutes without any resolution, transfer the call to your floor manager.

Thank you for your continued hard work and we hope this will help you.

備忘錄

日期：六月二十一日

最近有一些關於快遞延遲送達以及接著我們的客服代表又處理不佳的相關抱怨。我們知道快遞延遲送達並不是我們所能掌控的，但我們可以掌控對待客人的方式。

在處理顧客抱怨時，請謹記下方的技巧：

• 保持冷靜並認可顧客的抱怨。就算顧客所抱怨的事項並非你所能控制的範圍，仍然要表明你理解他們的問題。

• 小心地解釋你並沒有辦法掌控包裹的運送，因為它們經手第三方。但別只是提供解釋而已！主動協助顧客向快遞公司追蹤貨品後續的運送狀態。你有兩個選擇來協助他們。第一是提供有關於訂單的聯絡細節以及必要的資訊。第二個選擇是用電話會議讓快遞公司加入你與目前顧客的通話。這樣做會花上比較久的時間而且可能並不理想，但是尤其在面對難以應付的顧客時會是一個可能的選擇。

• 請不要承諾會重新出貨，除非已經沒有辦法將原訂單商品送給顧客。

• 請不要感到生氣或者掛掉電話。顧客可能會很難以應付或要求很多，但如果你自己生氣了只會讓問題更嚴重。如果通話已經超過了五分鐘但仍然沒有解決方案，請將通話轉給你的樓層經理。

感謝你的不懈努力，我們希望這個可以幫助到你。

153 What should representatives let unhappy clients know?

(A) That they can't control the client

(B) That they can't share contact details

(C) That they can't help the client

(D) That they understand the client's problem

客服代表應該要讓不滿意的顧客知道什麼？

(A) 他們無法控制顧客

(B) 他們無法提供聯絡資訊

(C) 他們無法協助顧客

(D) 他們了解顧客的問題

正解 **(D)**

本題詢問客服代表要讓不滿意的顧客知道的事。由第一個技巧所說 . . . still acknowledge that you understand their problem「仍然要表明你理解他們的問題」，可知符合邏輯的答案為 (D)。

---

154 What should representatives do to help clients?

(A) Give the client a refund immediately

(B) Get mad and hang up the phone

(C) See if they can offer a better deal

(D) Give them the details for the delivery company

客服代表應該做什麼來協助顧客？

(A) 立即給顧客辦理退費

(B) 生氣並掛掉電話

(C) 看看是否可以提供更優惠的價格

(D) 提供他們快遞公司的聯絡方式

正解 **(D)**

本題詢問客服代表該協助顧客的事。由第二個技巧提到 Offer to help the client follow up with the delivery company . . . give them the contact details and necessary information regarding their order. 可知應協助顧客與快遞公司取得聯繫，因此 (D) 為正解。

Questions 155-157 *refer to the following news article.*

Plain Retail Park is set to open next month near the National University's East Campus on Pine Road. —[1]—

The retail park, which is just under 3,000sq ft., will have student accommodation and academic buildings to one side and a shopping mall and gym on the other side. —[2]—

Macey Trent, Retail Operations Manager, said "Before we built this retail park, students had to cross a busy road to get to a store or gym. So this is much more convenient for them. And the student residences are just a short walk away so we are expecting to get a lot of business."

—[3]— The estate manager for Plain Park has confirmed that the rent will be controlled by an independent real estate agency. Students and potential buyers can contact park management to find out more. —[4]—

平凡購物商圈預計將於下個月在國家大學東部校區附近的松樹路開幕。

購物商圈占地大約三千平方英呎，一端會有學生宿舍和學院大樓，而另一端則是購物中心和健身房。

商圈營運經理梅西‧川特說：「在建立這個購物商圈之前，學生要到商店或是健身房需要穿越繁忙的路況。因此對他們來說，這樣會更加方便。而距離學生住宅區只間隔一小段路程，因此我們也預期生意會非常好。」

大多數的公寓已經售給國內外的投資者，他們會將這些房產租給學生使用。負責平凡商圈的地產經理已經證實當地的租金會由獨立的房地產公司掌控。學生以及潛在買家可以聯繫商圈的管理部門來獲取更多資訊。

155 What will Plain Retail Park most likely NOT have?
(A) Student dorms
(B) A gym
(C) A library
(D) Clothing stores

平凡購物商圈最有可能沒有什麼？
(A) 學生宿舍
(B) 一間健身房
(C) 一間圖書館
(D) 服飾店

正解 (C)

本題為除外題，詢問商圈並未具備什麼。由第二段中 will have student accommodation . . . and a shopping mall and gym. 得知選項 (A)、(B) 和 (D) 皆具備，唯獨 (C) 沒提到，故為答案。

156 What problem will the Retail Park most likely solve?

(A) Students having to pass through traffic to reach a store

(B) Students not having any accommodation

(C) Students not having access to a gym

(D) Students not being able to get to their classes on time

購物商圈最有可能解決什麼問題？

(A) 學生要到達商店需要穿越繁忙的交通

(B) 學生沒有住宿的地方

(C) 學生無法進入一間健身房

(D) 學生並沒有辦法準時上課

正解 (A)

本題為推論題，詢問購物商圈可能解決的問題。由第三段商圈營運經理所說的 Before we built this retail park, students had to cross a busy road to get to a store or gym. So this is much more convenient for them「在建立這個購物商圈之前，學生要到商店或者健身房需要穿越繁忙的路況。因此對他們來說，這樣會更加方便」，可知答案為 (A)。

---

157 In which of the positions marked [1], [2], [3], and [4] does the following sentence best belong?

"Most of the apartments have already been sold to local and international investors who will rent the properties to students."

(A) [1]

(B) [2]

(C) [3]

(D) [4]

以下句子最適合放入文章中標示 [1]、[2]、[3]、[4] 的哪個位置？

「大多數的公寓已經售給國內外的投資者，他們會將這些房產租給學生使用。」

(A) [1]

(B) [2]

(C) [3]

(D) [4]

正解 (C)

本題為篇章結構題，詢問題目句該放在文章中的位置。本句說到會將這些公寓租給學生使用，位置 [3] 後方接續說明公寓租金的相關事項，與題目句語意連貫，故 (C) 為正確答案。

Questions 158-160 *refer to the following letter.*

Belmont Clinic

112 Main Road

Milkey City, CA 94966

www.blmclinic.org

30 November

Dear Mr. Gerton,

You had an appointment on Monday, 30 November at 11:30 a.m. with Dr. Pearson. Unfortunately, you did not cancel the appointment or notify us in advance that you needed to reschedule it. As such, your health insurance will be charged the full amount of the missed appointment.

Since this appointment was a follow-up on your blood tests from last week, we strongly urge you to schedule a new appointment as soon as possible. These results were part of your **oncology** treatment and are therefore very important for your future treatment. The doctor would like to discuss your test results and possible treatment plans.

It is a time-sensitive matter and the doctor would like to see you within the next two weeks. Please call our reception desk at 502-315-6480 to schedule a new appointment.

Yours in Health,

Belmont Clinic

貝爾蒙特診所

緬因路 112 號
加利福尼亞州麥爾奇市 94966
www.blmclinic.org

十一月三十號

親愛的戈頓先生：

您有預約在十一月三十號星期一上午十一點半跟皮爾森醫生看診。很遺憾地，您並沒有取消預約或者提前通知我們要另外安排時間看診。因此，您的健康保險會被收取未到診的全額費用。

由於這次的約診是您上週血液檢查的回診，我們強力催促您盡快安排新的看診時間。這些結果是您腫瘤治療的一部分，也因此對於您將來的治療相當重要。醫生想要跟您討論您的檢查結果以及可行的治療計畫。

這件事的時間至關重要，醫生希望可以在未來兩週內見到你。請撥打 502-315-6480 聯繫我們的接待櫃檯進行新的預約。

祝身體安康，
貝爾蒙特診所

• oncology *(n.)* 腫瘤學

158 Why is the Belmont clinic writing to Mr. Gerton?

(A) He missed an important meeting.

(B) He missed a doctor's appointment.

(C) He missed an important test.

(D) He needs to get blood tests done.

貝爾蒙特診所為什麼寫信給戈頓先生？

(A) 他錯過了一場重要的會議。

(B) 他錯過了與醫師的約診。

(C) 他錯過了一個重要的考試。

(D) 他需要完成血液檢測。

正解 **(B)**

本題為主旨題，詢問貝爾蒙特診所寫信給戈頓先生的主要目的。由第一段中 . . . you did not cancel the appointment or notify us in advance that you needed to reschedule it. 得知戈頓先生預約看診卻沒有到診，故答案為 (B)。

---

159 Why should Mr. Gerton make another appointment urgently?

(A) His medical insurance will be charged.

(B) The doctor wants to do blood tests.

(C) The doctor wants to give him test results.

(D) The doctor wants to discuss doing more tests.

為什麼戈頓先生應該趕快預約另一個會診？

(A) 他的醫療保險會被收取費用。

(B) 醫生想要進行血液檢查。

(C) 醫生想要跟他說明檢查結果。

(D) 醫生想要討論做更多檢查。

正解 **(C)**

本題詢問戈頓先生應該趕快預約另一個會診的原因。由第二段最後一句 The doctor would like to discuss your test results . . . 「醫生想要跟您討論您的檢查結果」，可知正確答案為 (C)。

---

160 What should Mr. Gerton do?

(A) He should request to be given a full refund.

(B) He should call his medical insurance.

(C) He should make an appointment to get tests done.

(D) He should make an appointment before December 14.

戈頓先生應該要做什麼？

(A) 他應該要要求全額退費。

(B) 他應該要打電話到醫療保險公司。

(C) 他應該要進行預約好完成檢查。

(D) 他應該要預約在十二月十四之前看診。

正解 **(D)**

由最後一段第一句 . . . the doctor would like to see you within the next two weeks. 「醫生希望可以在未來兩週內見到你」，又根據信件開頭的日期得知當天是十一月三十號，因此可知戈頓先生應要安排在十二月十四日之前看診，故 (D) 為正解。

Questions 161-164 refer to the following online chat discussion.

Margo Diaz [7:18 a.m.]

Roll call! I want to know who's working the Bakersfield job next April. I'll be leading the project, and I'd like to start planning ASAP.

Tarik Smith [7:31 a.m.]

I don't know if I'm working Bakersfield or not. Have the assignment details been posted yet?

Margo Diaz [7:31 a.m.]

They haven't. Since planning isn't complete, there really aren't any details to post at this point. But you should have been informed if you're working the job.

Bev Maki [7:33 a.m.]

I was told that I'm being sent somewhere in April. I'm assuming it's Bakersfield? "You're going out on a job in April." That's what I was told.

Morris Yeun [7:34 a.m.]

Same here. I could really use a confirmation.

Margo Diaz [7:34 a.m.]

All right, I'll double-check regarding your placement. But for now, I'll **tentatively** mark you two down. I can also give you some very intial details. It's a factory-cleaning job in Bakersfield—a chocolate factory. Do you two have any experience with that?

Tarik Smith [7:35 a.m.]

I know you weren't asking me, but I actually have quite a bit of experience there. Back when I was in Ohio, I was assigned to a jam manufacturer pretty consistently. I cleaned the walls and the **ventilation ducts**.

Bev Maki [7:35 a.m.]

I don't have any experience with that.

Morris Yeun [7:35 a.m.]

Me neither.

Margo Diaz [7:36 a.m.]

OK. Tarik, I'm going to talk to Dave tomorrow and request that you come on this assignment too. I'll need your experience on this one. I'm also going to need you to help Bev and Morris get the hang of things.

- roll call *(n.)* 點名
- tentatively *(adv.)* 暫時地
- ventilation *(n.)* 通風（設備）；空氣流通（系統）
- duct *(n.)* 管道；管線

瑪歌・狄亞茲 [上午 7:18]
點名了！我想知道明年四月誰會去貝克斯菲爾德工作。我會領導這個案子，我想盡快開始規劃。

塔瑞克・史密斯 [上午 7:31]
我不知道我是否要去貝克斯菲爾德工作。有公布工作的細節了嗎？

瑪歌・狄亞茲 [上午 7:31]
還沒。由於還沒完成規劃，所以現在還沒有什麼細節可以公布。不過，如果你有被指派這份工作，應該會接到通知。

貝夫・馬奇 [上午 7:33]
我被告知四月要外派。我猜應該就是貝克斯菲爾德？我被告知說：「你四月要被外派。」

莫里斯・育恩 [上午 7:34]
我也是。我真的需要確認。

瑪歌・狄亞茲 [上午 7:34]
好吧，我會再次確認你們的工作安排。但現在我暫時先登記你們兩位。我也可以告訴你們一些初步的資訊。是一份在貝克斯菲爾德的工廠清潔工作——一間巧克力工廠。你們兩位有任何相關經驗嗎？

塔瑞克・史密斯 [上午 7:35]
我知道你沒有問我，但我其實在那方面很有經驗。我在俄亥俄州的時候，我經常被派到一間果醬製造廠工作。我負責清理牆壁和通風管道。

貝夫・馬奇 [上午 7:35]
我沒有任何相關經驗。

莫里斯・育恩 [上午 7:35]
我也沒有。

瑪歌・狄亞茲 [上午 7:36]
好的。塔瑞克，我明天會跟戴夫要求也讓你參與這項工作。我需要你在這方面的經驗。我也要請你協助貝夫和莫里斯熟悉這些作業。

161 Who most likely is Margo Diaz?

(A) A custodian   (B) A chocolatier

(C) A project manager   (D) A financial planner

瑪歌‧狄亞茲最有可能是誰？

(A) 一名監護人   (B) 一名巧克力師傅

(C) 一名專案經理   (D) 一名財務規劃師

正解 **(C)**

本題為推論題，詢問瑪歌‧狄亞茲最有可能是誰。由瑪歌在上午 7:18 所說 I'll be leading the project「我會領導這個案子」，因此最符合邏輯的選項為 (C)「一位專案經理」。

(A) custodian *(n.)* 監護人；監管人。

---

162 What does the Bakersfield job entail?

(A) Installing new ventilation ducts

(B) Building new walls at a candy shop

(C) Washing machinery at a jam manufacturer

(D) Cleaning a chocolate factory

在貝克斯菲爾德的工作需要做什麼？

(A) 安裝新的通風管道

(B) 在一間糖果店建造新的牆壁

(C) 清洗一間果醬製造公司的機台

(D) 清洗一間巧克力工廠

正解 **(D)**

本題詢問在貝克斯菲爾德的工作需要做什麼。由瑪歌在上午 7:34 所說 It's a factory-cleaning job in Bakersfield—a chocolate factory.，可知答案選 (D)「清潔一間巧克力工廠」。

---

163 At 7:34 a.m., what does Morris mean when he writes, "I could really use a confirmation"?

(A) He doesn't know anything about the job.

(B) He was given the wrong information.

(C) He's not sure if he's going on the job.

(D) He would like more responsibilities.

在上午 7:34 時，莫里斯寫道 "I could really use a confirmation" 的意思為何？

(A) 他不知道關於那個工作的任何事情。

(B) 他被告知了錯誤的資訊。

(C) 他並不確定他是否被指派到該項工作。

(D) 他希望承擔更多責任。

正解 **(C)**

本題為句意題，詢問 "I could really use a confirmation" 的意思。由本句的前一個訊息貝夫‧馬奇提到他會被外派去工作，但地點並不明確，而莫里斯回說 Same here. 可得知莫里斯也不確定自己是否會被外派到一開頭瑪歌所說的那個地點工作，因此希望能夠確認，故答案為 (C)。

---

164 What will mostly likely happen next in preparation for the Bakersfield job?

(A) The team will go to Bakersfield.

(B) Tarik will refuse to join the assignment.

(C) Margo will ask that Tarik join the project.

(D) Bev will study in order to get ready for the job.

接下來前往貝克斯菲爾德工作的準備事項中，何者是接下來最可能發生的事？

(A) 團隊會前往貝克斯菲爾德。

(B) 塔瑞克會拒絕參與任務。

(C) 瑪歌會要求讓塔瑞克加入專案。

(D) 貝夫會透過讀書來為該項工作做準備。

正解 **(C)**

本題詢問關於前往貝克斯菲爾德工作的準備事項中，何者是接下來最可能發生的事。由瑪歌說 OK. Tarik, I'm going to talk to Dave tomorrow and request that you come on this assignment too「好的。塔瑞克，我明天會跟戴夫要求也讓你參與這項工作」，故知答案選 (C)。

Questions 165-168 *refer to the following e-mail.*

To:	maggie@mail.com
From:	johnmc@invest.co
Subject:	Financial Portfolio

Dear Ms. Jones,

Thank you for your inquiry about our financial services. Your e-mail didn't specify which products or services you might be interested in, so I will list the main ones here:

- Financial Portfolio: we can help to set up, maintain, or grow your financial portfolio through various products including bonds, dividends, investments, etc. To get started, we will need your current financial statements and monthly or yearly budget. From there, we will discuss your financial goals for the future and see how we can help you meet them. Contact finport@invest.co

- Tax Consultancy: should you need it, we offer comprehensive tax services. We can help you with individual or company taxes for the current or previous fiscal year. For taxes older than five years, we will need to work with our corporate office in New York. Contact taxcon@invest.co

- Retirement Planning: if your financial portfolio doesn't include a retirement plan, or if you would like an additional one, we can help you. We offer several different plans that start with a minimum contribution as low as $100 per month and can go as high as you would like. We also offer local and international investments at high, medium, or low risk. Contact retplan@invest.co

收件人：maggie@mail.com
寄件人：johnmc@invest.co
主　旨：財務投資組合

親愛的瓊斯女士：

感謝您詢問我們的財務服務。您的電子郵件並沒有特別說明您對哪個產品或服務感興趣，所以我把主要的產品列在這裡：

- 財務投資組合：我們可以透過各種包含債券、股利和投資等產品幫忙設立、管理或壯大您的投資組合。一開始，我們會需要您目前的財務明細以及每月或每年的預算。然後，我們會討論您未來的財務目標並看看我們可以如何幫您達成目標。請聯繫 finport@invest.co。

- 稅務諮詢：如果您有需要，我們提供全面的稅務服務。我們可以協助處理個人或是公司今年或是去年財務年度的稅務。對於五年以上的稅務，我們將需要與紐約的分公司合作。請聯繫 taxcon@invest.co。

- 退休規劃：如果您的投資組合不包含退休計畫，或者您想要額外的退休計畫，我們可以協助您。我們提供數個不同的計畫，它們的金額由最低每月一百美元到您所想要的最高金額。我們也提供國內外高、中、低風險的投資。聯繫 retplan@invest.co。

- Business Services: aside from our tax consultancy, we can also manage your company's finances for you. You don't have to hire a full-time accountant to do your books once a month. Instead, you can make use of our business services and only pay us for the time we spend on your company. We also offer financial advice and recommendations. We want to work with you to make your company a success. Contact busserv@invest.co

This is an overview of our main service areas. Please contact the relevant departments for more information. Or feel free to set up an appointment with me, if you are unsure of what you need or if you need more than one of these services.

We look forward to being of service to you.

Kind regards,

John McGuire
Financial Representative
Invest in Now

- 商業服務：除了我們的稅務諮詢，我們可以幫您管理您公司的財務。您並不需要雇用一名全職會計師只為了每月做一次帳。反之，您可以利用我們的商業服務並只須依我們花在您公司上面的時間來支付費用。我們也提供財務意見和建議。我們想要跟您合作讓貴公司達到卓越。聯繫 busserv@invest.co。

這是我們所提供的主要服務的概述。請聯繫相關部門獲取更多資訊。或者，如果您並不清楚您所需要的服務或您需要的服務不只一項，請不吝直接與我安排會面。

期待能為您服務。

謹致，

約翰‧麥奎格
財務專員
當下投資

---

165 Why is Mr. McGuire writing to Ms. Jones?
(A) Ms. Jones is looking for a tax consultant.
(B) Ms. Jones wants to start saving for her retirement.
(C) Mr. McGuire wants to introduce himself.
(D) Ms. Jones asked about their services.

麥奎格先生為什麼寫信給瓊斯女士？
(A) 瓊斯女士正在尋找一名稅務諮詢師。
(B) 瓊斯女士想要開始為退休存錢。
(C) 麥奎格先生想要介紹自己。
(D) 瓊斯女士詢問他們的相關服務。

正解 (D)

本題為主旨題，詢問麥奎格先生寫信給瓊斯女士的目的。由信件開頭提到 Thank you for your enquiry about our financial services . . . list the main ones here「感謝您詢問我們的財務服務……把主要的產品列在這裡」，可知麥奎格先生是回覆瓊斯女士對於他們公司財務服務的詢問，因此正確答案為 (D)。

---

166 Which e-mail address should Ms. Jones write to if she wants individual tax consultancy, retirement planning, and an accountant for her company?
(A) finport@invest.co   (B) taxcon@invest.co
(C) johnmc@invest.co   (D) busserv@invest.co

如果瓊斯女士想要個人稅務諮詢、退休規劃以及一名為她公司處理事務的會計師，她應該要寄信到哪一個電子郵件？
(A) finport@invest.co   (B) taxcon@invest.co
(C) johnmc@invest.co   (D) busserv@invest.co

正解 (C)

由信件最後寫道 Or feel free to set up an appointment with me, if you are unsure of what you need or if you need more than one of these services，得知需要不只一項服務時可直接跟麥奎格先生聯繫，麥奎格先生的電子郵件即是寄件者，所以答案為 (C)。

167 Which financial service does Invest in Now NOT offer according to the e-mail?

(A) **Monthly budgeting**　(B) Saving for the future

(C) Managing finances　(D) Getting tax returns

根據電子郵件，哪一個並非當下投資所提供的財務服務？

(A) 提供每月預算　(B) 為未來儲蓄

(C) 管理財務　(D) 取得退稅

正解 (A)

本題為除外題，詢問何者並非當下投資所提供的財務服務。(B) 可見退休規劃中 start with a minimum contribution as low as $100 得知有存款計畫；(C) 可見商業服務中 manage your company's finances 得知有管理公司財務；(D) 可見稅務諮詢中 we offer comprehensive tax services. 得知有處理稅務；唯獨 (A) 並未提及有此服務故為答案。

168 Why would a business make use of Invest in Now's Business Services?

(A) To help them make more profits

(B) To help them find new clients

(C) **To avoid hiring a full-time bookkeeper**

(D) To avoid hiring full-time employees

公司為什麼要使用當下投資的商業服務？

(A) 為了讓自己獲利更多　(B) 為了幫自己尋找新客戶

(C) **為了避免雇用全職記帳員** (D) 為了避免雇用全職員工

正解 (C)

本題詢問公司使用當下投資的商業服務的原因。由商業服務中 You don't have to hire a full-time accountant to do your books once a month. Instead, you can make use of our business services ... 「您並不需要雇用一名全職會計師只為了每月做一次帳。反之，您可以利用我們的商業服務……」可知正確答案為 (C)。

Questions 169-171 refer to the following online advertisement.

The Tuck Shop: A Taste of Back Home

Living out in Asia, we're lucky enough to be able to sample all kinds of wonderful cuisine. —[1]— However, **every now and then**, we yearn for a taste of back home, and there are some treats that are almost impossible to get your hands on.

When was the last time you had a Cadder's Cream Crunch or a Blaster Bar? How about a Big Forest Fudge or a Roly-Poly Surprise? —[2]— We're betting that the answer is a long time ago, unless you managed to get Mom to send you a package of some of these **goodies**.

We were sick and tired of having to wait on those packages too. That's exactly why we opened The Tuck Shop. Here in our little store, we have a massive selection of chocolate, candy, cookies, and other types of **confectionery**. —[3]—

So what are you waiting for? If you've got a **sweet tooth** and miss the tastes from when you were a youngster, get on down to The Tuck Shop now! —[4]—

塔克之店：家鄉的滋味

住在亞洲的我們有幸品嚐各式各樣的美食。然而，我們偶爾會想要嚐嚐家鄉味，而其中有些美食是你幾乎不可能吃得到的。

你上一次吃到凱德爾奶油脆餅或是響響棒是什麼時候？那麼大森林蛋糕或是驚奇捲呢？我們敢打賭，答案是很久以前。除非你想辦法讓老媽寄一個裝有這些好料的包裹來。

我們非得等這些包裹寄來也等得很煩了。那正是我們為何要開塔克之店的原因。在我們這間小店裡，我們有各式各樣的巧克力、糖果、餅乾和其他種類的甜食。<u>如果在你家鄉是一種受歡迎的美食，我們就很可能有賣。</u>

所以你還在等什麼呢？如果你喜歡吃甜食，並且想念你年輕時的那種滋味，現在就過來塔克之店吧！

- every now and then *(phr.)* 間或；偶爾；有時
- goody *(n.)*（常指）好吃的東西
- confectionery *(n.)* 甜食；糖果；巧克力
- sweet tooth *(n.)* 嗜甜；對甜食（尤指糖果和巧克力）喜愛

169 The phrase "yearn for" in paragraph 1, line 2, is closest in meaning to

(A) To intensely dislike

(B) To strongly desire

(C) To clearly remember

(D) To amusingly observe

第一段第二行的 "yearn for" 意思最接近

(A) 極度地不喜歡

(B) 強烈地想要

(C) 清楚地記得

(D) 有興致地觀察

正解 **(B)**

本題考同義字詞，詢問與 "yearn for" 意思相近的字詞。yearn 是「渴望；嚮往」之意，且後方又說有些美食是你幾乎不可能吃得到，可推測在這裡是指很想要吃家鄉美食，所以答案為 (B)。

---

170 What does the advertisement say people have to do to get some items from back home?

(A) Shop online

(B) Get help from their parents

(C) Have friends send them packages

(D) Fly back home

廣告中說到，如果人們想要取得一些家鄉的物品的話，他們需要做什麼？

(A) 網購

(B) 跟父母尋求幫助

(C) 讓朋友寄送包裹

(D) 飛回家鄉

正解 **(B)**

本題詢問廣告提到人們必須做什麼才能得到一些家鄉的物品。由第二段開頭詢問有無吃過幾樣家鄉的食物，而最後說 . . . unless you managed to get Mom to send you a package of some of these goodies. 得知要吃到只能請媽媽寄送，答案為 (B)。

---

171 In which of the positions marked [1], [2], [3], and [4] does the following sentence best belong?

"If it's a popular treat back home, we've most likely got it."

(A) [1]   (B) [2]

(C) [3]   (D) [4]

以下句子最適合放入文章中標示 [1]、[2]、[3]、[4] 的哪個位置？

「如果在你家鄉是一種受歡迎的美食，我們就很可能有賣。」

(A) [1]   (B) [2]

(C) [3]   (D) [4]

正解 **(C)**

本題為篇章結構題。根據前文句意，[3] 的前一句說到店裡有賣各式各樣的甜食，而題目句「如果在你家鄉是一種受歡迎的美食，我們就很可能有賣。」再次強調了店內商品應有盡有，與前面語意連貫，故答案選 (C)。

SECTION C 模擬測驗

Questions 172-175 refer to the following article.

Many people complain about a lack of energy in winter; a physical and emotional experience that feels like finding yourself weighed down by a heavy blanket. It's hard to get out of bed and easy to find reasons to take a nap. You crave **carbohydrate**s and fats, and probably gain weight. You feel lazy and cancel social outings. In short, you behave like a bear ready for winter **hibernation**. In fact, nature may have written the same type of instincts into our genetic code.

This finding is important because it **sheds light on** the higher incidence of **depression**-like symptoms reported starting in the late fall. In other words, there is nothing wrong with us; we **are** just **at the mercy of** insufficient light and falling temperatures.

However, since humans are not bears and do not enjoy this experience, there are coping **mechanisms** to overcome the winter blues and keep your body and emotions running smoothly. Check the box of symptoms below and their corresponding remedies.

SYMPTOM	WE TEND TO	BETTER YET
Craving sweets	Have too many carbs, resulting in low energy	Skip the yo-yo feeling of sugar highs and crashes by loading up on high-nutrition-**laden** vegetables, and healthy proteins.
All-day sleepiness	Sleep in and then force ourselves awake with caffeine	Get up with your alarm and do some simple exercises. At lunchtime, go for a walk to soak up sunlight.
Feeling sad	Isolate ourselves	Join social events and stay in touch with friends or family for a natural boost to your mood.

- carbohydrate *(n.)* 碳水化合物（= carb)
- hibernation *(n.)* 冬眠
- shed light on *(phr.)* 為……提供解釋；使……較容易理解
- depression *(n.)* 憂鬱症
- be at the mercy of *(phr.)* 任由……的擺布；完全受……的支配
- mechanism *(n.)* 機制
- laden *(adj.)* 裝滿的（-laden 常如文中用法構成形容詞，表示「充滿……的；有大量……的」）

很多人都會抱怨冬天的時候整個人無精打采；也就是在身體和心情上感覺自己好像被一張厚厚的毯子給壓得喘不過氣一樣。覺得很難起床，找理由打個盹卻很容易。你會渴望吃到碳水化合物和脂肪，體重可能會增加。你會覺得很懶惰，並且取消社交戶外活動。簡言之，你的行為就好像是一隻準備冬眠的熊。事實上，大自然可能已經將同樣一種本能寫進了我們的遺傳密碼中。

這項發現很重要，因為它說明了為何從深秋開始，通報的憂鬱症類似症狀頻率比較高。換言之，我們並沒有生病；我們只不過是受到了日照不足和溫度下降的影響。

不過，既然人類並不是熊且不享受這樣的經驗，因此有了克服這種冬季憂鬱的機制，並讓你的身體和情緒保持正常運作。看看下方表格中的症狀，以及這些症狀相對應的治療方式。

症狀	我們會想要	改善方式
想吃甜食	吃太多碳水化合物，導致活力不佳	避開那種糖份帶來的情緒極端起伏，多吃營養成分高的蔬菜和健康的蛋白質。
整天昏昏欲睡	賴床，然後用咖啡因逼自己清醒	鬧鐘響了就起床，做一些簡單的運動。午餐時間出去散散步，曬曬太陽。
感到悲傷	孤立自我	參加社交活動，和朋友或家人保持聯繫，自然而然地提振自己的心情。

172 Which would be a good title for the article?

(A) Lessons from Bears

(B) The Secret to Good Sleep

(C) Reasons to Throw a Party

(D) Shake Off the Winter Blues

下列何者為適合本文的標題？

(A) 從熊身上學到的事　　(B) 良好睡眠的秘訣

(C) 舉辦派對的原因　　**(D) 擺脫冬季憂鬱**

正解 (D)

本題為主旨題，詢問何者為適合本文的標題。由開頭說冬季人類會變得懶惰，接著又說深秋開始憂鬱症狀的人就會變多，以及下方提供了這些症狀相對應的治療方式，故可知本文主要在探討如何改善冬天的憂鬱症狀，所以答案選 (D)。

---

173 What is compared to lying under a heavy blanket?

(A) Getting sick

(B) Experiencing tiredness

(C) Feeling cold in the winter

(D) Being controlled by the weather

躺在厚厚的毯子下是在比喻什麼？

(A) 身染疾病　　**(B) 感覺疲憊**

(C) 在冬天時感到寒冷　　(D) 被天氣操控

正解 (B)

本題詢問躺在厚厚的毯子下是在比喻什麼。由第一句 Many people complain about a lack of energy in winter, a physical and emotional experience that feels like finding yourself weighed down by a heavy blanket. 得知是形容人無精打采、疲累的感覺像是被厚毯子蓋住一樣，所以答案選 (B)。

---

174 According to the article, which illness can lack of energy in winter seem similar to?

(A) Obesity

(B) Depression

(C) Social phobia

(D) Muscle pain

根據文章，冬日倦怠與哪一種疾病相似？

(A) 肥胖

(B) 憂鬱症

(C) 社交恐懼症

(D) 肌肉痠痛

正解 (B)

本題為細節題，詢問冬日倦怠和哪一種疾病相似。由第二段第一句 This finding is important because it sheds light on the higher incidence of depression-like symptoms reported starting in the late fall.「這項發現很重要，因為它說明了為何從深秋開始，通報的憂鬱症類似症狀頻率比較高。」，說明前一段所說在冬天時會感覺無精打采原因正與憂鬱症有關聯，故選 (B) Depression「憂鬱症」。

(C) phobia (n.) 恐懼；懼怕。

---

175 What is recommended to combat wanting to sleep all the time?

(A) Drinking coffee

(B) Getting more rest

(C) Pressing the snooze button on your alarm

(D) Doing physical activity

作者建議如何克服總是想睡覺的感覺？

(A) 喝咖啡　　(B) 多休息

(C) 在鬧鐘響時按下貪睡鍵　　**(D) 做運動**

正解 (D)

本題詢問作者建議如何克服總是想睡覺的感覺。由表格的第二列的改善方式提到 Get up with your alarm and do some simple exercises. At lunchtime, go for a walk to soak up sunlight.「鬧鐘響了就起床，做一些簡單的運動。午餐時間出去散散步，曬曬太陽」，故選 (D) Doing physical activity「做運動」。

Questions 176-180 *refer to the following e-mail and listings.*

To:	john@stcloudreal.com
From:	barbwalsh@yakoo.com
Subject:	Real Estate Listings

Dear Mr. Cloud,

My husband and I just got married and we're looking for our first house. We are hoping to live in the downtown area near both our offices. Here is a list of our requirements:

- Quiet neighborhood, preferably with families
- A large porch at the front or back of the house
- Three bedrooms minimum, two bathrooms
- One floor with an open-plan living room and kitchen
- Old English architecture with brick face, not cement in front
- Close to schools, shops, and doctors

Ideally, we would like it to have a basement and double garage as well. We don't mind doing a bit of renovation ourselves. So feel free to send us any fixer-uppers that are cheaper. We have a meeting with our bank manager tomorrow to discuss mortgage rates and loans.

Please let me know if you have any listings that meet our needs. We could set up an appointment as early as next week to start looking at properties.

Kind regards,

Barbara Walsh

收件人：john@stcloudreal.com
寄件人：barbwalsh@yakoo.com
主　旨：房地產列表

親愛的克勞德先生：

我跟我先生最近才結婚，我們正在尋找我們的第一間屋子。我們想要住在兩人公司附近的市中心區域。以下是我們的需求清單：

- 安靜的社區，最好是有家庭的
- 屋子前面或後面有一個大的門廊
- 最少有三間臥房，兩間浴室
- 其中一層樓要有開放式客廳和廚房
- 外觀為老式的磚砌英式建築，而非水泥牆面
- 鄰近學校、商店和醫院

理想情況下，我們也想要一個地下室以及雙車庫。我們不介意自己動手翻修一小部分。所以請儘管寄給我們任何需要整修但較為便宜的房屋物件。我們明天會跟我們的銀行經理會面討論房貸利率以及借貸事宜。

如果您有符合我們需求的資訊請讓我知道。我們可以預約下週盡早見面以便開始審視這些房產。

謹致，

芭芭拉・瓦許

Stanley Cloud's Real Estate Listings	
SC-Portside-1001 • Two bedrooms • One bathroom • Large balcony • Two floors • Open-plan kitchen • Quiet neighborhood • Close to shops	**SC-Portside-1015** • Three bedrooms • One bathroom • Large front porch • Open-plan living room and kitchen • Quiet neighborhood • Close to schools and shops • Basement
SC-Portside-1020 • Four bedrooms • Two bathrooms • Large front porch • Brick-face • Quiet neighborhood • Close to shops and schools • Remodeling could create an open-floor kitchen and living room	**SC-Portside-1022** • Three bedrooms • Two bathrooms • Large porch • Open-plan kitchen • Close to shopping mall • Close to highway • Double garage • Needs renovation

史丹利・克勞德房地產列表	
SC 房地產－港口區－編號 1001 • 兩間臥室 • 一間浴室 • 大陽台 • 兩層樓 • 開放式廚房 • 安靜的社區 • 鄰近商店	**SC 房地產－港口區－編號 1015** • 三間臥室 • 一間浴室 • 大前門廊 • 開放式客廳與廚房 • 安靜的社區 • 鄰近學校和商家 • 地下室
SC 房地產－港口區－編號 1020 • 四間臥室 • 兩間浴室 • 大前門廊 • 磚塊外觀 • 安靜的社區 • 鄰近商家和學校 • 更改結構之後可以隔出一間開放式廚房與客廳	**SC 房地產－港口區－編號 1022** • 三間臥室 • 兩間浴室 • 大門廊 • 開放式廚房 • 靠近購物中心 • 鄰近高速公路 • 雙車庫 • 需要翻修

176 What is the purpose of this e-mail?

(A) To ask a landlord some questions

(B) To complain about problems with a house

(C) To inquire about finding a home

(D) To inquire about cheap agents

這封電子郵件的目的為何？

(A) 為了向房東詢問一些問題

(B) 為了抱怨一間房子的問題

(C) 為了詢問有關尋找房子的事宜

(D) 為了詢問有關便宜仲介的事宜

正解 **(C)**

本題為主旨題，詢問寄發電子郵件的目的。由信件開頭提到 ... we're looking for our first house. 「……我們正在尋找我們的第一間屋子」，以及後方說明理想中的房屋物件需求，可知寄件者想要買房，故 (C) 為正解。

177 Why would Mrs. Walsh need a mortgage or a loan?

(A) She wants to build a house.

(B) She wants to rent a house.

(C) She wants to renovate their house.

(D) She wants to buy a house.

瓦許太太為什麼需要房貸或借貸？

(A) 她想要蓋一間房子。

(B) 她想要租一間房子。

(C) 她想要整修房子。

(D) 她想要買一棟房子。

正解 **(D)**

本題詢問瓦許太太為什麼需要房貸或借貸。由電子郵件上的購屋條件以及倒數第二段最後一句說 We have a meeting with our bank manager tomorrow to discuss mortgage rates and loans. 得知瓦許太太要為買房貸款，答案為 (D)。

模擬測驗

178 What does Mrs. Walsh mean when she says, "So feel free to send us any fixer-uppers that are cheaper"?

(A) They want to buy a house up the street.

(B) They might buy a house that has been fixed.

(C) They might buy a house that needs renovation.

(D) They are not willing to do any work on the house.

瓦許太太提到"So feel free to send us any fixer-uppers that are cheaper" 的意思為何？

(A) 他們想要購買街道盡頭的房子。

(B) 他們可能會購買已經翻修好的房子。

(C) 他們可能會購買需要翻修的房子。

(D) 他們不願意在房子上付出任何心力。

正解 (C)

本題詢問瓦許太太說 "So feel free to send us any fixer-uppers that are cheaper" 的意思。由於本句的前面寫道 We don't mind doing a bit of renovation ourselves.，可推知他們不介意自行整修，故可推測他們會願意購買雖尚待翻修但價格較低的房子，答案為 (C)。fixer-upper 指「屋況不佳、需要整修的房子」。

---

179 What is wrong with SC-Portside-1022 according to Mrs. Walsh's requirements?

(A) It has two bathrooms.

(B) It doesn't have a living room.

(C) It needs remodeling.

(D) Nothing, it's perfect.

根據瓦許太太的需求，SC 房地產－港口區－編號 1022 有什麼缺點？

(A) 它有兩間浴室。

(B) 它沒有客廳。

(C) 它需要整修。

(D) 沒有任何缺點，它很完美。

正解 (B)

本題為整合題，詢問根據瓦許太太的需求，編號 1022 的房屋物件有什麼缺點。根據電子郵件中瓦許太太所列的第四項條件是 One floor with an open-plan living room and kitchen「其中一層樓要有開放式客廳和廚房」，可知瓦許太太希望有一間開放式客廳；而對照房地產列表中編號 1022 的房屋物件卻沒有客廳，所以答案是 (B)。

---

180 Which of the following would be most suitable for Mrs. Walsh?

(A) SC-Portside-1015

(B) SC-Portside-1001

(C) SC-Portside-1022

(D) SC-Portside-1020

下列何者最適合瓦許太太？

(A) SC 房地產－港口區－編號 1015

(B) SC 房地產－港口區－編號 1001

(C) SC 房地產－港口區－編號 1022

(D) SC 房地產－港口區－編號 1020

正解 (D)

本題為整合題，詢問哪一個房屋物件最適合瓦許太太。根據瓦許太太的電子郵件中所列條件，對照房地產列表可知編號 1020 所滿足的條件最多且符合瓦許太太的需求。雖然此物件需要整修才能隔出廚房跟客廳，但她在郵件中有提到不介意自行進行小部分整修，因此選項 (D) 為最合適的答案。

TOUR CAPE TOWN!

Join us on our well-equipped, luxury tour bus, for an unforgettable tour of Cape Town!

Day 1: Arrive at Cape Town International Airport and travel to hotel via shuttle bus

Day 2: Explore the V&A waterfront and Table Mountain*

Day 3: Hout Bay and Boulders Beach to see penguins in their natural habitat[1]

Day 4: Wine and dine! We will visit the largest wine cellar in the world, KWV, to enjoy wine, brandy, and whisky tastings. After that we'll enjoy a fabulous dinner at La Colombe.

Day 5: Robben Island. We will return to the V&A Waterfront and take a ferry to the historical landmark of Nelson Mandela's prison on Robben Island.[2]

Day 6: Long Street and see ancient artifacts at the Iziko South African Museum.

* If the weather is unpleasant, we will return to Table Mountain on Day 5.

Optional extras:

1. The adventurous tourist can join a sea-kayaking trip to the penguin habitat on Boulders Beach.

2. You can include a trip to the Two Oceans Aquarium on this day as well.

Contact us at: info@greattours.com

開普敦觀光行！

加入我們設備齊全的豪華巴士行程，來一場難忘的開普敦觀光行！

第一天：抵達開普敦國際機場並搭乘接駁巴士到飯店

第二天：探索維多利亞阿爾弗雷德碼頭廣場和桌山 *

第三天：到豪特灣以及去巨石灘企鵝的自然棲息地看企鵝[1]

第四天：美酒佳餚！我們會參觀世界最大的酒窖 KWV，並品嚐紅酒、白蘭地和威士忌。在那之後，我們會到 La Colombe 享用美味晚餐。

第五天：羅本島。我們會回到維多利亞阿爾弗雷德碼頭廣場，並搭乘渡輪到具有歷史性的地標，就是羅本島上關押納爾遜‧曼德拉的監獄[2]。

第六天：到長街以及去看收藏於南非自然歷史博物館的人類遺產。

* 若氣候不佳，我們會在第五天再到訪桌山。

額外自選行程：

1. 熱愛冒險的旅客可以參加海上獨木舟的行程前往巨石灘上的企鵝棲息地。

2. 您也可以在當天到兩洋水族館參觀。

聯絡方式：info@greattours.com

SECTION C

模擬測驗

To:	info@greattours.com
From:	mel345@homail.com
Subject:	Cape Town Tour

Dear Great Tours,

I am really interested in the tour of Cape Town, but I have a few questions.

1. What kind of accommodation do you provide? Can I book my own or stay with locals?

2. What are the costs for the optional extras on Days 3 and 5?

3. Do I need any experience for the optional extra activity on Day 3?

4. Are the tastings and meals included in the price on Day 4?

5. I'm not really interested in history. Could I skip those activities?

I look forward to your reply!

Kind regards,

Melanie

收件人：info@greattours.com
寄件人：mel345@hotmail.com
主　旨：開普敦觀光行

親愛的卓越行：

我對於開普敦的觀光行很感興趣，但我有一些疑問。

1. 你們提供什麼樣的住宿條件呢？我可以自己預訂住宿或者是留宿當地人的住家嗎？

2. 第三天和第五天的額外自選行程費用是多少呢？

3. 參加第三天的額外自選行程需要有任何經驗嗎？

4. 品酒和餐點的費用有包含在第四天的費用之中嗎？

5. 我對於歷史不太感興趣。我可以不參加那些行程嗎？

期待收到您的回覆！

謹致，

梅蘭妮

---

⑱ How will the tour participants get from the airport to the hotel?

(A) They will take a tour bus.

(B) They will take a ferry.

(C) They will rent cars.

(D) They'll take a shuttle bus.

觀光行的參加者會如何從機場到飯店？

(A) 他們會搭乘觀光巴士。　(B) 他們會搭乘渡輪。

(C) 他們會租車。　　　　　**(D) 他們會搭乘接駁巴士。**

正解 (D)

本題為細節題，詢問參加者會如何從機場到飯店。第一天的行程中提到 . . . travel to hotel via shuttle bus，可知他們會搭乘接駁巴士從機場到飯店，故正確答案選 (D)。

---

⑱ What happens if the weather is bad on Day 2 of the tour?

(A) They will stay at the hotel.

(B) They will go to Hout Bay instead.

(C) They will go back to the aquarium.

(D) They will go to Table Mountain on Day 5.

如果行程的第二天天候不佳，會發生什麼事？

(A) 他們會待在飯店。

(B) 他們會改去豪特灣。

(C) 他們會回到水族館。

(D) 他們會在行程的第五天去桌山。

正解 (D)

本題詢問如果天候不佳，第二天的行程會做什麼事。第二天之後的星號引導到行程底部的註釋，其中提到 If the weather is unpleasant, we will return to Table mountain on Day 5.，因此可得知如果氣候不理想，他們會在第五天再去桌山，因此 (D) 為正確的選項。

183 What is implied about the sea-kayaking trip?

(A) **It's not for people who don't like adventure.**

(B) It's not recommended for tourists.

(C) It's only recommended if you have experience.

(D) It's a good activity for elderly people.

關於海上獨木舟的行程，文中有何暗示？

(A) **不適合不喜歡冒險的人。**

(B) 並不建議旅客參加。

(C) 只推薦給有相關經驗的人。

(D) 對於長者是很好的運動。

正解 **(A)**

本題為推論題，詢問關於海上獨木舟行程的暗示。由額外自選行程第一項提到 The adventurous tourist can join a sea-kayaking trip...，可推知海上獨木舟比較適合愛冒險的旅客參加，選項 (A) 符合邏輯，故為正解。

---

184 In the flyer, the phrase "wine and dine" on Day 4 is closest in meaning to

(A) Tasting wine and other beverages

(B) **Drinking good wine and eating good food**

(C) Tasting food from different places

(D) Making wine and cooking food

在廣告中第四天提到的字詞 "wine and dine" 意思最接近於何者？

(A) 品酒和其他飲料

(B) **喝美酒和吃美食**

(C) 品嚐來自不同產地的美食

(D) 釀酒和烹飪美食

正解 **(B)**

本題為同義字詞題，詢問 "wine and dine" 的意義為何。由第四天行程提到 We will visit the largest wine cellar ... to enjoy wine ... enjoy a fabulous dinner at La Colombe 可知當天的行程包含美酒和美食，因此最符合邏輯的選項為 (B) Drinking good wine and eating good food「喝美酒和吃美食」。

---

185 Which activities would Melanie most likely want to skip?

(A) The V&A waterfront and Table Mountain

(B) Long Street and Boulders Beach

(C) **The Iziko South African Museum and Robben Island**

(D) Two Oceans Aquarium and Hout Bay

梅蘭妮最可能想要跳過哪些行程？

(A) 維多利亞阿爾弗雷德碼頭廣場和桌山

(B) 長街和巨石灘

(C) **南非自然歷史博物館和羅本島**

(D) 兩洋水族館和豪特灣

正解 **(C)**

本題為整合題，詢問梅蘭妮可能不想參加什麼行程。由梅蘭妮電子郵件中的第五個疑問 I'm not really interested in history. Could I skip those activities? 可知梅蘭妮對於歷史相關的參觀景點不感興趣。又根據廣告傳單中的行程，由第五天及第六天行程中的關鍵字詞 historical landmark 及 ancient artifacts 可知 Robben Island 與 The Iziko South African Museum 這兩處景點與歷史及古老文化相關，因此答案選 (C)。

Questions 186-190 refer to the following test results, patient information, and e-mail.

Patient Code	Description	Value	Units	Range	Flag
TAY-12-001	White blood cell count	12.62	X10^9/L	3.0-10.0	High*
TAY-12-002	Red blood cell count	4.80	X10^12/L	4.4-5.8	
TAY-12-003	**Lymphocytes**	4.27	X10^9/L	1.2-3.65	High
TAY-12-004	**HCT**	0.439	L/L	0.37-0.50	
* Young or elderly patients should be careful if accompanied by high fever or vomiting.					
Other Test Results					
H1N1 virus: negative Influenza A: negative					

- Lymphocytes *(n.)* 淋巴球
- HCT *(abbr.)* 血球容積（為 Hematocrit 的縮略語，指紅血球在血液中所占體積的百分比，可了解貧血程度）

檢查項目代碼	說明	值	單位	參考區間	標記
TAY-12-001	白血球數	12.62	X10^9/L	3.0-10.0	高*
TAY-12-002	紅血球數	4.80	X10^12/L	4.4-5.8	
TAY-12-003	淋巴球	4.27	X10^9/L	1.2-3.65	高
TAY-12-004	血球容積	0.439	L/L	0.37-0.50	
* 年幼或年長的病人要注意是否伴隨高燒或嘔吐等症狀。					
其他檢查結果					
H1N1 病毒：陰性 A 型流感：陰性					

Patient Information	
Name: Patrick Taylor (TAY-12)	Date of Birth: 1945 – 05 – 30
Age: 75	Blood Type: A
Allergies: Peanuts	Address: 103 Main Road, Sherry Town, 116
Consultation Date: May 8	
Patient presented with flu-like symptoms: high fever, cough, blocked nose	
Patient also complained of diarrhea and stomachaches	
Diagnosis:	
Blood and **influenza** tests ordered Antibiotics and pain killers prescribed	

- influenza *(n.)* 流行性感冒

病患資料	
姓名：派翠克・泰勒（TAY-12）	出生日期：一九四五年五月三十日
年齡：75	血型：A
過敏：花生	地址：116 雪利鎮緬因路 103 號
診斷日期：五月八日	

病患有類流感症狀：高燒、咳嗽、鼻腔阻塞
病患也抱怨有腹瀉和腹痛症狀
診斷：
安排血液和流感檢測
開抗生素和止痛藥

To:	taylorpat@yadomail.com
From:	drb@medcare.com
Subject:	Blood Test Results

Dear Mr. Taylor,

The results of your blood test and influenza tests have arrived. Please see the results attached. Luckily you don't have to worry about the flu. But it does seem like you have an infection since your white blood cell count is high.

I suggest you get some rest over the next few days and drink a lot of water. Continue taking the Keflex until you finish all the pills. You can stop taking the ibu+ when your fever and pain goes away. I'd also recommend you stay away from coffee, spicy foods, and dairy for the next week. It will give your stomach time to recover.

If you are still feeling sick after two days, please come see me again. However, if your fever suddenly goes up or you start vomiting, please go to the emergency room immediately.

I hope you feel better soon.

Regards,
Dr. Bennison

收件人：taylorpat@yadomail.com
寄件人：drb@medcare.com
主　旨：血液檢驗結果

親愛的泰勒先生：

您的血液及流感檢驗結果已經到了。請看附件的檢測報告。好消息是您不需要擔心流感。然而，由於您的白血球數量比較高，因此您似乎有受到感染。

我建議您接下來的幾天多休息並喝大量的水。要持續吃完 Keflex 藥丸。如果發燒跟疼痛的症狀消退了，可以停止服用 ibu+ 藥錠。我也建議您接下來的這一週遠離咖啡、辛辣食物以及奶製品。如此一來您的腸胃才有復原的時間。

如果您兩天之後仍然感覺不適，請再來看我。然而，如果您的發燒症狀突然變得更嚴重或者您開始嘔吐，請立刻到急診室。

祝您早日康復。

謹致，
班尼森醫生

⒙ Why did Mr. Taylor go to see Dr. Bennison?
(A) Because his red blood cell count was high
(B) Because he had many symptoms
(C) Because he had H1N1 virus
(D) Because he had influenza

泰勒先生為何去看班尼森醫生？
(A) 因為他的紅血球數量很高　(B) 因為他有諸多症狀
(C) 因為他感染到 H1N1 病毒　(D) 因為他感染到流感

正解 (B)

本題詢問泰勒先生去看班尼森醫生的原因。由病患資料的底部提到 Patient presented with flu-like symptoms: high fever, cough, blocked nose . . . also complained of diarrhea and stomachaches，可知泰勒先生有諸多身體不適的症狀，故答案選 (B)。

187 Why does Dr. Bennison say that Mr. Taylor doesn't have to worry about the flu?

    (A) He doesn't have flu-like symptoms.

    (B) He has diarrhea instead.

    (C) His test results are negative.

    (D) His red blood cell count is high.

為什麼班尼森醫生說泰勒先生不需要擔心流感問題？

    (A) 他沒有類似流感症狀。

    (B) 他有腹瀉而非流感。

    (C) 他的檢測結果為陰性。

    (D) 他的紅血球數很高。

正解 (C)

本題詢問班尼森醫生說泰勒先生不需擔心流感的原因。由檢驗報告書上所寫的 Influenza A: negative「A 型流感：陰性」，得知泰勒先生並沒有感染上流感，故 (C) 為正確答案。

---

188 Why does Dr. Bennison think Mr. Taylor's stomach needs time to recover?

    (A) Mr. Taylor complained of diarrhea and stomachache.

    (B) Mr. Taylor has the H1N1 virus and needs to rest.

    (C) Mr. Taylor has been eating too much spicy food.

    (D) Mr. Taylor needs to recover after the flu tests.

班尼森醫生為什麼覺得泰勒先生的腸胃需要時間復原？

    (A) 泰勒先生抱怨有腹瀉和腹痛的症狀。

    (B) 泰勒先生感染到 H1N1 並且需要休息。

    (C) 泰勒先生吃了太多辛辣食物。

    (D) 泰勒先生在流感檢查後需要復原。

正解 (A)

本題詢問班尼森醫生認為泰勒先生的腸胃需要時間復原的原因。由病患資料上 patient also complained of diarrhea and stomachaches，得知泰勒先生有抱怨腹瀉和腹痛的症狀，又電子信件中醫生建議他遠離咖啡、辛辣食物以及奶製品來讓腸胃有時間恢復，所以答案選 (A)。

---

189 What type of medicine is Keflex most likely?

    (A) A pain killer

    (B) An antibiotic

    (C) A pill for vomiting

    (D) A pill for blood tests

Keflex 最有可能是什麼藥？

    (A) 止痛藥

    (B) 抗生素

    (C) 嘔吐藥

    (D) 血檢用藥

正解 (B)

本題為整合題，詢問 Keflex 最有可能是什麼藥。由病患資料中的 Antibiotics and pain killers prescribed，可知目前開了抗生素和止痛藥兩種藥品；又從班尼森醫生的電子郵件中 You can stop taking the ibu+ when your fever and pain goes away，可推知 ibu+ 為止痛藥，故可推論 Keflex 最有可能是醫生所開的另一種藥品，即選項 (B) 的「抗生素」。

190 Why does Dr. Bennison advise Mr. Taylor to go to the emergency room if he starts vomiting?

(A) Because the doctor's office isn't open

(B) Because Mr. Taylor is older

(C) Because he is very young

(D) Because Mr. Taylor is allergic to peanuts

為什麼班尼森醫生建議如果泰勒先生開始嘔吐，需要去急診？

(A) 因為診所沒有營業　　(B) 因為泰勒先生比較年長

(C) 因為他非常年輕　　　(D) 因為泰勒先生對花生過敏

SECTION C　模擬測驗

正解 **(B)**

本題為整合題，詢問班尼森醫生建議如果泰勒先生開始嘔吐，需要去急診的原因。由檢查報告書上寫道 Young or elderly patients should be careful if accompanied by high fever or vomiting.；又根據病患資料表可知泰勒的年齡為七十五歲，因此正確答案為 (B)。

Questions 191-195 refer to the following letter, online review, and magazine article.

On Body and Beauty

Dear valued customers,

New Product Line On Sale

We would like to announce an exciting new range of products, Liquify. These products will address a number of skin-care concerns such as sunburn, acne, dry or flaky skin, rashes, and oiliness. The range of products can be used safely on all areas of the body and for all ages, including infants and pregnant women. Over the next ten days, you will receive a 10% discount on all Liquify products as an introductory special. We trust you will love these products as much as we do!

Clearance Sale

We are also clearing out old stock this month. Enjoy products from BodyLove, Purify, and Lotioness at 50% off. Stocks are limited and we won't be ordering again, so don't miss out!

Blog Posts

This month's blog posts are all about ethical choices, from buying products to ordering a rideshare.

Recipe

Our recipe for this month is a dairy-free, meat-free lasagna that's better than the alternative!

We look forward to serving you in store. As always, feel free to stop by with any vegan-related problems or questions. Our staff members are well-informed on all the products we stock, as well as being familiar with a wide range of natural cures.

Yours in good health,

On Body and Beauty Management

美體美容舖

尊貴的顧客：

新品系列上架

我們想要宣布一個讓人振奮的新系列產品，麗葵菲。這些產品處理一系列護膚相關問題，包含曬傷、痘痘、乾燥或脫皮肌膚、紅疹或者出油症狀。這系列產品可以安全使用在各個身體部位，且適用所有年齡層，包含嬰兒及孕婦。在接下來的十天有新品優惠，所有的麗葵菲商品都打九折。我們相信您會跟我們一樣熱愛這些產品！

清倉拍賣

我們這個月也將出清一些舊庫存。您可以半價的優惠取得芭狄樂芙、普莉菲以及樂旋納斯的產品。庫存有限，且我們不會再補貨了，可別錯過喔！

網誌貼文

本月的網誌貼文全都是關於道德選擇，從購買產品到預約共乘。

食譜

這個月的食譜是無與倫比的無奶素食義大利千層麵，比葷的還好吃！

我們期待在門市為您服務。一如往常，請不吝帶著素食相關疑難雜症駐足。我們的同仁對於所有架上的商品和各式自然療法瞭如指掌。

祝身體健康，
美體美容舖管理部

Reviews

4.5 out of 5 ★★★★⯪
1,002 customers recommend On Body and Beauty

Mary-Anne Lewis recommends On Body and Beauty

1 day ago

"What a great store! The staff members really know their stuff and were very willing to help me, even if it meant recommending a product that they didn't currently have in stock. They went so far as to tell me where I could buy it, since it was an emergency. I browsed through most of their products and was impressed by the wide selection. I ended up buying a bottle of BodyLove's "Body4U" lotion for just $10 because it was on offer, and have loved it. I'd say about 70% of their brands have the Flying Rabbit logo which is way above other shops who also claim to stock ethical products."

Can cruelty-free be trusted?

A recent report in the *Bulk Times* has revealed that a number of companies that claim to produce cruelty-free products are actually not doing so.

Although they themselves don't test their end products on animals, the ingredients they buy from third-party suppliers do. This means that even though there is less animal-testing than with other companies, there is still more than people are led to believe. The companies range from herbal medicine giants like Pfiper to smaller local operations such as BodyLove Cosmetics.

Most of the companies did not respond to the **allegations** in the report. Two companies claim that they did not know about the animal testing, as their suppliers faked reports and data when they first agreed to order from them.

They now vow to find other suppliers who don't do any animal testing and bear the Flying Rabbit logo from Green Corp. This logo means that the product has been ethically sourced in every way possible. No slave labor, animal testing, or harmful chemicals were used during its production. Consumers can look for this logo to ensure their products really are cruelty-free.

As consumers become more aware of these **breaches**, companies will have to be more transparent about their entire operation. **In a bid to** improve customer relations, major cosmetic retailer, On Body and Beauty, is already making efforts to get rid of products that have been connected to animal cruelty. The hope is that more stores **follow their lead**.

- allegation *(n.)* （尚未證實的）指責；指控
- breach *(n.)* 違反
- in a bid to *(phr.)* 力圖；為了
- follow sb.'s lead *(phr.)* 以某人為榜樣；效法某人

評論

4.5 星評價（滿分五顆星）
1,002 名顧客推薦使用美體美容舖

瑪莉－安・路易斯推薦美體美容舖

一天前

「多麼棒的一間店！員工真的很清楚他們販售的東西，也很願意提供協助，就算是建議一個他們目前沒有庫存的商品。由於我急著要，他們甚至告訴我哪裡有賣。我瀏覽了他們大部分的產品，對他們豐富的選項印象深刻。我最後用特惠價僅僅十元就買到一瓶芭狄樂芙的「芭狄寵愛」乳液，我非常喜歡。我覺得他們大概有七成的品牌有飛行兔標誌，比起其他也聲稱販售符合道德規範產品的商家多出太多了。」

零殘忍是否值得信賴？

最近一則《公牛時報》的報導揭露一些聲稱製造零殘忍產品的公司其實言行不一。

儘管他們本身並不使用動物來測試他們已製成的產品，但是他們從第三方供應商購買的原料有進行動物實驗。這意味著就算相較於其他公司有較少的動物實驗，但仍然比人們被誘導相信的更多。這些公司從大到像霹菲珀的草本醫學巨頭到小到像芭狄樂芙彩妝公司的當地企業。

大部分的公司並未回應報導中的指控。兩家公司聲稱其供應商在他們最初同意下單時偽造了報告和數據，因此他們對於動物實驗並不知情。

他們現在誓言要尋求不做任何動物實驗並且有從綠色集團取得飛行兔標誌的其他供應商。這個標誌表示該產品在各個可能層面都以符合道德規範的方式取得所有來源。製造過程中沒有壓榨勞工、不經動物實驗，亦未使用有害物質。消費者可以從這個標誌來確保他們的產品確實是零殘忍。

由於消費者已更加意識到這些違規行為，公司對於他們的整體營運將得更透明化。為了改善顧客關係，美妝用品的主要供應商美體美容舖已經試圖出清與動物實驗有關的產品。希望更多商店以他們為榜樣。

191 Why might On Body and Beauty be selling all their BodyLove products?

(A) Because of recent customer complaints

(B) Because new products are cheaper

(C) Because they want to get rid of some old stock

(D) Because they have a bad relationship with BodyLove

美體美容舖販售他們所有芭狄樂芙產品的可能原因為何？

(A) 因為近期顧客的抱怨

(B) 因為新產品比較便宜

(C) 因為他們想要清掉一些舊庫存

(D) 因為他們與芭狄樂芙的關係不好

正解 **(C)**

本題詢問美體美容舖出清所有芭狄樂芙產品的可能原因。由第一篇信件中的清倉拍賣裡提到 We are also clearing out old stock this month. Enjoy products from BodyLove . . . ，可知美體美容舖正在出清庫存，答案選 (C)。

---

192 What was the price of one bottle of Body4U before it was discounted?

(A) $10 (B) $17

(C) $20 (D) $40

一瓶芭狄寵愛折扣之前的原價是多少？

(A) 十美元 (B) 十七美元

(C) 二十美元 (D) 四十美元

正解 **(C)**

本題為整合題，詢問芭狄寵愛折扣之前的原價為何。由信件中提到 Enjoy products from BodyLove . . . at 50% off 可知芭狄樂芙的產品打五折，又根據評論中瑪莉－安・路易斯說到她以一瓶十美元的價格取得芭狄樂芙的芭狄寵愛，故可知原價為 (C) 二十元美金。

---

193 What is true about BodyLove?

(A) It is an internationally established company.

(B) It has only ever used ethically-sourced products.

(C) It has received some negative publicity.

(D) It doesn't want to change its prices.

關於芭狄樂芙，何者為真？

(A) 它是一間跨國知名企業。

(B) 它只使用過符合道德來源的產品。

(C) 它收到了一些負面的關注。

(D) 它不想要更動價格。

正解 **(C)**

本題為是非題，詢問關於芭狄樂芙何者為真。由雜誌文章第一段開頭提到一則報導揭露一些公司並不是真正製造零殘忍用品；又根據第二段最後一句 The companies range from herbal medicine giants like Pfiper to smaller local operations such as BodyLove Cosmetics，可知芭狄樂芙便是報導中非製造零殘忍產品的公司之一，故答案選 (C)。

模擬測驗

⑲ Why does Mary-Anne mention the Flying Rabbit logo?

(A) She likes the logo and thinks it's cute.

(B) She only buys products with that logo.

(C) She knows it means the company is ethical.

(D) She thinks it's a good brand.

瑪莉－安提及飛行兔標誌的原因為何？

(A) 她喜歡那個商標，並覺得它很可愛。

(B) 她只購買有那個標誌的產品。

(C) 她知道這表示公司有符合道德規範。

(D) 她認為它是一個很好的品牌。

正解 **(C)**

本題詢問瑪莉－安提及飛行兔標誌的原因。由其評論最後一句 I'd say about 70% of their brands have the Flying Rabbit logo which is way above other shops who also claim to stock ethical products. 可知她認為有飛行兔標誌才是真正有符合道德規範的產品，故 (C) 為答案。

⑲ What does the article say companies have to start doing?

(A) Offer better deals to customers

(B) Be more honest about their production process

(C) Put the Flying Rabbit logo on all products

(D) Respond to allegations of unethical practices

文章提到公司應該要開始做什麼？

(A) 提供更優惠的價格給顧客

(B) 對於產品製程更加誠實

(C) 把飛行兔標誌放在所有產品上

(D) 回應針對非道德作法的指控

正解 **(B)**

本題詢問文章中提到公司應該要開始做的事。由雜誌文章的最後一段第一句提到 . . . companies will have to be more transparent about their entire operation.「……公司對於他們的整體營運將得更加透明化」，最符合答案的選項為 (B)。

Questions 196-200 refer to the following job posting, e-mail, and response.

Digital media site looking for **dynamic** new hires

Copy Editor

- Candidate must have 1+ years' experience in Web content editing
- Must be familiar with *The Chicago Manual of Style*
- Must have background with a wide variety of content
- All articles written in American English
- Must know how to use the software package *NewLayout*
- Strong communication skills a must
- Competitive salary
- Contact tim_bendes@mediamate.com

數位媒體網站徵求
充滿活力的新員工

文稿編輯

- 應徵者必須具備一年以上的網站編輯經驗
- 必須熟悉《芝加哥論文格式》
- 有做過各種不同內容主題的經驗
- 所有文章須以美式英文書寫
- 必須知道如何使用新排版套裝軟體 NewLayout
- 必須具備良好的溝通技巧
- 具有競爭力的薪水
- 聯絡方式：tim_bendes@mediamate.com

- dynamic (*adj.*) 思維活躍的；活潑的；充滿活力的

To:	tim_bendes@mediamate.com
From:	jjenks@jmail.com
Subject:	Position of Copy Editor

To Whom It May Concern,

I am writing in connection with the position of copy editor that I saw advertised on the MediaMate site on Thursday. Attached is my **CV**. As you will see, it includes many years of experience at a variety of companies in traditional print and web media. My most recent role was at the Daily Scoop's website, where I was in charge of the sports desk.

Although most of my positions have been working for the sports sections of **publications**, I have also helped out in the business and politics departments from time to time, so I consider myself a **jack-of-all-trades**. In addition to my fine eye for detail and great copy editing skills, I am **adept** in a number of software packages, including the layout program InDesign.

I hope you will give my application some thought.

Best wishes,
Jez Jenkins

- CV *(abbr.)* 履歷（書）；簡歷（curriculum vitae 的縮寫）
- publication *(n.)* 出版物
- jack-of-all-trades *(n.)* 萬事通
- adept *(adj.)* 擅長的；熟練的；內行的

To:	jjenks@jmail.com
From:	vtomlinson@trendingdaily.com
Subject:	Copy Editor application

Dear Mr. Jenkins,

Many thanks for your application for the position of copy editor. Unfortunately, the role has already been filled, but we will keep your details on file.

I have a question: Are you from the UK? The reason I ask is that you use the word CV rather than résumé. Speaking of the résumé, it seems your eye for detail **deserted** you this time as you didn't attach it!

Anyway, thanks for your interest in the position and good luck with the job search.

Regards,
Vera Tomlinson

- desert *(v.)* 喪失（某資質）；背棄

收件人：
tim_bendes@mediamate.com
寄件人：jjenks@jmail.com
主　旨：文稿編輯職位

敬啟者：

我寫這封信是因為我星期四在媒體伴網站上看到了文稿編輯職位的廣告。附件是我的個人履歷。如你所看到的，履歷中包含了我多年在不同傳統印刷和網路媒體公司的經驗。我最近的職務是在每日獨家的網站中負責運動版面。

雖然我大多數的職務都是負責出版品中的運動版面，我也不時會幫商業和政治組的忙，所以我認為自己樣樣都懂一些。我除了善於注意細節和具備絕佳的文稿編輯技巧外，我對於一些套裝軟體很在行，包括排版程式 InDesign。

希望您能考慮我的求職。

祝好，
傑茲‧詹金斯

收件人：jjenks@jmail.com
寄件人：
vtomlinson@trendingdaily.com
主　旨：應徵文稿編輯職位

親愛的詹金斯先生：

非常感謝你應徵我們的文稿編輯職務。很可惜，這個職位已經找到人了，但我們會把你的資料建檔。

我有個問題，你是英國人嗎？我之所以這麼問，是因為你用了 CV 這個詞，而非 résumé。說到履歷表，你善於注意細節這件事這次似乎沒有發揮作用，因為你沒有附加履歷！

無論如何，感謝你對這份職務感興趣，祝你謀職順利。

謹致，
維拉‧湯林森

196 Which is a requirement in the job posting that Jez mentions in his e-mail?

(A) Familiarity with *The Chicago Manual of Style*

(B) Strong communication skills

(C) Proficiency in required software programs

(D) One or more years of experience in Web content editing

傑茲在電子郵件中有提到徵才廣告中的哪項必要條件？

(A) 熟悉《芝加哥論文格式》

(B) 良好的溝通技巧

(C) 熟悉必要的軟體程式

(D) 一年或多年的網頁內容編輯經驗

正解 (D)

本題為整合題，詢問傑茲在電子郵件中有提到徵才廣告中的哪項必要條件。由傑茲的電子郵件提到 ... it includes many years of experience at a variety of companies in traditional print and web media. 得知他有多年在網路媒體公司當編輯的經驗。對照徵才廣告正好符合第一項條件，所以答案選 (D)。

---

197 What is indicated about MediaMate?

(A) It is a newspaper.

(B) It is hiring a copy editor.

(C) It helps people create résumés.

(D) It forwards job applications to clients.

關於媒體伴，文中有何暗示？

(A) 它是一家報社。

(B) 它正在招募一位文稿編輯。

(C) 它幫人們編寫履歷。

(D) 它將求職信轉寄給客戶。

正解 (D)

本題為推論題，詢問媒體伴是什樣的機構。由傑茲的電子郵件可知他寫求職信到媒體伴，收件者電郵為 tim_bendes@mediamate.com，而下一封電子郵件卻是由湯林森小姐回信，且寄件者的電郵地址並非 @mediamate 而是另一家公司，可推知媒體伴有將求職信轉給職缺需求公司的湯林森小姐，因此推斷媒體伴應是求職網站，答案要選 (D)。

---

198 What is true of the job?

(A) It is too difficult for Jez.

(B) It is already taken.

(C) It involves filing.

(D) It would require relocating.

關於這份工作何項敘述正確？

(A) 對於傑茲來說太困難。

(B) 已經找到人了。

(C) 工作內容需要歸檔。

(D) 有調派需求。

正解 (B)

本題為是非題，詢問關於這份工作何項敘述正確。由維拉‧湯林森在電子郵件中所提及 Unfortunately, the role has already been filled ... 得知職缺已找到人，所以答案為 (B)。

199 Which of the following skills does Jez NOT say he has?

(A) Enough years of total job experience

(B) Knowledge of the required software

(C) A fine eye for detail

(D) A background with a variety of content

下列何者並非傑茲提及擁有的技能？

(A) 總計工作經驗已累積足夠年份

(B) 必要的軟體技能

(C) 細心度高

(D) 各種不同內容主題的經驗

---

200 What did Jez forget to do?

(A) Write a résumé

(B) Use correct English

(C) Specify which role he wants

(D) Attach a document

傑茲忘記做什麼？

(A) 寫履歷

(B) 寫正確英文

(C) 明確指出他想要哪一個職位

(D) 附加一個文件

正解 (B)

本題為除外題，詢問何者並非傑茲提及所擁有的技能。(A) 可見於傑茲電子郵件中的 . . . many years of experience at . . . 可知其工作經驗符合徵人廣告要求的一年以上；(C) 由 In addition to my fine eye for detail . . . 可知他很細心；(D) 由 . . . helped out in the business and politics departments . . . 可知有提到有做過不同內容的經驗。唯獨並沒有提及 (B) 熟悉徵人廣告中所要求的 NewLayout 的套裝軟體（他所提到的是另一種排版程式 InDesign），故為答案。

正解 (D)

本題為細節題，詢問傑茲忘記做的事。由維拉・湯林森電子郵件中第二段最後一句提到 Speaking of the résumé . . . as you didn't attach it! 得知傑茲沒有附上履歷的附件，故答案為 (D)。

NOTES